Melissa McTernan writ loves grumpy heroes, s
tales. She won the Stile
novella and *A Curse of B*
new trilogy The Wolf Brothers series.

When she's not writing, she's most likely reading or wrangling her kids as a stay-at-home mom. Melissa lives in upstate New York with her husband, kids, cats, puppy, and full bookshelves. She writes romance to keep her sanity.

X x.com/melissamcternan
facebook.com/Melissa-McTernan-Author
instagram.com/melissamcternan

A CURSE OF BLOOD AND WOLVES

Wolf Brothers
Book 1

MELISSA MCTERNAN

One More Chapter
a division of HarperCollins*Publishers* Ltd
1 London Bridge Street
London SE1 9GF
www.harpercollins.co.uk
HarperCollins*Publishers*
Macken House, 39/40 Mayor Street Upper,
Dublin 1, D01 C9W8, Ireland

This paperback edition 2024

First published in Great Britain in ebook format
by HarperCollins*Publishers* 2023
Copyright © Melissa McTernan 2023
Melissa McTernan asserts the moral right to be identified
as the author of this work

A catalogue record of this book is available from the British Library
ISBN: 978-0-00-864302-7

Printed and bound in the United States

24 25 26 27 28 LBC 7 6 5 4 3

Playlist

Don't Blame Me - Taylor Swift ♥
vampire - Olivia Rodrigo ♥
Running With The Wolves - AURORA ♥
Eat Your Young - Hozier ♥
A Drop in the Ocean - Ron Pope ♥
Meet Me In The Woods - Lord Huron ♥
Never Say Never - The Fray ♥
Can't Catch Me Now - Olivia Rodrigo ♥
I Did Something Bad - Taylor Swift ♥
Howl - Florence + The Machine ♥
Motion Sickness - Phoebe Bridgers ♥
Poison - Rita Ora ♥
Die For You - The Weekend ♥
like that - Bea Miller ♥
Dark Paradise - Lana Del Rey ♥
The Wolves - Ben Howard ♥
Bruises - Lewis Capaldi ♥
Youngblood - 5 Seconds of Summer ♥
greedy - Tate McRae ♥
Heaven - Julia Michaels ♥
Out Of The Woods - Taylor Swift ♥
Radio - Lana Del Rey ♥
invisible string - Taylor Swift ♥

To anyone who grew up but never outgrew fairytales. Here's a grown up one just for you.

Chapter One

R uby kept her pace steady even as the hairs rose on the nape of her neck, a familiar breathlessness squeezing her lungs. She felt the stranger's gaze tracking her as she traipsed through the woods. Dry leaves crunched under her feet on the overgrown trail, the smell of dirt and pine drifting up to her nose.

Beneath the terror of knowing she was being watched, a deep sense of relief settled into her. He was still here, still waiting.

Any sensible woman wouldn't be traveling through these woods after dark. *She* shouldn't be here. But she was not a sensible woman. Every night after leaving her shift at the bar, she promised herself she would take the long way home, stick to the well-lit streets through town, and stay out of the woods. And yet every night she found herself back on this same path, her black boots stomping through the underbrush, sticks and vines lashing across her bare legs. And always the stranger's eyes on her.

Her pulse leapt again at the thought. He was here

somewhere just beyond the glow of the moon. He kept to the shadows, so quiet she sometimes wondered if she imagined him. But then the sound of a snapped twig underfoot, or the slight rustling of leaves, and she would be convinced all over again that he was there.

She supposed she should be afraid. Her body seemed to think so anyway. Her heart raced in her chest and her breathing was unsteady. It took all her strength not to glance behind her with every step, to not give in to the tingling awareness at the back of her neck. She had to fight every instinct not to break into a run until she made it to the safety of the little house she shared with her sister.

But beneath the thrumming fear of her body, she wasn't afraid at all. She was excited. Alive. Aroused. Further evidence that she was just as screwed up as everyone said she was. Rumors had swirled about her for years: she was a witch, she communed with the dead, she fucked ghosts. Whatever the hell that meant.

Leaves whispered alongside the trail and a shape moved through the shadows beside her. Goosebumps raised along her arms despite the heat of the night. Maybe she was just as weird as everyone said. Maybe she would fuck a ghost or whatever it was that was following her because damn it if she wasn't trembling at the thought.

She picked up her pace, closing in on the path that led to her backyard. The house she shared with her sister sat on the edge of town. The girls bought the tidy fixer-upper with the money their aunt left them when she died. Ruby strode toward it now, the light from an upstairs window shining through the trees. Their closest neighbor's house was already dark. It must be past midnight.

Ruby was nearly in her own yard when she dared a glance over her shoulder.

She froze, pinned to the spot by a pair of silver eyes shining out from the darkness. *Holy shit.* A hulking shape stepped from the shadows and into the light spilling from her window.

A strangled sound left her lips, fear and panic clamoring to escape her throat.

He was massive. The man, her stranger, was huge. He hadn't come any closer, leaving enough space between them that she couldn't make out his features in the dark, except for his glowing eyes and the dark hair that hung to his shoulders.

Run. The word tore through her thoughts but her feet remained stuck, her body refused to obey her mind. So this was how she died. A fitting death, she supposed. Just as weird and macabre as she was. Strangled to death by a stranger in the woods. What would it feel like to have his hands around her throat? Her breath caught, a choked whimper in the silence between them.

The man shifted, his eyes flashing in the darkness. His enormous chest rose and fell nearly as fast as her own, as though he was just as affected by this moment. Why had he followed her? And why the hell had she wanted him to?

Why even now, when she was sure he was about to crush her with the huge hands fisted at his sides, did she not want to leave him?

Screwed up, for sure.

The man took a step forward and another. Ruby's breath burned in her throat, her heart threatening to tear through her rib cage. He could reach out and grab her now if he wanted to. He could wrap those hands around her and do whatever he wanted to her.

Ruby's survival instincts finally kicked in.

She ran.

Shit.

Rafe slumped against the closest tree, watching the woman flee from him. She raced across the small yard, her short black skirt flapping around her legs. She yanked open the back door and disappeared inside without a backward glance. Of course. Why the hell would she look back? He had obviously just scared the living hell out of her.

But for a minute there it had seemed as if she might…

Rafe shook the thought from his head. Sometimes he really was as stupid as his father always said he was. He spat on the ground at the memory of the old bastard and turned from the little cottage at the edge of the woods.

He strode back toward home, easily finding his way in the dark. He walked fast, letting the humid night air fill his lungs. Maybe if he breathed deeply enough he could wash the scent of the woman from his nose. He forced his body to move faster, his long legs eating up the distance between her house in town and his cabin in the woods.

His efforts were wasted. Even as he dragged in breath after breath of piney air, the woman's spiced scent lingered in his nostrils. It had been driving him mad for weeks. He'd never hated his wolf senses more.

Rafe lowered himself with a groan onto the steps of the small porch at the front of his cabin. He couldn't be closed in by walls right now, not with that woman's terrified face still imprinted on his mind.

Her wide eyes, her heavy breathing, the small whimper that

4

had escaped her ruby lips. His cock twitched at the memory. Damn it. What the fuck was wrong with him?

He knew he was a literal fucking monster, but he'd never wanted to chase a woman before. To pin her down in the dirt and—

Rafe shook his head. Hard. He was normally much better at controlling his beast than this. He'd spent the last five years wrangling that side of himself, denying that side of himself, trying his damnedest to act human, to *be* human. But lately, his control was slipping. Ever since she'd started walking through his woods. Her scent drove him wild. He couldn't stay away.

Shit. She had been so fucking beautiful up close. He'd never gotten that close before, had never seen her in the light. But tonight he followed her farther than usual and in the light of her house, she'd been perfect. Terrified, but perfect.

Her skin was like moonlight, her lips a deep blood red, and the rest of her dark pools of shadow, black hair, and black clothes. And that spicy cinnamon scent. Christ, he'd nearly reached out and grabbed her. And for a minute, he could have sworn she wanted him to.

He ran a shaking hand down his face, the ever-present stubble scraping against his palm. He needed to get a grip. There was a reason he lived out here on his own, and stalking innocent women through the woods was not it. Quite the opposite. He lived out here, at least partly, to protect women like her. He'd hurt enough people in his life and he had no intention of adding to the list. The look of terror on her face should have been a reminder to stay the hell away. It's what he should have done the last time a woman looked at him like that. He shuddered at the memory.

Rafe stood and stretched, his muscles protesting nearly as much as the old wooden steps. He may have overdone it last night in his wolf form. He'd run for miles after following her, trying to purge her from his system. He'd returned home exhausted and still couldn't sleep.

Tonight would be worse. Now he had images of her beautiful face to add to her scent and the sound of her footsteps through the woods. Now he had even more to torment him in his dreams.

He pushed open his front door and flicked on the light. The cramped interior greeted him, crowded with books and overstuffed furniture. He had outgrown the space long ago but hadn't had the energy or the desire to move. He strode to the refrigerator and pulled out a beer, popping the cap on the edge of the counter.

He could go to the woodshop out back and work on his latest order, but he didn't feel up for it tonight. Making furniture had paid his bills since moving out on his own, and he liked the work. And the solitude. But tonight he couldn't focus. He'd probably end up making a three-legged table or something. He took a slug of beer and dropped onto his couch, sinking into the well-worn cushions.

What would have happened if he'd spoken to her? If he'd acted less like an animal stalking its prey and more like a goddamn human? He suddenly found himself dying to know what her voice would have sounded like, what she would have said.

Shit. He really was an idiot. He'd spent far too long alone in this cabin, and most of the time that was fine with him. But lately, the loneliness had opened up its black jaws and threatened to swallow him whole.

Maybe that's all this obsession was, his own loneliness demanding companionship. But even as he thought it, even as he tried to explain away his attraction to this woman, he couldn't shake the feeling that there was more to it.

Things had been quiet for far too long in these woods. The pack, *his* pack, had been quiet for far too long. And that made Rafe uneasy. It made him want to protect this woman of the woods from whatever was coming next. From his brother. From his kind.

Rafe knew that was exactly how he would rationalize it to himself when he went out to find her again tomorrow.

Chapter Two

R uby slammed the door and bolted the lock, her breath sawing painfully in and out of her lungs. She thumped her back against the door and slid down to the floor. Holy shit. What was that? *Who* was that? Ruby squeezed her eyes shut and rested her forehead on her knees, waiting for her heart rate and her breathing to return to normal. But when she did, the man's silver eyes stared at her from behind her closed lids. She blinked them open again, shaking the image from her head. Her heart still rammed painfully against her chest and her breath was ragged. She needed to get a grip before she passed out.

She ran her hands over her bare legs and then over her arms, convincing herself that she was fine. Alive and well. Completely unharmed. Totally fine, she repeated to herself over and over until finally she could breathe without panting and the panicked beat in her chest lessened. Whoever he was, he hadn't hurt her.

This time.

Ruby pushed the unhelpful thought from her head. The man had had plenty of opportunities to hurt her and he never did.

She was home and she was safe. And even though she had run, she still had a hard time believing he would actually harm her. Which was probably further evidence that she was screwed up. More for the townies to whisper about.

Not that she cared. Ruby stopped caring what other people thought of her a long time ago, right around the time her parents died and the other kids in her third-grade class decided dead parents were contagious and stopped talking to her. Ruby decided she didn't need them anyway. Moving in with her mother's great-aunt in her crumbling old Victorian only solidified her reputation as a weirdo.

She didn't let it bother her. Most of the time she steered right into it. With her entirely black wardrobe, her affinity for Edgar Allen Poe, and her habit of reading in the town graveyard, she let herself become a caricature. It didn't matter that she loved wildflowers just as much as she liked dead poets. Or that she read in the cemetery to feel closer to her parents. Or that despite her black clothes her fingernails were always painted a different bright color every week.

No one bothered to learn anything else about her. Not that she wanted them to. Not that she cared. It was still her mantra even now at twenty-five. She told herself she didn't need anyone besides her sister, Lena. And she didn't.

Besides scaring away the townsfolk, her parents' death had knocked the ability to feel real fear about anything out of her. What did she have to be scared of when the worst possible thing had already happened? It made her immune. Death was inevitable and it had visited Ruby early in life. Not that she particularly wanted to die, but she'd made her peace with it much earlier than most people.

She rose from her seat against the door and stood on shaky legs. She might be immune to most fears, but apparently her flight-or-fight instincts still worked. Her body left her no choice but to flee from that big hulking man in the shadows. But now from the safety of her house, her thoughts ran back to him, over the width of his chest and the intensity of his gaze and the size of those hands. She would bet they were rough and calloused. They would scrape against the soft skin of her thighs, easily holding her in place—

The stairs creaked, pulling Ruby from her daydream.

"Lena?" she called, but it was Lucifer, their sleek, black cat that rounded the corner, not Ruby's sister. Ruby leaned down to give the little demon a scratch between his ears before heading upstairs to find her sister.

The small upstairs hallway led to two bedrooms and a bathroom. Light seeped out from beneath Lena's door. "Lena?" Ruby pushed the door open and found her sister staring out the window toward the woods. Had she seen Ruby run? Had she seen the man?

"Lena." Ruby squeezed her sister's shoulder, but Lena didn't budge. "Lena!" Ruby shook her sister, her voice rising. "Not again, not again," Ruby muttered as she turned Lena in her chair, forcing her to look away from the window. "Lena, can you hear me?"

Lena turned toward the sound of Ruby's voice, but her pale eyes were blank and unblinking, like she wasn't seeing Ruby's face in front of her own. Ruby swallowed the panic in her throat and squeezed her sister's arms, giving her another shake. "Lena, it's me, Ruby. Can you hear me? Come back to me, please." She had to cut off the sob rising to the surface. Crying would get her nowhere; panicking would get her nowhere. It never had in the past.

Memories of her aunt sitting in her old rocker with the same blank expression on her face crowded into Ruby's mind, but she pushed them away. Her aunt was gone and Ruby had no one to ask about her strange habits, about what was happening to Lena.

Finally, Lena's unseeing gaze settled on Ruby. Her pale hair hung around her face and even though she was two years older than Ruby, right now she looked so young, so helpless. Ruby shook her fiercely. "Snap out of it, goddamn it!"

Lena cocked her head, as if hearing something no one else could. "They're coming."

Ruby froze, her fingers digging into her sister's flesh. "Lena, please." Her voice was nothing more than a choked wail.

Lena blinked. "Ruby?"

Ruby collapsed into her lap with a sob. "You're back, you're back, you're back," she repeated until Lena tugged her upright again, worry etched into her features.

"What did I say this time?" she asked as Ruby plopped down onto the floor at her feet.

"The usual. They're coming." Ruby sighed, running her hands through her long hair. Her sister was getting worse. These episodes were coming on more and more frequently, and she didn't know what to do about it. Her aunt had never mentioned her episodes after they happened, and Ruby convinced herself her aunt was just old and tired.

But Lena was young and vibrant. Or at least she used to be.

Lena pressed her fingers against her temples and squeezed her eyes shut. "I don't know what it means." She shook her head, dropping her hands in her lap. "I'm sorry, Ruby."

"Don't be." Ruby patted her sister's knee through her pink fuzzy bathrobe. "You don't need to apologize. It's not your fault. We'll figure it out." It was the same every time. The same apologies, the same promise to figure it out. But Ruby still didn't have any answers. "Come on, I think there's leftovers in the fridge from yesterday."

She grabbed Lena's hand and tugged her up. Her fingers were cold and clammy and Ruby held them tight, warming them the best she could.

Downstairs, under the soft yellow light of the kitchen, Ruby studied her sister as they ate their cold lasagna in silence. They sat at the tiny kitchen table, just big enough for the two of them. They never had guests anyway.

Lena picked at the food on her plate, a furrow of worry between her brows. In the wake of their parents' deaths, Lena had grown soft where Ruby had developed hard edges. Lena was well-liked, well-behaved, and accepted by her peers. She always had plenty of friends and their parents seemed to want to coddle her, to take her in and comfort her. Invitations to sleepovers and birthday parties were never in short supply for her sister, while Ruby stayed home with their octogenarian aunt and watched reruns of *Murder She Wrote*.

It didn't matter. Ruby loved her aunt and her sister. She completely understood why they loved Lena because she did too. But her sister was falling apart and no one had stuck around to help. No one but Ruby.

Ruby scraped the edges of the pan, getting every last bit of crispy cheese.

Lena gave her a tired smile. "I'm sorry you've been working double shifts."

Ruby waved her fork as though she could brush away their problems. "It's fine, really. I don't mind."

Lena had to quit her job at the local preschool when her mind drifted away during story time. Ruby maintained that the incident only proved what an amazing teacher Lena was. Not a single child moved from their seat as they waited patiently for

Lena to start up the story again. Unfortunately, her assistant teacher had returned from bathroom duty and found her unresponsive on the brightly colored alphabet carpet, *The Very Hungry Caterpillar* in her lap.

Every doctor they'd visited had found nothing wrong with her. The bills for CAT scans and MRIs were crammed in Ruby's desk drawer away from Lena's worried gaze.

Ruby reached across the table and took her sister's hand again. "It's going to be okay, Lena. I promise."

Her sister sighed and shook her head.

"It will," Ruby insisted. "Now go get some sleep."

Lena's pale blue eyes met hers. She looked as though she might say more, but instead, pulled her bathrobe tighter around her and shuffled back up the stairs to her bedroom. Shuffled, when she used to run 5K's for fun, when she used to be the center of every party. Lena was the popular sister, the beauty, the beloved one. Now she spent most of her days asleep and Ruby had no idea how to help her.

Ruby listened to her footsteps overhead, the sound of her door clicking shut, the creaking of her old mattress as Lena sunk into it. And only then did she let her thoughts slip back to the man in the woods.

Ruby's face hurt from the fake smile she plastered there. Surly girls don't make good tips, she reminded herself as she set the customer's beer down on the bar.

"Can I get you anything else?" she asked, not recognizing the bubbly tone in her own voice. But she needed those tips. Bad.

The man in front of her—overly styled hair, wide perfect

grin, far too much cologne, distinctly not her type—let his gaze linger a beat too long on her chest before bringing his eyes up to meet hers.

"I'm good for now, sweetheart." He flashed more shiny white teeth at her, and Ruby had to bite the inside of her cheek to keep from telling him to fuck off for calling her sweeheart and for staring at her tits.

"Okay, let me know if you change your mind." She turned to go, but the man grabbed her hand.

She stared at where his hand covered hers on the bar and then looked up into his smirking face.

"I'd enjoy my beer more if you stayed here and talked with me for a minute."

The cloying scent of his cologne mingled with her rage and nearly choked her. How dare he touch her? He still hadn't moved his hand, so she yanked hers out from underneath him.

"I really need to get back to work," she ground out, still needing those tips, still thinking about that stack of medical bills, still fucking smiling.

The man glanced around the nearly empty bar. Damn it. It was a Wednesday night and the dinner crowd had cleared out hours ago. She literally had no work to get back to. Maybe she could marry the ketchups? Slice more limes? Do anything rather than stand here and talk to this asshole.

He grinned. "I think you could spare a minute."

Ruby sighed.

There were only two types of guys that went after Ruby. The first type knew her sad backstory. They knew all about poor orphaned Ruby and her odd quirks. The problem with living in the same small town she grew up in was that this type was all too common. They wanted to comfort and protect her. They got off on her tragedy. She despised type number one.

The second type was convinced that girls who dressed in black and wore dark red lipstick were kinky in bed, and was just dying to find out if it was true. This type could be fun, sure, but with them she always felt like she was playing a role. Ruby, the kinky goth girl. It was exhausting.

Ruby assumed from the fact that she'd never seen this guy around town and from the way he kept glancing at her breasts in her tight black tank top that he was type number two. And she was not in the mood for type number two.

"Ruby?" Ruby's manager cut in before she could stab a little pink drink umbrella into the man's eye. "What are you still doing here? Your shift ended half an hour ago."

Ruby turned toward her boss, finally letting the smile fall from her lips. "Thanks, Macy. I guess I lost track of time."

Macy's knowing gaze flitted to the man at the bar and back again. "You've been here since lunch. Go home." She shooed her away from the bar, her purple braids spilling over one shoulder.

Was that a wrinkle of concern on Macy's face? Ruby wasn't used to having outsiders care about her. It was unsettling.

"Okay, sure. I'm heading out now." Ruby didn't bother with a backward glance at the asshole at the bar. She'd been standing since noon and it was now well past eleven. All she wanted to do was to get home and land face-first in her bed, boots and all. Which she was sure Mr. Type Number Two would find sufficiently kinky.

She tossed her bar apron into her locker in the back room and grabbed the boxed-up leftovers Macy had set aside for her from the fridge. Still pondering what all these nice gestures from Macy meant, she pushed the door open into the alley. The night air was hot and sticky and did nothing to improve her mood.

She was wearing her typical work outfit, black tank top, short black skirt, black boots. The only thing that changed in colder months was an added black cardigan and black tights. Red lipstick all year round. Without it douche bags might never hit on her, but she liked her red lips and she wasn't about to give them up.

She twisted her long dark hair in a knot on top of her head in an attempt to stay cool on her walk home but it didn't work. By the time she reached the path to the woods, she was a sweaty, tired mess.

Ruby stared into the darkness beyond the trees. She could stay in town and walk home through the well-lit neighborhoods. She *should* do that. But the path through the woods was so much shorter. And she was so tired.

And why shouldn't she be able to take any route home that she wanted?

She was being reckless.

He might be there.

It was dangerous.

A new warmth spread to her core. A tingle of anticipation ran down her spine.

Maybe she was just as kinky as people assumed. She shifted the leftovers to her other hand, grabbed the pepper spray out of her purse, and strode into the woods.

Chapter Three

S he was back.

Rafe pushed away from the tree he'd been leaning against, waiting. Waiting like a goddamn stalker. He still didn't know what the hell was wrong with him, but again he'd been pulled from his cabin and back to this spot. He would swear to anyone who asked that it hadn't even been a choice. He *needed* to be here.

Or that's what he'd told himself, anyway, as he'd hurried to the place where he usually saw her, cutting in from town through the overgrown trail at the edge of the forest. He'd had a choice, of course. There was always a choice. But not going to see her meant staying home and being tortured with thoughts of her, her scent drifting in through his windows, seeping in through the cracks in the house even when he closed everything up.

His wolf side had never come with more than the instinct to run and hunt, increased senses, and an occasional anger that he struggled to keep tamped down. But it was different with her. His need to throw himself around her and not let anything harm her was stronger than anything he'd felt in hundreds of years. Stronger than what he'd felt for a different human woman, so long ago he'd thought maybe he'd finally forgotten. Except he could never forget how things ended with Scarlet, and now here he was repeating his mistakes.

But he couldn't stop.

This woman called to him.

Maybe if he was still with his pack, things would make more sense. Or at least he'd have someone to ask, but Rafe hadn't seen his older brother in years and he barely tolerated the younger one, not that he would admit any of this to them. His father was dead, a fact he liked to remind himself of whenever he felt anxious. And he'd never known his mother.

He was raised by his stepmother, and the thought of Nell left Rafe with an ache in his chest. She would have something to say about this woman, some bit of advice for him. But he hadn't been brave enough to see her in years either.

Rafe had been alone for so long, without his pack, without his family. It was what he wanted. It was necessary. But maybe he was forgetting what it was to be a werewolf. Maybe he was losing more than just his people.

The woman moved down the path and Rafe followed just out of sight, his feet silent on the soft leaves. She strode purposefully tonight, her purse thumping against her hip, her skirt flapping over the curve of her ass. He refused to look at that ass. This was not about sex. It was about … protection. Safety. She looked small, walking through the towering pines. Her hair was piled on her head with a few stray pieces trailing down the delicate curve of her neck. Her blood red lips were set in a firm line, a crease between her brows.

He wanted to know what upset her. He wanted to make sure it never did again. He was losing his mind.

Rafe followed along beside her, far enough from the path that she couldn't see him, hopefully couldn't hear his footsteps through the leaves, but her scent pulled him along as though he were on a leash. He nearly cursed out loud at how much he didn't hate that idea. What the fuck was wrong with him?

"I'm not afraid of you." Her voice cut through the relative quiet of the woods, rising above the sounds of crickets and cicadas. She stopped on the trail and turned to face him, staring into the shadows.

Rafe froze. For a moment it seemed she could actually see him, but then he noticed how her eyes scanned the darkness. She was just guessing at where he was.

"I'm not afraid so you might as well come out and stop being such a creep." She put a hand on her hip, waiting for him to emerge. He thought about last night, the fear on her face when she'd seen him. What if she ran again? If she was smart, she would. He shouldn't have come.

He stepped closer and he could see the rapid rise and fall of her chest, her eyes wide in the light of the moon. Her words might claim she wasn't afraid, but her body betrayed her. He moved slowly, not wanting to startle her even more, until he was finally out of the shadows. Only a few feet separated them and her eyes widened further when he came into view.

"What's your name?" she asked. The pulse in her neck jumped wildly even as she kept her voice steady, strong. He noticed the pepper spray clutched in her fist and he almost smiled to know she was ready to protect herself.

"Rafe." It was more like a sound than a name. His voice was rusty from disuse. It had been days since he'd spoken to another human. He cleared his throat. "I didn't mean to scare you."

She scowled at him. "Oh really? So stalking women through

the woods at night is a friendly neighborhood service you provide?"

He winced. God, he was a monster.

"I, uh … I never meant to…"

She waved his stuttering away with a flutter of her hand. "Never mind. Just cut it out, okay?" She turned on her heel and continued down the path. Cut it out? He wished he could. The leash tightened and he followed her.

"I will use this pepper spray if you get any closer," she told him without turning around.

"Understood." He dropped back a few paces but couldn't stop his feet from continuing down this path. It was as though she held him by the throat. He couldn't breathe and yet he knew without her nearby it would be even worse.

She didn't look at him again until they reached the end of the path. Light from her windows spilled into the yard like the night before, and for the first time he wondered who was home waiting up for her.

She turned to him, that same defiant look on her face, the one that dared him to hurt her. She looked like she might say something but his question slipped out before she could.

"Why aren't you afraid of me?" He hated the growly edge to his voice, and he tried to soften it. "You should be."

Her eyes widened slightly at that, but she didn't run. "I'm not scared of most things," she said, rolling her shoulders back, and he believed her. He wanted to ask why. He wanted to know what had made her so fearless, but she had her own questions.

"Why have you been following me?"

Rafe hesitated. How could he possibly tell her that he was drawn to her like a magnet, that her scent called to him every night, that he was convinced she was in danger? He couldn't. Not without sounding like a complete psychopath.

He ran a hand through his hair. "I just wanted to make sure you were safe."

Apparently, it was the wrong thing to say.

Her mouth turned down and her dark brows drew together. Her fingers tightened around the pepper spray. "I don't need your protection."

He took a step toward her, but she held up a hand to stop him. He froze, his heart thundering in his ears. The urge to touch her was so strong, he jammed his hands in his pockets and prayed for strength.

"I don't need anyone's protection." Her dark eyes flashed in the moonlight. "I'm not broken. I'm not helpless."

Of course she wasn't. Anyone who thought so was clearly blind. That wasn't what he meant at all. It was just this damn feeling he had, this horrible sense that she was in danger. He opened his mouth to tell her that, but snapped it shut when she glared at him.

She adjusted her bags again. Whoever was waiting for her, she was bringing them dinner. He could smell it. "Quit following me or next time I'll call the police."

The police. He'd dealt with the police enough in his lifetime and it never ended well.

He held his hands up in surrender. "I'm sorry. You won't see me again. I promise."

Some shadow of an emotion crossed her features but it was gone before he could figure it out. "Good," she said, turning away from him again.

"Just be careful." He couldn't stop the warning even though he knew it would piss her off even more.

"Will do, Grandma." She tossed the words over her shoulder and he couldn't help the smile that crossed his face. She was halfway across the yard now, but he needed one more thing from her.

"What's your name?" His voice was quiet, not wanting to wake anyone, and for a second he wasn't sure if she'd heard him. Or maybe she just didn't want to answer. She got to the back door and put a hand on the knob. The thought of never seeing her again tore through him like claws across his skin, a pain he knew all too well.

But then she turned, and offered him her name.

"Ruby," she whispered into the darkness.

Ruby.

Protect her? Protect her! Who the hell did he think he was? How dare he! Ruby tossed the leftovers onto the counter and plopped into a kitchen chair. She yanked off one boot and then the other and sighed in relief.

Protect her. What a dick.

She wiggled her toes and let the cool night air skate across her skin. She considered getting up to close the window. There was a man stalking her through the woods after all. But she hadn't lied to him. She wasn't afraid.

Curious.

Intrigued.

Attracted.

One thought about his broad body emerging from the shadows, his silver gaze on hers, raised goosebumps up and down her arms. Okay, maybe a little afraid. But in a good way. God, she found the weirdo stalking her attractive. What the actual hell was wrong with her?

It didn't matter anyway. He'd ruined it as soon as those

words'd left his mouth. Words about protection and safety. The last words she wanted to hear from her dangerous stranger.

His eyes on her these last weeks had made her feel alive. Exhilarated for the first time in a long time, maybe ever. Like finally her existence was more than just a series of long hours at work and even longer hours taking care of her sister. Like maybe someone saw her for her bared-down self. The self that walked home every night tired and frustrated. The self that was both eager to get home and dreading what she would find. The self that wasn't the sad goth girl. She had somehow convinced herself that whoever was watching her had seen all of it and still found her interesting, desirable.

But she was wrong. He was just another man who saw her as a small and broken woman. One that needed protecting. One that needed fixing.

Ruby got up from the table and poured herself a tall glass of water from the pitcher in the fridge before she had to head upstairs to check on Lena. In the back of her mind she knew she was being unfair to this Rafe character. She'd told herself repeatedly that it was stupid and reckless to walk alone at night on that damn path. He was only telling her what she already knew.

Or maybe she was being too fair? Maybe had she been a normal woman she'd have called the police a long time ago. But she wasn't and she hadn't.

And now even her creepy stalker had disappointed her. There was no end to the ways she was screwed up.

Lucifer circled her feet and she nearly tripped over the silent cat.

"Damn it, Lucy. Are you trying to kill me?" The cat gazed up at her with yellow eyes and an expression that said he just might be plotting her demise. Wouldn't that be ironic? Survive her nightly strolls through the woods just to die tripping over her own cat.

Lucifer continued to stare until Ruby took the hint and filled his food and water dish.

"There. Now let me live to see another day."

Lucy set to eating, not bothering to glance back in her direction, so Ruby grabbed her boots and dragged herself upstairs, praying her sister was lucid tonight. Complicated feelings for a stalker were enough drama for one day.

Chapter Four

I t had been three days since she'd told Rafe to get lost, and he'd actually listened. Ruby shifted her bag of leftovers to her other hand and peered into the darkness between the trees. Nothing. No hulking shape in the shadows, no footsteps on the leaves, no silver eyes flashing in the moonlight. She was back to being alone. Well, good. That's what she wanted. Right? That's what she asked for and surprisingly, he'd given it to her.

Ruby ignored the pang of disappointment in her chest and kept walking toward home. It was another hot night, humid and sticky, and sweat trickled down her back and between her breasts. The bar had been swamped, endless hours of pouring drinks and taking orders. Just putting one foot in front of the other now seemed to take an inhuman amount of energy. And focus to not crash into a tree. Her cell had died hours ago, depriving her of a flashlight.

She probably should have taken Macy up on her offer for a ride home but sitting in a car with her would have meant talking one on one, like about personal stuff. The thought made panic flare in Ruby's stomach. Small talk freaked her out more than a large dark stranger following her through the woods. Her therapist would eat that shit up. Too bad she couldn't afford to pay him anymore.

A stick cracked somewhere off the trail and Ruby's heart lurched in … fear? Anticipation? Excitement?

"Hello?"

The only answer was the buzz of the cicadas.

"Rafe?" Ruby took a step off the trail. The moon was covered by the clouds that had been threatening a storm all day and the darkness was thick around her. She could barely see a few steps in front of her face but she inched further into the trees away from the trail. Her heart rammed against her ribs, warning her to stay away, stay out. But the thrill of danger only made Ruby move closer.

A rustle in the leaves to her left and she swiveled just in time to see silver eyes flash in the dark.

"Rafe, is that you? You can come out. I won't be mad."

A breathy huff stopped her in her tracks. She could make out the shape in the shadows now, and it didn't belong to a human.

"Holy shit," she breathed. Less than a few feet away stood the biggest wolf she had ever seen in her life. Although to be fair she hadn't come face to face with any wolves in her life, but this one was huge.

Now what? Her panicked brain scrambled for an answer. Play dead? Run? Try to look bigger than she was? She had no freaking idea. Where the hell was the large man who so badly wanted to protect her when she really needed him?

The wolf hadn't moved since she'd spotted him. He just watched her with those silver eyes. Ruby put up both hands and backed away slowly.

"I'm just going to go now," she whispered. "No need to eat me. I'm sure I taste terrible anyway."

The wolf gave a low growl. Ruby took another step backward. Her heel snagged on a root and she tumbled back. She hit the ground hard, knocking whatever shaky breath she had from her lungs. Her bags scattered around her and pain shot up her tailbone.

Everything stopped. Her heart, her breath, her swirling thoughts. This was surely how she died. She waited.

But instead of teeth tearing the flesh from her bones, she felt soft fur beneath her fingers. She looked up to find the wolf nudging her hand with his big head. He huffed a warm breath against the skin of her wrist and the sensation skittered up her arm. *Holy shit.*

Ruby sat up. She was vaguely aware of being covered in dirt and the dull ache in her back, but the looming animal in front of her robbed her of all coherent thought. The wolf cocked his head and the movement was so dog-like, the fear constricting Ruby's lungs loosened. Maybe he was tame? A pet?

Ruby's gaze took in the dark shadowy animal. Pet or not, he was huge. The wolf leaned down again and nuzzled Ruby's hand. She lifted it from the dirt and ran her fingers through his thick fur. He made that breathy sound again like he was pleased.

"Good dog," she whispered. The wolf seemed to narrow his eyes at that, in a look that was almost human. "Uh … good wolf." He huffed again. Ruby got slowly to her feet, dusting the dirt from her butt and legs. She moved cautiously, afraid any sudden moves would upset the beast beside her. But the wolf sat patiently on the edge of the trail while she gathered her things. Macy had packed the leftovers so tightly, they hadn't even spilled from the bag.

"Okay, well … I'm going to go home now." Ruby straightened, glancing at the wolf. She took a few tentative steps along the path but the animal fell into step beside her. His head reached her elbow and every few steps she could feel his fur tickle the skin of her arm. She couldn't help but reach out and sink her fingers back into the thick fur at his neck. It was coarse on the surface but delightfully fluffy underneath. She gave him a scratch and the wolf let out a low growl of contentment. Or she assumed he was content anyway when he didn't try to kill her.

They reached the end of the path and the light from her windows illuminated the creature beside her. He was beautiful. Gray and black fur with white around his face. He cocked his head again and she scratched between his ears the same way she did with Lucifer. He pushed his head against her hand and she giggled.

"Oh, you like that, huh?"

Was it possible for wolves to smile? She didn't know, but she was pretty sure this one just did.

"Such a good boy," she crooned. But maybe that was a step too far. The wolf's ears flattened against his head and a low growl emanated from his throat.

"What—" Ruby backed away, but the wolf was staring at the trees behind her. He wasn't growling at her.

He was growling at the other wolf. The one that was lunging right for her.

In the blink of an eye, he'd gone from the heaven of Ruby's fingers in his fur to the hell of seeing another wolf, teeth bared, barreling toward her. He'd let his guard down for one damn minute. Berating himself for that would have to wait until later.

Ruby's startled cry broke through the quiet of the night and sent him hurtling for the other wolf.

They met in a clash of fangs and claws, Rafe's rage burning hotter than it had in years. For once he let it burn. He pounced on the other wolf and managed to roll him onto his back in the long grass of Ruby's backyard. The wolf beneath him growled, exposing his huge fangs. Rafe's claws dug deeper into the wolf's flesh, pinning him to the earth. He tried to push up but Rafe grabbed the wolf's neck with his teeth and thrashed his head. Blood filled his mouth, hot and metallic. A million memories flooded in with it. This wasn't who Rafe was anymore. And yet...

Whoever this bastard was had come after Ruby and that was reason enough to tear his throat out. The wolf yelped and squirmed, his claws lashing Rafe's flesh. The scent of his own blood filled the air.

Rafe was only vaguely aware of Ruby's whimpering, too blinded by rage and fear to really remember he wasn't alone in this yard. He dug his teeth in deeper. The other wolf's pulse throbbed against his tongue. He could finish him off right now. But a movement at the periphery of his vision stopped him. He lifted his head, blood dripping from his mouth.

Ruby was on the ground. She must have been knocked over when the two wolves ran past her. Her eyes were huge. Huge and terrified. She scurried away from the fight like a crab on the shore, her legs already covered in dirt from her earlier fall. But it was her eyes that stopped him. She was looking at him like he was a monster. Like the monster he was. He hadn't wanted anyone to look at him like that again. Especially not her.

For the second time that night, Rafe let his guard down for a moment too long. The other wolf reared up and latched on tight to Rafe's shoulder, tearing through fur, skin, muscle. Pain seared through him, but it only incensed him further. The other wolf rolled him over, but Rafe refused to let him get the upper hand. They twisted and snarled, lashing claws and fangs. The other wolf was still bleeding profusely from the neck, but now Rafe had his own wound to worry about.

The wolves stirred up grass and dirt, their own fur and blood flying as well. It was all too familiar, too much like his old life. And Rafe was settling back into it all too easily. He tore at the other wolf, leaving another gaping wound on his front leg. The wolf yelped and backed off, limping. Blood streaked his mostly white fur, staining it black.

Rafe growled a low warning, placing his body between the wolf and Ruby. He didn't dare look at her again, afraid of what he might see. The other wolf's eyes narrowed, his gaze flicking from Rafe to Ruby as though assessing if she was worth the trouble. Apparently deciding she wasn't, the other wolf backed down. Rafe didn't take his eyes off of him until he had disappeared into the woods.

It wasn't until he was gone that Rafe noticed his own wounds. His fur was matted with blood and each move of his shoulder sent pain slicing through him. He had to get home. He needed to lie down for a while and heal.

He took a step and stumbled, his shoulder screaming in protest. *Damn it.*

"You're hurt." Ruby's voice was shaky but strong. She got to her feet and reached out a hand. He wanted with his whole body, no, his whole soul, to lean into that hand. But he couldn't. Not like this. Not after what she'd just witnessed. He tried to back away but stumbled again, his front leg giving out beneath him. His face hit the dirt. The earth tipped. He'd lost too much blood. He was dizzy and nauseous. And too damn weak. He gave up and let his body collapse onto the cool grass.

Ruby dropped to the ground beside him. "Oh no, no, no," she whispered, stroking between his ears. "I'm going to help you. It's going to be all right." He wanted to tell her he just needed a few hours to rest, to heal himself, and then he'd be fine. But of course he had no way to do that.

He nudged her hand with his head and huffed a breath across the delicate skin of her wrist. She smiled a little at the sensation.

"You saved me." Her lips quirked up in the corner. "But don't tell anyone. You'll ruin my reputation."

If wolves could laugh, he would have. But he had to settle for a low growl. Ruby scratched between his ears again.

"And now I'm going to save you." She said it with such determination that Rafe instantly believed her. He had no idea what she meant but he had complete confidence in her ability to do it. She stood, giving Rafe an upfront view of her black boots. She looked like she could kick the shit out of someone in those boots and he liked that.

"I'll be right back."

The boots walked away, taking Ruby with them. Rafe drifted in and out of consciousness with Ruby's words echoing through his head. *You saved me. And now I'm going to save you.* Wouldn't that be nice, he thought before he slipped under again.

Chapter Five

"What in the name of all that is holy…"

Ruby really wished she had an answer to her sister's whispered question, but she was just as shocked as Lena. Maybe even more so. Last night she had dragged an injured wolf into their living room and now, in its place lay a completely naked man.

"Shhh…" Ruby hustled her sister out of the living room and into the kitchen.

Lena's pale eyes were wide in disbelief when Ruby turned to face her. "What is going on? Who is that? What should we do?" Her sister's voice rose with every question and Ruby shushed her again. She needed to think before he woke up.

"I don't know," she admitted, pacing from the small breakfast nook to the kitchen counter and back. She took a lap around the table before stopping in front of Lena. Her sister twisted the belt of her bathrobe between her fingers.

"Should we call the police? Or an ambulance? He's bleeding." Lena glanced down at the bloodstains that trailed from the back door, through the kitchen and into the living room at the front of the house.

Images from the night before flashed through Ruby's mind: the wolf following her home, the terrifying fight, the blood, and her insane determination to help the animal that had saved her life. She'd rolled him up in an old rug she found in the shed and dragged him home. Well, she'd dragged him halfway across the yard and then gave up. She'd managed to coax him to his feet and got him to limp the rest of the way inside.

And then what? She'd gotten as far as the living room and collapsed on the couch, the wolf asleep at her feet, figuring she'd call the vet in the morning, with only a vague notion in her mind that bringing a giant injured animal into her home was a terrible idea.

Except now instead of an injured wolf she had an injured man instead. A perfectly normal Sunday morning.

"No police. I know him."

Lena's eyebrows shot up to her hairline. "You know him?"

Ruby nodded, striving for casualness, as though having a naked man lying on their living room floor was a typical occurrence in the Bellerose household.

"And what is he doing in our house?" Lena waited, her gaze boring into Ruby. Even before her strange episodes, Lena had always been able to see straight to the heart of her. "Ruby, what is going on? Are you in some kind of trouble?"

She didn't have time to think up a lie before a groan from the living room abruptly ended the conversation. They both hurried out to the living room to find Rafe still sprawled out in all his glory in front of the sofa like some kind of erotic coffee table. The thought of placing her coffee mug on Rafe's impressive abs nearly sent Ruby into a fit of hysterical giggles.

He groaned again and ran a hand down his face. The

muscles of his arm bunched and flexed, his stomach going taut with another groan, and while one part of Ruby's brain was still frantically trying to figure out what the hell was going on, the other half paused to take a moment and appreciate the creature in front of her.

She already knew he was big, but in the confines of her tiny living room, he looked massive. Dark hair covered his broad chest and trailed down his abs to his ... dear God. Ruby snapped her gaze away. He was asleep, for goodness' sake. She wasn't that much of a pervert.

Although there weren't many places she could look that didn't make her cheeks heat. The other two times she'd seen him, it had been dark, but now sun streamed in through the windows and streaked across Rafe's golden skin. His hair that had seemed black before was actually chocolate brown and hung down to his shoulders. Ruby's fingers curled at the memory of sinking into the thick fur at the wolf's neck.

His eyes were still closed but she remembered their silver stare. Dark stubble covered his face and his mouth was set in a pained grimace. Pained. Right. He was hurt and here she was gawking. His shoulder was still bloody, but somehow didn't look nearly as bad as it had last night. The flesh seemed to have knit itself back together and other than some ugly teeth marks and a few bruises, it looked significantly better. How—

Rafe stirred again, fluttering his eyes open with another low groan. Next to her Lena tensed, still worrying the ends of her robe. Ruby watched the realization of where he was slowly dawn across his face. Rafe turned to look at them from his position on the floor.

"Shit." He let out a long sigh, still not bothering to sit up or cover any part of his very distracting anatomy. His gaze stayed locked on Ruby's and she gripped the edge of the couch tighter, glad it stood as a barrier between them. She needed as many shields as she could get right now.

Lena cleared her throat and tossed him a throw blanket. He caught it with his good arm and pulled it over his lap, slowly working his way to a seat.

"Sorry. Uh … I'll get out of your hair."

Ruby let out a strangled laugh and Lena looked at her as though she'd lost her mind. She probably had. "You're not going anywhere."

Rafe raised an eyebrow.

"I have questions."

"Right, okay. I will go grab you some clothes then." Lena hurried out of the room, the steps creaking under her feet as she made her way upstairs. Ruby could only imagine what she was thinking, that this was some kind of bizarre lovers' spat.

Ruby climbed over the back of the sofa and perched on top. Rafe's mouth tipped into a small smile. He wrapped the blanket more firmly around his waist and maneuvered gingerly into the old armchair.

"What the hell is going on?" she asked as soon as Lena was out of earshot. "Last night I dragged a wolf in here, a wolf with your exact injury, and now…" She waved a hand in the general direction of all his muscle-y nakedness.

Rafe studied her, his silver gaze lingering on her bare feet. She tucked them under the nearest cushion. He raised his eyes back to hers and sighed.

"That was me."

"That was you? That wolf?"

"Yes."

Ruby pinched herself hard under the arm. "Ow, damn it."

"Why did you do that?"

"Just making sure." She rubbed her arm, ignoring the small

smile dancing around Rafe's lips. "So the wolf was you and this is you, so that makes you..." She couldn't bring herself to say it. It was too absurd.

"That makes me a werewolf." He winced a little at the word as though the admission hurt him, but he still held her gaze.

"Jesus Christ."

He huffed a laugh that sounded so similar to the wolf sound he'd made last night she nearly tipped backward off the couch. She ran her hands through her hair, combing it with her fingers and then twisting it into a knot. It was long enough that she could tie it up like that, no hair tie needed. Rafe watched every movement like she was the most interesting thing he'd ever seen. Goosebumps broke out across her skin and heat pooled in her belly.

"Here you go." Lena's voice broke through the sudden tension in the room. She tossed Rafe a pair of sweatpants and a T-shirt, apparently not wanting to get close enough to him to hand them over. They must be left over from Trevor, the last boyfriend who'd been scared away by Lena's "issues", as he'd so kindly called them.

Lena's gaze flicked between them. "I'm going to make some coffee. Anyone want some?"

"Yes. A lot." Ruby said with a nod.

Rafe huffed again and the phantom memory of his wolf breath skated across her skin.

"He'll take a cup too. We still have things to discuss."

Rafe gave Lena a sheepish smile. "I'm Rafe, by the way. Thanks for the clothes."

"Lena. Nice to meet you." She gave Ruby a questioning look before wandering back into the kitchen, but Ruby had no answers for her at the moment. At least none that didn't make her sound like a lunatic.

She swung her gaze back to Rafe and struggled with what to say next.

God, she was even more beautiful than he first thought. The way she was perched on the top edge of the couch gave him the perfect view of her long legs and firm thighs. He wished he wasn't quite so naked right now because the sight of her slender neck, exposed when she lifted the mass of hair off her shoulders, was enough to make his dick harder than it had been in weeks. Or possibly ever.

But it wasn't the sight of her lush curves or dark gaze or even the slightly smudged red lips—the lipstick worn off just enough it made her look thoroughly kissed—that sent his heart racing. No, it was the sight of those little bare feet. So vulnerable, so personal. He felt like he'd seen something he was never meant to. Her toenails were painted bright pink.

Unfortunately, besides being intimate and adorable, her tiny feet had only sent his blood racing at the memory of last night's attack. She could have been killed. She was too vulnerable. What if he had actually stayed away like she'd asked? A cold dread sank into his stomach at the thought.

He didn't recognize her attacker. Definitely not a member of his former pack, or at least no one he had known. But he wouldn't be surprised if his brother was somehow behind this whole thing.

"What are you thinking about?" Ruby asked, sliding the rest of the way onto the couch.

Her cinnamon-spiced scent assaulted him in the small room. He discreetly pressed down on the blanket in his lap.

"Nothing really." He cleared the raspiness from his throat. "Why?"

Ruby shrugged, still watching him. "Your face went all dark and frowny like you were angry."

He shook his head, his hair brushing across his bare shoulders, reminding him how exposed he was. "Uh ... maybe I'll get dressed before we talk?"

Ruby nodded, her face flushing pink. "Of course, sorry. The bathroom is right through there."

He followed the small hallway to a laundry room and half bath. The room was barely big enough for him to fit into but he managed, struggling into the too-small sweats and T-shirt in the cramped space. He felt ridiculous. The shirt clung to his body and the pants were too short by several inches. Not to mention they didn't exactly leave him enough room to have any hope of concealing his feelings for Ruby.

Christ. He raked his hands through his hair, wincing at the ache in his shoulder. It still wasn't fully healed but by tonight he should be fine. He wondered how the other wolf was doing and where the hell he'd come from.

He emerged back into the living room to find Ruby curled up on the couch with a fresh cup of coffee in her hands. His coffee sat on the small side table between the chair and sofa.

"How's your shoulder?" Ruby asked when he sat.

"Better." He took a sip and closed his eyes in relief. Healing took a lot out of him. Not to mention fighting, which he hadn't done in years. The memory of the other wolf's blood spilling into his mouth nearly had him spitting out his coffee. He had sworn he would never taste that again. And yet just the memory of it had him wanting to hunt down that wolf and finish what they'd started.

"You're doing it again."

He looked up to find Ruby staring at him over the rim of her mug.

"Doing what?"

"That angry stare thing. Like you want to kill someone."

He swallowed his next sip too fast. It burned the back of his throat. "I would never hurt you."

Ruby's eyes widened slightly but then returned to normal. "I know."

Her confidence in him was unnerving. He'd given her no reason to believe he wasn't a monster. In fact he'd just confessed to the exact opposite and yet she still sat across from him.

"But you would have killed that other wolf. Werewolf?"

He nodded yes to both her questions. It had been a while since he'd been around people and he couldn't seem to string together enough words. She waited quietly.

"I would have killed him, if I had to. And yes, he was a werewolf."

It was Ruby's turn to nod and sip her coffee. It had been a long time since he'd confessed to anyone what he really was and he was shocked that she hadn't run away yet. Instead she studied him with a focused curiosity.

"So why did that werewolf attack me?"

Chapter Six

R afe glanced toward the kitchen, not sure how much of his story Ruby would want her sister to hear. He wasn't sure how much he wanted to tell her either.

"My sister went out to grab some breakfast."

Rafe ran a hand through his hair, replaying the attack in his head. "I don't know why he attacked you. It's not done anymore. We have a strict policy..." Rafe trailed off, noticing the sick expression on Ruby's face.

"Anymore?"

Rafe swallowed hard. This was when she learned the truth about him. This was when she'd run. "We used to hunt humans. For sport."

"You what?" Ruby pulled the closest pillow onto her lap as though she could use it as a shield.

"We didn't kill them. Usually." Rafe ran a hand up the back of his neck, no longer able to meet Ruby's eye. "Just scare them."

"*You* did that? You terrorized humans?" She squeezed the pillow tighter.

43

"Yes." He could barely get the word past his lips. He deserved every ounce of disgust that dripped from her words.

"Why?"

He could try to explain the way he was raised. The pressure from his father to train and hunt and fight to be the best Alpha, the one that would take his place some day. He could blame the horrible things he'd done on his need to please that old bastard. But he wouldn't do that. He'd done those things. He'd chased terrified humans through the trees, listened as they begged for their lives, tackled them to the ground and growled as they pissed themselves, letting them go only when he was through toying with them. He was a fucking monster and he wouldn't lead Ruby to believe anything different.

He shrugged. "It's just what we did back then." It was only one item on his list of sins.

Ruby narrowed her eyes. "Back then? How old are you?"

Rafe shifted in his seat, wishing these damn clothes weren't so tight. He couldn't breathe with Ruby's eyes on him and this extra small T-shirt wasn't helping matters.

"Pretty old." He shrugged, his shoulder aching in protest.

Ruby sighed like she was getting tired of his terse answers.

"We haven't hunted humans in at least two hundred years," he added. "It got more dangerous for us than for them. We lost a lot of wolves. So I don't know what the hell that wolf was up to." Just the thought of that wolf lunging toward Ruby had his stomach twisted in angry knots. The need to go after him, track him down, and rip his throat out burned hot beneath his skin. Humans were off limits but animals, even other wolves, were fair game.

"So you're immortal?" Ruby asked instead of digging deeper into why she'd been attacked. Some of her earlier disgust was already being replaced with curiosity. Her death grip on the pillow loosened.

"No. Werewolves are perfectly capable of dying. It just takes us longer." There had been days, in fact, when he'd wished it wouldn't take quite so long, days when he wished for the end.

Ruby took another sip of her coffee and uncurled her legs. She stretched them out in front of her and wiggled her pink toes. He was mesmerized by the action.

"Were you born like this?"

"Yes." His gaze ran from her feet, over her calves and up her lush thighs. When he reached the edge of her short skirt he lifted his head and met her eyes. Her pale skin was flushed a delicious pink.

"Can someone turn into a werewolf, though? Like if you ... bite them?" She hesitated on the word "bite", her voice catching on something. Fear? Disgust? Desire?

Damn these tight pants. Rafe pressed what he hoped was a discreet hand over his lap, but the way Ruby's eyes flicked down, her blush deepening, told him that it wasn't as discreet as he hoped. But it was impossible to deny that the idea of biting Ruby's soft flesh made him hard as hell.

"No. Werewolves are born, not made." His lust quickly cooled with the unwanted memory of the last time he'd confessed to what he really was. It had been over a century ago, but the scars were still there, though they were worn smooth by the years. He'd been foolish enough at the time to think that Scarlet would see past the monster. The memory of the look on her face when he'd told her the truth of what he was... It had been an expression of pure horror. He had been wrong. She only saw the beast.

And now here he was confessing it all again. He shook the

memories from his head, the memories of his confession and every horrific thing that had happened after.

This time would be different. And he had completely different reasons for telling Ruby the truth. First of all, he didn't have much of a choice. Ruby had caught him in the act, so to speak. And secondly, if any of this knowledge kept her safe then he would freely give it.

She was still studying him with a look of fascination on her face. Her eyes were such a dark brown they appeared black and they were rimmed in dark lashes that contrasted sharply with her pale skin. And those lips. Fuck him, those lips were enough to drive a man out of his mind.

"O-kaaay..." she said finally, drawing out the second syllable. "So, you're a reformed werewolf who lives in the neighborhood." She smirked a little. "But why have you been following me?"

She moved closer, leaning on the arm of the sofa, her pillow carelessly tossed aside. What he wouldn't give to drag her onto his lap and...

He ran a hand through his hair, tugging harder than necessary, trying to regain his composure. It didn't work. Now he was thinking about Ruby's fingers in his hair, his head between her legs. What was wrong with him? He was acting like a fucking animal. Something he had avoided for years.

"I told you, I was trying to protect you."

"And I told you to cut it out."

He leaned toward her, bracing his forearms on his knees. Mere inches separated them now. "And what if I had listened?" His voice was a low growl and Ruby's dark eyes widened. "Not all werewolves are reformed."

A slight tremor went through Ruby's body, but she didn't take her eyes from his face. She shivered with fear, but her face

46

was eager, bright. Like she liked it. Like she liked *him* despite what he'd done last night or centuries ago. He could get addicted to that look, but he knew how that story ended. He pulled back, struggling against the gravity of Ruby's gaze.

"How did you know I was in danger? Are all werewolves psychic?"

He shook his head. "No. But with you, everything is different."

"Different" was an understatement. In the past twenty-four hours, Ruby had witnessed a brawl between wolves, woken up to a naked stranger in her house, discovered werewolves were real, and was having a very confusing physical reaction to the one sitting in her living room.

But despite everything Rafe had just told her, Ruby still found herself wanting to curl up in his lap like a damn cat. All the old black and white werewolf movies she used to watch with her aunt had not done the real thing justice. Rafe, a reformed werewolf, in living color in the middle of her living room, was overwhelming her senses.

Rafe stared at her like he was waiting for her to run, but she didn't have time to ask more questions before her phone rang. She jumped, startled by the obnoxious music. No one called her unless it was bad news. No one called anyone unless it was bad news. Wasn't that some kind of rule?

"Shit." She patted the cushions next to her but had no idea where her phone had ended up last night. She was exhausted after hauling the wolf, uh ... Rafe, into the house and she'd collapsed onto the couch where she'd apparently dozed off until Lena woke her up this morning with a strangled gasp.

Ruby stood up, frantically yanking pillows off the couch. It must have slipped between the cushions. Rafe jumped up too, sliding his hands in between the cracks in the couch. Ruby winced, just imagining the years of dust and crumbs he must be brushing up against right now. But he yanked the phone up, a triumphant smile on his face. That smile. Ugh. Damn it. She did not need to see that right now, so instead she grabbed the phone and answered it with a breathy hello.

"Ruby, hey. It's Nathan."

"Uh, hi?" Nathan Greene. She'd known him since kindergarten but why the hell was he calling her?

"I ran into your sister at the café and uh … she wasn't feeling well, so I'm going to bring her home."

Shit, shit, shit. "Thank you, Nathan. Seriously, I'm so glad you were there."

"No need to thank me. We'll be there in less than five."

Ruby blew out a long slow breath and hit end. She never should have let Lena go out alone but she was too damn distracted by…

She looked up and found Rafe staring at her. Like a predator watches its prey. He cocked his head just slightly, asking her without words what was wrong. Okay, so not like a predator, more like a guard dog. She would have smiled at her own joke if she wasn't so keyed up about Lena.

"You have to go." The words left her mouth before she really considered them, but she needed him out of here. It was bad enough that Nathan and whoever was at the coffee shop had witnessed Lena's latest episode, she didn't need Rafe seeing it too.

"Why?" His voice was rough every time he spoke, and his words were curt and brief like he wasn't used to speaking to people. Something sharp brushed against Ruby's heart at that thought. Sharp and sad. What was his life like?

She shook her head. No time to feel sorry for the wolf-man. She had Lena to worry about and that was plenty.

"My sister's not feeling well. You need to leave." She glanced down at his feet. Could she kick out a man with no shoes? Didn't matter, she was going to anyway. She put her hands on his chest and pushed to move him along, to jolt him out of his frozen stare.

Oh, big mistake.

He was solid and warm and real. It was as though even after this whole insane conversation she still hadn't thought of him as a real thing until she laid her hands on him. And now that she had, she wasn't sure she could take them off. It was like she was being electrocuted and the only way to break the current would be for someone to come by and kick her away from him.

His muscles twitched beneath her palms like he was holding himself still but it was becoming harder and harder to do. His breath hitched, pupils blown wide, turning his silver gaze black.

Ruby believed in a lot of things: ghosts, astrology, bad luck, the way the right shade of toenail polish could improve one's mood. But she had never believed in having an instant connection to someone until right now.

Rafe backed away and cleared his throat. "I can't leave. It's not safe."

Hold on just a minute…

Ruby didn't have time to argue with her wolfy protector before Nathan and Lena were coming in the back door. She gave Rafe her best glare, hoping she communicated just how she felt about his last statement before hurrying out to the kitchen.

"Are you all right?" She went right to Lena's side, ignoring a nervous-looking Nathan in the doorway and a scowling Rafe at her back.

"I'm fine. Really." Lena waved her concerns away with a hand. Ruby scanned her for damage but other than looking a bit paler than usual, she seemed all right.

"Thanks, Nathan. For bringing her home."

"Sure thing." He glanced over Ruby's shoulder at the glowering shadow behind her, but Ruby did not feel up to introductions at the moment. "Well, I'm sure you have a busy day ahead of you at the golf course. It's going to be another hot one."

Ruby moved toward the door, hoping Nathan would take the hint and get the hell out.

"Yeah, definitely." He dropped his voice so only Ruby could hear. "It's just that your sister was saying some strange things. Kinda freaked me out." His concerned gaze flicked back to Lena. The poor bastard was probably one of the many that had a crush on Lena since high school, but Nathan's feelings were not Ruby's main concern at the moment.

Ruby let out a stiff laugh. "Yes, well. You know us Bellerose girls. Big giant weirdos. Anyway, thanks again—"

Nathan put a hand on her shoulder to stop her rambling. Ruby could have sworn she heard a low growl from Rafe's corner of the kitchen. She ignored it.

"She said, 'They are coming.' What does that mean?"

"Uh ... gee. I'm not sure. Isn't that some kind of *Game of Thrones* reference?" Ruby wiggled free of Nathan's grasp and opened the back door for him.

"Anyway, thanks again!" She nearly shoved him out the door and then shut it with a sigh of relief.

"Who was that?" Rafe growled.

Ruby put her hand on her hip. "An old friend. Not that it's any of your business."

Lena raised her eyebrows, her gaze jumping back and forth between them.

"Lena, why don't you go upstairs and rest."

Her sister looked like she might protest, her stare lingering longer on Rafe, but her episodes exhausted her. She didn't argue but, as she walked past Ruby on her way out of the kitchen, she whispered, "What about him?"

"I told you, he's a friend. He … uh … got into a bit of a fight at the bar last night. So I let him crash here." There. That was a perfectly reasonable explanation. Ruby was about to congratulate herself on a lie well done when Lena asked,

"And what happened to his clothes?"

Ruby coughed. "He … uh … lost them in a particularly ruthless game of strip poker. Now off you go."

Lena looked at her like she didn't believe a damn word she said. She smiled like she had developed an entirely different theory about why there was a naked man in their house, but mercifully she left without asking any more questions.

Leaving Ruby alone with the wolf.

Chapter Seven

"What's wrong with your sister?" Despite his best efforts, every word out of Rafe's mouth was a growled demand.

Ruby narrowed her eyes. He'd pissed her off again. But he would be damned if he was going to leave her alone in this house before he figured out what that wolf wanted with her and who else was involved.

"Nothing's wrong with her," she snapped. She moved to the counter and poured herself another cup of coffee. "She just... She..." Ruby sighed and sank into one of the chairs at the kitchen table. Rafe lowered himself into the one across from her. It groaned beneath his weight.

Ruby rested her forehead on the table, exposing the nape of her neck and a few dark curls nestled there.

"She has these episodes sometimes and no one can really explain them." She spoke down at her lap and it was the first time since he'd met her that she sounded defeated. He fucking hated it. If there was something he could kill to make this go away for her, he would.

"That guy said she said something. Does she always?"

Ruby raised her head. "How did you hear him? He was whispering across the room from you."

Rafe shrugged, the tightness in his shoulder already better. "Wolf hearing."

Ruby frowned like she didn't like this little invasion of privacy, but he needed to know. He needed all the information he could get to figure this out.

Ruby sighed. "It doesn't matter."

"It does," he insisted.

"Why? You're here to protect *me* from some other wolf, right? Not my sister."

Rafe let out an impatient growl. "It might matter. I don't know what we are dealing with."

Her eyes flickered with concern, her teeth digging into her bottom lip, reminding him of all the shit she'd been through in the past day. About how this whole world was foreign to her. About how damn brave she was to still be sitting across from him.

Ruby blew out another long sigh. "When it happens, it's like she can't see me anymore. She goes somewhere else and I can't get to her." She slumped in her chair. "And she always says the same thing. ' *They're coming.*'"

They're coming? Well, that was ominous.

"When did it start?"

"A few months ago."

"Does she see anything? Like a vision or something?" He leaned forward, his arms on the table. Even in this tight space his body was drawn to hers, like he couldn't get close enough.

"A vision?" Ruby scrunched up her face. "She's not some kind of fortune teller."

"Then what is she?" He tried to keep his voice gentle but it came out gruff anyway.

The glare Ruby sent his way may as well have been a punch to the throat. "She's my sister. That's what she is. And you need to leave." She pushed back from the table and stood as though she were ready to escort him out, but there was no way he was leaving.

"Something's not right, Ruby. About any of this. That wolf. Your sister's ... episodes." He stood too, and even towering over her he felt like she could knock him over with a touch. "I can't just leave you alone."

Ruby crossed her arms over her chest, her dark eyes narrowed. If she had her boots on, she'd probably kick him in the shins. But he wasn't going to give in on this. If he'd listened to her before, that other wolf would have killed her.

"I am perfectly capable of taking care of myself."

"You are reckless and naive."

Her eyes widened and her red lips hung open. "How dare you? You don't even know me." She tried to storm past him into the living room, but he grabbed her and held her arms. A slight tremor ran through them both.

"I know that if I wasn't there last night, you wouldn't be here right now."

She wanted to argue with that. He felt it in the tension in her body and the fury in her stare. But she couldn't argue with the facts. As much as she hated to admit it, she needed him right now. She deflated a little in his arms and it took all his strength not to pull her to him, to press her body against his. He was a sick man.

"I'll sleep outside. You won't even know I'm here," he said, even as he already hated the idea of being separated from her again.

She let out an annoyed laugh. "You'll sleep outside? And how am I supposed to explain that to the neighbors? Oh, just disregard the enormous man camping out in the backyard. He's our new guard dog."

"Guard dog?" he growled. He tugged Ruby closer and she had to tilt her head back to look at him. A small smile crossed her face. He wanted to kiss it off her lips.

"Sorry. That was rude." She sighed and that glimmer of a smile disappeared. "You can sleep inside. I assume you're housebroken." She bit her bottom lip but the giggles burbled up out of her anyway.

Rafe couldn't help the laugh that escaped his mouth. He was just so damn relieved that Ruby wasn't upset anymore. She put a hand on his chest, still laughing, and he felt the shock of her touch jolt through him. By the sudden surprised look on her face, she felt it too.

Ruby cleared her throat. "You can let go of me now."

Rafe dropped his hands and Ruby pulled hers away too.

"What are you going to tell your sister?" he asked, pretending he didn't feel the absence of her touch like a kick in the gut.

"We'll tell her you need a place to crash for a few days. She won't mind."

The tension eased a bit in Rafe's shoulders. It was a start.

"But I have conditions," Ruby went on, retwisting the hair that had tumbled down during their argument. "First of all, Lena doesn't need to know about this, about what you are or about what happened last night. I don't want to stress her out any more than she already is."

Rafe had a feeling Lena was a bigger piece of this puzzle than Ruby wanted to believe, but he wasn't going to push her on it. Not yet anyway. If she didn't want her sister to know the truth about him, he wouldn't tell her.

"Fine." He nodded and Ruby continued.

"Secondly, I'm not a prisoner in my own home. I still need to work and live my life." She frowned a little, twisting a stray hair around her finger. "Although, I guess, living my life is basically just working. But it's non-negotiable."

"I'll go with you."

She laughed. "No. You won't."

Rafe felt the low rumble of a growl building in his chest but he swallowed it. "Fine, but I'll walk you to and from."

"Don't you work? Won't this keep you away from your own life?"

Rafe thought about his cramped cabin and his workshop filled with half-finished projects. "I can step away from it for a while. No one will miss me."

Something flickered across Ruby's face and when she met his gaze again, her eyes were softer. "But you'll stay out of the woods," he grumbled and her frown returned. Better she thought of him as an asshole than whatever that sweet expression meant.

"Fine," she gritted out. "Lastly, I want complete honesty from you. I want to be a part of whatever this is. It clearly involves me and my sister. Anything you know, I want to know." Her hands were on her hips now, the look of determination back on her face.

He couldn't help his smile. "Deal."

"Okay, deal." She let out a long breath, blowing the wisps of hair out of her face. "Now pour yourself another cup of coffee because I have a lot more questions."

"So, can you change whenever you want or do you have to wait for a full moon?"

Rafe gave her an amused smile. They were sitting on her back deck; the late afternoon sun was low enough now that the trees at the edge of the woods cast long shadows across the backyard. Ruby could see the torn-up grass where Rafe had fought that other wolf. She didn't let her gaze linger there. The rest of the yard was wild and unmowed. Dandelions waved in the breeze. Her bare feet hung over the edge of the deck, the wood rough beneath her palms. They'd never bothered to put furniture out here.

"No, that's a myth. I can change whenever I need to."

Interesting that he said need instead of want, like he never changed just for the fun of it, but Ruby didn't get to delve into that further. It was Rafe's turn. They'd been trading questions for most of the afternoon.

He studied her for a minute before asking, "I thought you only wore black."

Ruby peered down at the Care Bears tank top she'd found at the thrift shop and her purple terry cloth shorts. They'd both taken the time to shower and change, despite Rafe's reservations about leaving her for even an hour to go get stuff from his house.

She flashed him a smile of her own. "That's also a myth."

Rafe laughed, the sound like a roll of thunder in the distance. It was quickly becoming one of Ruby's favorite sounds. It was her turn but she was running out of general werewolf questions: were there other paranormal creatures out there? Yes. Full moon required? No. What did he eat? Mainly hamburgers and Snickers bars, but the occasional rabbit if he felt like hunting.

"What does it feel like to be a wolf?"

Rafe hesitated, thinking, his eyes fixed on the forest beyond the yard.

"Brighter," he said. "Like all your senses are magnified, but your self-control is weaker too. Like you want to run and run forever. Wild."

Wild. Ruby's blood rushed faster through her veins at the idea of running wild. What would it be like to leave it all behind? Her job, her sister, her bills ... and just run. She breathed in the fantasy together with the wildflower-scented air.

They were quiet for a long time before Rafe asked, "Favorite food?" An easy one.

"Chicken Parm."

"Fancy."

She could go with another easy one, but she wanted to know more. She wanted to know everything. Talking to Rafe was easy, even while it was intense. Like she wanted to unpack all the tangled-up shit inside her and lay it out for him. Like she already knew he wouldn't mind. And she wanted him to do the same.

"You mentioned something about your pack..."

Ruby could feel his body tense beside her. He sat the same way she did, with his long legs dangling over the edge of the deck, leaning back on his hands, face tipped toward the late day sun. But now he turned to look at her.

"You don't have to tell me. I was just wondering what happened to them." Ruby had been on the other end of this question enough times in her life to know what was going through Rafe's mind, the calculations being made. How much should you share? How would the other person react? No matter how many years went by, she still hadn't found a good way to tell people about her parents' death. There was no good way.

When Rafe finally spoke, his voice was rough and his gaze was on the treeline as if he could see all the way to his past. "I left five years ago and I haven't gone back."

He didn't elaborate and Ruby didn't ask. If he wanted to tell her more, he would.

"Does anyone else in your family have episodes like Lena?" he asked, shifting his big body so he could look at her.

She wasn't expecting that one, but she supposed she had it coming after asking about his family. She turned too, criss-crossing her legs in front of her.

There were those times when Aunt Millie's mind had seemed to leave the room even while her body stayed behind. But she was so old, ancient by the time Ruby and Lena had gone to live with her. Wasn't that just typical for someone her age? Plus she never relayed creepy messages afterwards like Lena did. She usually just asked the girls if they wanted ants on a log for a snack and they all moved on with their day.

A different memory flickered through her, one that had only gotten fuzzier over time. Had she really dreamt about her parents' accident before it happened? She had never been sure, but that couldn't be what Rafe was talking about. It wasn't the same as what was happening to Lena. Just a strange coincidence. One she hadn't thought of in years. She pushed the crazy idea that it mattered now out of her head.

"Uh ... not that I know of. My Aunt Millie was pretty into seances for a while, but I know she was the one pushing that ouija board thing. She denied it but I'm sure she was cheating."

Another low-thunder laugh had Ruby spilling more than she intended.

"She was just trying to cheer me up. After the accident..."

Ruby paused. She could leave the story here and never tell Rafe about her parents. Never give him the chance to pity her. Or add the tragedy to her pile of personality quirks. Fun facts about Ruby: wears black, favorite color red, sad little orphan.

Rafe leaned forward, resting his forearms on his thighs. His hair hung forward, half obscuring his face, but his silver eyes flashed from the shadows. "You don't have to tell me either. We all have shit in our past that we'd rather forget."

But that was just it, she didn't want to forget. She stopped telling people about her parents because it made *them* uncomfortable, not her. "My parents died in a car accident when I was eight. I went to live with my great-aunt in her big old house. And I was sad, of course I was. It was obviously the worst thing that ever happened to me; it still is the worst thing. And I was attacked by a werewolf ... so that's saying something."

Rafe's lips tipped into a smile, his gaze never leaving her face as she spoke.

"But I loved my aunt. She was smart and hilarious and she took good care of us. And I had my sister. Lena has always been my best friend. But..."

Ruby shifted, the sun-warmed wood comforting beneath her palms.

"But?" Rafe's voice was soft, not pushy or demanding, just curious.

"But after it happened, it was all anyone saw when they looked at me. Oh, there's poor Ruby, the girl who lost her parents. I was the sad girl and then the weird girl and then the creepy girl and now occasionally the weirdly hot girl when guys have a particular goth kink."

A low growl from Rafe on that particular comment curled

up inside Ruby like a pet. It was possible she could get used to this protective shit. From him anyway.

She shrugged. "Anyway, my aunt would take out the ouija board when we got sad. She would say, 'Let's call up Mom and Dad and tell them about your day.' I know that sounds insane and kind of morbid, but it helped. I still talk to them." She was rambling, telling this man, whom she hardly knew, way too much, but she had never been good at small talk.

"That's why you're not scared."

Ruby huffed a quiet laugh. "When the worst has already happened, there's not much left to be scared of."

"Oh, Ruby." Rafe's voice was a low whisper, caressing and gentle. "Things can always get worse."

Chapter Eight

Ruby stiffened, the ease they'd found this afternoon evaporating as soon as the words left his mouth. Shit. Why had he said it like that? He only meant that she should be careful, that she shouldn't let her guard down just because one terrible thing had happened to her. He knew from experience that life had plenty of space for more than one bad thing. But instead he'd uttered what basically sounded like some cryptic threat.

She cleared her throat. "Yeah, I guess you're right." She stood, not bothering to look down at him. "I have to get ready for work. If you really plan to escort me, I'm leaving in half an hour."

He absolutely planned on escorting her, but he didn't have time to say that or to apologize for being an asshole after she spilled her guts to him, before the screen door slammed behind her. God, his interpersonal skills had really taken a hit lately. Way too much time alone.

Apparently, there was more than one reason wolves lived in packs. It wasn't just for protection. More and more Rafe felt like he was losing both his wolf and his human side. Like he couldn't blend in with humans, couldn't talk to them, but also like he was forgetting how to be a wolf after being away from his pack for so long. And now he was a walking disaster that stalked and scared young women.

Who was he kidding? That wasn't new.

Rafe was still thinking about everything Ruby had told him when she hurried back out thirty minutes later. He had a few theories about Lena but nothing solid enough to mention.

"Hop to it, wolf-man. Or I'm going to be late."

He was currently sprawled out on the deck, soaking in the last rays of sun. Ruby stood above him, close enough that he could see the freckles on her legs, but not so close that he could see up her skirt. Not that he would have looked.

"Wolf-man?" He stood and stretched and pretended he didn't notice Ruby's gaze roaming across his chest and down his torso.

"You know this is totally unnecessary," she said, turning away and tromping down the stairs into the yard. Each one groaned like it might be its last day. A chipmunk scampered out from under the bottom step and raced through the tall grass. Rafe tracked it with his eyes.

"Hungry?" Ruby asked, laughter clear in her voice.

He gave her his best wolfish smile. She could tease him about whatever she wanted as long as she was smiling again. He'd totally fucked up their earlier conversation. He didn't need her believing he was some sort of nice guy but he also didn't want to hurt her. Ever.

"Nah, chipmunks are too small for me. I go for bigger game."

Ruby huffed a disbelieving laugh and strode ahead of him. They walked around the side of the house and onto the sidewalk out front. There were only two other houses at this end of the street, with neat yards and window boxes below each window.

Rafe glanced back at Ruby's house. The tiny bungalow must be at least one hundred years old. The lawn out front was just as unkempt as out back, more of a meadow than a lawn. Wildflowers swayed in the evening breeze. The rest of the house was tidy despite its age, giving the yard a deliberate and not neglected vibe. He would bet Ruby loved those wildflowers.

He picked up his pace to keep stride beside her as they made their way through the rest of her neighborhood and on to the small main street in town. There were exactly two bars in this town and Rafe was assuming Ruby didn't work at the biker bar on the south side, although he was learning that Ruby was full of surprises.

"I can handle it from here," she said, nodding to a passing couple. "I'm not going to get attacked by a wolf in the middle of town."

Rafe leaned toward her, lowering his voice. "Are you embarrassed to be seen with me, Ruby?"

She sputtered, "Uh, no." She picked up her pace. Rafe matched her step for step. "But the more people see us together, the more questions they're going to have. This is a small town."

"Just tell them we're friends."

Ruby stopped short. "Friends?"

"Yeah."

"A friend who walks me to work every day?"

"I'm a very nice friend." He grinned.

Ruby bit her bottom lip, her white teeth sinking into her blood red flesh. *Friends*, he reminded himself.

She sighed through her nose like he was exasperating her, which he found more entertaining than he probably should.

"Okay, well, I'm here now. So you can go."

They'd stopped in front of the Sligo Pub, the other bar in town. He just happened to love their burgers. "I think I am hungry, after all."

Ruby's eyes widened and her mouth hung open in protest but he waltzed by her and pushed open the door into the dark interior of the bar. He heard Ruby stomping in behind him, her boots making every ounce of her displeasure known. Rafe ignored her and headed for the bar, settling himself on his usual stool.

She disappeared into the back for a minute and then came out, tying a short black apron around her waist. She pulled a small notepad from the front pocket and stood on the other side of the bar in front of him.

"What can I get you, sir?"

He raised his eyebrows. Now it was "sir"? Ruby smirked.

"Hamburger, rare. No onions. And a Guinness, please."

"Coming right up."

She spun away from him, her long hair swinging around her shoulders. Her cinnamon-spiced scent trailed behind her, but he didn't feel the familiar longing to follow her. Something about knowing he could be near her had calmed something in him.

But he shouldn't let his guard down. He scanned the crowded interior: booths along the wall, a few high-top tables in the middle, and a small stage in the back corner for live music. The bar was about half full already, and he was sure it would be packed in another hour or two. Ever since Macy took over as manager, the bar had been pulling in more and more business, but he hadn't been in here in months, since before Ruby started working here, apparently.

Not finding anyone that made the hair on the back of his

neck rise, Rafe turned back to the bar just in time for Ruby to slide his plate in front of him.

"Thanks."

"You are very welcome. Let me know if I can get you anything else," she said in a syrupy sweet voice he'd never heard from her. She was about to turn back to her other customers, when Macy emerged from the kitchen.

"Rafe! Is that you?"

He raised his burger-free hand in greeting. "Hey, Mace."

"Where the hell have you been? You haven't been in in months. I thought maybe I offended you." Macy leaned her elbows on the bar, her long purple braids swinging over her shoulder.

"Oh no, nothing like that. Just been busy." Busy taking a break from pretending to be human, busy repeating past mistakes.

Ruby was watching their exchange with rapt attention.

"We've been getting so many compliments on the tables," Macy said, her smile bright in her light brown face.

"Glad to hear it." He took another big bite of his burger.

Macy tapped a hand on the bar in front of him. "I'll let you get back to your meal. Glad you're here, Rafe." She worked her way down the bar, refilling drinks and taking orders. Ruby stood frozen.

"Don't you have work to do?" he asked, taking a swig from his beer.

"You know Macy? How?"

"This is my favorite bar."

"How come I've never seen you in here then?"

He shrugged. "I haven't been in town in a while."

Ruby narrowed her eyes like she didn't believe that he ever came into town.

"I do need supplies every now and then. And I like Macy's burgers." He shrugged again and took another bite. "Sorry if I ruined the wolf-man mystique for you. I don't always prowl in the shadows."

A scarlet blush ran up Ruby's cheeks. So maybe she did have a bit of a primal kink.

"That's not it at all. I'm just surprised." She put her hands on her hips, still studying him. "What did Macy mean about tables?"

Rafe lifted his head from his meal and gestured vaguely behind him. "I made the tables. I'm a woodworker."

Ruby's eyebrows raised to her hairline. "You made them?"

"Yep."

"Hmm."

He flashed her a grin before she was called away by another customer.

Rafe being a woodworker should not have been the most surprising thing Ruby learned today. And yet, something about him being an actual person and not just some shadowy figment of her imagination had really thrown her for a loop.

That and the fact that he'd hung around for her entire shift. His gaze followed her around the bar, tracking her movements, like a familiar caress. It shouldn't have been hot. It should have been annoying. But she was having a hard time convincing her body of that.

With about a half hour left in her shift, Ruby found Rafe in a corner booth with a few of her regular customers.

"Hey, guys, what can I get you tonight?"

Callie pushed her long blonde braid over her shoulder. "Just fries and a coke for me."

"Bacon cheeseburger, fries, and a Sam Adams for me." Sawyer flashed her a grin. "Actually, can we also get an order of wings for the table?"

Callie raised her eyebrows, her blue eyes wide. "Really, Sawyer?"

He laughed. "I'm hungry."

Callie leaned into his side with an ease Ruby had never felt with another person. Her gaze flicked to Rafe, who looked more and more like a deranged lumberjack next to these two fresh-faced lovebirds. His five o'clock shadow was nearly a full beard even though he'd shaved this afternoon. He'd tied his long hair back while he ate, making his silver eyes that much more noticeable. He had one arm slung across the bench on his side of the booth, the muscles flexing in his forearm as he gripped the edge of the seat.

"And for you, sir?"

"Stop pretending you don't know me, Ruby," he grumbled.

Callie's eyes shot from Ruby to Rafe and back again. "You two know each other?" she asked.

Ruby shifted from tired foot to tired foot. "We just met," she said at the same time Rafe blurted out, "We're old friends."

Well, there goes keeping their story straight.

Callie's forehead crinkled in confusion. "So, you reconnected recently?"

"Something like that," Ruby mumbled and then quickly changed the subject. "How do you two know Rafe?"

"Uh ... well..." Callie stumbled over her words. Apparently, it was her turn to be flustered over her connection to Rafe.

"I'm a friend of her grandmother's. From way back," Rafe said, his gaze steady on Ruby.

Realization dawned on her slowly. "Her grandmother? Oh…" *From way back.*

Callie smiled up at her. So she knew what Rafe was. It wasn't until Ruby walked away to put in their order that she thought to wonder what the hell Callie might be.

Chapter Nine

By the time they were walking home, Ruby was exhausted, as usual. And Rafe, by her side, insisted on staying in town and avoiding the woods, making the walk even longer. And making Ruby even grouchier.

The night was hot and humid, the air heavy with the threat of thunderstorms. It was past one o'clock and the streets were deserted, especially when they hit the residential side of town. Ruby shifted her bag of leftovers to her other hand and adjusted the purse on her shoulder. She could feel the heat of Rafe's gaze on her even though they hadn't spoken a word since they left the bar. His presence was as warm and ominous as the storm clouds overhead.

He tried to take the bag from her hand but she tightened her grip.

"What are you doing?"

"Let me carry it." He tugged again on the bag. "You're tired." His voice was a low rumble and while part of her wanted to argue that she was perfectly capable of carrying her own bag, the other part of her was really fucking tired. So she let him take it. Then he lifted the purse from her shoulder and slung it over his own.

Ruby glanced over at him. Her purse looked absurdly tiny against his huge chest. The laugh burst from her lips so fast and loud, she clapped a hand over her mouth to quiet it.

He quirked a small smile. "What?"

"You look ridiculous," she told him between snorts.

"Well, you sound ridiculous." He pulled the purse strap higher on his shoulder and looked down at her with a haughty expression that had her doubling over in giggles. He let out an exasperated sigh, but his smile grew.

She nudged him with her shoulder and he didn't budge. "Thanks for carrying my stuff." They started walking again, crossing the bridge over the highway that led to her neighborhood. A few cars raced underneath, their engines loud in the quiet night air. "And thanks for the whole saving my life thing," she went on, the bridge safely crossed. "I don't think I ever said that."

Rafe's gaze was heavy on her again, his looming presence towering over her. A familiar trail of goosebumps broke out along her arms, the hairs rising on the back of her neck. She didn't dare look at him, for fear of those flashing silver eyes.

"It was my pleasure," he rumbled, every word coming from some place deep in his chest.

"So, is Callie a wolf like you?" she asked, suddenly needing a change of subject.

Rafe cleared his throat, his eyes back on the sidewalk in front of them. "No, she's not like me."

"What is she then?"

"I'm not really in the habit of outing other people."

A sudden chill raced up Ruby's spine, despite the heat of the night. How many others were there? "Right. Sorry, I shouldn't have asked."

"It's a lot to take in, all in one day."

"That's an understatement."

Rafe huffed that wolfy laugh and heat pooled in Ruby's stomach. They turned onto her street and the realization that Rafe—a man she barely knew, one that was capable of turning into a wolf— was going to sleep in her house tonight hit her hard in the panic center of her brain. The fire alarm started going off in her skull, drowning out whatever it was Rafe had said last.

"Uh ... what?" She turned to face him as they stopped on her front path.

"I said, I can sleep outside." He cleared his throat. "I mean, in wolf form."

Right, wolf form. That did make a heck of a lot more sense than him sleeping outside in man form, which was what she'd imagined when he'd brought it up earlier.

"Do you like sleeping outside?" she asked, tipping her head to look up at him. The scent of fresh cut grass and electricity hung heavy between them.

He shrugged. "It's not bad. I used to do it a lot when I was younger."

Ruby nodded, her gaze running across his wide chest to where her purse dangled from his shoulder. Her leftovers were clutched in his other hand. It was hard to be scared of a man while he was holding your purse. She let out a long sigh.

"I don't want to make you uncomfortable," he said, dipping his head to rumble quietly in her ear. "I just want to keep you safe, but we'll do this however you want." His breath was a cool breeze against her overheated skin. He smelled like pine and sawdust. Ruby wanted to climb him like a tree.

She shook her head. *Yikes. No climbing the werewolf, Ruby.*

"You can sleep inside." Her voice shook and she cleared it. "We wouldn't want the neighbors calling animal control."

"Right." Rafe nodded once, his gaze never leaving her face, like he could read her every dirty thought about him. She was in so much trouble.

"Lead the way." Rafe gestured toward the door.

Fireflies flicked on and off in the dark yard, creating a pattern that only made sense to them. Ruby took a deep breath and led the wolf back into her house.

The enormity of how bad an idea this was didn't hit Rafe until he was standing alone in Ruby's living room. She'd crept upstairs to check on her sister and to find him some blankets and a pillow. Her scent clung to him like a second skin. He should have slept outside in the dirt. He should keep his distance from this woman who looked at him like he could be human, like he could be redeemed. But Lord knew he was beyond redemption. His father had made sure of that long ago. The old bastard had never failed to remind his sons of their true selves. They were monsters and he made sure they acted like it.

Even now, with his pack life behind him and his father cold in his grave, Rafe couldn't shed that truth. What happened to Scarlet couldn't be undone. But Ruby's eyes on him in the dark made him long to start over.

Her footsteps on the stairs interrupted that dangerous line of thought. For now.

She stopped in front of him, the exhaustion clear on her face. She worked so damn hard. He'd seen it for weeks, of course, her bone-tired steps through the woods, her weary trek toward home, but now he knew she had been heading home to more work. More caretaking. He'd wanted to carry more than her purse tonight. He'd wanted to lift her over his shoulder and carry her home.

The thought that she probably would have kicked him brought a small smile to his lips. Ruby frowned.

"So I might have made things worse," she said.

"Worse?"

"Uh, yeah." Her arms were suspiciously empty of blankets. Good. Outside would be better. "I may have told Lena we're sleeping together."

"You what?" He nearly choked on his surprise.

Ruby winced. "I'm a terrible liar! Especially when it comes to Lena. She was looking at me with those moonbeam eyes of hers and I panicked!"

Moonbeam eyes. That was a perfect description of her sister's eerily pale eyes, but Rafe didn't have time to appreciate Ruby's flowery language right now. Not when she'd said out loud the thing he had been trying very hard not to think about. Sleeping with Ruby. A growl started low in his throat and he couldn't stop it from spilling out into the quiet of the little house.

"You panicked and the first thing you thought to tell her was that we're sleeping together?"

Ruby's pale skin flushed pink. "It didn't make sense that you were some friend she's never heard of and that all of a sudden you needed a place to sleep." She put her hands on her hips in that way he already liked too much, the way that said she wasn't backing down.

"So you told her…"

Ruby blew out a sigh like he was the one being difficult. "I told her we're seeing each other and that we met at work. I said you might be spending some nights here. That's all. No big deal." She tilted her chin up to look at him and goddamn if he didn't want to take that ruby red bottom lip between his teeth and ruin her makeup completely.

"Okay," he said because he was an idiot who was never finished punishing himself for past sins.

"Okay." Ruby nodded once and then turned back toward the stairs. "Come with me."

He followed her up the creaky steps, worn smooth with age. He kept his eyes on her bare feet instead of her ass. Mostly anyway. That damn skirt was flapping at him like a red flag to a bull. Upstairs, Ruby led him down a narrow hallway to the second bedroom on the left. She pushed open the door and he followed her in like a puppy.

The room was small like everything else in this house. It was clearly built by gnomes or something. Ruby's bed took up one entire wall. Under the only window sat a desk covered in stacks of books and a small lamp. Two closet doors filled the other wall. A worn braided rug hid most of the old wood floor. He leaned against the faded daisy wallpaper next to the door as Ruby's scent wrapped around his throat like a vice. He would not survive the night.

Ruby's gaze flitted around the room like she was seeing it for the first time.

"Maybe this was a terrible idea."

Rafe looked at the thin rug and then at the full-sized bed. Neither option was particularly promising. Not that he would dare to think he could sleep in the bed.

"How light of a sleeper is your sister?"

"She sleeps like the dead."

"Perfect. Turn around."

Ruby's eyes widened but she obeyed. She'd had enough

shocks for one day. The last thing he wanted was for her to see him shift. He closed his eyes, letting his body rearrange itself. Bones shifted and muscles transformed. Fur sprouted from his skin. His hearing sharpened. His sense of smell nearly killed him. But this was better. He'd be more comfortable on the floor as a wolf and he'd be ready if anything happened to threaten Ruby.

Most importantly, as a wolf he couldn't do any of the incredibly stupid shit he was thinking of doing right now. With him as a wolf, Ruby was safe.

When he was done shifting, he brushed against Ruby's hand. She sunk her fingers into the fur at his neck and if wolves could purr he sure as fuck would have.

"All right, wolf-man, let's go to bed."

Rafe woke up to the sound of soft laughter. He lifted his head from where it had been tucked beneath his tail. It was still dark, but a soft glow was emanating from Ruby's bed. Rafe stretched and ambled over to her bedside. He rested his chin on the edge of the mattress.

"Sorry," Ruby whispered. "Did I wake you?"

Rafe huffed and nudged her free hand. She immediately dug her fingers into his fur. God, he was getting way too used to that.

"I couldn't sleep. Bad dream." She waved her phone at him. "Thought I would watch a little *Golden Girls* to calm me down."

Had he been in human form he would have loved to tease her about that, but as it was he just huffed again. Ruby cocked her head, studying him for a minute before patting the spot beside her.

"Do you want to come up?"

He should not come up. There was no scenario in which coming up was a good idea. And yet...

Rafe glanced over his shoulder to find his damn tail waving like a sail in the wind. Son of a bitch. His own body betrayed him.

Ruby smiled.

He jumped up.

Apparently, being in wolf form was not going to help him as much as he hoped. He circled twice out of habit and dropped down on the blankets beside her. She kept her distance at first, holding up her phone so they could both watch, laughing quietly at every snarky remark from Sophia and every absurd comment from Rose. But slowly, her hand began to droop and she slouched lower into her pillows. Her phone dropped into her lap and Rafe nudged it with his nose, pausing Blanche's dirty jokes and the audience's canned laughter.

Ruby sighed softly in her sleep and snuggled in closer to him, her body warm and soft against his side. He could feel every breath she took, every twitch in her sleep, every dreamy murmur. He lowered his head to his front paws and watched the clouds sweep past the moon out the window, casting shadows on the bed.

Sleep was no longer an option. Not with Ruby's hand resting on the top of his head, her chest rising and falling against his back. It was the perfect torture. And it gave him far too much time to think, to remember.

Chapter Ten

Scarlet's hand was small and warm in his. She smiled shyly up at him as they walked down the dusty road. The summer sun was setting behind the tops of the tall pines and the sky burned with oranges and reds.

"Thanks for walking me home," she said, her voice as sweet as the heavily perfumed air. Wildflowers lined the roadside and bobbed in the evening breeze. Everything was pinks and yellows, bright and cheery. It was all so different from Rafe's days in the shadows of the trees, none of it felt real.

Scarlet gave his fingers a light squeeze. Real. She was real. And she was speaking to him and letting him hold her hand.

"You're welcome," he said, struggling to remember how to speak to a human. His interactions were usually limited to short visits into town for supplies and wolves weren't big on manners. His trips to the general store for his father's smokes and whatever else the pack needed never mattered to him before. Not until Scarlet took over for her aging father. Not until she smiled at him, slow and shy, a slight blush creeping up her cheeks.

No one had ever looked at him like that before. Like he was something other than the second son of the Alpha, or like the giant stranger that came into town every so often. Humans tended to keep their distance like they sensed something was off about him. They weren't wrong.

It wasn't all that long ago that he used to chase the local settlers just for fun. For the thrill of it, to calm the beast inside him. Although the humans never seemed to find it fun.

Theo would have laughed at that. His younger brother found morbid shit like that funny, but Rafe knew he wouldn't repeat it to him later. Things had changed between him and his brothers lately. Not that they had ever been close. They'd butted heads their whole lives, all three of them too different to see eye to eye. Their father made sure to drive the wedge between them deeper over the years, turning everything into a fight. A competition. The past few months had been worse than they'd ever been.

"This is my house," she said, coming to a stop beside a stone-lined path. The walkway led to an old farmhouse with a wide front porch. Two rocking chairs sat side by side. Cozy, welcoming. Rafe had never lived in a house with four solid walls, but the thought was suddenly appealing, like maybe he might enjoy that. Like he might also enjoy rocking beside Scarlet in those cozy-looking chairs.

Wouldn't that image make his father choke.

"Will I see you again?" he blurted out, not wanting his time with her to end. "At the store, I mean."

Scarlet's smile grew. "I'm there every day, helping out my dad."

Rafe nodded, already trying to figure out the next time he could slip away into town.

"So, you'll be back in again soon?" she asked, lifting her chin to look at him. The setting sun lined her in gold.

"Soon as I can."

She put her hands on his chest, her blush deepening. His heart raced beneath her fingers. Could she feel it? She lifted up on her toes and brushed her lips across his, so soft, so gentle. It brought back the only other gentle memories he had, his stepmother, Nell, caressing his forehead as he fell asleep.

But then he wrapped an arm around Scarlet's waist and pulled her closer and a breathy sigh escaped her lips. He wasn't thinking about his stepmother then. No, he was thinking about Scarlet's hands wrapped in the front of his shirt, and her mouth pressed against his, and her heart beating frantically against his chest.

Stop, he needed to stop. She was so delicate, so fragile, a butterfly he was trying to catch with his big, monstrous hands. He let her go and she smiled up at him, dazed from their kiss.

"I like you, Rafe," she said, stunning him even further into silence. "See you soon." She turned and walked away from him, her words repeating on a loop in his head. She *liked* him?

He must be doing a damn good job pretending for that little slip of a woman to like him. He just didn't know how long he could keep it up.

Chapter Eleven

T he next few days passed in a warm summer haze. Walking to and from work with Rafe, the streets empty and dark, had Ruby feeling like she was existing somewhere between a dream and reality. Somehow, the sexy fantasy she'd been having for the past month had materialized and was walking beside her like everything was normal. Like requiring a werewolf bodyguard was all perfectly regular. But the really odd part was how normal it did feel. How right Rafe felt next to her.

The night air was thick and warm, a weight heavy on her shoulders as they walked home. Ruby wished the heatwave would end but every storm seemed to only bring more humidity. Rafe's hand brushed against hers and despite the weather, shivers raced up her arm. She glanced up at him, his face stoic and strong in the light of the street lamps. He caught her looking and heat flared in her cheeks.

"What?" he asked, brow furrowed.

"Nothing. Just thinking it's nice to have someone to walk with."

He looked at her a moment too long and she glanced away, her pulse thrumming in her ears. Why did he still have this effect on her? She was acting like a horny fangirl. But seriously, a sexy werewolf had been her wet dream since puberty. It was a lot to take in.

"Want to eat with us again?"

He'd sat around the kitchen table every night so far, eating leftovers from the pub with her and Lena, joining them in their little ritual.

Her sister had even taken to smiling and laughing again, teasing Rafe for his taciturn nature, always trying to pull more words out of him. It made Ruby remember why her sister was so adored. Lena charmed her way into everyone's hearts. And Ruby was glad her sister was comfortable with their little—giant—houseguest.

Lena's appetite was back too, and Ruby wasn't even mad when her sister scraped all the best bits of burnt cheese off the edges of the lasagna.

"Sure." Rafe's voice was a rumble in the darkness.

"Okay, great." Ruby ignored the odd squeak in her own voice and hoped Rafe did too. They walked up the front path to the house, the front door's cheerful yellow obvious even in the dark. She leaned into the door with her shoulder, pushing their way in. The old wood had a tendency to swell in the heat and it groaned in protest.

Rafe followed her through the living room and into the kitchen, his presence in her house never failing to send a jolt of nervous excitement through her.

"Lena! We're back. I brought dinner." Ruby paused, waiting for her sister's response, dreading the nights when Lena didn't answer.

"Coming!"

Ruby let out a sigh of relief and caught Rafe studying her. She gave him a quick smile and set the food on the table, busying herself with setting out utensils and plates. A large hand on the small of her back stopped her in her tracks. Lightning zipped up her spine.

"You don't have to serve anyone here," he said, his mouth dangerously close to her ear as he reached around her and took the plates from her hands. "You've been on your feet for hours. Go sit."

The gruff command sent her scurrying to her chair faster than she would ever admit. Rafe set the plates on the table while she opened the takeout containers. It was probably terrible for her body to eat such heavy food at one in the morning but Ruby ate breakfast at noon and the rest of the day was a crap shoot. She was starving. Her stomach grumbled at the smell of Macy's signature fries. Extra salty just the way Ruby liked them.

"Ooo … fries. Yum." Lena snaked a fry on her way to her seat and popped it in her mouth. "Hey, Rafe."

"Lena." He nodded as Lena dished up her food.

"How was work?"

"Work was good. Busy. Lots of tips." Ruby smiled at her sister, not wanting her to know the truth, which was that work was long, tiring, and soul-sucking. Lena felt bad enough about not being able to contribute to their bank account right now. Ruby didn't want to make it worse. But somehow, from Lena's doubtful expression, her sister already knew exactly how she felt about her job.

"What did you get up to today, Rafe?" Lena asked, turning her gaze to the giant man in their kitchen.

Rafe stuffed the remains of his burger in his mouth and gave Lena a noncommittal shrug. Ruby bit down on a smile, picturing him running through the woods chasing bunnies.

"I told you, Lena. Rafe's a woodworker."

"Right." Lena tipped her head. "You do have a bit of a lumberjack vibe."

Rafe grimaced.

"That's not the same thing," Ruby said with a choked laugh.

Lena waved a hand like it was inconsequential what Rafe did with his wood. *Settle down, Ruby.* She stuffed more fries in her mouth to stifle a giggle.

"So, are you going to finally tell me the real story of how you two met?" Lena asked, twirling her fork between her fingers. She used to do the same thing with her hair, twirl the long, blond locks around her fingers. Ruby had seen boys captivated by the motion, hypnotized by her beautiful sister. At the moment, Ruby was just glad she was eating.

"I told you, work," she jumped in before Rafe could answer.

"Right. After that intense game of strip poker."

Rafe's eyebrows rose to his hairline. Ruby shrugged apologetically, forgetting about that little lie.

"Just a friendly afterhours game."

"Of course," Lena said with a laugh. The girls weren't in the habit of policing each other's dating habits, but an injured naked man in the middle of the living room was unusual even for Ruby. "It must have gotten pretty rough. You were bleeding." Lena's tone had turned serious and Ruby shifted in her seat.

"I fell. On the way home."

Ruby nodded vigorously. *Yes, good job, Rafe. Very convincing.*

Lena's gaze swung between them but then she shrugged, apparently deciding to give up this mystery for now. Ruby blew out a sigh of relief. She wanted Lena to be comfortable having

Rafe here but there was just no way to explain that first encounter without spilling the whole insane story.

"You don't usually have … guests for this long, Ruby."

Ruby's face went up in flames and she didn't dare meet Rafe's eye. It was true Ruby wasn't one for long-term relationships but she really didn't need Lena making her sound like she tossed men away after one night. Although … that wasn't entirely wrong.

"Rafe's different." Different in that he's a werewolf. Different in that they were faking this whole thing. Different in that she wanted to keep him forever. Forever? Yikes. She needed to get a grip.

Lena smiled brighter, taking another big forkful of food. She could tease Ruby as much as she wanted if it meant she kept eating, kept smiling.

"Well, I'm glad you've stuck around, Rafe."

Color swept up his cheek bones. "Uh … thanks. Me too." His gaze flicked to Ruby, his eyes intent on hers. "I think I'll head upstairs."

"Goodnight!" Lena called sweetly after him and Ruby couldn't help a smile. She loved seeing her sister like this. Cheerful, happy. Healthy. "It's nice you're keeping this one, Ruby-red."

"Yeah, thanks for making me sound like some kind of loose woman."

Lena burst out laughing and Ruby joined in, their giggles filling the kitchen like old times. As popular as her sister had been, she'd always made time for Ruby, the two staying up late to talk about Lena's latest date or to dissect Ruby's current favorite movie. There was always a plate of late-night snacks between them, leftovers they'd scrounged from the fridge or whatever little cakes their aunt had bought for her daily tea. For so long, it had been just the two of them. Except for lately, when it had been just Ruby at this table, tired and alone.

Ruby wished she could bottle it up, this moment, for later when inevitably Lena's illness would return.

"Loose woman?" Lena gasped. "Okay, Aunt Millie."

Ruby grinned at the comparison to their aunt. "Whatever. I'm going to bed too."

"Enjoy!" Lena said, giggling into the rest of the lasagna.

Ruby climbed the stairs, thinking about what her sister had said. Lena was right. Ruby didn't keep men around like this and even though the relationship was fake it didn't make sense, this instant trust she put in him. Ruby could count on one hand the number of people she let into her life and still have fingers left over. But something about Rafe just made sense. His steady presence beside her lightened her load. Well, his presence and his tendency to carry her bags for her.

She found herself opening up to him, whispering things to him in the dark that she didn't admit to anyone. Her confessions filled the night. How exhausted she was. How she wished things with Lena would go back to normal. How she was sick of everyone in this town and longed to escape their judgment and their pity.

And Rafe listened. He listened and for the first time in a long time, Ruby felt like she had a friend. A friend she desperately wanted to kiss, among other things, but a friend nonetheless.

Some nights he stayed at the bar, but more often than not he left her alone to work. Even with Macy and Callie, he never seemed totally comfortable around others, like he worried they might find out more than he wanted them to, might see more than he meant to show them. She wished he would let her see more of him, wished her presence loosened his tongue the way his did to her. But so far, he'd remained frustratingly quiet.

Other than a few tidbits about woodworking, she hadn't gotten much more out of him since their first day together.

Ruby stroked his soft fur as he lay beside her on the bed. This was a new habit too. Rafe in her bed, his wolfy sighs lulling her to sleep. She wondered if he was as lonely as she was. Or had been before sneaking into her life. Maybe tomorrow she would ask him.

"What should we watch tonight?" she asked even though he couldn't answer. Not really. "How about *An American Werewolf in London*?"

Rafe narrowed his eyes.

"No? It's a classic!" Ruby bit down on a smile. "Okay, how about *The Howling*?"

Rafe huffed a wolfy breath against the exposed skin of her arm.

"You're right, too scary." Ruby kept scrolling through the movie options, her laptop balanced on her knees. "Oooo! *Frankenstein Meets the Wolf Man*!"

The wolf beside her let out a low growl and goosebumps rose along her arms but she couldn't help the giggle that escaped her lips. "You know you could have more of a say in the choices if you stayed in human form."

Rafe laid his head on his front paws, his ears twitching. Ruby couldn't help the thoughts that crept into her head about what it would be like to have a human Rafe in her bed. "Here, I know." Ruby clicked on *Teen Wolf* and snuggled down into her pillows. "You can't tell me you don't love this one. Everyone loves this one."

Rafe sighed, shifting his big body closer to hers. Ruby smiled to herself, thinking about what her preteen self would have done if she walked into the room right now to find Ruby snuggling in bed with a gigantic werewolf, her favorite movie playing on the screen. Again Ruby had the feeling that she was existing in some space in between, some dream that she would soon wake up from. She dug her fingers into Rafe's fur. She didn't want to wake up.

Rafe shifted, resting his head in her lap and she scratched between his ears. A growl rumbled low in his throat, the one she'd come to equate with a cat's purr. Maybe he was happy here too. Maybe even after this werewolf attack situation was ironed out he would stay. At the moment, it didn't seem like too much to ask for.

Chapter Twelve

R uby woke to find the bed next to her warm but empty and the smell of bacon wafting up the stairs. She stretched and glanced out the window. Dark clouds still filled the sky. The storm hadn't broken and the humidity hung heavy in the air. There were no giant wolves in the yard so she could only assume it was Rafe cooking breakfast. Lena would have burned the house down by now.

Ruby considered changing out of her pajamas before joining Rafe in the kitchen, but he'd already seen her butterfly-covered sleep shorts and the oversized David Bowie T-shirt she wore to bed every night. So why bother? Also she was starving and breakfast smelled amazing. Besides, fake boyfriends/bizarre temporary roommates saw you in your PJs, right?

Tugging the T-shirt back up on her shoulder, Ruby wandered downstairs to eat. She found Rafe wearing her *Wolf Man* circa 1941 apron and scrambling eggs in her kitchen. He froze when she walked in like he could sense her without looking.

He cleared his throat. "Morning," he rumbled, not turning away from the stove.

"Uh, morning." Ruby sidled into the kitchen and grabbed her favorite mug from the cabinet and poured herself some coffee. She couldn't remember the last time she'd woken up to fresh coffee someone else had made. Probably never. Every other day this week, she'd managed to beat Rafe to the kitchen, but today she'd slept in.

Rafe continued pushing eggs around the pan and flipping sizzling bacon, so Ruby prepared her coffee and sat at the table. She folded her hands. And then unfolded them. Her T-shirt slid down her shoulder again and she yanked it back up. Maybe she should have at least put on a bra. God, she was practically naked. Somehow this never seemed like a big deal when Rafe was a wolf, but now faced with a very human Rafe in her kitchen, Ruby was suddenly aware of every inch of exposed skin. On both of them.

She untied her hair and let it fall down her back, but was immediately too hot and twisted it back up. She tapped her fingers on the table, sipped her coffee, stared out the window. What the hell was one supposed to do while someone else made them breakfast?

Even during her last few years living with her aunt, Ruby was the one who made breakfast. Well, who made all the meals, if she was being honest. Aunt Millie was so old at that point and she'd taken such good care of them when they needed her most, Ruby really hadn't minded taking care of her for a while.

Needless to say, she had no idea how to handle the current situation. So she continued to fidget and sneak peeks at Rafe while he cooked. He had his hair tied back today in a knot at the base of his skull, revealing the strong lines of his face. He was freshly shaven this morning and wearing nothing but the apron and a worn pair of jeans. He moved fluidly around the kitchen, scooping eggs onto plates, buttering toast and plucking bacon from the grease. It was like he'd always been here. Ruby blinked and shifted in her seat suddenly uncomfortable with just how comfortable she was around this man. Again she was shocked by how quickly it had happened. How seamlessly he had fit into her life.

Rafe grabbed a plate in each hand and set one down in front of Ruby and then slid into the chair across from her.

"Thanks for breakfast. You really didn't have to."

Rafe shrugged. "If we really were sleeping together, I would have."

Ruby inhaled too quickly—the image of Rafe braced over her in bed tearing through her mind—and sucked a perfectly cooked piece of egg into the back of her throat. "Ack!" She coughed and sputtered. Rafe jumped up from his seat, rattling coffee mugs and patted her, hard, on the back.

Ruby waved him frantically away, his firm touch only adding to the panicked flutter of her heart and the very inconvenient constricting of her airway. Rafe backed away but continued to stare at her with a furrowed brow until she finally stopped coughing.

"I'm fine. I'm fine," she said between gasps. "Really. I just swallowed weird."

Never taking his eyes off her, like she could suddenly die at any moment, Rafe lowered himself back into his seat.

"You sure you're okay?"

She smiled reassuringly and scooped more eggs into her mouth. Damn, they were so fluffy. "Yep, totally fine."

He quirked an eyebrow.

"Really. Fine."

He nodded and tore into a piece of bacon, followed by a

huge forkful of eggs, and a bite of toast that obliterated nearly half the slice. His Adam's apple bobbed as he took a gulp of coffee. Ruby traced the column of his neck with her eyes down the V of the shirt he'd put on to eat, to the dark shadow of hair beneath it. Her fingers curled around the edge of her chair at the memory of her fingers in his fur.

Rafe cleared his throat and Ruby tore her gaze up to find him smirking, his silver eyes flashing stormy in the morning light. Heat crept up Ruby's neck. Busted.

"No one ever makes me breakfast," she said, tugging her shirt up on her shoulder again.

"I know."

"How could you possibly know that?" she asked, a small shiver of fear running up her spine. Had he been watching her at home too?

He shrugged and leaned back in his chair, his breakfast long gone already. "Well, I assumed."

Ruby stared at him until he finally went on.

"You take care of everyone. That's clear right away." He held her stare. "It's time someone took care of you."

Ruby's eyes widened. Why did he say that out loud? Why did he imply he should be the one to take care of her? God, he really was an idiot.

He stood too quickly, rattling the plates again. He grabbed his empty dishes and walked them to the sink, leaving Ruby staring after him in confusion. He needed to get to the bottom of whatever the hell was going on with this other wolf and fast. And then he needed to get far away from Ruby.

"I'm going to see my brother today." It had only been a vague plan but it came out of his mouth like an edict.

"Your brother?" She'd followed him into the kitchen and now stood leaning against the counter, cradling her coffee. Hot pink letters said, *Fuck off, I'm reading* on the side. He bit down on a smile.

"Yeah, maybe he'll have some insight into what's going on." Rafe actually had very little hope that his younger brother, Theo, knew anything, but he had to get out of here and he had to do something that at least felt remotely helpful. He had gotten way too damn comfortable here over the past week. It was time to snap out of this false sense of domestic bliss. He wasn't built for this shit.

"You can't leave the house while I'm gone. I'll be back before your shift." He peered at her out of the corner of his eye. He was still facing the sink, his hands braced on either side of it, like this piece of plumbing could save him from all the things he wanted to do right now.

Ruby's shirt had slipped down her arm again, revealing the pale curve of her shoulder, the soft line of her neck, her clavicle bone just beneath her delicate skin. He'd been avoiding looking at her breasts all morning and it had taken a nearly Herculean effort. He let his gaze slip lower now, over the outline of her tits beneath the soft shirt. Lower still her thick thighs made those tiny shorts look even tinier. Goddamn it. He ground his teeth so hard his jaw ached. *This* was why he slept in wolf form.

He pushed away from the sink, practically launching himself back into the center of the kitchen. "I'll leave soon and be back before sundown."

Ruby plunked her coffee mug down on the counter and turned to face him, her hands on her lusciously wide hips. Fuck him. Maybe he should just shift and run like hell out of here. She'd never catch him.

"Nope. No way." She stepped closer. "You promised me you'd be honest with me."

"Nothing I've said this morning has been a lie."

Another step closer. The smell of cinnamon and coffee clung to his nostrils. "Maybe you haven't lied, but you haven't told me anything. And now you're just going to run off on your little mission and leave me here wondering what the hell is going on? Nope. Not happening."

A low warning growl tumbled from his lips but Ruby didn't back up. In fact, she stepped closer.

"Fine," he ground out. "What do you want to know?"

Ruby grinned. "First of all, who is this brother of yours?" She held up one finger in front of him and it took all his remaining strength not to suck it into his mouth and run his teeth along her sensitive skin.

"His name is Theo. He's my younger brother."

Ruby raised an eyebrow, waiting for more. Rafe had nothing else he needed to say. Theo was his younger brother. He'd seen him only sporadically in the last five years, much like his older brother and everyone else he'd grown up with. Theo was a spoiled fuckboy who spent his days screwing women he barely knew and shirking all responsibilities. Rafe was the one who made that life possible for Theo all those years ago, and it pissed him off that he chose to waste his second chance at life. But none of that seemed relevant right now.

"And is he still with your pack?" Ruby asked, trying to draw out more information. He'd been stingy with it, with stories about himself, while Ruby had opened up to him a little more every day. He already knew it was a privilege she afforded to very few people. But he couldn't reciprocate.

Rafe ran a hand down his face, pressing down all memories of his damn pack and both his damn brothers. He never should have mentioned it. He should have just said he was going to look for clues or something.

"No, he isn't. He left when I did. But he may have heard from our other brother."

"There's three of you?"

Rafe nodded. There were three of them and that had always been the problem. "Our older brother, Knox, is the current Alpha of our pack. It's possible Theo has heard from him." He could go straight to Knox for information, but he doubted his older brother would even bother to meet with him.

"And you'll talk to him for me?"

Rafe blinked. "Of course. Why wouldn't I?"

Ruby's lips tipped into a small smile. "Well, you clearly don't want to. You're obviously estranged from this family of yours and you're still willing to go talk to him for me."

Ruby stepped forward again until there was nothing more than a sliver of cinnamon-scented air between them. Rafe stepped back, colliding with the wall behind him.

"Stop looking at me like that, Ruby," he growled.

"Like what?"

"Like I'm the hero here."

Her smile grew.

Rafe shook his head, his hair rasping against the wall behind him. Ruby took the last step and laid her hands on his chest, right over his racing heart. He had to go. *Now.*

"Then what are you, Rafe?" Her breath skated over the skin of his neck. Her face was tipped up to look at him and her lips were right there, so fucking close. He could have her if he wanted her. She was making that abundantly clear. And goddamn, he had never wanted anyone more, not since Scarlet. Not since the last time he'd made this same mistake.

He grabbed her by the arms and held her back. Her eyes filled with hurt.

"I'm the monster."

Rafe's fingers dug into the flesh of her upper arms as he held her away from his body. His words, *I'm the monster*, hung in the air between them. Ruby watched the rapid rise and fall of his chest. His hair had come loose, shadowing his face again, but not before Ruby saw the desperate desire in his eyes, the same desire that was tearing through her body, but he was fighting it. Fighting it so hard his hands trembled against her skin.

"Monsters don't cook breakfast," she said.

"Ruby, don't." He shook his head.

"Monsters don't watch old movies with you in the middle of the night." She wriggled out his grasp.

"Ruby." Her name was a growled warning but she didn't listen.

"Monsters don't carry your purse." She pushed the hair from his face and tucked it behind his ear. The muscle in his jaw ticked. She leaned in, rising on her toes just enough to brush her lips against his. She felt the rumble in his chest as it vibrated through her, but his hands remained at his sides, his huge body rigid against her kitchen wall.

"Rafe," she whispered against his mouth. "Kiss me." She pressed her body against the full length of his and his restraint broke.

He grabbed her ass with both hands and lifted her, his lips crashing against hers. His kiss was hungry and wild, like he hadn't done it in a long time but like he'd really fucking missed it. She slid her hands through his hair and he groaned, breaking the kiss only to scatter more kisses along her cheekbones, his lips feather-light. God, she loved that about him, this gentleness sprinkled in with his roughness. He claimed her lips again, his tongue sweeping in and tangling with hers.

Ruby was suddenly very aware of the thinness of her shirt, the rub of it against her breasts as she squirmed against Rafe's chest. She tugged his hair again just to hear another low growl, to feel it vibrate between her legs.

Rafe shifted and turned them so Ruby was the one pinned against the wall, so he could take a hand off her ass and skate it up her useless shirt, so she could feel his calloused fingertips against her stomach, tickling the dip in her waist, running across the underside of her breast. Rafe's breath caught, a soft stutter against her throat.

"Shit, Ruby. You're so fucking soft." He nuzzled against her neck, kissing and sucking, his fingers still toying with her, his thick erection pressed into her middle.

God, she wanted him. She had never wanted like this, like she was on fire. She squirmed between him and the wall, shamelessly pressing herself into him, needing to get closer…

"Uh … good morning?" Lena's voice broke through Ruby's fog of lust. Rafe dropped her so fast she nearly landed on her ass.

"Shit," he muttered, backing away from her and running a hand through his hair.

"Morning," Ruby squeaked, attempting to smooth down her shirt and act like this was all perfectly normal. She cleared her throat. "Rafe made breakfast."

"Did he? How nice." Lena's gaze flicked between the two of

them, a smile dancing on her lips. "What a productive morning you two are having. Thanks, Rafe."

Rafe wouldn't meet her eye and instead seemed to be finding the old linoleum floor to be infinitely interesting. He muttered some unintelligible response and moved toward the door.

"I need to go."

"Don't rush out on my account," Lena chirped, filling her plate at the stove. "But you might want to move your after-breakfast activities to Ruby's room."

With Lena's back to them Rafe finally looked up. His pupils were still blown wide, the black swallowing up the silver, and his lips were swollen from kissing her. He took a quick step toward her.

"Stay inside. I'll be back soon." The words were a rushed growl against her cheek followed by a rough push of his lips against hers and then he was out the back door and gone.

Lena carried her plate to the table with a smirk on her face. "Did he just run out of here barefoot?" There was laughter in her voice and color in her cheeks and it was enough to distract Ruby from whatever the hell had just happened between her and her wolf-man. Lena looked healthy again this morning.

"He ... uh ... I think he left them out back on the deck."

Lena nodded, chewing thoughtfully. "He's an odd one, Ruby-red, but I like him."

Ruby noticed she had a hand on her chest over her rapidly beating heart. She glanced out the back window and could have sworn she saw a flash of gray fur tearing through the trees.

"Yeah, I like him too."

Chapter Thirteen

"You think you're better than us, Rafe. That's the problem. You think you're human." His father's breath smelled like cigarettes and stale coffee. "When will you embrace who you are?"

Rafe wasn't in the mood for this today. He wanted to keep the feel of Scarlet's smooth skin and her burnt sugar scent a bit longer. He had no desire to replace it with flying fur and the smell of blood. But his father had set up the sparring ring again and Knox was already inside, pawing at the dirt like a damn bull or something.

Knox was big in wolf form, intimidating and fast. He eyed Rafe with narrowed eyes, flashing silver in the sunlight. Rafe huffed out a breath. There was a time when he interacted with his brothers without trying to tear them apart, a time when they used to spar for fun, for no other reason than their wolf side demanded the release. But more and more now his father insisted on a winner, insisted on a fight that ended with one brother pinned and humiliated and the other victorious in front of the pack.

Other wolves, some in human form, had gathered to watch the fight. The Alpha loved parading his sons out for the pack to see. To show them who their next leader would be, who they should fear. Rafe despised it. This false show of strength. If he ever was the Alpha, he sure as hell wouldn't lead the way his father did, through ruthless displays of strength and manipulation.

"Is this really necessary?" Rafe asked, leaning in closer. His father would only make things worse for him if he made a scene in front of the pack. He knew. He'd tried it before when his father started these matches a few months ago. Rafe had refused to get in the ring with Theo and instead he'd ended up bloody and beaten beneath his father's claws and a growled promise of "more where that came from" in his ear.

His father wouldn't be around forever and these tests of strength would be how he chose his successor. A thought that made Rafe sick to his stomach.

The Alpha sneered. "Where were you today, Rafe?"

"Town."

"You've been spending an awful lot of time there. Been sniffing around some human pussy?"

Rafe's whole body recoiled at his father's words. If his father found out about Scarlet, Rafe didn't know what he'd do. Fear tightened his gut.

"Course not."

His father circled him as though taking his measure. The man was getting older, as even werewolves did eventually, and those human cigarettes he loved so much weren't doing him any favors. But the old man was still strong and he fought dirty. Rafe knew better than to challenge him again. It wasn't just his father he'd have to fight this time. Packs thrived on hierarchy. His father surrounded himself with werewolves that were loyal and he rewarded them at every turn. If he wanted to take down the Alpha, he'd have to take down the whole top third of the pyramid too. And everyone else was just afraid. Simple as that.

They needed each other to survive, to hunt enough to feed themselves, to protect their land. There weren't many wolves willing to strike out on their own. Wolves exiled by the Alpha didn't last long as far as Rafe knew. They were either killed by humans or died of exposure. Starvation. A wolf on his own was vulnerable.

So when he looked out into the crowd, he didn't find a single sympathetic face, a single wolf willing to stand up to the Alpha.

Rafe sighed. He was so tired of this bullshit. And it had only gotten worse. The old ways were failing them. Civilization was closing in and the pack was finding it harder and harder to find space and isolation. The pack needed to run, needed to hunt. With humans taking up more room, the pack had to adapt. If they wanted to survive, they'd need to interact with humans more, but his father didn't want any part of that. The old man wouldn't allow it. Beyond a few supply trips here and there, Devon felt werewolves and humans shouldn't mix. If the man wasn't so addicted to nicotine, he might ban trips into town altogether.

Scarlet's throaty laugh ran through his mind. Maybe Rafe didn't want to be isolated anymore. Maybe he could leave—

"Whatever crazy bullshit you're thinking, son, forget it," his father growled, knowing Rafe's thoughts before he could even think them. "You were born a beast and you'll die one. There's no point in trying to be something you're not." His father stalked off toward the ring. "They don't want you anyway," he added with a cackle that deteriorated into a hacking cough.

He remembered Scarlet's hand on his, the taste of her

mouth, the way she said his name. What if she knew what he really was? Would she still want him?

He yanked his shirt over his head and tossed it on a nearby branch. Toed off his shoes and stripped off his pants. He had already shifted by the time he reached the ring and lunged for his brother's neck.

It wasn't hard to imagine what Scarlet's reaction would be if she were here now.

He fucking hated it when his father was right.

Chapter Fourteen

Rafe ran.

He ran until his lungs burned and the scent of cinnamon and coffee and Ruby was finally replaced with pine and dirt and dead leaves. He ran until the trees blurred together and the earth beneath his paws nearly erased the feel of Ruby's soft skin beneath his fingers. Nearly but not completely. And nothing could stop the sounds of her moans and whimpers from playing over and over in his mind. The wind through his fur only reminded him of Ruby's fingers in his hair, tugging and demanding.

He had fucked up. He'd given in when he'd only wanted to protect her. Especially from himself, because regardless of what Ruby said, he was a monster. A fact that had been drilled into him for years, decades. His father, the old Alpha, had made sure of it. He made sure that no werewolf in his pack ever forgot what they truly were, especially his sons.

But she'd been so damn soft and she smelled so fucking good and when she pressed her body against his, it made him weak. So damn weak. Too weak to protect her at all.

If he was being honest, they were lucky Lena didn't find them with Ruby bent over the kitchen table, her ass in the air and Rafe thrusting into her from behind.

Goddamn it. That was not a helpful image.

Oh, if his father could hear him now, pining over another human woman. Rafe could hear the old man's sneering voice, could feel the scrape of the man's claws over his skin.

Rafe shook off the memory, pushing himself to run faster.

He was the largest of his brothers, huge from the day he was born, killing his mother on his way into the world. His father had refused to get medical attention for her, the mother Rafe never met. If she was strong enough, she would survive. That was the old bastard's way of thinking.

Rafe should have taken over as Alpha. It's what his father had wanted. But Rafe never did. Never wanted to fight his brothers like his father had insisted; claws and fangs were the only language he knew for so long.

He'd left all that behind, but now he felt it dragging him back. Back to those fights, back to his father's demands, back to his backward, dying pack. The pack that his father had refused to bring into the modern world, leaving them fending for themselves in the backwoods of Maine. Rafe had left all of it, like the coward that he was.

He wouldn't let Ruby make him forget the things he'd done. The life he'd lived. He would figure out who was after her and then he'd go back to his cabin and forget Ruby. Ruby and her soft skin and red lips. Ruby who took care of everyone. Ruby who thought she had nothing to fear.

Rafe let his wolf brain take over, letting the world become nothing more than smells and sounds: a family of skunks in a nearby log, a snake slithering beneath the dried leaves, the sun warming his back. Simple sensations. Simple thoughts. Maybe he should be a wolf more often.

It didn't take long to get to Theo's cabin, not in wolf form anyway. He shifted in the overgrown front lawn and grabbed some clothes from the front porch. They always left some lying around for moments like this.

Rafe was bigger than his brother and the T-shirt stretched tight across his chest. He took a peek around the house, looking for signs of life. The cabin was similar to Rafe's, small, isolated, an old pickup around back for trips into town.

But Theo's house had two chairs out on the front porch and window boxes with flowers in full bloom. He wasn't alone out here. Rafe swallowed the swift rise of jealousy and rapped his knuckles on the door.

No answer.

He knocked again, louder this time and threw in a shouted "Theo" for good measure. He didn't have time to waste, not if he wanted to get back in time for Ruby's shift at the bar.

Shuffling sounds and a muttered curse came from behind the door, and then Theo tugged it open, blinking in the sunlight.

He squinted up at Rafe. "Oh, fuck. What are you doing here?" He stepped aside, rubbing a hand over his stubbled jaw and let Rafe into the dim interior. All the curtains were drawn tight against the daylight.

"It's after noon. Why were you still asleep?"

Theo flipped on the light and gave his brother a lopsided grin that Rafe was sure some people would find charming. He found it irritating to the extreme.

"I had company last night."

Rafe grimaced. "Still fucking every human, nymph, and witch in a fifty-mile radius?" There was no shortage of pretty, available creatures in these woods or the surrounding towns and his brother seemed to be acquainted with all of them.

Theo clapped a hand on Rafe's shoulder like they were pals. They had never been pals, not even before their father pitted them against each other. They had been brothers who fought, argued, wrestled, and drove Nell crazy. If he was honest, it hadn't been all bad, but Rafe chose not to remember that. Then he would have to acknowledge what he'd lost. One more thing his father had stolen from him.

"You know I don't fuck witches. Not since that last one put a hex on me." He shuddered and shuffled into the adjoining kitchenette.

"That wasn't a hex. It was chlamydia," Rafe grumbled.

Theo's laugh filled the tiny house. "Funny." He poured two cups of coffee and held one out to Rafe. He accepted but only to have something to do with his hands that didn't involve punching his brother in the face.

Theo had always been the pretty one, the one all the pack women doted on when they were young. He took after his mother, Nell, the woman their father jumped on so quickly after Rafe's own mother's death. His eyes were an eerie green like hers, and his hair black and curly when he let it grow. It was short now. Too short. The scar that ran from temple to his jaw was too visible.

"Where's Phoebe?"

That wiped the smirk off his brother's face.

"What do you care?"

"Does she know you're still fucking around?"

Theo leaned his hands on the counter separating them, his eyes flashing. "That's none of your business."

"I didn't get you out of the pack so you could fuck everything that moves. I thought you and Phoebe—"

Theo cut him off with a slam of his hand on the counter. "She's none of your business. *We* are none of your business."

Rafe held his stare but his little brother didn't back down. This was a fight they'd had before. Rafe thought he saved him that day, thought he'd spared his little brother's life. His father wanted a fight to the death, but he didn't get it. And when Rafe caused enough of a distraction for his younger brother to slip off into the night, he thought for sure he'd run off with Phoebe, the little dryad he'd been in love with for years.

But smarts did not run in the family.

Phoebe was around. Rafe could see her touch everywhere. But his idiot brother was still pretending she was nothing more than a friend. What an asshole. Rafe didn't have time for that today.

"Did you come all this way just to bust my balls? Seems like a text would have done the job." Theo's voice was a low growl. In the old days they would have shifted and taken this little discussion out back, but it wasn't the old days. And as much as he hated the damn thing, Rafe did have a cell phone, but he'd needed to do this in person.

He cleared his throat and ignored Theo's question. "Have you heard from Knox?"

None of the tension left Theo's body with the move from one uncomfortable topic to the next, but the defensiveness left his gaze.

"No, of course not. Why?"

"How about anyone else from back home?"

Theo's eyes widened. He stood up from the counter and folded his arms across his chest. "I talk to some people. Why do you care about the pack all of a sudden?"

Rafe ignored the sudden pang of guilt he felt at the thought of the people he'd left behind. "I think something's going on."

"You're going to have to be more specific."

Rafe nearly growled. Now that it was time to talk about Ruby out loud he was finding it hard to do. How the hell was he supposed to explain this to Theo?

"My neighbor was attacked."

Theo's eyebrow rose. "Your neighbor?"

Rafe cleared his throat. "Distant neighbor."

"Okay, so? Cut the two-word answers and fill me in if you want my damn help."

Help? Who said anything about help? Rafe ran a hand through his hair, memories of the night Ruby was attacked racing through his mind. Okay, maybe a little help would be all right.

"My neighbor was attacked by a wolf. No one that I recognized, but definitely one of us. If I hadn't been there..." He had to clear his throat again, the panic of that night suddenly clamping tight around his windpipe. "I was there, though. That time. I just need to figure out who's behind it and why."

At some point he'd started pacing and the amusement on Theo's face had grown as he spoke.

"And who is this neighbor, exactly? A sweet little old lady? Or maybe a family with adorable kids?"

"It doesn't matter who it is. They're in danger." Something in Rafe's jaw cracked as he ground his molars together.

Theo smirked and shrugged, bringing his mug to his lips. "Maybe it was just a wolf out for some fun."

"That kind of fun isn't allowed anymore."

Another infuriating shrug. "Don't tell me you never get the urge to chase some pussy through the woods, Rafe. Tackle her in the dirt, hold her down..."

"Shut. The. Fuck. Up."

Theo's cackle made Rafe think maybe his father was right.

Maybe he should have killed this asshole when he had the chance. He slammed his mug down on the counter and turned toward the door. "Never mind. You clearly don't know shit."

"What makes you think this is more than a one-time attack?"

Theo's question made him stop in his tracks, one hand on the door. *They're coming.* Lena's visions or episodes or whatever the hell they were had to mean something. It couldn't be a coincidence that Ruby was attacked and her sister has some kind of power. But should he tell Theo?

He turned around to face his brother again. The smirk was gone, replaced by actual curiosity.

Rafe sighed. "Her sister has these visions or something. It feels like it might be related."

"What, like a seer?"

It was Rafe's turn to shrug. He had no idea what Lena's deal was. There hadn't been a known seer around in decades. At least not one that anyone had heard about. But if she did have clairvoyant powers, it would definitely be something people would be interested in. Like willing-to-do-some-damage-to-get-their-hands-on interested in. The power to see what was coming, who wouldn't want that?

"Shit. That's wild."

"Yeah, well. If you hear anything let me know." Rafe shifted, the old floorboards groaning beneath his weight. "Anything about Knox or the pack going after humans again. Just let me know."

Theo nodded, his brow knit together in concentration. "I don't think he would, man."

Rafe's skin prickled. He had no desire to listen to Theo defend their older brother.

"I've heard that he's done a lot for the pack," Theo went on.

Rafe snorted. "I'm sure he is. Feel free to go crawling back whenever you like."

A low growl rumbled from Theo's chest. "Fuck you, Rafe."

"Same to you."

He was out the door and shifting again before he had time to think about how much he wanted to throttle his little brother and how much it pissed him off that he'd bothered to save his life if he wasn't going to do anything with it.

Another pleasant visit and nothing to show for it.

Chapter Fifteen

Rafe loped into Ruby's yard a couple hours later, his muscles aching from the long run, but his lungs filled with fresh piney air. He'd almost completely shaken off the bullshit with his brother when Ruby's cottage came into view.

Rafe stopped dead in his tracks. The yard reeked of another wolf. More than one. And still nobody he knew. Rafe sniffed the grass around him, the trail leading straight to Ruby's back door.

Ruby.

He was shifting as he ran, tugging on the gym shorts he'd left on the back deck. He ran a hand over the claw marks on the door and his heart stopped. Shit. He never should have left her. Oh, God what had he done?

He nearly tripped head-first into the house, his shorts still not fully covering his ass, his pulse pounding in his ears, to find Ruby and Lena at the kitchen table playing cards.

Their heads snapped up, wide-eyed, when he stumbled into the room.

"Uh, hi. Welcome back," Ruby said, a small smile playing

around her lips. She'd painted them bright red. Blood red. Goddamn this woman.

"Come with me." He grabbed her arm, tugging her up from the table and nearly dragging her from the room. He was being an asshole. He was being a barbaric asshole. But all he could imagine when he smelled those other wolves and found those claw marks was Ruby's body torn to pieces, her blood staining the floorboards. The memories of another woman's blood staining his hands flooded his thoughts. His throat tightened, strangling him.

Ruby tugged her arm back when they made it to the living room. "What the hell is wrong with you?" she hissed.

"I..." Rafe squeezed his eyes shut, willing the image of Ruby's bloody flesh from his mind. "I just..." He couldn't breathe. His lungs forgot how. What if they'd gotten to her? What would they have done?

Then Ruby's hand was on his arm. "Okay, big guy. Take a seat." She guided him to the couch and sat beside him. Her hand was cool on the back of his neck as she gently pushed his head between his knees.

"Just breathe," she whispered and slowly, slowly his throat loosened and his lungs took up their job again.

When he finally managed to look up at her again, there was so much damn concern in her eyes it nearly sent him into a tailspin all over again. He pressed his fingers into his thighs, digging in until the pain distracted him from the soft look on Ruby's face. He did not deserve that soft look.

"What happened?" she asked, sitting back on the cushions, her legs crossed beneath her.

"Did you go anywhere?"

"No. You said not to, so I didn't—"

"Good." His voice was rough. Too rough. Everything he said

sounded like he was angry with her. But it wasn't her. It was everything else.

Her hand was on his arm again, her fingers tracing his muscles. He hadn't bothered with a shirt.

"What happened?" she asked again and he remembered he'd promised her honesty.

He let out a long sigh and glanced toward the kitchen. They could hear Lena shuffling around, cleaning up.

"Come with me." Ruby tugged him up from the couch and led him upstairs to her room, resettling on her bed. He sank down beside her, his feet on the floor, forearms resting on his thighs, his gaze on the floorboards.

"There were more wolves here. Today. I could smell them in the yard."

"Oh." Ruby's voice was quiet. At some point it had started to rain. Thunder rumbled in the distance.

"I wasn't here—" He lifted his face to look at her and found her big dark eyes staring at him. "You could have been hurt." He couldn't help it; he had to touch her. He cupped her face in his hands and swept a thumb across her cheek bone. She softened under his touch. So soft, so willing. Her lips parted and he suddenly wanted that red lipstick smeared across his body.

Goddamn it. He nearly growled, pressing his forehead to hers, and her lashes fluttered closed.

Chase her through the woods, tackle her in the dirt, hold her down…

Theo's words ran through his head. It was all too easy to picture: Ruby beneath him, her breath coming fast and needy, her whimpers and moans, her lush thighs wrapped around him…

Shit.

He pulled away, running his hands roughly through his own hair. Ruby blinked her eyes open and raised a dark brow, but she didn't push him. Didn't comment on the raging erection that was so obvious in these damn shorts.

"Did you find out anything from your brother?" Her question was casual but the throaty quality to her voice told him she was just as affected as she was.

Rafe huffed. "Nothing. It was a wasted trip. Just reminded me how much he pisses me off."

She laughed a little at that and shifted next to him. Lightning flashed and lit the dim room, thunder louder than before.

"What time do you need to be at work?"

"We don't have to leave for another hour."

Rafe nodded. The storm should pass by then. He glanced down at his lap. Not sure he could say the same for his current problem.

Ruby moved closer, her breath skating across the skin of his arm. "What should we do to pass the time?"

Rafe jumped up from the bed as though Ruby had bitten him. She actually didn't hate that idea. All that exposed skin, all those muscles.

"I should go check the area. Make sure they're gone."

"It's pouring outside." Ruby glanced toward the window and then back to the enormous man in her bedroom. His eyes were wild, like he wanted to run. His cock still strained against the front of his shorts. Ruby might have been insulted at his hasty retreat if it weren't for the physical evidence that he wanted her too.

"Still, I should check." Rafe ran a shaky hand through his

hair. He had been so worried about her when he stumbled into the house. She'd seen the fear gripping his face.

"Rafe, just wait—"

He turned and rushed from the room before she had a chance to stop him. Ruby let out a long sigh and flopped back on the pillows, trying to ignore the ache between her legs.

What was up with this guy? Their conversation from this morning ran back through her head. All that bullshit about being a monster. Like she was some perfect flower that he didn't want to sully with his dirt. She didn't know what was floating around in Rafe's past that made him believe he wasn't good enough for her, but in the last week she'd learned everything she needed to know about her wolf-man.

And she knew that she wanted him. Not just because he was the sexiest person to ever grace her bedroom, or because that make-out session from this morning was still causing aftershocks. But because Rafe was the first person who made Ruby feel cared for. And as it turned out, that was super sexy.

Ruby ran her hands over her stomach, over the soft T-shirt she'd worn to bed. Her nipples peaked beneath the thin fabric. She hadn't bothered changing after Rafe left this morning. She could still smell him on her, pine and sawdust. She remembered the feel of his hands on her skin, rough and gentle at the same time as he pinned her against the wall. The taste of his mouth, the searing heat of him as he pressed himself against her.

She could not go to work like this. She was too keyed up.

She slipped a hand beneath the waistband of her shorts, imagining it was Rafe's hand, feeling the rough calluses on his fingertips and his breath across her neck. Ruby's fingers dipped between her legs as she pictured Rafe bracing himself above her.

She knew how it would go. Gentle at first, so slow and soft,

Rafe trembling with the effort to hold back until they were both so strung out with desire that they snapped. And then he would fuck her into the mattress until she screamed, those huge hands digging into her hips, her thighs, holding her open for him.

Ruby's soft moan filled the room as her fingers sped up and slowed down, bringing herself closer and closer to the edge. She was so wet and so close. Her fantasy of Rafe pounding her into the bed was so real she could smell him even stronger now, like he was here, like his cock really was sliding in and out of her when it was only her own fingers.

A low growl and a muttered curse pulled Ruby out of her daydream. She cracked open her eyes to find Rafe standing in the doorway, his hair wet, drops of rainwater following the dips and valleys of his chest and abs.

Dear Lord.

Ruby froze, her hand still between her legs, her breath coming in rapid gasps.

"Don't stop." Rafe's voice sounded like it was scraped from his throat. His eyes never left her face. His hand gripped the door jamb so tight, a part of Ruby's brain wondered if he might crack it.

But the other part of her brain screamed at her to finish what she'd started. She circled her fingers faster and harder but with Rafe's dark gaze on her, it didn't take long. Her back bowed off the bed, her heels digging into the mattress. Pleasure shot through her, lighting up stars behind her eyelids. She squeezed her eyes shut, letting wave after wave of release wash over her.

She sighed. Her body felt heavy, sated. A small smile played over her lips, but when she opened her eyes, the doorway was empty.

Rafe was gone.

Chapter Sixteen

The walk to the bar was long and quiet. It was taking every ounce of Rafe's humanity to not tackle Ruby onto the closest lawn and fuck her brains out. He could not erase the image of her on her bed, hands between her thighs, her cheeks pink from pleasure. Fucking herself because he couldn't do it. *Goddamn it.*

"You look like you want to kill someone again."

Ruby's teasing tone broke him out of his thoughts. At least she wasn't pissed at him for watching her like some pervert and then running away. Again. But he also didn't think she'd appreciate him telling her it was for her own good that he was keeping his distance. So they hadn't said anything about it at all.

"Uh, no. Not at the moment."

Ruby huffed a small laugh. The way she took everything in stride unnerved him. She didn't take things seriously enough. It was dangerous.

He stole a glance at her from the corner of his eye. She was dressed in her usual work wear, black tank top that made her tits look fantastic, short black skirt that made her thighs look edible, and her black boots for kicking the shit out of people that thought about her like that.

Her lips had a fresh coat of red lipstick and her dark hair was tied up in two knots on top of her head, exposing her long pale neck. His cock twitched at the memory of kissing that neck this morning.

"You coming inside tonight?"

Somehow in the midst of Rafe's lust-filled musings they'd arrived at the pub. Ruby looked up at him expectantly. He needed space. He needed to get away from her before he did something stupid.

He took a step back. "No. I'm going to ask around. See if anyone knows anything."

Ruby raised her eyebrows but didn't question him. She'd be safe here. No werewolf would be dumb enough to attack a human in the middle of town. And he'd be back before she had to leave. He turned to go, but Ruby grabbed his hand, tugging him close.

"Be careful," she said, her lips only inches from his throat.

Rafe swallowed hard. "Don't worry about me."

Ruby's lips twisted into a scowl but she let go of his hand and marched into the bar, her skirt flapping around those thighs. Rafe ran a hand through his hair and headed back toward the woods. His brother was useless but it was possible there were others who knew what the hell was going on.

There were two organized werewolf packs in Northern Maine, with another one right over the border in Canada. Not that wolves cared about arbitrary human borders, but that just happened to be where they were located. There were also quite a few lone wolves out there, like him and Theo.

The modern world had made a lot of things difficult for wolves, except for one, leaving the pack. What used to be a death sentence was now possible thanks to convenience stores and short-term rentals. When Rafe had first considered leaving over a century earlier, he would have been taking a huge risk. But after the last fight with his brothers, he'd stalked off, packed his few meager possessions, and left. Just like that.

Sure he'd had to sleep outside for most of that summer, hunting for whatever food he could find, but eventually he'd found work in town. First painting houses and then doing general handyman work for every old lady that would hire him. It had taken a few years to build a life for himself, but he'd done it. For whatever it was worth, he'd done it.

But lone wolves still made packs nervous. They were unpredictable and loyal only to themselves. Or at least that was the tale the packs sold to keep the hierarchy in line. The truth was, Rafe was just tired of the bullshit and the violence that pack life held for him. If he hadn't left, he would have been pushed out. Or, if their father had his way, killed. There wasn't room for more than one Alpha and his brother was more than happy to take the title.

Wolves without packs mostly lived in or near small towns, trying their best to fit into human society. They couldn't stay in one place for too long. They were drifters, unrooted, and alone. The fact that they aged so slowly made it impossible to stay put or to form bonds with humans. A shudder ran through him at the thought of Scarlet. How could he have watched her grow old while he didn't change?

But he'd learned from that experience. And now he kept to himself. Thanks to the miraculous human invention of the internet, he could sell his furniture pieces to anyone without ever leaving his home. But somehow, word still traveled around, news of the packs still reached his ears. A wolf would stop by; Theo would mention some news from home; one of the nosy little nymphs that shared these woods would drop some message for him.

Rafe wasn't nearly as isolated as he tried to be.

So now it was time to track down some of these wolves and see what they knew.

He shifted as soon as he entered the darkness of the trees, leaving his clothes draped over a nearby branch. Werewolves didn't have to shift on the full moon, but they did need to spend at least some of their time as wolves. It was essential to their health, to their sanity. Rafe knew that from experience too. Too much time spent as a human had nearly driven him mad.

It was why even when they left their packs, wolves stayed near a forested area. They needed space to run, to hunt. If he couldn't hunt the local fauna, it endangered every human around him. As much as he tried, his instincts couldn't be denied. The memory of Ruby's horrified face after his little confession about chasing humans flashed through his mind. She *should* be horrified. He deserved that look.

The creatures that lived in these woods liked to talk, to whisper through the branches, and Rafe had gotten wind of the improvements his brother had made over the years since he'd left the pack. He wasn't quite the asshole their father once was. But the pack still lived on the fringes of society. Most wolves had jobs like he had, jobs that didn't require any pesky paperwork or tax ID numbers. Whatever Knox's big plans were, Rafe hadn't seen much evidence of them so far.

Rafe shook himself out, his fur ruffling along his back. He didn't want to think about Knox right now. Certainly not in any sort of positive light. He preferred to remember his brother as the asshole who'd tried to tear his throat out. It was easier that way.

Rafe took off toward the closest wolf cabin. It was time to get serious about figuring out who was after Ruby.

Ruby tried to lose herself in the monotony of her work. Smile, pour drink, smile, take order, keep smiling, pour another drink. But the memory of Rafe's gaze on her while she touched herself would not leave. If she was being honest, she'd be surprised if it ever left. She'd be a little perverted old lady still daydreaming about the hottest moment of her entire life. Because it definitely had been. And then he'd fled the scene like he'd been caught gawking at a car wreck.

She shook her head, wisps of hair escaping from her updo. Rafe had acted like nothing happened. Other than the murderous glare returning to his face, he seemed completely unaffected by what he'd seen, so Ruby pretended the same. Even though just walking beside him set her skin on fire and melted her insides.

If Rafe wanted to pretend that there was nothing between them, she would just have to play along. She wasn't that desperate. How many times could she throw herself at the man and maintain any sort of self-respect? She was pretty sure it had already been too many, but she was stopping now. That was it. Rafe could hide all the unwanted erections he wanted, Ruby was not going to fight him on it anymore.

She nodded once to herself as though sealing some sort of deal and set her tray down on the bar to pick up the next drink order. It was a Friday night and the bar was slammed. Ruby

123

glanced at the clock on the wall above the shelves of liquor bottles. It was past midnight. Last call was at one. She was almost done.

The crowd had gotten sloppy, mostly full of frat boys from the college town next to this one. They were young and stupid and overly confident in their ability to hold their liquor. Half of them looked ready to keel over.

Ruby caught Macy's eye from over the bar. Time to cut them off or they wouldn't be able to stumble their way back to their shitty off-campus apartments. She put down a couple of waters in front of two particularly tipsy bros and they gave her two sloppy smiles.

"We didn't order water." The man looked like the villain in an 80s movie. Blonde hair, perfect teeth, polo shirt, far too much cologne. Ruby nearly gagged.

Instead she smiled sweetly. "Drink up or you'll feel even worse in the morning."

"I'd feel better in the morning if you came home with me." Blaine, she decided his name must be, or maybe Chad, grinned at his friend like he was being clever. His friend nearly tipped out of the booth, but laughed like a deranged donkey anyway.

Ruby wanted to say she doubted he'd be able to get it up in his current condition, but she worked for tips, so she didn't.

Her face ached from smiling. "Cute," she said. "But no thanks."

"Blaine" narrowed his eyes, shifting in the booth closer to her. But Ruby was only half paying attention to him. Something else had shifted. The air in the bar. Awareness prickled along the back of her neck. She would bet her life that Rafe was back and watching her, but she didn't turn around to check.

"Oh, come on, I think we could have fun together," Blaine was saying. "You look like you like to have fun."

Ruby's eyes hurt so bad from the need to roll them that she had to squeeze them shut. And that's when that drunk little fucker slid his hand up her skirt and grabbed a handful of her ass.

Ruby didn't smile. She didn't think.

She scraped her boot along his shin and stomped so hard on his foot that he yelped like the man-child that he was.

"Shit! That hurt." He was standing now, yelling in her face but Ruby didn't back up. She already knew what she would run into if she did. She could feel him like a solid wall behind her, unmoving and radiating pure rage.

Blaine's friend saw Rafe first and his eyes went wide.

"That's how you treat customers?" Blaine was yelling. "Acting like a fucking tease, flaunting your tits in my face all night? And then you assault me?"

Ruby almost laughed. Frat boys were so fucking fragile.

He finally paused his tirade long enough to raise his gaze to the shadow looming behind Ruby. Whatever he saw there caused the color to drain from his face. Ruby was vaguely aware of the fact that the rest of the bar had gone eerily quiet.

"You have sixty seconds." Rafe's voice had never sounded less human. It was an animal growl, a monster's rasp. It sent shivers up Ruby's arms.

"Sixty seconds for what?" Blaine asked, puffing up his chest because frat boys never learned.

Rafe leaned forward, his solid body pressing into Ruby's back. "A sixty-second head start before I chase you down and tear you limb from fucking limb."

Blaine's eyes widened, a bead of sweat ran down his temple. "Ha. Yeah, okay, man. We were leaving anyway."

"Clock's ticking," Rafe growled, his breath brushing against Ruby's neck.

Blaine's friend tossed some bills on the table.

"Better be a good tip," Rafe added and the friend tossed on a couple more. Ruby bit down on her bottom lip. She would not laugh until they were gone.

The men scrambled out of the booth, giving Ruby a wide berth on their way.

"And don't bother coming back!" Macy yelled from behind the bar.

Ruby let her laugh tumble out as she leaned back against Rafe's solid chest. His breathing was ragged against her ear. She turned to face him and his eyes were dark and dangerous. Shit.

"You can't really go after them."

A muscle in his jaw ticked.

"I'm serious, Rafe. You can't actually hurt them." She grabbed his arms and squeezed, trying to bring him back to himself. "It's not a big deal. Just let it go."

He squeezed his eyes shut and let out a long unsteady breath. "He put his hands on you."

"It's not a big deal. That's what the boots are for." She gave him a smile, hoping to break the tension but it didn't work. He still looked very murder-y. "Here, have a seat. I'll grab you a drink."

He looked like he might protest, or rip the bar down around them, but he slid into the booth.

"Don't go anywhere," she said before hurrying off to pour him a beer and ask their cook, Dominick, to throw one last burger on the grill.

She came back to find Rafe hunched over, elbows on the table and his head in his hands. She slid the food and drink on the table and sat across from him. He flicked his gaze up to hers and she felt it down to her toes.

"He touched you."

"Just another drunk asshole." She tried to brush it off again but the rage was still simmering in Rafe's eyes. "If you kill every drunk asshole, I'll be out of a job."

He huffed at that and leaned back in the booth, still watching her. She crossed her arms over her chest as though she could protect herself from his stare.

"You should have let me kill this one, as a message to the others."

She was pretty sure there was a joking tone there. She hoped he was joking.

"I can't have you murdering people for me. There are enough rumors about me as it is." Again she tried for humor but his mouth tightened like he now wanted to murder anyone who'd ever spoken ill about her.

"Just eat," she said. She always felt less like killing people after she ate, so maybe he would too. She watched him devour his burger in less than six bites and down the beer in several large gulps. He was a beast. She swallowed hard.

"Did you find out anything?"

Rafe shook his head. "Nothing. Nobody seems to know anything."

"Hmm. Are they lying?"

"Could be, but wolves are terrible liars. We can smell it on each other."

Ruby shivered. What could he smell on her?

He smirked a little as though reading her mind. "You smell delicious," he rumbled. Ruby nearly slid out of the booth into a horny little Ruby puddle on the floor. She gripped the edge of the worn plastic seat with both hands.

She cleared her throat. "Uh, good. I guess?"

He leaned forward again and suddenly the booth was way too small. "About earlier…"

"Oh, God. Yeah. We don't have to talk about that. Like ever." Ruby squirmed in her seat as warmth crept up her neck.

Rafe reached out and wrapped his huge hand around hers. "You're sexy as hell, Ruby."

Shit. Why did his voice sound like that? Like dark promises and aching need.

"But it's not a good idea." He let go of her hand and she ran her palm over the smooth wood of the table, the table he'd made.

"Why not?" *Let it go, Ruby.*

Rafe's gaze raked over her, lingering on her lips before meeting her eye. "It's just not safe."

Fuck that.

Ruby slapped both hands on the table and rose from her seat. She didn't miss Rafe's gaze flicking to her tits before landing on her face. His eyes were dark, pupils blown wide.

"It's not safe for who? Are you afraid of me, Rafe? Because I'm not afraid of you."

He leaned across the table, so close now that his ragged breath fanned across her chest as she looked down at him. "Goddamn it, Ruby. You should be afraid. You could have been killed. I couldn't even protect you from some asshole sticking his hand up your skirt. The least I can do is protect you from myself. From the things that happen to people who hang around me for too long."

Ruby shook her head. "I'm a big girl. Big enough to make my own decisions." He opened his mouth to protest, but she kept going. "You're the coward. Not me."

"Ruby—"

She ignored him and hurried out of the booth. "I'm clocking

out," she said over her shoulder. "You can escort me home after that."

She turned and left him hunched over his empty plate, his chest rising and falling in angry breaths. So much for pretending she wasn't affected by him.

Chapter Seventeen

Coward? Well, that fucking hurt. Rafe sat and waited for Ruby to be ready, grappling with what he'd done wrong. He'd let the bastard stroll out of here with his skin still on, against every instinct roaring through his body. What more did she want from him?

The memory of Ruby's flushed cheeks and panting breaths flooded in and reminded him of exactly what she wanted from him. But Rafe already knew how this ended. Humans were not for him, no matter how bad-ass they thought they were. This whole mess would only end with one or both of them hurt and that was only if Ruby made it out of whatever this was alive.

Again, Scarlet hovered around the periphery of his memory. Her blood, bright red in the morning sunlight. Rafe shook his head, scattering the image. This wasn't the same. He'd make sure this time things ended differently.

Ruby strode across the bar toward him, her usual bag of leftovers clutched in one hand, anger still darkening her expression. He'd fucked things up with her again.

"Ready?" she asked, not meeting his eye.

He stood slowly, unfolding himself from the cramped booth, and followed Ruby out the door. Somehow the walk home was even more strained than the walk there. Ruby didn't bother teasing him about the scowl he knew was on his face. He wanted to carry her bags again but had the distinct feeling that if he tried, his foot would get the same treatment as the guy who groped her. An unexpected smile crept onto his face. He liked seeing those boots be put to good use.

"I'm sorry," he said, finally into the heavy silence between them.

"Oh?" Ruby kept her gaze straight ahead.

Rafe cleared his throat. Apologies felt foreign on his tongue. "You are clearly capable of taking care of yourself."

Ruby paused to look up at him, surprise on her face. They were near the path to the woods now and the shadows called to him. Fireflies flickered through the trees. The breeze lifted the small wisps of hair on Ruby's neck.

"Thank you."

"In most situations," he went on, not stopping even when her eyebrows rose and her hand went to her hip. "You can handle frat boys at the pub, Ruby, but these wolves are something else entirely. You need to take this more seriously." They were on the hunt. The yard reeked of it. And yet every asshole he'd talked to tonight didn't know a damn thing. How was that possible?

She opened her mouth to protest but then clamped it shut. A small shiver ran through her as though she was remembering the wolf that attacked her. He knew he was.

"Fine," she said, finally. "But you're not those wolves. I don't need to be protected from you."

He wanted to argue. He should argue. But God, how he wanted those words to be true. He also wanted to lean down and taste her lips, her tongue, that spot on her neck that made her practically purr. But he knew how this ended. Eventually, Ruby would see his true self, the monster beneath the man and she would stop looking at him like that. And that was the best-case scenario. That meant she was alive.

Besides, Ruby deserved far better than him. What she said at the bar was true. He was a coward. A coward who abandoned his family. A coward who did his father's bidding for centuries. A coward who didn't want his heart torn out again.

Humans were not for him.

He cleared his throat, breaking the moment, and they continued their walk in silence.

By the time they walked up the path to Ruby's cottage, Rafe had decided he would sleep outside tonight. If he stayed on the edge of the woods, he could watch the house and still stay out of sight from the neighbors. It was for the best, he told himself as Ruby pushed open the front door.

The living room was dark when they stepped in.

"Lena must have gone to bed," Ruby whispered, flicking on the light, but the house felt unsettled, awake. The hairs rose on the back of Rafe's neck. He grabbed Ruby's arm and tugged her close.

"Wait."

A quiet murmuring filled the room, like someone praying.

"Lena." The name tore from Ruby's lips.

Ruby's sister was lying in a heap on the floor, words tumbling from her pale lips. Ruby strained against Rafe's grasp but he wouldn't let go. Not until he'd scanned the room. No blood on the floor, no movement in the other rooms. He couldn't smell anything other than Ruby's fear and the coffee and bacon from their breakfast.

Ruby yanked her arm and this time he let her go. She

collapsed in front of Lena, placing her sister's head in her lap. Lena's hair looked silver in the moonlight as it spilled over Ruby's legs. For the first time since he met her, Ruby looked truly terrified. Rafe's guts twisted inside him. Every instinct in his body roared at him to make it stop, to make Ruby stop hurting. It was worse than seeing that asshole grope her, although that had nearly sent him into a murderous rage. This feeling was helpless. No amount of violence was going to cure Ruby's sister.

He dropped down on his knees beside them. Lena's eyes were open but unseeing. She stared up at the ceiling. Ruby stroked her hair, her hand trembling.

"They're coming," Lena whispered over and over.

"Is that what she always says?" Rafe asked, his voice also a whisper as though he didn't want to wake the woman.

Ruby just nodded, her dark eyes rimmed with tears.

Rafe put a hand on Lena's shoulder. Her body was light and fragile compared to Ruby's lush curves. "Lena, can you hear us?" He gave her shoulder a small shake and Lena's head rolled to the side. She stared at him without seeing and a chill crawled up Rafe's spine.

"Lena," he said again, letting his voice grow louder. "What do you see?"

She paused her litany and her eyebrows knitted together as though she could hear him and was considering how to answer.

"Wolves," she said, the word hanging in the still air of the house.

Ruby's gaze snapped to his, her eyes wide. "She's never said anything like that before."

Lena reached out a hand and Rafe took it in his, wrapping his fingers around her chilled ones. Lena's eyes widened for a moment and she blew out a long sigh.

"I see blood," she told him. "So much blood. You're not safe."

Rafe's body had gone cold. What wolves? Whose blood? He needed to know more, but Lena's eyes had shut, her breathing gone slow and steady like she had fallen asleep. He wanted to shake her. He wanted to yell. He wanted to grab Ruby and run until she was safe.

But he couldn't do any of those things.

So instead, he sat back on his heels and looked at Ruby and told her the truth.

"I think your sister is a seer."

"Tell me more." They were at the kitchen table, each with a cup of camomile tea. Lena was tucked up in her bed. Her eyes had fluttered open when Rafe'd lifted her in his arms, but she hadn't remembered anything she'd said or seen during the episode. He'd carried her upstairs and laid her down with so much care, Ruby had to swallow the emotion in her throat again just thinking about it.

He let out a long sigh and leaned back in his chair. It groaned under his weight and he stilled, but the little chair held.

"I think Lena's a seer, someone who has visions about the future." He ran a hair through his dark hair. "I haven't heard of one around here in a long time."

"So what does this mean?" Goosebumps covered Ruby's arms despite the mugginess of the kitchen. It was one thing for her to be in danger, but for her sister to be involved made her stomach cramp. And why did that word "seer" echo deep inside her? The dream about her parents' accident floated to the surface of her thoughts. Had she really had it the night *before* the accident? Maybe she'd just had it so many times since, she couldn't tell anymore.

But her own dream wasn't the issue right now. "Why was she talking about wolves? She's never said that before."

Rafe grimaced but didn't hold back, just like he'd promised. "It must be related to the wolves that have been stalking you. Maybe that's what she's seeing. Maybe she knows…"

He didn't need to finish his sentence. Ruby knew from the anguish on his face what he was going to say. Maybe Lena knew what was going to happen to her. Maybe she'd seen Ruby's fate and it wasn't good.

Rafe swallowed hard. "I won't let anything happen to you." The force behind his statement sent heat through Ruby's body.

"Why?" she asked and his silver eyes widened.

"Why what?"

"Why do you care about what happens to me? Why were you following me for so long? What am I to you that you would fight so hard for me?"

Rafe shook his head like he didn't want to consider what she was to him. He swallowed again, his Adam's apple bobbing beneath his stubble. For a minute, Ruby thought he might give her some bullshit answer about wanting to do the right thing and protect an innocent life, but he didn't.

Instead he held her gaze, his silver eyes flashing in the moonlight, and he told her the truth.

"I don't know. I don't know what it is about you. I haven't given a shit about any human in decades. I've avoided them at all costs." He leaned forward, his arms braced on the table between them, the muscles in his forearms tensed and rigid. "I don't know why I can't stay away from you, why you haunted me even before I knew you. I don't know why I'm here and why I can't leave. But I know I can't. I know that even if I went home now, I'd be tormented by thoughts of you, of your scent and the taste of your lips and the feel of your skin, but mostly by the sheer terror of thinking you weren't safe, and I know I would run right back here."

Ruby sucked in a deep breath, drowning in his words, in his confession, in the intensity of his stare.

"I don't know anything except that I would kill for you."

She didn't know if he said those last words to shock her or simply because they were true, but it scared her how much she loved them.

She met his stare and smiled. "Okay."

Rafe blinked. "Okay?"

"Okay. I'll allow you to do your caveman protector thing. If it helps you sleep at night."

He slumped back in his chair and his bark of a laugh surprised them both. He ran a hand down his face and shook his head like she was the mythical creature and not him.

Ruby stood and held out her hand. He hesitated and then took it.

"Come on, wolf-man. Let's go to bed."

Ruby sunk her fingers into Rafe's soft fur, his warm body curled around hers. He still insisted on sleeping as a wolf. For safety. Ruby didn't argue, just patted the bed beside her and invited him up. She'd stroked between his ears until his wolfy breath came out in soft, snuffly snores. He smelled like pine even in his wolf form and she let the comforting scent surround her.

Rafe's confession still rumbled through her, about his inability to stay away. She knew that staying in his wolf form was a compromise with himself, a way to stay close to her without crossing the line he'd set for himself.

She'd let him stay on that side of the line for now, until he was ready. Until he saw that she wasn't going anywhere.

She sank lower into her pillows and let Rafe's soft breaths, the steady rise and fall of his body, lull her into a dreamless sleep.

Chapter Eighteen

"I told you, I feel fine." Lena glared at her over the rim of her mug. Dark circles hung below her eyes today, her skin sallow in the morning sun shining through the kitchen window. The charming sister Ruby had had back for the past week was gone again. This sister, the sullen, exhausted one, the one she didn't know, was back.

Ruby sat across from her sipping from her own cup, still thinking about what Lena had said last night and what it might mean. Rafe was outside, sniffing around the perimeter in human form, checking to make sure all was safe. A chill ran down Ruby's spine at the thought of what he might find, or worse—what he might do if he found something.

But what scared her the most was watching her sister waste away before her eyes.

Rafe had said she was a seer, but what did that even mean? What were they supposed to do now? Whatever this thing was, it seemed to be eating her from the inside out.

Lena gave her a weak smile. "What are you thinking about? Your face has gone all scrunchy."

Ruby blew out a laugh. She still hadn't told Lena the truth about Rafe, about his theory about her episodes. "Nothing. Just thinking about running some errands today."

"Sounds good." Lena stood and shuffled to the sink to rinse her plate. "I think I'll read in bed for a bit."

Ruby nodded and watched her go. Reading in bed meant she'd be asleep in a matter of minutes. Many times Ruby had found her sister sound asleep with a book open on her chest. Ruby sighed.

Lena had once been so vibrant, so loved by all who met her. But one by one, her old friends had abandoned her, either bored or afraid of her affliction. It happened slowly, a slow atrophying of her old life. Lena was too tired to go out, afraid of having an episode in public. At first she would just go blank. She would sit and stare. It happened one night in the middle of a crowded club, another time in the middle of an old friend's baby shower. She stopped getting invited to parties after that.

A few friends lingered. They would pay her little visits, keeping their voices low like Lena was sick, like Lena was dying. After a while Ruby stopped letting them in. She hated their whispers, their sympathetic smiles.

But maybe Lena wasn't sick at all. Ruby clung to Rafe's words from the night before. Maybe Lena had a gift. Maybe she just needed to figure out how to use it.

"You okay?" Rafe's voice startled her out of her musings. She hadn't heard the back door open or his light footsteps into the kitchen.

"Yeah. Just worried about Lena."

Rafe nodded, pouring himself some coffee and lowering himself gingerly into the chair across from her.

"So what's the plan for today?" she asked.

Rafe's eyes widened a fraction of an inch as he studied her. "The plan for what?"

"Who are we interrogating?"

Rafe choked a little on his coffee. "We?"

Ruby nodded. "Yes. We. I can't sit around here all day waiting for you to get back. I need to help." She swallowed the thick emotion that had bubbled up in her throat. "We need to do something for Lena. She's getting worse and if her condition is somehow linked to this whole wolf attack thing then I need to help."

She folded her arms across her chest, waiting for him to argue, but he nodded, finishing off his coffee in a final swig.

"I'll call my brother."

"For what?"

Rafe's fingers drummed on the table top. "I don't think the wolves are after Lena." He swallowed hard. "They've only gone after you, but I still don't think it's a good idea to leave her here alone." He stopped drumming and pulled his phone from his pocket. "Theo can come stay with her."

"He'll do that?"

Rafe shrugged. "He owes me." He prowled from the room to make his phone call. All Ruby could make out were some gruff sounds, an occasional growl, and few "fuck you's" before Rafe came back and told her Theo would be there within the hour. Nothing about his grim face said he was looking forward to the visit.

Ruby had just finished getting dressed when there was a knock on the front door. She hurried quietly down the hall past Lena's bedroom. The fact that Lena had been too tired to protest the fact that "Rafe's brother was in town and would be hanging out at the house for a few hours" only made Ruby's anxiety grow. Rafe still hadn't told her where they were going today, but at least she was doing something to help her sister.

"I'm not a goddamn babysitter." The voice that spoke was smooth like honey even though the words were sharp. "You saved my life *once*; you don't get to call in unlimited favors."

Ruby found Rafe face-to-face with a beautiful stranger in her living room. They both looked up when she hit the last step.

The man's full lips slipped into a slow smile. His skin had a golden tan and his eyes were like tropical waters. A shock of black curls covered the top of his head and despite the harsh line of a scar down the side of his face, he was very pretty. Ruby couldn't help the matching smile that crossed her own lips.

"Oh, I see now," the man crooned.

"Don't say another fucking word," Rafe warned, a low growl in this throat.

"I'm Ruby." She held out a hand and the man took it in his.

"Theo," he purred.

"Oh, for fuck's sake," Rafe grumbled. "Ruby, this is my asshole brother. He'll hang out here for the afternoon."

"Thank you so much," she said and realized he was still holding her hand. She tugged it away and he smiled wider. "My sister is upstairs resting, but she knows you're here."

Theo nodded. "At your service, Ruby."

She could feel the anger rolling off Rafe like it was a physical entity in the room. That whole "if looks could kill" saying had never made more sense to her.

"Now it's 'at your service'? A minute ago you weren't a babysitter."

Theo shrugged, drawing attention to his toned shoulders and chest. He wasn't as tall as Rafe or as wide, but he was covered in long, lean muscle. Damn, werewolf genes were no joke.

"Ruby convinced me." His grin was downright wicked now and Ruby felt the heat rush to her face. Rafe vibrated next to her.

"Cut it out, Theo. You're going to make his head explode."

Ruby blinked. A small, redheaded woman emerged from her kitchen clutching Ruby's favorite mug.

"You brought Phoebe?" Rafe asked, anger still creasing his face.

Theo shrugged again. "She wanted to meet the seer."

"Nice to see you too, Rafe." Phoebe practically floated into the room and landed beside Rafe. Her head only reached his shoulder but she stood on her toes to place a peck on his cheek. Rafe continued to glower but Ruby noticed the softening in his stance.

"Hey, Fee. It's nice to see you away from your grove."

The woman smiled up at him. "I am allowed to leave it every now and then." Her hair was short and coppery, her skin a creamy peach. A swarm of freckles covered her face and shoulders and ran down her arms. She was thoroughly speckled.

"What grove?"

The trio turned their attention back to Ruby, who braced herself for whatever insane bit of news she was about to receive next.

"Phoebe is a dryad. A forest nymph," Rafe explained. Phoebe smiled at her.

"Right. Of course." And there it was. A nymph. Of course she was. There were now two werewolves and a forest deity in her living room. Ruby reached back into her memory of Greek and Celtic mythology but all she could remember was that dryads were considered forest spirits, often found in sacred groves. She was dying to ask if Phoebe could make a tree grow in the middle of the living room, but that somehow seemed inappropriate at the moment.

Theo had dropped the flirty charmer act as soon as Phoebe came into the room and now shifted closer to her. Ruby didn't miss how he watched her, the blatant need in his eyes. She glanced at Rafe, eyebrows raised, but he just shook his head in annoyance.

"So is this the seer?" Phoebe asked.

"Oh ... no, I'm just Ruby. Uh, human."

Phoebe tilted her head, studying Ruby with interest. "Hm ... are you sure?"

Sure about what? Being human? Ruby nodded stupidly, her brain refusing to piece together Phoebe's question. Of course she was human. Lena was the one having visions, not her. One maybe prophetic dream and a bit of a nutty aunt did not mean this little quirk ran in the family. Did it? Ruby opened her mouth to ask more questions of the dryad, but Rafe cut her off.

"We have to go," Rafe practically barked. "We'll be back by sunset."

"He makes it sound so cryptic. My shift starts at eight, that's all," Ruby said, dropping the subject for now. Helping Lena was the most important thing; that was Ruby's focus. Or it should be anyway.

Phoebe grinned. "It's a family trait. These boys have a flair for the dramatic."

"Hey." The brothers spoke in unison, causing both women to laugh.

Rafe grumbled and grabbed her hand. "Let's go." He tugged her toward the door, but she glanced back to see Theo move closer to Phoebe. He ran a single finger up from her wrist to her elbow. Ruby watched the other woman shiver but then move away.

Ruby had a million questions she was sure Rafe would not want to answer. But that didn't mean she wasn't going to try.

"You and your brother don't look much alike."

Theo's truck bounced over a pothole as Rafe glanced at Ruby from the driver's seat. He was distracted, hoping that his old friend would be able to give them some answers.

"He's the pretty one." His comment came out embarrassingly bitter.

He could feel Ruby's gaze on him, but he kept his eyes on the road.

"I think you're pretty," she said and he could hear the smile in it. She was teasing him.

He huffed. "We have different mothers. He looks like his." Rafe did not mention that he looked like his father. He'd never liked those comparisons, no need to bring it up now.

"What's the deal with him and Phoebe?" She shifted in her seat and he dared another glance. She faced the road now, one leg tucked up underneath her, her thighs peeking out from her skirt. He wondered how many of those black skirts she owned. His fingers twitched on the steering wheel with the need to slide a hand up one of them.

He cleared his throat. "It's a long story."

"Tell me."

Rafe sighed. He did not pretend to understand the inner workings of either of his brothers, but he could give her the basic facts. "They've been friends for years. I suspect he loves her." He shrugged. "I assumed when we left the pack they would get together. My father never would have allowed it, mating with a nymph. He didn't tolerate half-breeds." Rafe swallowed hard. His father's hateful words felt slimy in his mouth.

"Your father sounds like a real dick."

A startled laugh puffed from his lips. "Yeah, he was."

"So they're not together?" Ruby shifted again, facing him once more.

"No. Theo fucks whoever he wants and still calls Phoebe a friend." An uncomfortable thought slithered into his gut. "Why? You interested?"

Ruby laughed. "Why? Are you jealous?"

Rafe ground his back teeth together. "No. But you should know he's an asshole."

"But is he an asshole who's good in bed?"

Rafe nearly drove the truck off the damn road. His hands were clenched so tight around the steering wheel his knuckles had gone completely white. The idea of his brother fucking Ruby was enough to make him want to...

Ruby's hand slid onto his thigh and his thoughts skidded to a halt. "I'm just kidding." She gave a little squeeze and his cock jumped at the proximity. "Stop looking so murder-y," she added with a laugh.

He tried to let out a breath, but his lungs were tight and hot. "This is just my face," he said.

She leaned across the center console and brushed her lips against his cheek. "I like your face," she whispered before sitting back down.

He could still feel the heat of her mouth when they pulled into the parking lot. He secretly hoped her lipstick had left a mark.

Chapter Nineteen

R uby hopped down from the truck before Rafe could do something absurd like open her door and help her out. He gave her a bemused smile as they walked across the parking lot to the front door of the apartment building. It was an old gray building clearly designed for function over beauty. It seemed to be surviving the years but doing nothing for the aesthetic of the neighborhood. The rest of the street was filled with even older Victorian houses that had been split up into apartments for the local college students years ago.

The sun was already high in the sky and the black top radiated heat right back up at them. A bead of sweat rolled down Ruby's back.

She'd promised herself she was done throwing herself at Rafe, but that one little kiss seemed necessary. Rafe looked positively homicidal at the thought of her lusting after his brother. She couldn't pretend she didn't sort of like it. A lot. Anyway, the kiss had been purely to make sure he didn't drive them into a tree. It had nothing to do with the way his stubble was scratchy beneath her lips or the small intake of breath he'd made when she did it. It had nothing to do with the fact that even now when she'd renewed her vow to respect his wishes her body still screamed at her to get closer.

Rafe opened the door to the old building, an eyebrow raised in question. "You okay?" he asked with an infuriating smirk. God, must her every lusty thought always be written on her face?

"So who are we visiting?" she asked, ignoring his question. "This building doesn't seem terribly werewolf-y." She wrinkled her nose at the musty smell of the lobby. Silver mailboxes lined one wall and the maroon carpet had seen better days. There was no elevator so they began the climb while Rafe explained.

"Callie might have some insight. She lives here with her boyfriend."

Callie? The girl from the bar? Ruby was more intrigued than ever about how that sweet little blonde girl and her even sweeter boyfriend could have anything to do with werewolf attacks and ancient seer abilities. But she didn't have time to ask any more questions before Rafe had stopped at the second landing and strode down the short hallway to the apartment at the end. Ruby hurried to catch up, her boots stomping loudly in the tight space.

Sawyer opened the door wide, an easy smile on his face. "Hey, guys, come in."

"Thanks." Rafe clapped him on the shoulder and Sawyer winced a little before grinning at Ruby.

"Nice to see you outside of the bar," he said and Ruby returned the smile.

"It's nice to be outside of the bar."

Sawyer laughed and gestured for her to come inside. The door opened into the living room where Callie was already perched on the couch, laptop in her lap.

"Hi, Rafe," she said, glancing up. "Hi, Ruby."

"Finals are this week," Sawyer said with a shrug. "She'll be done in a minute."

Rafe shifted on his feet. He looked like an enormous storm cloud in the middle of the bright apartment. Ruby bit down a smile.

Despite the dreary exterior, Callie and Sawyer's apartment was as colorful as its occupants. Patterned blankets were draped over the couch and chair, a braided rug covered the worn floor, and plants filled the windows.

"You guys want something to drink?" Sawyer asked. "I guess it's kinda early for a beer. Coffee?"

Rafe gave a curt nod in agreement and Sawyer grinned again like he really got a kick out of Rafe's gruff, silent type.

"How about you, Ruby?"

"Coffee is good. Thanks." It was possible Ruby was just as bad at human interaction as Rafe was, but she was more likely to get an odd look than make the other person run away in terror. Sawyer nodded and disappeared down a small hallway off the living room.

Callie slammed her computer shut and finally looked around the room, blinking like she'd just woken up.

"Hey. Sorry about that. I was kind of in the zone." She smiled, her long blonde braid sliding over one shoulder. "Please, sit down!"

Rafe took the only chair, one that looked older than Ruby, so she folded herself up on the other end of the couch. Awkwardness crawled over her skin. Should she have taken off her boots before she came in? She thought they were going to be questioning more silent wolfy types, not chatting with a sunny co-ed.

Ruby could fake chattiness at the bar. Anything for tips. And for whatever reason, Rafe's stoic growliness set her completely at ease. But put her in a room with peers and tell her to make small talk and Ruby was at a loss. Friends had never been her thing. Ruby played with ghosts and monsters, not other little girls.

Callie smiled and Ruby could have sworn the clouds parted from the sun outside the window. "So, what's going on?"

Rafe cleared his throat. "Ruby was attacked."

Callie's eyes widened. "By wolves?"

Rafe nodded. "No one I know. But they're still sniffing around. Have you heard anything?"

"You know I'm new to all of this." She shook her head. "But no, I haven't heard anything."

"What do you mean new?" Ruby asked.

Callie smiled at her, tossing her braid to the other side. Sawyer returned and handed Ruby and Rafe their coffee before settling on the floor at Callie's feet.

"She's a witch," he said with a grin and Callie kicked him playfully in the shoulder.

"I have certain atmospheric-related powers," she clarified.

"She can control the weather," Sawyer added, clearly delighted by this whole situation.

"Sometimes, sort of. Anyway, it's only been a year or so since I really figured it all out."

"Uh-huh." Ruby nodded. *The day started with a nymph and now we're throwing a witch into the mix. Because why the hell not.*

"I was hoping we could talk to your grandmother about something." Rafe leaned forward, resting his forearms on his knees, his eyes flashing with intensity.

"She's still in Arizona. I doubt she would have heard anything about wolf attacks out here."

"It's about something else." Rafe glanced at Ruby as though

asking for permission to go on. She gave him a small nod. "We think Ruby's sister might be a seer."

"She has visions?" Callie's eyebrows rose to her hairline. "My grandmother told me seers are rare."

"Very," Rafe said. "Haven't heard of one around here in decades."

"She needs help," Ruby cut in, shifting her weight on the cushions. "My sister, I mean. The visions are... They seem to be hurting her."

Callie's brow scrunched in concern. "Let's see what we can do."

Thirty minutes and several cups of coffee later, Callie's grandmother appeared on the screen in front of them.

Ruby and Rafe sat on either side of Callie now, the laptop on the coffee table in front of them.

"Grandma, can you hear us?"

"Oh, there you are, sweets! I see your beautiful face!" The old woman leaned toward the computer and her cheerful face filled the screen.

Callie smiled. "Lean back a bit. Okay, that's better."

"How are you? Do you have friends over? Don't tell me you replaced Sawyer with that big fellow there."

Rafe grumbled and Ruby swallowed her laugh.

"No, no. This is Rafe. You know each other."

The old woman squinted, peering through the screen at Rafe. Her eyes widened in recognition. "Devon's son? You look just like him!"

Rafe choked on his coffee.

"You haven't aged a bit," Callie's grandma went on, ignoring Rafe's reaction. "Gosh, I do envy those werewolf genes. How long has it been?"

"Must be close to fifty years. How are you, Eloise?"

Ruby watched the blush creep up Callie's grandmother's cheeks at the sound of her name rumbling off Rafe's tongue. Well, at least she wasn't the only one.

"Oh, I've been all right, but somehow I feel like this isn't just a social call."

Rafe cleared his throat. "We're hoping you can help or at least give us some insight."

"I'll do my best. Lay it on me."

Ruby smiled. She liked this woman.

"I left the pack a while ago," Rafe started.

"Oh?" Eloise's eyebrows rose. "I heard your father passed."

Rafe grumbled in the affirmative.

"I figured you'd be the next Alpha, but I take it that's not what happened."

"Knox took the position."

"Hm." Eloise looked like she wanted to say more but Rafe pushed ahead, clearly not wanting to talk about his brother or the pack. Ruby was itching to know what happened between them but now wasn't the time to press him.

"The point is, I'm not with the pack anymore, but lately Ruby's been followed by a few strange wolves and one attacked her."

"A werewolf attack? What is the world coming to? Or going back to?" She waved a hand in front of her. "Not good either way." The old woman shook her head and gray wisps fell from her braid.

"Right. I'm trying to figure out who it might be and what they want with Ruby." Chills ran up Ruby's spine. Hearing her current situation laid out for someone else made the whole thing more real. Maybe Rafe was right. Maybe she hadn't been taking this whole thing seriously enough.

Wolves. Blood. You're not safe. Lena's last words rang through her mind and panic seized her throat. Rafe leaned forward, body tense as though he could feel Ruby's fear.

"Her sister is having visions. Ones about wolves and blood, but she can't hold on to them. Can't tell us more than a few words."

Callie let out a small gasp. Fear tightened in Ruby's gut. *Wolves. Blood.* This wasn't her morbid imagination or one of Aunt Millie's special breed of bedtime stories or some decades-old dream. Her life was in danger. It was what Rafe had been trying to tell her all along, but for some reason it didn't sink in until she'd heard Callie's own gasp of fear and saw Eloise's solemn face through the screen. She was in actual danger.

"Do you know anything about seers? Any way we can help her?" Rafe paused, sucking in a breath. "The visions seem to be hurting her. She's weakening."

The old woman's brow was knitted in concern. "It's been a long time since I've heard of anything like this," she said after a moment. "My grandmother used to speak of them, how they were hunted and often killed for their knowledge. Or captured. A powerful seer could be a valuable asset."

Ruby's heart squeezed so tight she nearly yelped in pain.

Callie put a hand on her knee and left it there, the warm weight of it helping to ease the panic just enough so that Ruby could breathe.

"Hold on a minute," Eloise said. "Let me see what I can find on the subject." She stood and shuffled off screen.

Sawyer blew out a long breath from across the room. "Holy shit. You okay, Ruby?"

Ruby offered him a weak smile. "Yeah, I'm okay."

Rafe grumbled softly, his intense gaze on the screen, waiting for Eloise to return. Callie's hand was still on Ruby's leg and she gave it a light squeeze.

"We'll figure something out. Don't worry." But even as she said it, rain pelted the window and a rumble of thunder echoed in the distance. "Ignore that," she said with an apologetic smile.

A soft brush of fur ran across Ruby's calves and she looked down to find a gray cat staring up at her with amber eyes. She reached down and scratched between its ears. The cat purred in response.

"Oh, that's Iggy. He likes you," Callie said with a smile.

Ruby let the little cat's purr vibrate through her fingers, focusing on that instead of her racing heart. She hadn't seen her own cat in days, she realized now. He must be hiding from their new house guest or hanging out in Lena's room away from the giant wolf that had taken up residence in Ruby's.

Iggy weaved in and out of her legs before settling on top of her boots.

"He used to breathe fire," Sawyer said with a grin.

Ruby's gaze shot to his, but she didn't get to ask any questions before Eloise appeared back on the screen. She set a stack of books on the table with a thud.

"Now, let's see what we've got," she said with grim determination and opened the first one.

The ride home was quiet, both of them processing everything they had discussed with Eloise. She'd given them exercises Lena could try to still her mind and access her visions as well some history she'd found about this power. But none of it would help if they didn't actually tell Lena what was going on. That was something they could argue about tomorrow.

Rafe pulled the truck in front of the tiny bungalow. Ruby didn't budge when he turned off the engine. She just sat, staring straight ahead. She'd been afraid today. Truly afraid. He could smell it on her, the panic and the terror. The scent mimicked the one she'd been bathed in when the wolf lunged for her.

It was what he'd wanted all along. For her to take this threat seriously, but that smell, that knowledge that she was scared tore him apart.

"Should we go in?" he asked, his voice gruff even when he didn't want it to be.

Ruby turned to look at him. "I'm sorry," she whispered.

"Sorry? For what?"

"For not taking this seriously. For fighting you every step of the way. For…" Her cheeks lit up pink in the dim interior of the truck. "For being too distracted by my attraction to you to think about anything else." She picked at the hem of her skirt, not meeting his eye, and he wanted to haul her into his lap and show her just how distracted he was by her.

He took her chin between his fingers and tilted her head up. "You have nothing to be sorry about." His voice was husky, practically dripping with the need he felt for this woman. "None of this is your fault."

Ruby gave a small nod against his fingertips but she didn't look convinced.

"Maybe we just need to get it out of our system." The words were out of his mouth before he could think better of it. Ruby's eyes widened, her cheeks flushing darker pink. Rafe barreled forward, flinging himself off the cliff of terrible ideas. "This thing between us, it *is* a distraction. So, maybe we just need to…"

He swallowed hard, losing his nerve.

But Ruby was brave. "Yes." She breathed the word into the space between them. "Yes, that makes sense. We just need to get it out of our system. Then we'll be able to focus on helping Lena and figuring this all out." She gave him a small smile, those red lips curving up, beckoning him.

He moved his hand from her chin to the side of her face, cupping her jaw, allowing his fingers to burrow into her hair. Soft. So fucking soft. She leaned closer, close enough to taste. And he could have her. Just this once. Just to get rid of this need that wouldn't stop clawing at his insides, demanding to be released.

"Wait. Theo."

Nothing could douse the flames of Rafe's arousal faster than hearing his brother's name from Ruby's lips.

She shook her head, the small smile still playing around her mouth. "I mean, Theo is still here. Shouldn't we send him home before we... I mean we're in his truck."

Rafe blinked, remembering his surroundings for the first time since turning to face Ruby. Right. He absolutely under no circumstances would be fucking Ruby in Theo's truck. The late evening sun shone through the front windshield reminding him of another unfortunate detail.

"You have to be at work soon."

It was Ruby's turn to look startled back into reality. She slumped in her seat. "I forgot." Those perfect blood red lips turned down at the corner and Rafe couldn't stand it.

"Later, then."

Ruby's gaze slid toward him, full of promise. "Okay. It's a deal. Later. To get it out of our systems."

Rafe nodded. Yes, this made sense. Ruby never said she wanted some big love affair with him. He'd only jumped to that conclusion because of his history with Scarlet. This thing was purely physical and tonight they would take care of it like two consenting adults. Human adults. He could be human for one night. He'd done it before for far longer even if it had ended in disaster.

Tonight wouldn't be like that. Tonight would be him and Ruby working out this thing between them...

Ruby cleared her throat, pulling Rafe back to the present. "I should probably check on Lena."

"Of course."

She popped open her door and jumped out of the cab while Rafe frantically thought about everything from his idiot brother to roadkill to get his dick to calm down. The last thing he needed was to prove Theo right.

With a sigh, he hopped down from the truck. It was going to be a long shift.

Chapter Twenty

We're just getting it out of our systems. It made sense. She repeated the words to herself like a mantra while she worked. She'd had the hots for Rafe since before she'd even seen him. How many nights had she fantasized about her stranger in the woods? How many times had she touched herself imagining him chasing her and everything she'd let him do once he caught her?

And then he'd emerged from the shadows like some big hulking sex god. How could any red-blooded woman be expected to concentrate with that type of energy around her? And she needed to concentrate. That much had become clear during their conversation with Eloise today. If the visions themselves didn't kill Lena, someone else might. Ruby's stomach rolled at the thought.

She glanced up to find Macy looking at her with a concerned furrow in her brow. Ruby gave her a tight smile and arranged the drinks evenly on her tray.

The bar was busy but Rafe hadn't stuck around. He didn't want to leave Lena alone for too long, so he had walked Ruby here and had left with warnings not to step outside the bar without him. For once, Ruby hadn't bristled at his command. She had no desire to go anywhere alone.

As the hours wore on, fear and arousal twined together in her gut. It wasn't a new emotion for her. She loved to make out during horror movies and was never hornier than after a walk through a haunted house. It was one of the few parts of her goth persona that wasn't exaggerated. Fear got her off. But never before was it real. Never before was there an actual threat. But it turned out her body didn't know the difference. She was so keyed up, she could feel the dampness on her thighs.

"You okay?" Macy was studying her again as she poured the drinks.

Ruby leaned her elbows on the bar. It was after eleven. Only a couple of hours to go. "I'm fine. Just a little tired."

Macy's purple braids skated across her shoulders as she lined up the drinks. "You sure? You look pinker than usual."

Oh God, she really did need to get this out of her system if her boss could read it across her face.

"Nope. Everything's fine." She tried to make her smile convincing but what type of smile says, *I'm not aroused by the fact that my life is in danger because I am a perfectly well-adjusted person*? She smiled bigger and Macy narrowed her eyes.

"I'm fine, really."

"Where's Rafe tonight? I thought I saw him earlier."

Ruby could feel the heat flooding her blood just at the mention of his name. "He ... uh ... he dropped me off."

Macy continued her inspection of Ruby's face like she could read everything Ruby planned to do to the man as soon as she was done here.

"So are you two a thing?"

How many drinks had this table ordered and why was it

taking Macy so long to pour them? Sweat rolled down Ruby's spine, making her tank top stick.

"It's ... um ... it's new."

Macy smiled. "He's a good guy, from what I can tell. Amazing wood-worker."

Ruby nodded, eyes on the tap as Macy filled the last beer, a perfect head of foam on top.

"Not bad to look at either," she added with a grin. "If I had any interest in people with penises, I'd be jealous."

Ruby choked on her laughter. But it felt good to let some of the tension of the day go. Her shoulders relaxed until she had to lift the tray filled with drinks.

"Thanks, Macy," she said with an awkward smile. "For uh ... checking in."

"No worries. And keep me posted on the Rafe situation." She winked and Ruby found herself smiling as she weaved through the crowded bar. Maybe having people look out for her wasn't the worst thing that could happen.

Rafe found her immediately through the dwindling crowd. His hungry stare tracked her movements like the predator that he was. He knew how he must look, his bulky shape hiding in the shadows of the bar, his eyes following Ruby as she rang up her last customer of the night. He looked like a threat. And he felt like one, but he couldn't take his eyes off of her.

Her scent reached him even through the funk of spilled beers and fried food. It wrapped around his throat like a vice and squeezed. Any rational reason he had for sleeping with her had fled his mind as soon as he walked in the door and found her leaning over the edge of the bar, her short skirt skimming the backs of her thighs. He was an idiot to think he could ever get her out of his system. He knew that now, standing here, watching her laugh with Macy, noticing the way wisps of hair curled around her face. She was beautiful and fearless and sexy as hell. There would be no getting Ruby out of his system.

But maybe she could get him out of hers. She could live out whatever little fantasy she had about fucking a monster and be done with it. With him.

Rafe ignored the shards of glass in his throat as he swallowed that thought. He pushed off the wall and stalked toward Ruby. She turned, eyes wide in the dim bar.

"Ready?" he asked and her lips tipped up in a smile. She was ready. He could smell it and it nearly brought him to his knees.

"Ready." She grabbed her things from the bar and waved goodbye to Macy who waggled her eyebrows in a suggestive way that Rafe decided to ignore.

The night air was thick, expectant. Rafe's lungs felt tight. Silence hung between them as heavy as the humidity. Ruby's body next to him was a thing of tortuous dreams. She was so close. Soon she would be even closer. Her plush body beneath his, her thighs cradling his hips. Shit. He was so hard already, putting one foot in front of the other was a struggle. Walking had become a foreign concept. He needed to run. He blew out a ragged sigh.

Ruby's pinky brushed against his. Barely a touch but his body stood at attention, completely cued into hers. She slid her hand into his, their palms pressing together. She gave his fingers a squeeze and he felt it echo in his chest.

He was so screwed.

By the time they reached the house, Rafe could barely see

straight. It was all a blur, the overgrown lawn, the crooked path to the door, the squeaky hinges as it opened.

The only thing that was clear was Ruby—her small hand in his, her cinnamon scent bathing everything around them, her blood red smile as she opened the door. Ruby, Ruby, Ruby. Her name was the only thought in his head.

Until she peered into the house, looking uncertain, and he remembered the sight that had greeted them last time. He forced himself to unhook his hand from hers.

"I'll take a look around. Go check on your sister." He nodded toward the stairs and Ruby hesitated, uncertainty written on her face. "I'll meet you in your room," he added and her features softened again. Had she really believed he could change his mind about this?

He hurried back outside and strode around the property, forcing himself to pay attention, to notice if anything was off kilter. Everything seemed normal. Quiet. He let his wolf senses spool out from him but all he could smell was fresh cut grass from the neighbors' yard and the scent of an impending storm. No other wolves nearby tonight.

He walked the perimeter twice more to be sure he was right. And if he was honest, to calm down a bit before seeing Ruby again. The last thing he wanted to do was attack her like some beast as soon as he walked in the door. He sucked in a deep breath, forcing his body into submission. This was about giving Ruby what she needed and then backing off.

He could do this. Sex without feelings wasn't exactly his strong suit, but he could do this.

By the time he'd walked back inside, up the stairs and opened Ruby's door, he'd nearly convinced himself. But there she was. The full force of her struck him in the chest like a goddamn lightning bolt.

"Everything okay?" She was asking about the house, about the other wolves. She was asking about her safety, but all Rafe could feel was how not okay he was.

He swallowed hard and nodded. Ruby sat perched on the edge of her bed, still dressed except for her bare feet. Tension radiated from her body. She looked tired, her eye makeup smudged around the edges, but the idea of either of them sleeping right now was laughable. They'd come too far.

No, he had a choice. There was always a choice. And right now all he wanted was Ruby.

He crossed the room in two strides and dropped to his knees in front of her. She opened her thighs and made space for him to come closer. He let his hands fall to her hips, squeezed the flesh under her skirt. She ran her fingers through his hair, tugging at the ends until pinpricks of pain tingled against his scalp.

He leaned in, their faces so close now her breath fanned across his lips. "You sure this is what you want, Ruby?" he asked, his voice like gravel.

She nodded, her eyes on his.

"Say it," he growled.

"I want this," her voice was breathless but steady, sure. "I want you."

It was too much. He slammed his lips down on hers and stole the words from her mouth. *She doesn't want me. She wants the idea of me. She wants the monster in the dark.* So that's what he'd give her.

He devoured her mouth, biting and sucking and teasing until her moans filled her tiny bedroom. His fingers dug into her hips, holding her in place even as she tried to rub against him. He kissed down the long column of her neck, letting his teeth scrape against her sensitive skin. She shivered beneath his touch.

Rafe pulled his mouth away for long enough to pull the tank top over her head revealing the lime green bra beneath. Her full tits spilled over the top of the cups and a groan tore from Rafe's lips. She was fucking edible. He traced her curves with his tongue, dipping beneath the fabric. When his tongue grazed her nipple she gasped and arched toward him. Her fingers were tangled in his hair, pulling him closer.

He huffed a laugh against her overheated skin and dipped his tongue in again.

"Please," she whispered. "Rafe, please."

It wasn't Rafe's particular kink, to hear a woman beg, but goddamn, that word from Ruby's mouth set fire to his blood. He unhooked the bra with a flick of his fingers. Ruby's eyes met his in surprise.

He couldn't help the smile on his face. "You don't live hundreds of years and not learn how to unhook a bra."

Ruby's laugh tumbled out of her, low and bright, filling Rafe in ways he didn't want to think about. Not now. Not with Ruby half naked and smiling in front of him. He reached up and gently undid the knot of her hair, letting it tumble down her back. He ran his fingers through it and Ruby closed her eyes on a sigh.

"That feels so good," she breathed and Rafe wanted to do things that made her feel good over and over. Little things, big things, all the things. He leaned forward and took her nipple in his mouth. He swirled his tongue around it, savoring the hitch in Ruby's breathing. He sucked hard and she moaned low in her throat, the vibration shooting straight to Rafe's cock.

Ruby's thighs fell wider apart and she wrapped her legs around his torso. Her heels digging into his lower back kept him anchored in the moment. He licked and sucked at each breast like he was worshiping at the feet of a goddess. Nothing else mattered but this. Nothing else existed except for Ruby's lush body wrapped around him and her sighs and moans filling him and his name falling from her lips.

"Rafe, please." She tugged at his hair, pulling him away. Her cheeks were pink and sweat dampened her hair line. Little curls had formed around her face. He'd left marks on her breasts and almost felt bad about it, but he liked seeing them there.

"Make me come." She said the words while she held his stare, her chest heaving with every breath.

Rafe blinked, the world coming back into focus. *Make me come*. Those words. The look on Ruby's face. Shit.

Rafe put a hand up Ruby's skirt and tugged her underwear down over her ass. She wiggled out of them and reached for her skirt.

"Leave it on," he growled, running his hands up her thighs, spreading her wider. He sat back on his heels to admire the view. Ruby's perfect cunt was laid out in front of him. He ran a hand up her leg until he reached her center. She stilled, her breath catching. He palmed her thigh and let his thumb brush against her folds. She bucked, her hips meeting his hand involuntarily.

Ruby leaned back on her elbows, staring down at him, eyes glazed over with lust. She was so wet. He held her legs open with one hand and explored her with the other. His fingers traced over her, learning where she liked to be touched, watching for every intake of breath, every moan and whimper.

He could do this all night. All week. For the rest of his fucking life.

No, that's not what this is.

He was on his knees again, kissing up her legs, nipping and biting, loving how Ruby responded to every little spark of pain against the pleasure. The wolf inside him growled low with desire, with the need to claim her.

But Rafe wasn't a wolf right now. He was a human.

He ran his tongue through Ruby's wetness and his world fractured. *Human.* He was human. He couldn't hold on to it. To that thought. To his humanity. This taste. Ruby's taste. It was everything. He licked her again and again, broad and flat and then teasing and swirling. Over and over until Ruby was grinding against his face, her scent and her taste nearly suffocating him.

He'd never felt anything like it in his life and as Ruby came against his tongue, trembling and screaming his name, he knew why. The realization stole his breath, stole his senses. It couldn't be.

He stared up at Ruby while she trembled through the aftershocks, her dark hair streaming down her back like night itself, her lips red from kissing him instead of her lipstick. And he knew.

Ruby was his fucking Mate.

Chapter Twenty-One

R uby had just experienced the best orgasm of her entire life, but Rafe was the one who looked wrecked. He knelt in front of her, her wetness on his lips, his fingers still digging into her thighs, but his eyes were filled with something she'd never seen before.

Longing and desire mixed with … fear? Rafe was looking at her like he wanted to fuck her into oblivion and run from her at the same time. She grabbed tight to his arm. She wouldn't let him run.

"Fuck me, Rafe."

He shook his head, hard, like the words had rattled him out of his thoughts.

"I…" His voice was rough and choked like he couldn't bear the words he was about to say. Somehow Ruby knew she couldn't bear to hear them either. She leaned forward and claimed his mouth with hers, demanding he open for her, demanding he let her in.

For a moment he did, and Ruby sagged in relief. She ran her fingers through his hair and down his shoulders. He was still fully clothed which now seemed like a horrible oversight. She tugged at his shirt and he let her yank it over his head. He kissed her like a desperate man, like this was some kind of goodbye. But that couldn't be true. Despite all that "get it out of their system" crap, Rafe couldn't deny what existed between them. Not when it was so obvious, so bare.

Ruby pulled away and leaned her forehead against his. She let her hands trace the planes of his chest.

"That was amazing, but I don't want to stop."

Rafe's exhale was one of defeat. "You got what you needed." He pushed away from her, rising up. Ruby stood too, not wanting him to tower over her. Not now when he already held too much else over her. She'd been completely open with him and still he was pulling away?

"What I needed? I thought this was a mutual getting over it thing." She crossed her arms over her bare chest. Rafe grabbed her shirt from the bed and handed it to her.

"You said you were distracted. Hopefully, now you can concentrate better."

What the actual hell was happening here? Ruby tugged the shirt on, not caring that it was inside out and backwards. This whole night was falling down around her head. Outside rain pelted against the windows. The storm had broken.

"Are you kidding?" she asked, ignoring how hurt her voice sounded. "You're pretending that was just a favor to me?" She gestured to where Rafe's cock strained against the front of his pants.

The color rose in Rafe's cheeks, a pained expression crossing his face. "This is all I can give you, Ruby."

He stalked from the room before she could argue. Thunder rumbled through the house, drowning out his footsteps on the stairs. Ruby dropped back onto the bed, her legs still shaking from her soul-shattering orgasm.

She had never been so embarrassed in her life.

This wasn't possible. There was no way this could be happening. Not to him. Not with Ruby.

Rafe paced the woods beyond the house, his fur plastered to his body. He was soaked to the bone and the rain still hadn't let up. Every muscle in his body, every instinct was screaming at him to run back to her. But he couldn't. Especially not now. Not with Ruby's taste still on his tongue, the feel of her body still imprinted on his. He shook his fur out again, water spraying everywhere, not that it did any good in this downpour.

God, she must hate him. The look on her face when he pulled away, the betrayal and the anger, would haunt him forever.

But this couldn't be possible.

Rafe hadn't grown up with the fairy tale of fated Mates. His father shut down any whisper of it. The pack mated for strength and skill, not based on destiny or, worse, love. At a very young age, Rafe was convinced the concept didn't even exist.

Until he met Scarlet and he'd thought maybe...

The light in Ruby's bedroom went out, bathing the yard in darkness. She'd given up on him coming back. Rafe's chest cracked, letting the darkness in.

Good. She needed to give up on him. It was why he didn't fuck her. Why he couldn't, even as his body craved it like his next breath. Stories linger, even when they are suppressed. People whisper. Wolves talk. He knew the fairy tale even if he never believed in it. Werewolves were meant to mate for life. If they were lucky, they found their fated Mate, the wolf that was tied to their soul, the wolf they literally could not live without. It was all bullshit. Rafe had never met anyone who'd found their one, true Mate. It wasn't possible. It wasn't real.

Unless it was... Rafe shook himself again, his body still reverberating from the realization he'd had between Ruby's legs. The word *Mate* still ran through his blood, still screamed at him to pay attention to what was right in front of him.

Shit. He couldn't do it. Didn't want it. Humans were not for him. Not even that one, not even Ruby. He squeezed his eyes shut, trying to pull himself together, trying to slow his racing heart so he could think.

If the stories were true, the Mate bond wouldn't lock in place until he claimed her. In his current state, there was exactly one way Rafe could think of to claim his Mate and it didn't involve promise rings. Which was why he'd stopped before they went any further, before he lost himself in her and did things they'd both regret.

Just imagining being buried deep inside her made Rafe groan in agony, but she would have no choice, she'd be stuck with him forever whether she wanted it or not. Right? There was too much he still didn't know. Too many questions he'd never asked. He'd been afraid to ask them, to even think them, back then.

He knew one thing for certain, the last thing he wanted to do was force Ruby to be with him.

She was a human. Maybe she didn't sense the bond at all, maybe this was all one-sided. And what was he going to do, tie himself for eternity to this human for one little fuck? Follow Ruby around like a puppy for the rest of her life? He refused to think of what would happen to him after Ruby died and his damn werewolf genes kept him alive for several more centuries.

The terror that seized his heart at that thought was too much to bear.

None of this was fair to Ruby. She wasn't a werewolf. She was a human, another human that would be taken from him too soon. He refused to make that mistake again.

But even as he vowed to himself that he wouldn't claim her, that he wouldn't fuck her and make her his, even as he swore to himself that he would leave, his body rebelled. His feet wouldn't budge. He should find another way to protect her from afar. But even as he racked his brain for ways to do that, his heart laughed at what a liar he was, at what a fool he was.

It was too late. It didn't matter if he stayed away from Ruby for the rest of his life. It didn't matter if he ran to the ends of the earth to avoid her. It didn't matter if he never touched her again. She was already his. It was too damn late.

For him anyway. But maybe she could be the one to run. Just like Scarlet had, saving them both the trouble of wondering what could possibly happen next between a wolf and a woman.

The memory was vivid and real, like a movie played on the shadows of the forest.

Chapter Twenty-Two

"What are you saying, Rafe? I don't understand." Scarlet's eyes were wide, bright blue against her pale skin. The sun at her back brought out the gold in her brown hair. They stood by the quiet roadside, wildflowers lining their path. Birds chirped somewhere in the distance oblivious to the people arguing in their midst.

"I can't enlist."

She shook her head in confusion, but he kept going. "I can't because I don't exist in your world. Not really. I'm not..."

"You're not what?" She put her hands on her hips, her expression darkening. She thought he was a coward, that he was trying to get out of the war in Europe because he was scared of dying but that wasn't it at all. If he went, it would be all too obvious what he was. Not to mention he had no papers to prove his existence.

He reached for her and pulled her close, his fingers digging into the flesh of her upper arms. Her chest heaved against his. He hadn't known her for long, six months maybe. She was beautiful, petite and feisty. She'd let him kiss her behind the shop, let him run his hands over her waist and the curve of her breast. She looked at him like he was something other than the Alpha's son. She talked to him because she wanted to, not because she feared his father. She didn't know about any of that.

Rafe hadn't wanted her to know any of it, but now she was looking at him like he was a draft dodger, like he wasn't willing to lay down his life for her like her brothers were. And he couldn't stand it. It was worse than claws down his back, worse than teeth at his throat. The look of contempt in her eyes was worse than any fight he'd ever been in.

"I'm not human," he growled in her ear and she went rigid in his arms.

"Stop that. It's not funny." She put a hand on his chest and pushed.

They were far from town. He'd taken her on a walk hoping she'd let him do more than kiss her if they were away from prying eyes, but now she looked frantically at the empty fields around them.

He let her go.

"I'm sorry." He shook his head, trying to right his thoughts. "But it's true. There are things out there, Scarlet, things you don't know about but they're real."

She squinted up at him in the bright sun of the afternoon. "And you're one of those things?"

He nodded, his heart racing in his chest. Maybe she would understand. Maybe she would continue to look at him like he mattered even if she knew what he was.

"So what are you, Rafe?"

"I'm a wolf."

"A wolf?"

"Sometimes. And sometimes human." He wished he could be more human for her. All human. For the first time in his life, he wished he could shed the other half of him, ignore every instinct that urged him to run and kill, that whispered in his ear to be wild. He didn't want it anymore.

Her perfectly arched eyebrows rose to her hairline. "Like a werewolf?"

He nodded, not daring to say anything else, not daring to move toward her. Scarlet's gaze raked over his body, scanning him from head to toe. He never felt his size more. He knew what he looked like and it wasn't good.

"Show me," she said, her arms crossed over her chest.

This wouldn't end well. Rafe knew it already, but he did as she asked, some ridiculous bit of hope still lingering, still holding on. Shifting wasn't pretty. He ran from her so she wouldn't see it up close, the rearranging of his bones and muscles, his face transforming from man to beast, the hair growing over his skin. He crossed the meadow, far enough to lessen the blow but close enough that she could still see him.

By the time he ran back to her in his wolf form, Scarlet was trembling from head to toe. She held up a hand to stop him from coming any closer. He sat on the edge of the road and watched her.

"I thought you were lying. You can't be... It isn't possible." The words stuttered and tripped from her mouth, tumbling over each other to escape. Rafe watched as she processed what she saw and then shaped it into something new, something she could believe.

"What are you, some kind of magician? Where are you really, Rafe?" She raised her voice as though she thought Rafe was hiding somewhere. "Call off your dog!" She shook her head, backing away from him. Her eyes were wide, wild with fear. "You're a monster." The word sliced through him, the truth of it. "A ... a ... beast."

He was. Of course, he was. And now she knew it.

"Don't come around anymore," she whispered before running down the road. He sat and watched her go. The one pure and good thing in his life disappeared from sight. Life with his father, with his brothers had become nearly unbearable. Every day a battle, every minute a test. He was exhausted and now he wouldn't even have Scarlet's smile to look forward to. No more sugar-sweet kisses in the sun.

Rafe had managed to scare off the one bright spot keeping his miserable existence worth living. She didn't want him. Not the real him anyway. He should have seen that coming.

Movement caught his attention from the corner of his eye, pulling him from the painful memories.

Rafe pounced on the bunny and tore it to pieces just to have something to do. He was a monster after all.

Chapter Twenty-Three

R afe never came back to bed. Maybe he'd scampered off back home. *Good,* Ruby thought, running her fingers through her tangled hair. She twisted it into a knot and then swung her legs out of bed.

Just when she'd convinced herself she was glad he left, that she was better off without a werewolf in her bed, the smell of coffee wafting up from the kitchen told her Rafe hadn't gone anywhere. The bastard.

Her stomach heated at the memory of last night. She thought he wanted her as much as she wanted him. She didn't want some pity oral! Not that it wasn't amazing, but that was beside the point. He'd made her feel like a complete idiot and that was not the post-orgasm experience anyone wanted. And if he thought he was just going to run off again or pretend nothing happened, he had another think coming. Mr. King of Mixed Signals was going to get a piece of her mind this morning.

She'd slept in her tank top and nothing else, secretly hoping like the desperate pervert that she was that Rafe would come back, but clearly this outfit would not do for breakfast and telling wolf-man to go fuck himself. Ruby grabbed a fresh tank top, dark red like her rage. She pulled it on over a black bra. She didn't bother with fancy underwear because that furry bastard would not be seeing them today, but she did wear her shortest skirt just to spite him. She never wore makeup to breakfast in her own home but today, it felt necessary. Black eyeliner on her top lids with just a little swoop at the ends and her favorite lipstick color: *Sexy Red Riding Hood*. She smiled at herself in the mirror. She looked damn good for a morning of telling a guy off.

Ruby stomped down the stairs to the kitchen and found Rafe leaning against the counter, nursing a cup of coffee. He looked like shit. *Good.*

He didn't bother to smile when she walked in, just watched her. She lingered in the doorway not wanting to actually get close enough to him to get to the coffee maker.

"Morning." His voice was like black coffee, hot and rich. He had circles under his eyes and his hair was tied back messily at the nape of his neck. His stubble was dark and thick. Damn it, she was wrong. He didn't look like shit at all. He looked sexy as usual. How fucking dare he?

Ruby opened her mouth to tell him off but Rafe spoke first. "I'm going to the pack today. I'll get you their protection and then I can get out of your hair."

Wait. What? He was leaving? Just like that?

He turned away, avoiding her shocked stare and poured her a cup of coffee. Two teaspoons of sugar, no milk. Damn it. He remembered how she took her coffee. Could he be any more infuriating? He put the mug on the counter and slid it toward her. A peace offering. Well, screw that.

"You're leaving?"

He nodded. "I think that's best."

"Why?"

"The pack will be better able to protect you."

"No, Rafe. Why do you think that's best?"

He blinked and stared down into his mug. "Just drop it, Ruby."

"I won't drop it. Why are you so damn convinced that I shouldn't be around you?" She stepped closer, feeling the heat radiating off of him.

"I've told you before, I'm not what you think."

Ruby breathed out a frustrated sigh. This bullshit again. "And what am I supposed to think? So far you've been nothing but good and kind to me. You fought for me. You're protecting me and my sister. Are holding a girl's purse and giving her the best orgasm of her life supposed to be threatening actions?" Her voice rose with every word until she was practically shouting. His silver eyes flashed at the mention of orgasms but he stayed silent.

"I'm not scared of you, Rafe," she yelled.

He leaned forward until his face was level with hers. "You will be."

She pushed against his chest, shoving him back toward the counter. He let her. She was so damn frustrated with this argument she wanted to slap him.

"What does that even mean? I don't know what happened that made you believe you are so scary or terrible, but you're not, Rafe. You're just not!"

He swallowed hard, something shifting in his expression.

"I'm not a pet, Ruby. I'm not a dog. I'm a fucking werewolf." A muscle ticked in his jaw as he stalked toward her. She backed up until she hit the wall. He was close enough now that every breath pressed his chest against hers.

"I've terrorized entire villages. Chased people until they

pissed themselves. Torn out the throats of rival pack members without a second thought."

Ruby's breath caught. "Those things happened so long ago. That's not you anymore!"

He shook his head. "Do you want to know why I left the pack?"

He didn't wait for her response before he went on. "My father wanted me to kill my brothers, to take my rightful place as the Alpha. Not long ago at all, Ruby. Five years. That's it. We fought for hours, the three of us, round and round in that ring. By the time the rain started we were already exhausted and injured. Theo was the weakest. I could have picked him off easily.

"My father screamed at me from beside the ring. *Kill him! Kill him!* The old bastard was dying and wanted to see the new Alpha crowned before he left this world. I pinned Theo to the ground. My own brother, my own blood. He fought me, clawing and scraping. I slashed his face, blood pouring into his eyes. You saw it, Ruby. You saw the scar." He held her stare and she wanted to tell him to stop, that she'd heard enough, but he kept going.

"I could have ended it, but I hesitated. Knox barreled into us, his teeth at my throat. And I was happy, relieved. If he would just kill me, I could be done with it all. With everything my father wanted from us."

A small whimper escaped Ruby's throat. Rafe's eyes glowed bright silver, his voice a deep growl. Even his teeth seemed longer, sharper. She put a hand on Rafe's chest and she could practically feel the beast prowling beneath his human skin. She willed him to come back to her, to leave this awful memory behind. It was more words than he'd ever spoken to her, like he'd saved them all up and could no longer contain them.

"But then I saw her. Phoebe. She was hiding in the trees, watching, silent tears trailing down her face. Her eyes never left Theo. He lay in the mud, chest heaving, face covered in blood. I'd done that to him. My own brother. But Knox was at my throat. I was pinned on my back, the only thing stopping him from killing me was my paws on his chest. If I let him kill me, he'd kill Theo next. I did the only thing I could think of. A desperate, disgusting thing."

His breath came in long shuddering gasps like he'd just been in the ring, like the fight hadn't been over for five years. His eyes were dark with the memories.

"I shifted. Back into human form, right in the ring. It shocked the hell out of everyone. It's forbidden. I shamed my father and my pack. Knox didn't know what to do. I used everyone's surprise to my advantage. I screamed at Theo to run and he did. Sloppily and half blind he ran into the woods. My father came into the ring, raging but so old and sick I wasn't scared of him anymore.

"He spat at my feet, my bare, human feet drowning in mud. 'Get the fuck out of here. You are dead to us,' he screamed. So I did."

"You saved your brothers," she whispered and he laughed, low and mocking.

"Goddamn it, Ruby. Get it through your head. I've done nothing but fight and kill my whole life. And then in the end all I did was shame my people. I'm both a monster and a coward."

"But—"

"Stop." His voice was hard and cold, unmovable. "Stop trying to see me as something else. End this ridiculous infatuation. You are a silly little girl who likes ghost stories, but I am not a story, and I will hurt you."

She swallowed the sharp, angry tears clogging her throat.

She would not add crying to the ways she'd already embarrassed herself.

"Have it your way." She pushed against his chest but he didn't move, his eyes flashing with pain. "Maybe I am silly and ridiculous." He winced like he already regretted the words. "But you're the one still believing all the lies your father told you. You're the one with a completely warped view of himself. All this talk of protecting me when all you really wanted to do was protect yourself."

His eyes widened like her words hit him physically. She pushed him again and he backed up.

"So, big bad wolf, you can go fuck yourself." Ruby turned and spun away from him, not waiting for a response. She strode for the door, but it was blocked. By her sister. Who, judging by the wide eyes and blanched skin, had heard everything.

"Morning, Lena."

"Uh … morning."

The door slammed and Rafe was gone.

Chapter Twenty-Four

"Ruby, what the hell is going on?" Lena grabbed Ruby's arm and led her to the kitchen table. She shoved her into a chair and sat across from her. Apparently, Ruby wasn't going to get away with vague explanations and implausible stories this morning.

"Maybe you need some coffee first?" Ruby tried to stand but Lena pushed her back down. At least her strength was up this morning.

"Ruby." Lena's tone offered no possibility of stalling or lying so Ruby just went for it.

"Rafe is a werewolf and so is his brother Theo. And there's a third brother who I'm assuming is equally hot and he is the new Alpha of their pack, except Theo and Rafe haven't lived with the pack for years, because their father wanted them to fight it out in some sort of ultimate death match and so now Rafe thinks he's some kind of monster but I swear Lena's he's really not despite his overall glowering vibe—"

"Ruby, take a breath."

"Right. Sorry." She gave Lena a weak smile. "A lot has

happened and I hate lying to you but I couldn't figure out how to tell you and not sound crazy."

Lena pinched the bridge of her nose. "Well, I can't say you don't sound crazy."

Ruby snorted.

"Are you sure this isn't like the time you were certain Casper the Friendly Ghost was living in the attic?" Lena asked with a sigh, the exhaustion returning to her face.

Ruby shook her head. "Ha. Ha. You saw him, Lena. I'm sure you overheard at least some of that … uh … discussion we were having."

Lena nodded slowly, considering. "What is he doing here?"

"Well, that's kind of the part I didn't want to worry you about." Ruby fiddled with the ends of her hair. Her bun had tumbled down a while ago.

"Tell me." The force in Lena's voice was almost comforting. Her big sister voice. Her cut-the-shit voice. Ruby had missed that voice.

"I was sort of attacked last week. By a wolf."

Lena's mouth gaped open. "Oh, for God's sake, Ruby."

"But I'm fine obviously." Ruby gestured to herself showing off how perfectly fine she was even though her insides were a confused soup of anger, hurt, and lust. "Rafe was there and he saved me and then sort of took it upon himself to protect us, I guess."

"Mmhmm. So you're not dating?"

"Well … it's complicated."

"What were you fighting about?"

Ruby slouched back in her chair, allowing herself the pouting she'd wanted to do all morning. "He keeps trying to convince me he's dangerous or whatever and that I should forget about anything between us, but it's bullshit."

"I mean, he *is* a werewolf. Sounds kinda dangerous." Lena gave her a patronizing smirk.

Ruby rolled her eyes, slipping back into her little sister role like a pair of worn slippers. It was easy and nice.

"He's been perfectly civilized. Annoyingly so, actually. I don't know what his problem is."

Lena raised an eyebrow at that but didn't probe further.

"Anyway, he's now declared he's leaving us in the hands of the pack and just ditching us."

Ruby bit the inside of her cheek, refusing to get teary-eyed over this. So she'd been really hot for her sort-of stalker and now he was leaving. Big freaking deal. Except now she remembered the other reason why Rafe had been hanging around, and fear for her sister crawled back into her stomach, settling slimy and cold in her gut.

"There's something else."

Lena sighed. "How could there possibly be more?"

"Rafe thinks you're some kind of seer, like with psychic, future-telling powers."

Lena's eyes widened like two full moons. "What are you talking about?" She shook her head, her blonde hair slipping over her shoulders. It used to fall like golden waves but now it was thin and pale. Her sister was wasting away. "Don't start this crap again, Ruby," she warned. "I have enough to deal with right now. I don't need you adding to it."

"We need to get you help, Lena. You need to control the visions instead of letting them control you. It might be the only way—"

Lena stood abruptly, her chair legs scraping loudly across the wood floor. "Ruby, stop." Her face looked exactly the same as when they were little girls and Ruby would tell ghost stories before bed. Lena hated that. She hated that Ruby surrounded herself with the macabre after their parents' death. It made no sense to her. Just like everything Ruby just said made no sense now.

"Lena—"

"No. Just stop. You can play whatever kinky games you want to play with your boyfriend, but leave me out of it. Don't try to pretend my health is some kind of supernatural power. That's not how things work, Ruby." She gathered the ends of her robe in her hands like the train of a ball gown. "The doctors will figure it out. I'm sure of it. End of discussion." She turned and stormed from the room.

"Lena, wait!" Ruby shouted after her. "It's not a game! You can't keep pretending this is going to just go away!" Ruby's words were met with the sound of Lena's door slamming overhead and then nothing but echoing silence.

Shit.

Ruby put her head in her hands and groaned into the quiet. Kinky games? Did her sister really think everything Ruby told her was part of some sort of elaborate role-playing game between her and Rafe? Good Lord.

Did everyone think she was ridiculous?

Maybe she was.

Chapter Twenty-Five

R afe paced the yard waiting for Theo to show up, the memories clinging to his skin like sweat. He hadn't told Ruby the worst thing he'd done.

He hadn't left Scarlet alone. He couldn't. He was an animal. A beast. And he stalked her like one. He told himself it was for her protection. Her brothers were gone, her father was old and weak. This was werewolf country after all. Someone should look after her.

But he'd led death right to Scarlet's door.

Rafe followed her to and from the store each day, sticking to the shadows but remaining in human form. She didn't speak to him after the day he showed her what he really was; he didn't give her the chance to. He stayed hidden, still clinging to the ridiculous hope that she would change her mind about him, still planning to explain himself better one of these days. He was weak and stupid, but he couldn't stop.

Rafe strode into camp after walking Scarlet to the shop. The sun was barely up, but a few pack members were already up, cooking whatever they'd hunted for breakfast. Rafe smiled to himself. Wolves were hunters, but their human sides just couldn't resist a hot meal.

They were still working on more permanent structures at this site, having just moved here a few months ago. They'd overstayed their welcome in their last location and some members had been shot and killed raiding a farmer's chicken coop. It was a stupid move, but the pack was hungry. The pack was always hungry.

Before Rafe could even consider crawling back into his tent and sleeping another hour or two, his father emerged from behind the army green structure.

"Where have you been, boy?"

Boy. Rafe nearly laughed. He was over a century old and his father considered him a child. Alpha Devon never missed a chance to exert dominance.

"Doesn't matter."

The old man stepped closer. "It sure as hell does matter. I know you've been hanging around some woman."

If humans had hackles, Rafe's would be raised.

"There's no woman." Saying the words, Rafe felt the truth of it. There was no woman that wanted him anyway. He was just as pathetic as his father thought.

"Stay out of town."

"You control where I go now?"

His father's breath was a warm cloud of stale smoke. Rafe resisted the urge to flinch when he spoke. He'd received enough beatings as a child to know he should just take it like a man or it would last longer.

"I control where you go, what you eat, when you sleep," his father rasped. "I decide if you live or die. I'm the goddamn Alpha of this pack and you better not forget it."

Rafe stood stock still, letting his father's words roll over him. He didn't blink, didn't breathe until the man walked away. Rafe watched him go, his cocky swagger still in place despite his age. It was hard to explain why Rafe didn't push back. He knew, theoretically, that he was stronger than his father. If he really tried, head to head in a fight, Rafe could win.

But his father was right. He'd had complete control over Rafe's life forever. For decades it had been drilled into Rafe that his father could do no wrong, that he was the strongest, wisest wolf in the pack. And if he didn't believe it, if he didn't obey, he was punished. A wolf that goes long enough without meals, without the light of day, without the ability to run free, quickly learns to obey.

So even now, Rafe shuddered as his father walked away. Even now, his stomach tied in knots at the thought of getting caught back in town. But the fear didn't stop him.

By the time evening rolled around, Rafe was loping off back to Scarlet's store. He shifted to his human form before hitting the first residential street. It was a small town. Backwoods Maine wasn't exactly a bustling metropolis. He was the only one on the street as he waited for Scarlet to emerge.

She was dressed in light blue today. The color of the summer sky. She paused and took another glance at where Rafe stood in the shadows. His heart stuttered. It seemed she was staring right at him, but then she shook her head and started off down the street. Her steps were fast and frantic, like she was running from him.

And still he followed her.

When the old farmhouse Scarlet lived in with her father came into view, she stole a look over her shoulder. Fear glittered in her eyes. Rafe stayed tucked into the shadows of the trees and Scarlet pulled her cardigan tighter around her shoulders as she dashed into the house.

Despite her fear, despite his guilt, he kept coming back day after day, risking the wrath of his father, risking the scorn of his pack. Each day his plan to leave grew bigger. It solidified in his mind. Even if Scarlet never wanted him, he could go. He could build something just for himself away from his father and his brothers.

Once the thought had entered his mind it took hold and wouldn't let go. He could leave. He could leave.

It took months to build up the courage to do it. Rafe had no resources outside of the pack, but he could live off the land. He knew how. He'd go completely wild for now until he had a better plan. It was worth the risk. He couldn't stay here anymore. Not like this.

He walked slowly to town in the pre-dawn hours. He wanted to see her one more time before he finally did the right thing and left her alone.

Rafe stopped on the other side of the road from her house, his usual waiting spot, in the shadow of a giant oak. But something was off today. It was too quiet. Even the birds had stopped singing their good morning song to the sun. Everything was still except for the long grass in front of the farm house as it waved in the wind.

The creaky screen door on the house slammed shut in the breeze, sending Rafe's heart into his throat. Something wasn't right.

He raced across the road and the scent hit him so hard his knees buckled. Burnt sugar and fresh blood.

Scarlet's body lay in a heap on the grass, her dark hair spread out around her among the wildflowers. Rafe dropped beside her, the howl already rising up in his throat. He covered her body with his own, his head pressed to her chest, willing there to be a heartbeat even though he knew it was impossible. The wound to her neck was deep and precise. Teeth marks at her jugular left no room for mistaking what had happened here, and yet still he listened for a beat, still he prayed.

He didn't know how long he stayed there, the early morning dew seeping through the knees of his pants. Eventually, he lifted her small body in his arms and carried her onto the porch. He knocked on the door and faced her father. Watched as the man's face crumpled, as his arthritic hands shook. Rafe moved past him and laid Scarlet on the tattered couch in the family room.

The sheriff would be alerted, the neighbors. A hunt would ensue. The pack would have to move again.

His father had endangered everyone just to prove a point. To show Rafe just how much power the man still held over his life. He couldn't leave now. The old bastard would keep punishing people until Rafe submitted.

So he left Scarlet with her weeping father and went back to the pack, shifting before he even hit the woods. He was a monster, he might as well live like one.

A new painful thought gripped him, terror twisting his guts.

He'd done it again. He'd been following Ruby for weeks, longer than those other wolves. Had he led them to her? In trying to protect her had he led danger to her doorstep too? Rafe shook his head, the sob stuck in his throat. He wouldn't let history repeat itself. Scarlet would have been safer without him in her life. And so was Ruby.

The only way to save his Mate was to stay the hell away from her.

Chapter Twenty-Six

R uby was still sitting at the table, stewing, when Theo's soft knock came on the back door. She knew he was coming. She'd seen Rafe pacing the yard, cell phone to his ear, face grim. He was still worried about her even as he was leaving. Apparently, Theo was here to babysit until the pack was alerted to their current predicament.

"Come in," Ruby mumbled, and thanks to his super wolfy senses, Theo heard her.

"Good morning," Theo drawled, striding into the kitchen.

"Is it?"

He gave her his best charming smile. "The sun is shining; the birds are chirping. What more could you ask for, Ruby love?"

Ruby glowered.

Theo gave a knowing nod and dropped into the chair across from her. "Let me guess, my brother is being an asshole?"

Ruby couldn't help the surprised laugh that escaped her. Theo grinned. "It's a family condition but I think Rafe got the worst of it," he continued with an easy smile. He leaned back in his chair, taking up space like he belonged in her kitchen, like he belonged anywhere he wanted to be. He was a cocky bastard for sure, but Ruby liked him.

"He's very frustrating."

Theo nodded. "Stubborn as rock, his whole life." He ran a hand over his curls. "But ultimately, not a bad guy. Though I hate to admit it." He grinned again and Ruby could see how easy it would be to fall for a guy like Theo. Unfortunately, she didn't want a guy like Theo. Unfortunately, she liked big broody idiots. "So what did he do?" Theo asked.

"He didn't tell you?"

Theo blew out a breath. "Well, he said he was going to talk to Knox, which I admit nearly knocked me off my seat."

"Is it true that he saved your life?"

Theo paused mid stretch, his eyebrows touching his hairline. His eyes were like green pools, light against his tan skin. "Is that what he told you?"

"Not in so many words. He made it sound like it was all his fault, that he hurt you and your brother. That he shamed your pack."

"Typical." Theo huffed a wolfy breath. "He did save my life. My father wanted only one man standing and Rafe refused to do it. Of course he would see it as a failure though."

"A lot of daddy issues, huh."

Theo's laugh echoed through the kitchen. He shook his head, his eyes sparking in amusement. "You have no idea."

"He said he was dangerous and he had to leave. He called me ridiculous. It's like he doesn't trust me to decide that for myself." Ruby rested her chin on her forearms; the table was cool beneath them. The storm had brought drier air this morning and for the first time in days, Ruby wasn't sweating.

"Asshole." Theo glanced out the window to where Rafe was

still glowering in the yard. Why he hadn't left yet, Ruby had no idea. "Look, Ruby. That bullshit is not about you at all." His eyes cut to the window again and then back to her. "I probably shouldn't even tell you this and I don't really know the entire story, but there was another human woman."

"Oh." The word was as small and dejected as she felt.

"A long time ago," Theo rushed to add. "I knew Rafe was meeting up with her in town and my father hated it. He hated humans, really anyone that wasn't our kind." Theo's voice faded away. Ruby wondered if his thoughts had drifted to Phoebe.

"Anyway, it didn't end well. Like I said, I don't know the whole story, but the girl ended up dead. Killed by a wolf."

Some startled, strangled noise fell from Ruby's mouth. "But it wasn't... I mean he wouldn't..." She couldn't say it. The words refused to form.

Theo's eyes widened. "Oh God, no. It wasn't Rafe. The guy was wrecked afterward. He didn't eat for days. I had to practically force-feed him. No, I'm sure it was our beloved father reminding Rafe who was in charge and what happened to wolves who didn't fall in line."

"Jesus."

"Yeah, those were dark days." Theo leaned back in his chair again, stretching his arms overhead. "It was over a century ago, Ruby. But that's some hard shit to get over. He blames himself. He blames himself for everything."

Ruby rested her head on the table, trying to absorb everything Theo had just told her and everything she'd yelled at Rafe this morning. She'd accused him of only trying to protect himself when all he wanted to do was make sure she didn't end up like the last woman he cared for. God, she was the worst. She groaned and Theo huffed a small laugh.

"Let me go talk to him." Theo stood and Ruby peered up at him from the corner of her eye.

"I said some really shitty stuff to him."

"And he said some really shitty stuff to you. That's what fights are, right?" Theo grinned again, his perfect white teeth flashing. "I'm sure you two crazy kids can work it out."

Ruby groaned again and Theo strode toward the door. "Don't worry, Ruby love. I'll talk some sense into that asshole."

He left before Ruby could stop him.

Chapter Twenty-Seven

Theo sauntered out the back door. Rafe stood on the edge of the forest at the back of Ruby's yard. He should have left already. He should have left as soon as Theo showed up but he wanted to make sure Ruby was okay before he did. Which was idiotic because he was the one making her feel like shit.

Theo crossed the yard looking like the smug bastard that he was. Rafe should shift and run. He was positive he didn't want to hear what his brother had to say anyway, but he was rooted to the spot.

Maybe Ruby kicked him out. Maybe she didn't want Theo in her house. In that case Rafe couldn't leave. For safety reasons. Not for "feeling like his heart was being torn out every time he tried to leave" reasons.

"You really are an asshole, aren't you?" Theo asked, his smile growing wider.

Rafe growled in response.

"You have that pretty little thing waiting inside for you and you're going to ditch her just like that?"

"I'm not ditching her." Rafe's jaw tightened. He was going

to need extensive dental work after all this interacting with his brother.

"Oh really? She seemed to think so."

Rafe ran a hand through his hair. Theo was trying to get a rise out of him and it was working. "I need to go."

"Then go," Theo said with a lazy smile. "I'll keep the lovely Miss Ruby entertained while you're gone." The bastard winked. And Rafe saw red.

He shifted before he knew what he was doing, tearing right out of his clothes, like there was only one way to quell the blazing rage racing through his blood at the thought of Theo's hands on Ruby. Theo rolled his eyes, but tugged off his own clothes and shifted into his wolf form.

They growled and circled each other. *Good.* This he could do. This he could handle. He lunged for Theo, fangs glinting in the sun. They rolled, clashing and clawing at each other. Rafe bit down hard on Theo's leg and the metallic tang of blood filled his mouth. Theo growled low in warning and then he flipped them so he was on top, a wolfish grin on his face.

They fought until half the lawn was torn up and they were both bloodied and panting. Theo caved first, turning over on his back, belly up in submission.

"You win again, Rafe," he panted as soon as he was back in human form. He lay sprawled out naked in the sun and blood trickled from a wound in his arm. How many days had ended like this back when they were young and full of wolfish energy?

Rafe lay next to him, trying to catch his breath, memories of all the other times they'd done this racing through his head. It wasn't always bad. It wasn't always some forced show for their father and the pack. For a long time, it had just been him and his brothers pouncing on each other in the tall grass, for fun, for petty victories, to settle their latest argument. But it hadn't lasted. Their father wanted a winner.

"Keep your hands off Ruby," he muttered.

Theo laughed. "For fuck's sake, Rafe, you don't own the girl. You won't have her and you won't let anyone else have her either?"

Rafe sat up and Theo did the same, his green eyes flashing merrily in the sun. Everything was always a joke to him. The youngest, the prettiest. He never had to care about anything. Until they were in the ring and their father wanted blood. But even then it was left to Rafe to make the hard decisions.

"Stay away from her."

Theo's eyebrows raised. "You're serious? What are you going to do? Hang around here scaring off any guy that comes around?"

Rafe was ashamed to say the thought had definitely occurred to him. The idea of any man near Ruby sent his entire body on edge, every muscle coiled to pounce, every atom ready to act.

Theo saw it. He smelled it. The shift in Rafe's body chemistry.

"Oh my God—"

"Don't say it," Rafe warned.

"She's your—"

"Don't fucking say another word."

"Mate."

Rafe closed his eyes at the word, like he could hide from it.

Theo stood, yanking on his shorts. "She's your Mate! Holy shit."

"Keep your voice down."

"This is huge. What are you going to do?" Theo's face was lit up like a pup with a bone.

"I'm going to leave, just like I said." He had to leave. It was the only way to keep Ruby safe. Safe from him, safe from these other wolves, safe from whatever this damn Mate bond might mean for her.

Theo stopped in his tracks, staring down at where Rafe still sat in the flattened grass. "You're going to abandon your Mate? What the hell are you thinking?"

Rafe ground his teeth together. "It's for the best."

"For the best?" Theo shouted. "How could this possibly be for the best? Can you even leave her? I mean, physically. I heard wolves that try to leave their Mates go mad."

Rafe stood so they were nose to nose. He hadn't heard that one, but he'd been feeling like he wanted to crawl out of his skin since he figured out what Ruby was to him. Every moment he wasn't near her felt like being flayed alive, but he sure as hell wasn't going to tell Theo that. "She's human. I won't force her to be tied to me forever. She doesn't need any more of this werewolf bullshit in her life."

Theo blew out a long breath. "You didn't even tell her, did you?"

Rafe flinched.

"Christ, Rafe! You didn't even give her a chance to decide!"

"She's not one of us. She wouldn't understand."

"So make her understand! She's your Mate. That's ... that's ... amazing." Something wistful crossed Theo's face but Rafe ignored it.

"It's not amazing. It's impossible. I'm leaving." He didn't want her to understand. This couldn't work; none of this made sense. He had to get out of here before he did something rash, before he really did go mad with the need to touch her.

"I'm coming with you." They both swung around at the sound

of Ruby's voice. She strode down the back steps, a backpack slung over one shoulder. She'd changed from that absurdly small skirt into some shorts, but the tight red tank top remained to torture him.

How much had she heard?

"You can't." Rafe's response was immediate and gruff, taking every ounce of strength he had left after his never-ending night of denying his response to her.

Ruby put her hand on one hip and stared him down. Theo huffed a laugh. "You are so screwed," he whispered under his breath, but Rafe ignored him.

"I can and I will."

"Ruby..." Rafe's voice was nothing more than a growl.

"I have all the information now. The fighting with your brothers, the general terrorizing of humans, your... uh ... past lady friend..."

Past lady friend? Rafe's gaze whipped to Theo but the dickhead was already creeping toward the house.

"And I'm not worried about any of it," Ruby went on. "What I am worried about is my sister's health, so if your pack can help with that then I want to be a part of it."

Rafe stood speechless, still trying to figure out what exactly Ruby knew about Scarlet.

"Lena doesn't believe me about what you guys are, by the way," she yelled to Theo before he snuck in the back door. "So good luck with that."

Theo gave her an encouraging smile before he slipped inside. Ruby turned back to Rafe. "Let me come. Please."

Bad idea, bad idea, bad idea. Everything about this was a bad idea and yet Rafe couldn't seem to find the words to tell her that she couldn't come. He was at war with himself. His plan to keep her at a distance battled with his primal urge to keep her close. In the end it wasn't even a question. It hadn't been a fair fight.

He swallowed hard. "Fine."

It was her sister after all. Who was he to tell her that she couldn't try to help her own family? He ignored how his heart rate slowed as soon as he knew he would be near her. Everything in his body settled into a gentle thrum at the knowledge that Ruby would be by his side for the next two days at least. He would keep her safe until they figured this out and then he would let her go. He had to.

Ruby grinned. "Great." Her gaze flicked down and then back to his face. "So are you going to put some clothes on for this trip?"

Rafe's face heated. Shit. He'd completely forgotten he'd ruined his clothes when he shifted. He covered himself with his hands, already half-hard under Ruby's appraising stare.

"More than I got to see last night," she muttered, the hurt still fresh in her voice. But he couldn't have that conversation with her, especially not right now with him bare-assed in her backyard.

"I'll go get some things and meet you back out here in five."

"Aye aye, captain," she said with a smirk. He strode past her and tried to pretend he couldn't feel her gaze watching him walk away.

That ass, though. Ruby's plan to stop sexually objectifying Rafe was not going well. She'd come out here intending to let all that shit go. She only wanted to help Lena. Well, and also get away from Lena, who had thoroughly pissed her off for not taking her seriously. Her sister was the one person in the world she would walk into danger for even while being totally aggravated with her.

Anyway, after the wolves were done with their little wrestling match, she'd thrown some supplies in a bag and marched out ready to go, only to find Rafe in all his naked splendor. Damn him.

She was a grown woman and she could take rejection like an adult. It didn't mean she was just going to let Rafe pass her safety around from wolf to wolf without her say. He hadn't exactly spoken highly of this pack he was ready to hand her off to. She wanted to meet them for herself. And maybe this Knox guy would know what to do about Lena.

She was going. She could be around Rafe without throwing herself at him. Probably. She was not going to be a bystander in her own life. Not to mention she was not about to miss out on the chance to meet a real freaking werewolf pack. Ridiculous she may be, but she'd basically prepared her entire life for this moment.

Rafe's soft grumble let her know he was back and fully clothed.

"You need to work tonight?" he asked, coming up beside her.

"I called in."

He nodded. "We can take Theo's truck part way but then we'll hike in. We'll need to stay the night."

Ruby ignored the way her skin prickled at the idea. Rafe had already been staying in her bedroom. A little campout wouldn't be any different.

"Okay, great. Let's go."

Rafe let out a long-suffering sigh as they walked to the front of the house to Theo's truck. The white Ford pickup sat waiting for them and with it the memory of Rafe suggesting they get each other out of their systems. The suggestion that had taken their tenuous friendship and thoroughly killed it.

She climbed up into the seat, willing the memory of Rafe's head between her thighs from her mind. It didn't want to go. He'd just been so damn enthusiastic. Like licking her was his entire purpose in life, like she was his new favorite flavor...

"Buckle up."

Rafe's gruff command broke through her reverie. Thank God.

"Do you even have a driver's license?" she asked as they pulled away, the thought suddenly occurring to her.

"Of course."

"Is it real?"

"Uh..." Rafe paused. "Real enough."

Ruby laughed, putting her feet up on the dashboard. "All this concern for my safety and here I am driving with an unlicensed driver."

"I know how to drive," he grumbled. "I can't exactly get official documents for that sort of shit."

Right, the whole being hundreds of years old thing. It probably also explained why he was so grumpy all the time and how he got so good at oral. *Damn it, Ruby. Head out of the gutter!*

"What were you and Theo fighting about earlier?" Ruby watched Rafe's hands tighten on the steering wheel. The muscle ticked in his jaw.

"We're always fighting."

"But what was it this time?" she pushed, remembering the tension radiating off Rafe when she walked into the yard. And the bewildered excitement coming from Theo. It was weird.

"Doesn't matter."

"Hmm."

"Hmm, what?" Rafe's eyes cut to hers and then back to the road.

"It seemed like it did matter, that's all."

Rafe grunted in response so Ruby didn't bother probing further. Instead she watched the towering pines whizz past as they drove out of town. The sky was summertime blue with cotton ball clouds. The type of day that was perfect for a backyard cookout, the type with watermelon and lots of grilled meats made by a dad in an apron. Or so she assumed. Aunt Millie wasn't much for cooking out or cooking anything really. But she did make a mean cucumber sandwich, perfect for a picnic in the sunroom.

Ruby sighed. Sometimes the memories of what she did have and what she didn't conspired to make her sad in two completely different ways. She missed the childhood she didn't get to have, the one with her parents. The one where she wasn't a freak. The one with her family intact. But she loved living with her aunt. She'd given her and Lena the best childhood she could in her own quirky way. And now that she was gone Ruby missed her too.

More memories flooded in, memories of odd things her aunt would say. She spoke about history as though she'd lived through it, as though she'd been there. And there was the box of old photos Ruby and Lena had discovered the summer Ruby turned thirteen. Ancient pictures of a woman who looked so much like their aunt, but if the dates on the back were correct it would make her nearly one hundred and fifty. When asked, she'd waved an old weathered hand at them. "Ancestors," she'd said. Aunt Millie seemed to know so much, too much. Ruby was young; she thought her aunt was full of old person wisdom, but now she wondered—

"What are you thinking about?"

Ruby turned in her seat to stare at Rafe. He'd never initiated a conversation with her before. She'd assumed her chatter and constant questions were annoying.

"You want to know what I'm thinking about?" she asked.

He shrugged. "You got all quiet. And you keep sighing." He shrugged again and Ruby bit her lip to keep from smiling. "Makes a guy wonder."

"I was thinking about how I never got to have a proper cookout with my dad." Her theories about Aunt Millie still seemed too absurd to admit, even to a werewolf. Maybe she was misremembering. She'd been so young.

"Oh."

"Yeah. But then I was also thinking about my aunt's funny little tea sandwiches she used to make and how we used to dress up to eat them. Like a fancy tea party."

Rafe huffed a laugh. "I bet you were cute."

"I was super cute. The cutest." She smiled. "I used to set two extra spots for my parents. Lena hated it. She didn't want to hear about ghosts. Or any of my other ridiculous ideas."

"Ruby, I—"

"It's fine." She waved him away.

"It's not fine. I shouldn't have said that to you. I was being an asshole."

"True."

He huffed. "It's a chronic problem."

Ruby stifled a laugh. "Yeah, Theo mentioned." She shifted in her seat, not sure if she should bring up the subject of Rafe's former love, but also really, really wanting to. "He explained why you might be so … worried about me."

Rafe let out a long sigh, his hands clenching and unclenching around the steering wheel.

"Do you want to tell me about her?" she asked. "It might

help."

He shook his head a little, strands of hair tumbling loose from their tie. In the quiet, Ruby thought he might not tell her anything. And she would just have to respect that. Not everyone was as keen on talking about their dead loved ones as she was.

"It was my fault she died," he said finally. "I don't want to repeat that mistake."

God, the guilt this man had lived with for so long. Ruby swallowed the tears that had suddenly risen in her throat.

"What was she like?" she asked, steering the conversation from the woman's death back to her life.

"She was sweet," Rafe said, his voice hoarse with emotion. "She worked at the general store in town to support her and her father after her brothers enlisted in the war."

"The war?"

"First World War."

Ruby blew out a breath. "Shit, you are old."

Rafe barked an unexpected laugh. "Yeah, I know." He shook his head, but kept talking. Ruby let his low voice wash over her, the story of his lost love comforting even though she knew the ending. "She was in there working every time I'd make the trip into town for supplies. We didn't need much back then, mostly lived off the land, but I started stopping in more often. Making more excuses to see her.

"She smelled like candy, like burnt sugar and sunshine. Her hair was dark like yours, but she had light eyes and she was always smiling. Seeing her ... it was like for the first time I saw something outside of my own world. Something that wasn't violent or cruel." He paused, pushing his hair out of his face. Ruby didn't dare move or speak, afraid he would stop talking and she would lose this glimpse of his life, of his heart.

"She looked at me like…" He swallowed hard. "She looked at me like I was something good. No one had ever looked at me like that before."

He cleared his throat and Ruby swiped the tears from her eyes. "It didn't matter, though. In the end. She stopped looking at me like that once she found out what I was. What I am."

"Rafe, I'm sorry." Ruby pried one of his hands from the steering wheel and held it in her own. She pressed kisses to the back and to the palm until Rafe's body relaxed.

"I should have left her alone after that." His voice was rough and quiet. Endless trees flew past the windows and the road curved in front of them. "But I was a selfish bastard. I led my father right to her. I should have never—"

"Don't." Ruby squeezed his hand and he tore his eyes from the road to glance at her. "What your father did is on his soul, not yours."

His jaw clenched as he stared at the road ahead of them. "I've been stalking you for weeks, Ruby. I could have led that wolf right to your door."

She shook her head even though he wasn't looking at her. "No. You saved me from that wolf. I am nothing but glad you were there."

"I can't stay away from you." His voice broke on the last word and Ruby brought his hand to her lips again.

"I don't want you to. I want you with me."

Rafe blew out a long shuddering breath.

"I thought I'd been pretty obvious about that," she added with a smile.

"You've been stubborn, that's for sure."

Ruby laughed. "You should probably just give in."

He brought her hand to his lips this time, his breath warm across her knuckles when he spoke. "I might have to."

Chapter Twenty-Eight

"What did you do?" Rafe roared, his voice echoing off the trees, the pain of Scarlet's death still tearing through him. "Where is Devon?" he demanded of the pack members who stood around staring.

"Where the fuck is my father?" he asked again, stalking through the camp. He was met with a heavy, uncomfortable silence.

Knox found him first.

"What is it?" his brother asked, putting a firm hand on Rafe's chest. He stopped in his tracks, his chest heaving with angry breaths. Knox looked genuinely confused, a small comfort. His brothers weren't in on it then.

"Scarlet." The name burned his throat, but Rafe kept going. "He killed her. The bastard killed her."

"Christ." Knox blew out a harsh breath. "Why the hell would he do that?"

"To keep me in line. He did it to punish me." Rafe's voice shook with rage. "It's my fault." He shrugged off Knox's hand and continued his search, his brother trailing him.

"What are you going to do?"

"I'm going to kill him."

Knox grabbed his arm and pulled him back, hissing in his ear. "You can't say shit like that, Rafe." Knox glanced around. They both knew his father's top men were never far. "Just calm down. Who was this woman anyway?"

Rafe spun to face his older brother. "It doesn't matter. She was innocent, Knox. She was so fucking innocent and he slaughtered her."

They were outside Devon's tent now and Rafe didn't wait. The rage boiling under skin wouldn't allow him to think, to pause, to consider his actions. Those were things humans did and Rafe's last bit of humanity had just died in a sunny field. He tore open the flap of the tent followed closely by Knox. Their father sat sprawled in a camp chair, cigarette dangling from his fingers. He'd been waiting for them, of course.

"You," Rafe spit, lunging forward, but Knox had him by the arm and tugged him back.

His father chuckled. "I warned you," he growled. "I told you to stay away from town. To stop sniffing around humans." He took a long drag of his cigarette and then stubbed it out under the toe of his boot. "I'll give it to you though, she was a pretty little thing."

Rafe roared and lunged for him again, this time flinging Knox off his arm and knocking his father to the ground. He got in two punches before his brothers hauled him off again. He didn't know when Theo had shown up, but now all three of the Alpha's sons stood panting in front of him.

Devon sat in a heap on the dirt floor, surrounded by his usual cloud of smoke, his lip bloodied.

"My sons," he said with a sneer. "All think you're so much better than me."

"Father—" Knox started, but Devon cut him off.

"Someday, I'll kick the bucket and one of you assholes will take my place." He stood and dusted the dirt from his pants. "But until then, I am still your Alpha and you will obey me or you will pay the price."

Rafe spit at his feet. "Fuck. You." Theo and Knox each tightened their grip on his arms and he'd never hated them more. Never hated them more than when they held him back from giving their father what he truly deserved.

"Let him go," Devon growled.

"What?" Theo asked. "Devon, really…"

"I said, let him go. And get the hell out. I want to talk to Rafe alone."

"Shit," Knox whispered under his breath, but they both let go. Theo gave him one last glance before they left him alone with the Alpha.

Rafe's body coiled tight, ready to spring, but Devon assessed him coolly. "It should be you," he said, stepping closer, crowding Rafe against the side of the canvas tent.

Rafe gave a low growl of warning.

Devon chuckled. "You are the biggest and strongest of my sons, Rafe. And look at how the beast sits so close to the surface. I want it to be you."

"I don't want it."

His father grunted. "I know. I also know you've been planning to leave."

Rafe didn't bother to try and figure out how his father knew that. He knew everything.

Devon leaned forward until Rafe could feel his hot breath on his face. "But know this, son: that little human was just the beginning."

Rafe flinched and his father laughed.

"You've got friends here, yeah? Those brothers of yours too. Don't think I would hesitate to make their lives a living hell if you leave. Nell, too."

"Jesus Christ, Devon." Rafe's stomach rolled in disgust. "You'd use your own pack, your own goddamn family against me?"

"It's what's best for them in the end. Having a strong Alpha. It's what's best."

Rafe shook his head and nearly laughed at his father's logic. He was willing to torment some members of his pack just to get the strongest leader for them in the end? What a sick son of a bitch. But what choice did that leave Rafe with? Leave and try to make it on his own? At what cost to the rest of his family? Or stay and live with whatever little tests Devon cooked up until the day the old bastard died?

"I want the fights to stop. The sparring."

"What?" Devon's bushy brows rose in surprise. "You're trying to make a deal with me?"

Rafe shrugged, feigning a casual calm he didn't feel. He couldn't feel calm with Scarlet's blood still fresh on his hands and his father's latest threats ringing in his ears.

"You want me to stay? Then no more of these bullshit fights. I'm tired of it."

Devon stepped back, his mouth twisted into a frown as he thought Rafe's offer over. Rafe couldn't bring Scarlet back and the thought tore through him with fresh agony, but maybe he could make life slightly more bearable for him and his brothers.

His father turned back to face him, familiar silver eyes flashing. "Deal."

Devon kept his promise for a while, but as the old Alpha weakened he ramped up the competition for his place all over again. And Rafe had been too exhausted to stop him until the final fight, the one he'd refused to win.

Chapter Twenty-Nine

They drove the rest of the day in comfortable silence, broken only by Ruby's casual questions about his life. It was hard at first, talking about the past, like the words were stuck somewhere inside him. But Ruby just kept digging. She was like those archeologists that painstakingly brush the dust off dinosaur bones. Patiently working until the whole thing is revealed.

He told her about never knowing his mother and growing up with Theo's instead. About his father's expectations for him, about almost leaving the pack even before Scarlet died. None of it fixed anything, but he felt better, lighter just telling her.

He still didn't know what to do about Ruby possibly being his Mate and he couldn't bring himself to confess that piece of the puzzle, but God, it felt good to have her listen and still want to be near him. Maybe she'd been telling the truth the whole time. Maybe she wasn't scared of him. He let a tiny sliver of hope work its way into his heart.

By the time Rafe pulled off the road into the diner parking lot, the dipping sun painted the tree tops golden.

"How about dinner?" he asked, turning to an absurdly delighted Ruby.

"You're taking me out to dinner? Is this the part where you start to woo me?" She grinned and he bit back his own smile.

"No, I'm just hungry."

"Me too! But I figured you'd be hunting us some poor little creature and we'd roast it over a campfire or something."

"Would you rather that?"

Ruby wrinkled her nose and Rafe lost the battle with his smile. "I'll take my chances with the diner."

Rafe nodded and got out of the truck and around to Ruby's side fast enough to help her down. And she actually let him. *Damn. Opening up to a girl really works.*

"So, you know this place?"

Rafe took in the diner from Ruby's perspective. The current building was at least sixty years old, silver with several letters missing from the sign. Myrna's Diner, now read *My 's in r*, but the sign wasn't necessary anyway. Everyone around here knew the place and anyone that wasn't local didn't need to know. Tall grass grew around the front, stopped only by the gravel parking lot. There were three other cars in the lot, two pickups and a rusted old Civic with a hula dancer on the dash. A big crowd for Myrna's. But the hamburgers and milkshakes were the best. Or at least they always had been.

"Trust me," he said, taking her hand and pulling her toward the door.

"Be right with you, sweetheart." The old woman behind the counter didn't bother to look up when the bell over the door rang their arrival. Ruby looked up at him and smiled like she was having the best day. A ridiculous swoop of pride raced through him.

"Take your time," he said.

The woman spun at the sound of his voice, along with the heads of a few regulars sitting at the counter.

"Rafe, by God, is that you!"

"It's me, Gert."

She scurried around the counter and gave him a squeeze around the middle before smacking him hard on the arm. "Where on earth have you been?" She narrowed her eyes and smacked him again. "Making an old woman worry about you like that. We heard you left—" her eyes cut to Ruby "—uh ... town."

"It's okay, Gert."

Gertie looked Ruby over again, apparently deemed her not a threat, and turned back to Rafe. "We heard you left the pack a few years back. I knew you set up shop down south a ways, but it would have been nice to hear from you."

Tears welled in the old woman's eyes and Rafe cleared his throat. "I'm sorry. I should have checked in with you. I haven't ... I haven't been back in a while."

Gert glanced at Ruby like she already knew this little human was the reason Rafe was back in these parts.

"This is Ruby."

Ruby stuck out her hand. "So nice to meet you."

Gertie hesitated a breath and then scooped Ruby into a bone-crushing hug. "Aren't you just the cutest little thing. Where on earth did Rafe find you?"

"He stalked me through the woods," Ruby said with a smile and Gertie threw back her head with a laugh like a gunshot.

"I like this one, Rafe. She's a spitfire."

Rafe only nodded, suddenly getting whiplash from his past and present crossing paths.

"Rafe's been coming here since he was knee high to a

grasshopper," Gertie went on. "Back then my mama ran the place. Myrna that is. But she passed on a while back."

Ruby nodded and Rafe could see her mind racing, trying to piece together what Myrna was and how long she'd been slinging hamburgers by the roadside.

"Anyway, this one was as cute as a button when he was a pup. Didn't take long for him to grow into this..." Gertie gestured up and down his body and then made a face as though she didn't know what to make of him.

"There is a lot of him," Ruby said, grinning. "But I think it's part of his charm."

Gert cackled again. "Come with me, darling. I'll give you my best table." Gertie took Ruby's hand and led her to the last booth against the windows. It was exactly the same as all her other tables but Rafe followed along with a smile.

"I'm glad you're back, dear," she said with another fond squeeze of his arm before scooting off to tend to her other customers.

Ruby's eyes were sparkling with delight when he sat down across from her.

"Knee high to a grasshopper? When you were a pup?" she practically squealed. "This place is amazing. Gertie is amazing. Picturing you as a pup. Amazing!" She grinned and slouched back in her seat. "Thanks for bringing me here."

Rafe shrugged, feeling more exposed than he had all day. It was one thing to tell Ruby stories about his life while staring out the windshield, but to actually show her parts of it? And while she looked at him like that? This might have been a mistake.

But it was too late now because Gertie was already back, laying sticky menus on the table in front of them. And Ruby was already telling her she definitely wanted Myrna's world-famous vanilla shake with a hamburger and fries and Rafe was already muttering he would have the same and that was that.

Ruby leaned across the table when she'd gone to put in their order. "So, are you going to tell me?" she whispered.

"Forest nymph."

"Like Phoebe?"

Rafe nodded. "Phoebe's great-aunt or something like that." Rafe could not for the life of him keep track of the elaborate nymph family trees around these parts. There were hundreds of them and somehow they were all related.

Ruby shook her head in wonder. "Man, if I had known all this when I was growing up..." She trailed off and now Rafe leaned in, wanting her to finish. Needing her to.

"What would you have done?"

She shrugged but her smile had faded. "Don't know. Just felt less alone, I guess." He hated that she ever felt alone. That she ever felt sad or mistreated. He wanted to burn the world down to make sure it never happened again. Which was insane considering that since meeting her he'd made her feel like that more than once.

"Murder face," she said pointing at him.

"Huh?"

"You're doing the murder-y face thing again."

Rafe relaxed his brow.

"That's a bit better." Ruby smiled and tucked a strand of hair behind her ear. She'd left it down today and it hung like a dark curtain over her back. Her lips were stained red as usual and the black liner she'd used on her lids this morning somehow made her eyes look wider when she looked at him.

"So is this some kind of werewolf hang-out?" she asked, the teasing tone back in her voice. She'd done that all day, switched from serious to playful, never letting him sink too deep into a dark place.

"Something like that. We can't live entirely on bunny rabbits."

"Oh, of course not." Her smile grew.

Gertie came back with a tray full of food. "Here you are, loves. Enjoy." She scurried away but Rafe could tell by the way she studied him that he wasn't getting out of here without telling her more about why he was back.

"This all looks delicious!" Ruby took a slurp of her milkshake, her cheeks caving in as she sucked through the straw. The shakes were so thick he usually ate them with a spoon. "Mmm…" she groaned with a satisfied smack of her lips. "It *is* delicious."

Rafe's lips tipped into a smile. "I told you to trust me."

"I do trust you." The response was so quick it surprised him, but just as quickly the words burrowed down deep. Ruby trusted him. And he couldn't fuck that up.

"So what's the plan?" she asked, biting into her burger with a dedication he truly admired in a woman.

"Uh … well, I figure we'll camp around here tonight and then hike in tomorrow. It's only five miles or so."

Ruby's eyes widened. "A five-mile hike? You clearly think I'm in better shape than I am, Rafe."

He couldn't help his grin. "Your shape is perfect, Ruby."

Color crept up her neck into her cheeks. He shouldn't take such pleasure in that. Especially not when he had no intention of fucking her. But maybe another taste wouldn't hurt…

"And what happens when we get there?" Ruby's question tore him away from thoughts of her delicious pussy.

"Uh … not sure." He'd been so determined to leave, to find

another way to protect Ruby, a way that didn't directly involve him, that he hadn't really thought this plan through.

"Well..." Ruby leaned forward, her elbows on the table. "I was thinking we could see if your brother has any thoughts about Lena. Or about what her visions might mean."

"I don't know if that's a good idea."

"Why not?"

"I don't know if we can trust him."

"But you were going to leave my protection up to him." Ruby cocked an eyebrow like she knew it was all bullshit. And of course it was.

"So why are we going? I came so we could get help for Lena," she pushed. Rafe swallowed a growl. The idea of telling his brother about any of this was turning his meal into rocks in his gut. He must have been insane to think Knox could help them.

"I need to find out if he knows who the hell is following you. To see if he has any idea why some rogue wolves are attacking you outside your home."

"It only happened once."

"They came back, Ruby. More than one of them. It's only a matter of time before they attack again. And as much as I hate to admit it, my brother has pull around here. He's the Alpha. If something is going on, he'll know about it." He would decide how much to tell Knox later. Maybe they could get the information they needed without ever letting his Alpha brother know about Lena's powers.

Ruby watched him as she ate, taking it all in.

"He tried to kill you."

"Yes."

"Will he do it again?" she asked, fear threading in between

her words. And the shortsightedness of his actions slammed into him. He'd brought her here. He'd led her directly into danger. Again. Just so he could keep her near. Just because she asked.

This was why his father rejected the fated Mates story. It made wolves stupid and impulsive. He felt like a young wolf all over again, nothing but hormones and bad ideas.

He couldn't get the food past the lump in his throat. He swallowed hard, once, twice, until he could finally breathe. "I don't think so." Rafe tried to sound confident in his answer, but now that they were this close, he realized he had no idea how his brother would react to seeing him. Or any other pack members for that matter.

Maybe it was because they'd spent all day reminiscing but Rafe couldn't help but think of the times before his last few years with the pack. The times when his brothers were on his side. The times when they used to come here for burgers after beating the shit out of each other for fun. There weren't a lot of memories like that, but they were there. Mixed in between the demands of their father.

He didn't think Knox would hurt them. Not now that Devon was gone.

Ruby nodded like it was settled. "Okay. We'll suss him out first, but let's try to find something we can use to help Lena."

"We will."

"Thanks."

"Stop thanking me."

Her mouth turned down into a small frown. "I won't stop. You're helping me and my sister and I'm allowed to thank you for that."

He huffed and she stuck out her tongue at him. Gertie was back before he could argue further.

"So, what brings you back?" Gertie asked innocently as she cleared the table.

"I need to talk to my brother."

"Oh?" Gertie's silver eyebrows rose to her hairline.

"What's been going on over there, Gert? Have you caught wind of anything strange?"

The old woman's mouth twisted into a wry smile. "Anything stranger than a pack of werewolves? Not really."

Gertie made her business by not spilling everyone's secrets, a rarity amongst nymphs, who trafficked in gossip. And Rafe hadn't seen her in years. Her loyalty didn't lie with him anymore. He glanced at Ruby, not wanting to share stories that weren't his, but she nodded her permission.

"Ruby was attacked by a wolf a few days back."

Gert's eyes widened, her gaze flicking from Ruby to Rafe. "You think it was your brother's pack?"

"You tell me, Gert."

She brought a hand to her chest, forgetting about the tray of dirty dishes she'd rested on the table. "You boys had your differences, but Knox has done a lot for the pack since you've been gone. Things have changed."

Rafe grumbled. "So I've heard."

Gertie sighed. "That old man did a lot of damage to you kids, but he's gone now. You have to let the past go, Rafe."

"It's hard to forget someone's teeth at your throat."

"Don't forget yours were at his too," Gertie countered. "But neither of you went through with it."

"He would have," Rafe growled. He hadn't stuck around to find out, but he was sure that if he'd stayed in his wolf form, Knox would have killed him that day and then finished off Theo. Regardless of how the brothers felt about each other, Knox wanted it more than they did. The oldest son. He wanted

225

to be the next Alpha. He always had. Their father should have let him have it, but instead he made it a sick competition. Something like that was not easily forgotten.

Gertie laid her small hand over his and gave his fingers a squeeze. "I don't think your pack had anything to do with the attack, but I hope you find some answers."

"Thanks, Gert."

She turned her attention back to Ruby. "How was that milkshake, Red?"

Ruby grinned at the nickname. "The best I've ever had, thanks."

Gertie smiled in return. "Glad to hear it. Now you be careful out there and stay close to your big wolf-man here."

"I intend to," Ruby said, shooting him a dazzling smile.

Gertie laughed and lifted the tray with a small grunt. "Good girl."

"Let me get it for you, Gert." Rafe tried to stand but the woman was already turning away from him.

"And let you steal my tips? No way."

Ruby laughed as their diminutive waitress walked away. "Poor Rafe," she cooed. "Always trying to save us weak, defenseless women and always getting shot down."

"That's not what I'm doing…"

She met his eye, serious again. "I know," she said. "You're only being kind."

Kind? Is that how she saw him? A new warmth settled through him. A new glimpse at himself.

Ruby rustled around in her purse. "We can split the check."

"No. I got it." He waited for her to get pissed at him again or to tease him for being an outdated misogynist, but he'd seen the stack of medical bills on her desk. He knew how hard Ruby worked.

Instead, she just breathed out a dramatic sigh of relief. "Oh, phew. I'm broke." She laughed and slid from the booth. "Thanks for dinner, buddy." She clapped him on the shoulder as she said it, the word and the gesture combining in an awful gesture of friendship. *Buddy? What the hell just happened?*

His idiotic behavior from the night before came rolling back to him. He made her come and then he'd rejected her. He'd run away. No wonder she was acting like they were just friends now. What the hell did he expect?

It was what he'd wanted. For Ruby to stay away from him, for her to never find out she was his Mate, for her to be safe. But God, that word, that nickname: *buddy*. It was something you called an acquaintance, a neighbor whose name you always forgot. Something essential curled up and died inside of him at the thought of being Ruby's buddy.

Gert stopped him on his way out the door. "She's different, that one," she said, one hand on Rafe's arm. "Magic in the blood?"

Rafe swallowed hard, thinking about Lena. If Lena was a seer, then there was non-human blood in the family, right? Magic blood. Ruby couldn't be entirely human, could she? Questions he'd been trying not to ask flooded his brain. Seers lived nearly as long as werewolves. If Ruby was even part seer...

"She's human," he assured Gertie, not wanting to let himself hope. Not with everything else going on. But he tucked it away for later. For when he finally told Ruby what she was to him. When they finally had a chance to figure out where to go from here.

Gertie hummed a note of suspicion, but didn't argue. "Don't stay away so long next time."

"I won't," he promised and followed Ruby out of the diner.

His gaze raked over her as she waited for him by the truck. Ruby's shorts were no less erotic than her usual skirts, her lush thighs and ass filling them completely. She looked positively edible. *Friends sometimes go down on each other, right? Shit.* He was an idiot and he had no idea what to do next, although his cock had some very strong opinions on the matter. Any half-hearted plans he made last night to keep away from her were rapidly slipping through his grasp.

"You coming?" Ruby glanced back at him with a smile. He hadn't noticed he'd stopped walking and just stood staring at her from the door.

"Uh … yeah. I'm coming." He just had no idea what he was going to do when he got there.

Chapter Thirty

"This is so cozy," Ruby said as Rafe climbed into the bed of the truck.

His lips tipped into a sheepish smile. "I hope it will be comfortable enough. I hadn't really planned on camping."

"Right." A stab of guilt hit Ruby in the gut. She'd probably made this whole endeavor much more complicated than it needed to be. "How long would it have taken you without me?"

Rafe shrugged. "Depends on how fast I felt like running." He gave her a slow grin. "But I was feeling keyed up, so pretty fast."

Nerves fluttered low in Ruby's belly. Being Rafe's friend, not some weird pervert who keeps throwing herself at him, was going to be a lot harder if he kept looking at her like that.

After dinner they'd driven a few more miles north and then pulled off the road and parked beneath the towering pines. He'd filled the bed of the truck with sleeping bags and worn comforters, making a nest for Ruby to snuggle down into.

The sky was clear and filled with bright stars. Ruby lay on her back and breathed in the damp forest air, avoiding Rafe's gaze. The night was mercifully cool after another hot day and she was thankful for the blankets. With her head propped on a rolled-up sleeping bag, Ruby marveled at the inky blackness above her. It was a rare, clear night with the storm clouds finally gone and the stars were bright against the darkness.

Crickets and cicadas buzzed around them, the tree frogs adding their peeps and chirps. The forest felt full and alive and so did Ruby. Sure, they were trying to track down dangerous wolves, but Ruby was hard pressed to think of a better day than this one.

She smiled up at the night sky, remembering the horrified look on Rafe's face when she'd called him "buddy" at the diner. Her wolf-man was not so keen on being her "buddy". Good. She hated the idea too. But she also hated every guy that wouldn't take no for an answer. She wouldn't be one of those guys.

She burrowed down deeper into her nest. The truck shifted with Rafe's weight as he lay down beside her.

"This okay?" he asked even though their arms weren't even touching.

Yep, perfectly okay except for the fact that she could feel the heat radiating off of him and smell his comforting sawdust scent and picture his beautiful body … but it was all perfectly okay. She could be a gentleman.

"Yes, very comfortable. Thanks."

He shifted and his shoulder brushed against hers. Solid. He was so damn solid.

"Rafe." Her voice was breathy, giving her away completely, but she charged forward. "I need to apologize for something."

She kept her gaze at the stars even as she felt Rafe turn to look at her. "Ruby, I told you before, you have nothing to apologize for."

"No. I do. I just … I think I misunderstood you before or maybe pressured you … I'm not sure…"

He shifted again, propping himself up on his forearm to look down at her. "What are you talking about?"

"I thought we both needed to get things out of our system, but maybe it was just me. And I'm really sorry if I made you feel pressured or weird or, I don't know … objectified? It happens to me all the time at work and I never meant to…"

"Ruby, stop," Rafe growled, his silver eyes flashing. "Goddamn it," he swore, sitting up. Ruby followed and sat facing him in the dark. He shook his head, his hair brushing across his shoulders.

"I'm the one who should be sorry, Ruby. God, I never meant to make you feel that way. I want you so fucking bad." He breathed out the words on one pained sigh. "I want you, but I thought it was better for you if I kept you away, safer."

Ruby pushed the hair from his face, pressing her forehead to his. "I want you too. You are not dangerous to me." She whispered the words and he drank them in.

"Walking away from you last night was the hardest thing I've ever done."

Ruby held him tighter, digging her fingers into his hair. "Then don't walk away tonight."

He hesitated a breath longer before bringing his lips to hers. The touch was so soft she could barely feel it. She whimpered and Rafe's mouth tipped into a smile. "So last night wasn't enough to get me out of your system?" he asked, his words skating across her skin.

She huffed a small laugh. "Not even close."

Rafe groaned and tugged her into his lap. She straddled him, the nest of blankets tangled around her legs. She rocked into his rigid cock and he finally claimed her lips with his own, biting and licking until she opened for him. He tasted like vanilla and summer and home.

He kept a hand behind her head, holding her close and another on her ass, holding her closer. She was pinned against him, his arms locking her in place. The feeling of being caught zinged through her. She liked it, being captured by this man. This man who could hurt her but never would.

She rocked again, wrapping her arms around Rafe's neck and he deepened the kiss, licking into her, tasting her. They kissed like that, slow and languorous like they had forever, while fireflies lit up around them like nearby stars.

When Rafe finally pulled away his lips were swollen and his eyes dark with desire. His hair was mussed from her fingers and his breathing was fast and shallow. He looked positively feral and it made Ruby want to run. Run so he could catch her.

"God, Ruby," he murmured, running a thumb over her sensitive lips. "You are so fucking sexy. I've lived so long without you … and I've never … I…" He swallowed hard, pain crossing his expression.

"It's okay," she whispered. "It's okay."

He sat up, looking away from her face. "We can't … I'm sorry … not yet." He breathed deep, waiting for her response. The nervous furrow of his brow nearly broke her.

"We'll do whatever you want," she said, running a hand over his chest.

"It's just, it's complicated."

Ruby nodded. "Complicated werewolf stuff?"

"Yeah," he said with a relieved smile. "Complicated werewolf stuff."

"Okay, we'll wait." Ruby tried to move off his lap, but Rafe held tight to her hips.

"No." His fingers dug into her flesh. "I want to eat you

again. Like last night."

Heat flared in Ruby's gut. "Oh."

Rafe kissed her again, his tongue flicking over hers, mimicking what he'd done between her thighs the night before. Ruby moaned, but pulled back.

"Just to be clear," she said, her voice low and needy, as she squirmed in his lap. "We can't have … uh … intercourse because of werewolf reasons but everything else is on the table?"

Rafe huffed a laugh. "Intercourse?"

"Fine," Ruby said, nibbling on his lower lip. "We can't fuck, but hands and mouths are fair game?"

Rafe's smile turned wolfish, his eyes lit up like the stars. "Yes, exactly."

She didn't have time to ask why or to care before Rafe had flipped her onto her back and made quick work of her shorts and underwear. If the man wanted to go down on her again, who was she to argue?

And God, did he want to. He licked her like he was starving, like she held life's secrets between her thighs, like he'd waited for her forever. She grinned up at the night sky. Damn, he was good at that. Ruby ran her fingers through Rafe's hair, needing something to hold on to before she floated off into the stars above them.

He looked at her, his silver eyes flashing in the dark, his hands on her thighs, holding her open to him and Ruby got the very unsettling feeling that maybe this wasn't just lust. That maybe this thing between them wouldn't be solved by orgasms —although orgasms never hurt. The way he looked at her with not only hunger in his eyes, but something else, something softer, something like…

Rafe tore his gaze away and stroked her clit with his tongue until Ruby's back bowed off the bed of blankets.

"You like that, brave girl?" His voice rumbled against her flesh and she whimpered. He repeated the move with his tongue, applying more pressure this time, licking her with broad, flat strokes.

He squeezed her ass with one hand and slid a finger into her with the other. Finger fucking must be allowed, she thought, nearly giggling before her breath was stolen by another finger joining the first.

Rafe groaned, his fingers working in long slow strokes and already she felt so full. "Is it okay?" he asked, his silver gaze watching her reaction, his other hand running over her thigh.

"Yes, very."

He smiled and she needed him closer. She tugged him up to her face, his fingers never stopping their tortuous movements. His lips were soft and warm and wet. She licked them clean and Rafe growled against her mouth, dipping inside with his tongue, salty and sweet at once. He propped himself on his elbow with Ruby tucked into his side. His thumb traced her clit as his fingers thrust faster, but he didn't take his lips from hers, kissing and thrusting and holding her until she came hard against him, her cries filling the still night air.

Ruby slumped down onto the blankets and Rafe stayed propped up next to her, his own breathing nearly as hard as hers.

"Shit, Ruby," he murmured, leaning down to nuzzle into her damp hair and kiss along her neck. "You are so beautiful." He brought his fingers to his mouth and licked them clean, making her hot all over again.

"You're very good at that," she sighed.

His lips tipped into a smile. "Glad you enjoyed yourself." He had begun to trail kisses down her neck and chest, so he whispered the words against her skin. "This should go." He tugged at her shirt until she laughed and pulled it off.

He kissed along the top of her bra, groaning to himself. "God, these tits. So fucking perfect."

"Yeah, they're pretty good as tits go."

Rafe peered up at her, his laugh skating over her flesh. "They're amazing." He reached around and undid the clasp, freeing her breasts to the night air. "Perfect," he crooned as he sucked on one nipple and then the other, his tongue worshiping her all over again.

"Rafe," she gasped, the sensation too strong, like torture.

"Mmm?" He didn't look up from his ministrations, just sucked and licked, the heat building between her legs again. She slipped her hand down her stomach to where she needed more, more friction, more everything.

Rafe groaned when he realized what she was doing, but didn't stop teasing and biting and sucking and Ruby thought maybe he was right, her tits were perfect because right now they were making her feel amazing. It didn't take long between Rafe's beautiful mouth and her own hand before Ruby came again, sharp and strong and sudden.

"Fuck," she breathed and this time Rafe collapsed next to her, pulling her in close. Ruby let herself snuggle into him for a minute before she realized what was wrong.

"Why are you still dressed?"

Rafe's laugh rumbled through her. God, she loved that laugh already. When did that happen? Sometime between Rafe holding her purse and making her come, apparently.

Ruby sat up and looked down at him in the dark. He was still smiling. He looked happy and young. No sign of his murder face. This Rafe looked sweet and kind, like his insides were finally reflected on the outside.

She pushed the hair out of her face. "I'm serious. Get naked, wolf-man. I want to see you."

His eyes sparked. "This was just for you, Ruby." He ran a finger down her arm and she shivered.

"You said hands and mouths were allowed." She held up her hands in front of her, turning them back and forth for him to admire. "And I have those things too."

Rafe's gaze darkened, imagining the possibilities.

"So, strip."

He sat up, his eyes only leaving hers long enough to pull the shirt over his head and reveal all the glorious muscle underneath. Ruby kneeled in front of him, her hands on his shoulders. "Isn't that better?" she said, leaning in to kiss him again.

His hands traced over her back, dipping over the curve of her ass and back again.

"This ass drives me crazy every time you wear those short skirts," he growled.

She laughed, kissing him again. "Is that what you thought about when you followed me through the woods, my ass?" she asked, breathless.

"Tried not to," he said and bit her bottom lip. "But it didn't work."

She moaned, the feel of his fingers barely touching her driving her wild.

"Is that what you wanted, brave girl? You wandered through the woods hoping the big bad wolf would find you?"

She couldn't help the whimper that escaped her, the wetness that coated her legs. His words were so close to what she'd fantasized about for months.

"Not the big bad wolf," she breathed. "You."

Rafe pressed his forehead to hers, his hands still tracing her curves, still barely touching her when she wanted him to grab and push and hold.

"And what did you want me to do when I found you?" he asked, his voice like distant thunder.

Ruby swallowed hard.

"Everything."

Rafe groaned and cursed under his breath, his hands finally gripping her tight and pulling her to him.

"Ruby, I... We..." He struggled for the words and maybe she should have let him find them, maybe she should have let him try to explain but she didn't want it to end, this night, this moment, this whatever this was between them. She wanted to hold on to it for as long as possible. She didn't want him to pull away from her again.

"This is perfect, Rafe. This night is perfect." She pulled back so he could see she was serious. This sex was the best she'd ever had and whatever was holding him back from the rest was something they could work out later.

The pain was back on his face, the furrow back between his brows. She wanted it gone. Just for tonight, she wanted him happy. She tugged at his waistband.

"I want to make you feel good," she whispered.

A tremble went through him at her words. "Ruby—"

"I want to."

He held her gaze, his eyes black with desire. The shift in his expression was so subtle she would have missed it if she hadn't been staring at him. His restraint was snapping. She could see it with every twitch of his muscles, with every clench of his jaw. He was done denying himself, at least for tonight.

"And how are you going to make me feel good, brave girl?" he rasped, barely above a whisper and Ruby grinned.

"Well, first I'm going to suck your cock."

Chapter Thirty-One

He was in so far over his head he couldn't even see the surface anymore. All he could see was Ruby and her bright eyes and sinfully red lips. Lips that would soon be wrapped around his cock if he didn't stop her, if he didn't tell her no.

She held his gaze, searching and uncertain. And that look, the fact that she didn't know how bad he wanted her, it was what broke him. He wanted her more than he wanted his next sunrise, more than his next race through the woods, more than any part of his own worthless life. Wanting Ruby made existing possible. For centuries he'd only been living a half life and he was only now realizing it.

Ruby still toyed with the button of his jeans, her fingers slipping beneath the fabric, sending heat sizzling up his spine.

"Rafe?" she asked, still questioning, still uncertain, and it was his fault. His fault that she didn't know the truth. His fault for wanting her and pushing her away at the same time in some misplaced act of protection.

"Yes," he growled. "Wrap those ruby red lips around my dick like I've been dreaming about."

A slow smile bloomed on Ruby's face. "You have?"

He huffed. "Fuck, yes." He leaned against the side of the truck bed, lifted his hips and pulled the jeans and boxer briefs off and tossed them to the side. "Come here." His voice was barely human anymore, enough to scare away most people, but Ruby crawled in closer until she was kneeling between his thighs.

"I've wanted those lips on me since the first day I saw you. That damn red paint, Ruby, it's like a fucking beacon." He ran his hands over her hips and up to her tits, palming one and then the other. He rolled the nipple between his fingers and gave it a squeeze. Ruby whimpered and pressed her thighs together.

"What else did you want?" she asked, her voice a breathy whisper.

He couldn't help his smile, even as he dug himself deeper into whatever this was, even as he remembered that this woman was his Mate and he still didn't know what to do about that.

"I wanted everything, too. I wanted all of you. God, I still do."

She leaned in to kiss him at the same time as she gripped his cock in her fist. He groaned into her mouth and he felt her smile against him. And that smile. It was a victory. It was evidence that he'd done one fucking thing right in his life.

And then her hands were on his chest, his thighs, her fingers digging into her flesh as she took him into her mouth one slow inch at a time. He pushed her hair from her face and wrapped it around his fist, not wanting to miss a second of the obscene view. Those lips framed his cock perfectly. He tugged her hair just a little and she purred, the vibration nearly killing him. Of course she would like it a little rough, his brave girl who ventured into dark woods, who dreamt of dangerous strangers.

He tugged again, moving her how he wanted her, thrusting a little deeper with each stroke of her mouth. She squeezed her thighs together and pressed her sharp little finger nails into his legs, and let him fuck her mouth.

She was so good, so perfect, her mouth so fucking warm and tight and wet. It wouldn't take long. Already the orgasm was building, pleasure radiating out to his toes.

He let her go, let her come up for air, her hair cascading over her shoulder. She held the base of his cock in one hand and licked around the head, her lipstick smudged on her swollen lips.

"God, that's so good," he murmured, feeling all his senses, all his thoughts scatter to the night and join the constellations. He should be keeping her at bay but all he could do was be so damn grateful that the universe had sent him the perfect Mate.

"I want you to come in my mouth," she said between tortuous swirls of her tongue.

"Yes," he growled, unable to say anything else. Yes. Yes to this. Yes to anything this woman wanted. Yes to everything.

His hands were in her hair again and her mouth was moving, taking him in, all of him. Up and down until it was too much, the heat, the pleasure, the frisson of tension up his spine. He came hard with ragged breaths and Ruby's lips around him and only the night sky to witness the moment he came apart completely and was pieced back together by the look in Ruby's eyes when she sat up and smiled at him.

Ruby slept like some kind of deranged starfish. She currently had half her body draped over Rafe's torso and the other half spread across seventy-five percent of the truck bed. Or that was Rafe's best guess anyway. He was crammed into the remaining space and it couldn't be more than a quarter of the truck. She'd also stolen all the blankets even though her limbs stuck out of them at precarious angles. And she snored.

Rafe was tired, cold, and achy and yet couldn't seem to wipe the idiotic grin off his face.

Someday, he was sure he would complain about her nocturnal acrobatics and nighttime cover hogging…

Wait. Someday? One amazing night and what? He thought Ruby would be dying to tie herself to him forever? He scrubbed his free hand—the other one was trapped somewhere beneath Ruby—down his face, trying in vain to think straight.

He needed to tell Ruby about the Mate bond. He nearly had last night; he should have. But the more he thought about it, the more he realized he didn't know nearly enough. What it meant, or how to navigate it, especially for a human.

Ruby stirred and her cinnamon scent wrapped around him. Instead of choking him, now it warmed him, pulling him closer. He knew she was his Mate like he knew when he needed to hunt. Instinctually and without a doubt. Everything he'd felt about her made sense now. Why he couldn't leave her alone, why he felt compelled to protect her. Why he found her so damn sexy. She was his and he was hers.

But as far as what happened next, he was embarrassingly underprepared. Damn his father and his "mating for strength" ideology. Rafe didn't know a single Mate-bonded pair. His pack didn't operate that way. His father scoffed at any mention of it.

There had been wolves through the years that had left the pack, gone off on their own. And now Rafe wondered how many had left to be with their true Mate. Now that he'd met Ruby, he couldn't imagine being forced to mate with someone else if you knew who your true Mate was. It would be torture.

He didn't even know if sex was the only way to secure the bond. He thought he was being safe by not fucking her, but every moment with her felt like a claiming. Every story he shared with her, every smile she gave him, every touch, every bit of trust she put in him. She had claimed his heart the first time she spoke his name, the first time she sought him out in the dark.

He had to tell Ruby. He had to tell her right now. He attempted to free his arm and Ruby groaned, face down in her pillow.

"Too early," she mumbled. "Go away."

"Ruby." He rolled onto his side and pulled her closer using his trapped arm to reel her in. "Wake up." He kissed along her nose and she scrunched it up.

"No," she grumbled. "Too early." She didn't open her eyes as she pushed the hair from her face.

"Are you always like this in the morning?" he asked, unable to stop his foolish heart from imagining more mornings like this with Ruby grumpy and him slowly waking her. He could think of so many interesting ways to wake her.

"I work nights. I'm practically nocturnal," she muttered, cracking open one eye. "You know I don't wake up before noon. And it's too bright out here." She squeezed the eye shut again.

"We need to get an early start if we're going to make it there and back today."

Ruby groaned again, but Rafe ran a hand over her still naked hip and around to grab her ass, turning Ruby's groan into a squeal. He pulled her closer, so warm and pliant in the morning. He'd already forgotten what he needed to tell her.

He let himself forget. Why waste this moment by freaking her out?

He kissed down her neck, lingering over her racing pulse. She squirmed against him. "What happened to getting an early start?" she laughed as he continued his journey to her breasts, kissing and licking each one.

"I mean, we could spare a few minutes," he said grinning up at her. She smiled back, her eyes bright like the sun.

"No way, wolf-man. We have your asshole brother to question." She snatched up the blankets and scootched to a seat, leaving Rafe lying naked by himself. He didn't care. Her stare kept him warm.

He pushed himself up and dug around for his jeans from last night. He tugged them on, letting Ruby watch him with hungry eyes. Maybe it was finally time for him to have what he wanted. Maybe fate would be on his side this time. Thinking it felt like a jinx. He nearly leaned over the side of the truck to knock on a tree trunk.

What if telling Ruby about the Mate bond ruined everything? Theo was right, he'd go full howling-at-the-moon mad. Just because Ruby had been understanding about everything he'd told her so far did not mean she'd be cool with this sudden and intense escalation of their relationship.

He needed to figure out why wolves were stalking Ruby and her sister. Once Ruby was safe, then he could worry about what fate had in store for him. There was no use in sharing his suspicions about their Mate bond yet. Not if Ruby was still in danger. Not if her sister was still having violent visions about wolves.

First he needed to get to the bottom of the attack. Then he would deal with the rest. One life-altering crisis at a time.

"What's for breakfast?" Ruby asked, still watching him from her seat.

He hopped down from the bed, happy for the distraction, and walked to the front of the truck. He grabbed the bag he'd put in the back seat last night.

"Gert sent us home with pie."

"Pie!" Ruby's face lit up as she grabbed the bag. She was still wrapped in blankets, her bare arms a teasing reminder of all the skin beneath her covers. "Apple and blueberry! Gert is officially my new favorite person," she said, pulling the containers from the bag along with plastic forks and napkins. She laid it all in front of her like a picnic.

Rafe leaned against the side of the truck, his forearms resting on the side of the bed. "Favorite person, huh? After last night, I'm a little insulted."

Ruby smiled. "Oh don't be a sore loser, Rafe. You're a close second."

He laughed, loud and unexpected. It felt good. It felt like cracking open. Ruby giggled too and handed him a fork.

"Pass the blueberry."

Ruby leaned forward to pass him the container and he pressed a kiss to her apple-flavored lips. Her eyebrows rose in surprise. "You're awfully affectionate this morning, Rafe."

"Yes." He watched her, wanting her reaction, needing to know if she still wanted him or if she'd satisfied her curiosity. "I'll stop, if you want me to."

"No." Ruby's answer was quick and Rafe bit down on a smile. "Don't stop. I like it." She took a bit of pie, licking the crumbs off her lips. Her tongue traced slowly around those full lips and Rafe's human brain shut off. Fuck it. He should tell her. Tell her and then claim her. He should fuck her until she understood that she was made for him and he was made for her. Until nothing else mattered.

"Does this mean you're done running away from me?" she asked, interrupting his insane werewolf instincts.

He coughed. "Maybe."

"Maybe?"

"Still not convinced I'm good for you."

Then those lips tipped into a sinful grin. "Oh Rafe, you must know by now that I don't want things that are good for me."

Chapter Thirty-Two

She waited for him to argue with her. She expected him to. But the long list of reasons why she shouldn't be with him never left Rafe's mouth. Instead he leaned forward and pressed his lips to hers. Ruby melted into him but he pulled away before things could escalate again.

"We really do have to go," he said, pushing the hair from her face. This new Rafe, the Rafe that touched her and kissed her and looked at her like that, was enough to make her want to stay in the bed of this truck for the rest of her life. What if they walked away from here and everything disappeared? What if this tenuous, fragile thing between them broke as soon as they left?

But then Rafe smiled at her and she knew whatever was between them wasn't fragile at all. And she was damn well going to fight for it. This wasn't about sex anymore. One week with this man and she knew this was it. He was it. The certainty of the thought struck her hard in the chest, squeezing her heart. Rafe was it for her.

She finished her pie and got dressed as Rafe rolled up their bedding and threw it in the cab of the truck, letting this new realization settle into her bones. She was in love with a werewolf. She was in love with Rafe.

He paused to watch her apply the lipstick she never left home without. Hopefully he didn't notice her hand tremble as she smoothed it on.

He smirked. "Really?"

"It's my signature look, Rafe. I can't just go traipsing through the woods with pale lips." She grinned at him, feigning bravery. He huffed a laugh, shaking his head as he moved around the truck. He extended a hand and helped her down from the bed.

Her boots hit the dirt, and the bubble from last night was broken. Reality flooded in.

"Ready?" he asked.

Nerves flared in Ruby's belly and not the good kind. She was about to walk into a werewolf pack with a man the current Alpha tried to kill and all because her sister was slowly dying. The pie she'd been so excited about sat heavy in her gut.

Rafe laced his fingers with hers and gave a squeeze. "It's going to be fine," he said, but the relaxed lines of his face had tensed again as though the truth of the situation had settled on him too.

"Yep. Super fine."

Rafe tugged her along and Ruby tried to focus on the trail in front of her, and the birds in the trees, and the sunshine, and the breeze blowing across the back of her neck. But all she could really think about was Rafe's calloused hand in hers and what it felt like to be wrapped up with him last night and what the hell "werewolf reasons" were. And how she loved him. When her brain got tired of that it looped back around to what horrors they might find amongst this pack and how she would ever help her sister.

She would be lucky if the pie stayed down.

"You're quiet." Rafe's rough voice broke the silence, derailing Ruby's cycle of super-unhelpful thoughts.

Ruby glanced up at him. His hair was pulled back today, revealing the full force of his face. The strong lines and coarse stubble. The soft lips.

"Just thinking."

"About what?"

She smiled despite the chaos in her brain. "You really want to know? I thought you didn't like my chattering."

He flinched. "Why would you think that?"

Ruby shrugged. "I don't know. It seems to fluster you."

"Your questions fluster me. I'm not great at conversation." He cleared his throat. "But I like listening to you."

She moved closer, letting her shoulder rub against his arm as they walked. Their hands were still linked and Ruby thought about all the times they'd walked through the woods separately but together. She liked it better like this.

"Well, in that case, I was thinking about last night and how amazing it was."

A low growl of agreement from Rafe sent a shiver through her. He brought her hand up to his lips and brushed a kiss across the back, causing her thoughts to stutter again. She wanted to bring up his hesitancy to do more, but she also didn't want to push him. She could respect his boundaries.

"But I'm also really worried about today and about meeting your pack and about Lena." She blew out a long sigh.

Rafe was quiet and when Ruby stole another glance his brow was furrowed.

"I'll handle the pack," he said, gruffly. "My father's dead.

Whatever else I may think about Knox, I know my brother is a better Alpha than my father was."

"I'm sorry to make you have to face him again."

"Don't be."

Somehow Ruby found the return of his harsh two-word answers comforting.

"It's time I face my people again. I've stayed away too long."

Ruby hadn't really considered that there were others he'd left behind, others he might miss. He'd mentioned Theo's mother yesterday and a few wolves from his childhood, but it wasn't until right now that Ruby realized how much he'd lost. How much his father had stolen from him.

"Do you miss them?"

"Some of them. Sometimes."

"Do you miss her?"

Rafe stopped dead and she turned to see him frowning down at her. "Scarlet died over a century ago."

"I didn't know there was a time limit on missing people."

"I hardly knew her." He swallowed hard.

"You hardly know me."

Rafe's silver eyes studied her, the sun streaking through the trees and lingering in his hair, bringing out the warm brown in the strands. He looked at her like he *did* know her. Like he had known her forever. Ruby's breath caught in her throat and for a second she thought maybe she knew what "werewolf reasons" were. Maybe she knew exactly what she was to Rafe. And he to her.

She nearly asked. The word she had only ever heard in biology class and old werewolf movies caught in her throat.

Rafe brushed a wisp of hair away from her face. "Everything's different with you."

Her body ached like every inch of it longed to be with his.

This wasn't normal. This wasn't just a crush on a sexy man. This wasn't just love. The pieces began to slide into place. "Are we…? I mean, am I your…?"

His eyes widened, a look of alarm on his face, the look of a cornered animal. Ruby lost the nerve to finish her question.

She cleared her throat, glancing away from Rafe's startled stare. "We should probably keep going, right?" she asked.

Rafe blinked. "Uh … right. Yes." He grabbed her hand again and strode ahead on the path, pulling her along behind him. At least he hadn't run from her this time. His fingers were still wrapped tight around hers.

Was she right? Bits and pieces of everything Rafe had told her over the past few days raced through her mind. He couldn't stay away from her. She was different. His overwhelming desire to protect her. This insane physical attraction to each other. If everything she'd ever read about werewolves had even an ounce of fact in them, then maybe it was true. Maybe she and Rafe were—

"Not much farther." Rafe's gruff voice broke through her racing thoughts.

Ruby tugged on his hand and he slowed his pace a bit. "Can we slow down?" she huffed. "My legs can't keep up with yours."

Rafe peeked over his shoulder and gave her a sheepish grin. "Sorry."

Her heart stuttered at the sight of his smile. "So, what should I expect when we get there?" she asked, needing to change the subject, needing a distraction from everything swirling through her mind.

Rafe shrugged, slowing even further and walking beside her again. She squeezed his hand in reassurance.

"Back when my father was Alpha, things were pretty rough.

The pack didn't have a lot. He hated any mingling with humans, but it's become more and more necessary. He hated change."

Ruby nodded, taking it all in. "Are all werewolves artisans like you? How do they survive out here?"

"Artisans?" Rafe huffed. "I make tables, Ruby."

"Beautiful tables." She nudged his arm.

He paused to lean down and kiss the top of her head. Ruby felt it all the way to her toes.

"We mostly live off the land, but a lot of wolves do jobs in town. Day laborer type stuff. Jobs no one asks for papers for."

He helped her over a fallen tree blocking their way. The trail was barely a trail anymore and the white pines towered over them.

"It's so peaceful here," she said, breathing in the damp air of the woods. She tipped her head up to the sky. It was another clear blue day. After a week of humidity and storms, it was a welcome change.

"It is." Rafe came up behind her and nuzzled her neck. God, if they could just stay here like this all day and forget everything else...

"How long has the pack lived here?" she asked, trying to focus on her question and ignore the heat pooling in her core.

Rafe released her, his hand sliding around her waist, his fingers coasting over the skin beneath her shirt. Ruby shivered.

They started walking again, Rafe in front, Ruby behind, the path too narrow now to walk side by side.

"A while now. We moved around a lot when I was younger. But we've stuck around this general area lately. Nobody bothers us too much out here, as long as we don't cause any trouble."

"That's good, right?"

Rafe scanned the trees ahead, his body becoming more rigid as they went. Using those wolf senses apparently.

"It's good. It'd be better if the land wasn't always in threat of being developed. We need space to run."

Run, right. He was a *freaking wolf*. Could they even have a future together? Was it even possible? Werewolves lived for hundreds of years and humans … didn't. Panic raced through her at the thought of being separated from this man she'd only known a few days. What was happening to her?

"Rafe, look. I know this isn't the best time, but after last night and everything, I just think we need to talk about what we are—"

The words died on Ruby's tongue as the first few tents appeared in front of them. Glowing eyes watched them from the trees. A few people emerged from their homes and tracked their approach like they knew they were coming. Like they'd sensed it. Ruby swallowed hard, her heart thrashing in her chest.

One glance at Rafe as she came to stand beside him and she knew the smiling, laughing man from this morning was long gone. His jaw was set, his eyes flashing in the sunlight, every muscle was tense and ready to pounce. He was still human but his entire demeanor had shifted.

"We're here," he growled and Ruby braced herself for whatever happened next.

Chapter Thirty-Three

Five years. Five long and lonely years since Rafe had been with his pack. He didn't think he'd missed it. The posturing, the fighting, the bullshit with his father. But now that he was here, all the rest of it came back too. The companionship, the loyalty, the feeling that someone else understood who and what you were. Maybe he had missed it. A little.

They walked toward the encampment, Ruby tucked close to his side. The weight of his people's gaze on him was heavy enough to slow his footsteps. What if they turned him away? He swallowed hard, half expecting his father to emerge from the shadows. The old bastard died shortly after Rafe left, his lungs finally failing him, but a chill ran down Rafe's spine nonetheless. If anyone was going to come back as a vindictive ghost, it would be his father.

The camp looked the same as when he left it, clusters of tents around fire pits, a few trailers for the colder months. The state left them alone as long as they stayed out of trouble, but the threat of some developer buying the land was always looming.

Nothing was permanent. The pack had been here for years now but they still lived as though they might have to leave at any moment. Rafe remembered the times they'd had to leave in a hurry, usually after too many confrontations with local humans. Eventually, their neighbors fought back and as their weapons got better, the wolves became the ones being hunted. Nothing enraged his father more than being reminded that they were no longer the apex predators.

Rafe recognized the faces, wolf and human, peering at him as he and Ruby walked into the camp. He watched as their expressions went from shocked to questioning. No one looked outright hostile, which helped ease the tension in his muscles.

The old man is dead, he reminded himself, letting out a long breath. He grabbed Ruby's hand and she hung on for dear life. He was an idiot for bringing her here, but there was no turning back now.

One of the older women of the pack approached them first. Dina had known him longer than most. Her tan face was creased with age.

"You're back," she said simply, assessing Rafe with her gaze.

"I am."

Her dark eyes flicked to Ruby. "You brought a human."

"She's a friend." If Dina sensed Ruby was anything more than that, she didn't say it. She nodded once, but stayed in the way of the path.

"Did you come to bring trouble, Rafe?"

Shame flashed hot in his gut. This is what his pack thought of him even after all this time. That he'd come to stir up old battles.

"No, ma'am." He cleared his throat again, his words sticking. Ruby squeezed his fingers. He took a deep lungful of her scent and reminded himself why he was here. "Just came to talk to my brother." Dina's gray brows rose but Rafe put up a hand in surrender. "Talk, Dina. That's it. I didn't come to stir things up." This was what his relationship with his brothers had become. No one believed he would have any motive other than picking a fight. Why would they? He hadn't had a civil conversation with Knox in nearly a decade.

She studied him a moment longer and Rafe's skin prickled under her gaze. Wolves weren't like humans. They didn't bother with being polite. They stared and sniffed and took you in completely. You couldn't lie or pretend around a wolf. They knew you too well.

Other wolves had gathered around them as they spoke, several still in wolf form. They sniffed around Ruby's legs and she pressed closer to his side. He suddenly felt exposed, flayed open in front of everyone. Could they all see it? Did they all know she was his Mate? This thing that he'd never believed in was suddenly more real to him than anything else. He felt like the word was stamped across Ruby's forehead. He should have told her this morning.

Rafe nudged a sleek black wolf, Leo, with his leg. "Back off," he grumbled. The wolf huffed but backed up.

He glanced back at Dina to find a begrudging smile on her face. "It's been a long time, Rafe."

"I thought it was best."

She shrugged her small shoulders. "You may have thought wrong."

He didn't have a chance to untangle that comment before more wolves and people were coming out of their homes to see what the commotion was about. It wasn't easy to do anything around here without the whole pack knowing.

Rafe sifted through the familiar faces, some with hesitant smiles, some with furrowed brows. Faces of the people he grew up with. The people who did nothing to stop his father's abuse. His brother wasn't among them yet.

"You back for good?" Archer, a friend from a lifetime ago, patted him hard on the shoulder, daring to approach now that Dina had given her approval.

"No, just a visit." Rafe's answer barely made it past his lips. Sights and smells closed in on him from all sides, memories chasing them all. *Home.* The word, the feeling, struck him hard in the chest. Fur and pine and woodsmoke mingled in the air. Faces he hadn't seen anywhere but in his dreams, lined the path in front of him.

The last time he had seen them rushed to the surface. The rain and the mud, the shouts from the crowd. No one had tried to end it. No one had thought to stand against the Alpha. They would have let Rafe die. Bile rose in this throat, hot and acidic.

It was too much. How had he thought he could come back so easily?

"Rafe?" A woman's voice broke through the din of the growing crowd. Everyone else fell away. She looked the same as the day he left, except this time there were no tears streaming down her cheeks. Her olive skin and light eyes still made her strikingly beautiful, just like her son.

She approached slowly, blinking like she couldn't trust herself. "It's you," she said with a smile and then threw her arms around his neck.

Rafe held her tight, breathing in her familiar scent of lavender and strong tea. "Ma," he breathed. Her long curls tickled his arms as she hugged him.

Ruby cleared her throat, startling him out of a million memories of this woman caring for him, loving him when no one else did. She had been his soft place to land. The only one in a childhood filled with harsh lessons and even harsher punishments.

He put her feet back on the ground and she beamed up at him.

"Ruby, this is my ... uh ... stepmother, I guess you would call her. Ma, this is Ruby."

The only mother he ever knew, Nell, flicked her shrewd gaze to Ruby. A frown wrinkled her brow.

"Nice to meet you," Ruby said, and Rafe realized it was the first she'd spoken since they got here. Nell didn't speak right away, her gaze steady on his Mate.

More words tumbled out of Ruby in a nervous rush. "I met your son. Uh ... I mean your other son ... I mean Theo. He's very nice. So charming. He looks just like you."

Nell's lips tipped into a smile at the mention of Theo. "He's a good boy." She glanced over Rafe's shoulder. "Is he here?"

"Not this time. Sorry, Ma."

Her beautiful face fell in disappointment but she quickly recovered. "Well, I'm happy you're back, Rafe."

"Not back."

She flinched at his clipped answer and he softened his tone.

"Not back, just here to talk to Knox. It's important."

She studied him a moment longer before nodding once and gesturing for him to follow. She spoke over her shoulder as they followed her through the camp and the whispering groups of wolves.

"I'm sure Knox will be surprised to see you."

An understatement, but his stepmother was always one to downplay whatever issues her Alpha's sons were having.

"He's been busy since your father died. He has big plans for the pack."

"So we keep hearing," Rafe muttered.

Nell turned sharply to face him. "Your brother is the Alpha now, Rafe. If you've come to challenge that, you should leave right now."

Rafe ground his back teeth.

"He's here on my behalf, not his own."

Nell's eyes snapped to Ruby. "Oh?"

Ruby rolled her shoulders back and faced the female werewolf. "Rafe is only here to help me and my sister. I was attacked by wolves."

"Not one of ours." Nell's response was quick and defensive.

"No. But we thought Knox might have some answers."

Nell studied them both, her earlier smiles gone. It had always been this way with his adoptive mother. The pack came above all else. Even her sons.

"Please. We just want to talk to him." Ruby's voice was steady even as Rafe could smell the fear vibrating beneath her skin. He wanted to grab her and run. Far away from here.

They'd stopped in front of a big green army tent in the center of the camp. Tarps were hung over the outdoor kitchen space and various mismatched chairs were gathered around the fire pit. The pack lived most of the year out here until the weather turned to cold. Then they moved into the trailers or some left-to-rent places in town for the winter. They were squatters at best, drifters at worst.

Rafe's tiny cabin was a luxury compared to this. Whatever Knox's big plans were, they didn't seem to include housing upgrades, at least not yet. Not that he could do much if the pack didn't own the land they lived on. But Rafe wasn't here about any of that.

Nell waved a hand toward the chairs. "Knox is out hunting, but you're welcome to stay and wait." Her expression softened and she laid a hand on Rafe's arm. "I am happy to see you."

"Me too."

She raised on her toes to give him another quick hug. "Be careful with that human," she whispered.

Rafe's heart stopped and stuttered frantically back to life.

Nell gave him a knowing smile as she pulled away. "Good luck, Rafe. Don't stay away so long next time."

He stared at her as she walked away, leaving him and Ruby alone at Knox's campsite. Or as alone as they could be with wolves and people still wandering past to get a look at the former Alpha's disgraced son.

"Well," Ruby breathed. "That was … a lot."

Rafe huffed a laugh despite the emotions roiling in his gut. "Sorry. I should have prepared you better. They can be very intense."

"Which is surprising since you are so laid back," she quipped, sinking into the closest chair.

He shook his head, wanting to scoop her up and hold her close, wanting to return to this morning when he held her in his arms. But not here. Not with everyone watching them.

"Are you okay?" she asked, her gaze following him as he paced in front of her.

"Fine."

"Rafe." Her voice was soft, imploring. "Sit."

He obeyed, lowering into the chair next to Ruby's. "I wasn't expecting to feel so … conflicted."

Ruby took his hand and traced the lines of his palm with her finger. The touch sent tingles through his whole body. "Going home is always hard."

"I thought I hated all of this and all of them." He lowered his voice even though he was sure everyone's ears were perked up and listening. He didn't give a shit what they heard. "But being back here is more complicated than that."

"I get it."

He turned to look at her, and the sight of Ruby at his old home added to his tangled emotions. "You do?"

"Sure. Maybe not to the same extent, but right before we left, Lena basically told me she thinks I'm a ridiculous person who makes up scary stories to get off, and yet here I am trying to save her ass. So yeah. I get how families are complicated."

Rafe brought their entwined hands to his mouth and ran his lips over her knuckles. "It was a stupid idea to bring you, but I'm glad I did."

Ruby's smile grew, her red lipstick still perfectly in place. He wanted to kiss it off, to smudge it and wreck it. He wanted to do so many things to Ruby, but if he did ... what then?

A realization settled in his gut as Ruby smiled at him. He wanted her to want him not because of some fated paranormal bullshit reason, but because she actually just wanted him. For him.

It was as simple and complicated as that.

"Ruby, there's something you need to know."

She leaned toward him, giving him her full attention, but he didn't get to tell her everything that was on his mind. It would have to wait.

Knox was back.

The man that strolled into the campsite was obviously Rafe's brother. They had the same dark brown hair, the same eerie eyes, and the same murderous expression etched into their features. But where Rafe's hair was long and tied back at his nape, Knox's was short with silver at the temples. Ruby took in this tiny hint that werewolves did age eventually.

He'd allowed his beard to grow fully while Rafe kept his to a delightfully scratchy stubble. Both men were large, but Rafe had at least a few inches on his older brother.

Rafe stood and Ruby followed, keeping hold of his hand. Knox stopped in front of them, his cool gaze sliding from Rafe to Ruby and back again.

"Rafe."

"Knox."

The men greeted each other with a terse nod. Ruby could swear the entire pack went still around them. Goosebumps broke out across her arms.

"It's been a long time." Knox's voice was deep and smooth, lacking Rafe's rough edges. It was the voice of a leader, demanding yet comforting all at once. Under other circumstances, Ruby could imagine herself liking this man.

Rafe shrugged. "Didn't seem worth coming back."

Knox narrowed his eyes. "And yet, here you are."

Tension rippled through Rafe's body and into Ruby through their linked hands. "We need your help." How he got the words past his clenched teeth Ruby would never know.

Knox smirked. "I haven't seen you for five years and now you want my help?" He let out a low laugh. "Rafe who always thought he was better than us has come crawling home."

"Don't repeat Devon's bullshit. I never thought that."

Knox's eyes slid to Ruby and a chill ran up her spine. "You always preferred humans to us."

Rafe growled, taking a step in front of Ruby, shielding her with his body. "I didn't want to fight you then and I don't want to fight you now."

Knox sneered, his handsome face turning ugly with the expression.

Rafe went on, "You got what you wanted, Knox. You're the Alpha. Nothing left to prove."

Something shifted in Knox's face, a flash of regret before he schooled his features. "It's been five years. What makes you think you can walk back in here now?"

"After you almost killed me, it didn't seem worth the visit."

Knox scoffed. "I wouldn't have done it."

Rafe went rigid beside her, seething. "You sure as hell would have. And then you would have killed Theo too."

The other man's eyes went wide with shock and anger but when he spoke his voice filled with a deadly calm. "You seem to know everything I'm thinking: I wanted to be the Alpha; I wanted to kill my brothers, my own fucking blood. You're a goddamn mind-reader, Rafe."

Knox had stepped forward and the two men stood toe to toe in the dirt. Ruby clung to Rafe's hand as she cowered behind him. So much for not being afraid of anything.

"It was hard to think anything different when your teeth were at my throat," Rafe growled.

"I'm not the one that nearly blinded Theo."

Another wave of tension rolled through Rafe's body. "We were all in that ring. We didn't have a choice."

Knox smirked. "My point exactly, little brother." He emphasized the word little and Ruby bit down on an ill-advised giggle. "We all did things we regret." It wasn't an apology but some of the rippling fury seemed to leave Rafe's body.

"We did."

Knox nodded like something was settled between them. Ruby would have argued that all three brothers could use some time in extensive family therapy, but no one asked her.

"You said you need my help?"

Rafe nodded. "Ruby's in trouble."

Ruby peeked out from behind Rafe's huge form and gave Knox a small wave. He quirked a questioning eyebrow like he didn't quite know what to make of her, but he gestured for them to follow him.

"Too many ears out here," he said and the casually meandering wolves suddenly had places to be, scurrying off in various directions.

Knox led them to a trailer set back in the pines and they followed him into the dim interior. It was hot and stuffy inside compared to the shade of the woods.

"Something to drink?" Knox asked, wandering into the small kitchen. The entire space was a rectangle with a kitchen at one end and living room at the other. Ruby assumed the two doors off the living room led to bedrooms.

"Beer, if you have."

"Uh ... me too, please." If Ruby was going to survive this day, she needed a drink. Even if it was only beer.

Knox handed them each a bottle and Ruby took a swig, letting the cold, bitter liquid fortify her. She was still trying to come to terms with the fact that they were sharing a drink with the man who tried to kill Rafe, but she had the odd feeling that this was how the brothers' entire relationship worked. Neither man seemed particularly nonplussed by the situation.

"So what's the problem with Ruby?" Knox asked, leaning against the kitchen counter, arms crossed over his wide chest. Ruby made a mental note later to ask Rafe if werewolves worked out a lot.

"There's no problem *with* Ruby." Rafe grumbled. "Ruby is perfect."

Well, shit. This man was trying to kill her. Heat rose into Ruby's cheeks. She took another sip of beer and lowered herself into the closest kitchen chair. Her knees were suddenly weak.

Knox's eyebrows lifted to his hairline. "Then what is the problem?"

"She was attacked by a wolf. About a week ago. And then a few more came sniffing around her door."

Ruby's gaze flicked between the two men, Rafe dark and glowering, Knox deceptively calm. The Alpha kept his features carefully neutral, but Ruby could see the flash of interest in his eyes.

"They weren't ours."

"I know."

"Then why are you here, Rafe?" Knox spoke with a hint of impatience, a man who had too much to do to sit around and chat with his long-lost brother.

Rafe blew out a long, frustrated breath. "I was hoping you'd know something about it. Any other packs on the move? Have you heard of any attacks on humans?"

Knox stared at them, his gaze moving from one to the other like he was trying to piece together a puzzle. He shook his head. "I haven't heard of any other attacks." He took a swig of his beer. "But the pack up north has been getting antsy. Crossing the border more and more often to hunt."

Rafe ran a hand down his face, the rasp of his stubble filling the cramped space. Ruby longed for a simpler time when all she had wanted was the feel of that stubble between her thighs. A time before international werewolf incidents were a concern to her.

"Could have been them, I guess."

"But why attack a human?" Knox asked, gesturing at Ruby with his beer bottle. "What's so special about this one?"

The air in the tiny house shifted and whatever tentative peace the men had shared evaporated in an instant.

"Everything," Rafe growled.

Knox rolled his eyes. "Fuck, Rafe. When will you learn?"

"Ruby, go wait outside." Rafe didn't even glance at her as he gave the command.

"But … no. What about Lena? We didn't get to ask—"

"Go," Rafe snapped.

Ruby bit down on the spike of pain his words sent through her. She swallowed her hurt and her tears and got up from the table.

"Fine." She stomped out of the stale trailer air and perched on the top step outside the door. Fucking werewolves. One minute he says she's perfect and the next he's barking orders. Rafe had more mood swings than a premenstrual teenager during a chocolate shortage.

He was clearly an asshole.

But she still hoped his brother didn't kill him.

Chapter Thirty-Four

"What the hell is going on with the human?"

Rafe ran a hand through his hair, loosening it from its tie. "It doesn't matter." He needed to get out of here. He needed to get back to Ruby.

"It clearly does matter if helping her brought you all the way back here," Knox pointed out, still leaning against the counter. So still. So calm. But Rafe knew his brother. Once provoked, Knox was a mean son of a bitch and could shift in seconds.

But Rafe didn't come here for a fight.

Even though his fists were curled at his side and his blood was screaming through his veins, begging him to let the beast out.

"She was in danger, so I wanted to help. That's it."

"Oh Rafe, always the hero."

"Fuck you."

"Well, fuck you too, little brother." Knox threw back the rest of his beer and pushed away from the counter. The space was too small for two oversized men. The smell of sweat and beer filled Rafe's nose. "You left me here to pick up the pieces."

His brother's words were more shocking than a punch to the face would have been. "And what should I have done?"

Knox shrugged, but his tone was anything but casual. "You could have stayed. You could have … helped." Was that a flicker of uncertainty in his brother's eyes? What the hell was that about?

"Devon would have never allowed it."

Knox huffed. "The old bastard had one foot in the grave. We never should have let him manipulate us for as long as he did. I'll always be ashamed of that."

Knox's words hung between them. The truth of it. The shame of what they did to each other. Of what they'd allowed their father to do.

"I'm sure you're doing a better job than he ever did." Rafe cleared his throat. "Or than I could have done."

Knox held his gaze a moment longer, his silver eyes seeing more than Rafe wanted him to. Rafe had the same eyes, the eyes they'd inherited from their father. But maybe those eyes could be where their father's legacy ended. Maybe they could finally put the man to rest.

Knox glanced toward the door. "Tell me honestly, what's the deal with the girl?"

"I think she's my Mate." The word stuck in his throat, the confession too heavy for the thick air of the trailer.

"Please tell me you don't believe in that bullshit."

How did his brother have the ability to ruin every damn moment between them? After centuries of it, Rafe supposed he should be used to it.

"I didn't. Until I met her. And now I do."

"It's fairy tale nonsense, Rafe. Fated Mates are a lie."

And just like that their father raised his ugly head. Again. The old Alpha scorned the idea of a fated Mate. He called the shots in his pack. He had to approve every pairing and he only cared about strength and power.

But his father had been so wrong.

Rafe had never felt stronger than when he was with Ruby.

He shook his head. "It's more real than anything else."

"Look, I believe that you're attracted to this girl. That you want to fuck her. Maybe even that some ancient wolf part of your brain, or your dick, wants to claim her in some way, but there's no way you have some sort of cosmic connection."

"Fuck you, Knox. I'm out of here. Thanks for the lovely visit."

"Wait." Rafe turned to go, but Knox grabbed his shoulder. "Just be careful."

"What's that supposed to mean?"

"I know what happened with your other little girlfriend and I wouldn't want Ruby to end up the same way."

Rafe spun to face him, every nerve in his body begging him to attack this arrogant bastard. "Is that a threat?"

"Of course not." Knox dropped his hand. "But if there's one thing I agree with Dad about, it's that humans and werewolves shouldn't mix."

"He was wrong."

"Really? And have you told Ruby yet?"

Rafe stiffened.

Knox smirked. "You haven't. Because deep down you already know. You know this thing between you won't work. It can't."

"You don't know a fucking thing about it."

"I know that humans are weak. They live short little lives and then they die. Even if this one seems different."

Rafe was silent, thoughts of Lena and the magic blood that must run through both sisters racing through his mind.

"Fate wouldn't make a mistake. She's meant for me," he said, more to reassure himself than to convince Knox.

"And she wants you? Forever? You're certain of that?"

Rafe's stomach pitched and rolled as his brother laid his every fear out in front of him. Of course he wasn't certain and Knox knew it. His brother didn't bother to say it, just patted him on the arm like he was offering his pity. Rafe shook him off and strode toward the door.

"She'd be safer without you."

Knox's words stopped him in his tracks. He froze with his hand on the door knob.

"I'll send out some wider patrols to keep an eye on things. You should stay away from your human friend. For her own good."

"You don't know what she needs," Rafe growled.

He could hear Knox's low laugh, but he didn't stick around to hear any more even as his brother's words burrowed deep under his skin and began to fester.

Rafe flung open the door to find Ruby sitting in the dirt with a pile of pups in her lap. Three little balls of fluff wriggled and yipped as they vied for her attention. Werewolf pups were rare and Rafe's heart turned over at the sight of them. Three babies made a blessed year for sure. Figures everyone would be right about Knox being good for the pack.

Ruby giggled as a gray and white puppy licked her face. She scratched him behind the ears, and Rafe's anger drained out of him at the sight. He wanted to get in line for his turn.

"We should go."

Ruby's gaze shot to his, the joy dropping off immediately. "We need to ask about Lena."

"It's not a good idea."

Ruby nudged the wolves from her lap and they scampered off, tumbling over each other to chase a chipmunk through the trees. She stood up, hands going immediately to her hips, fighting stance. "Why the hell not? We came all this way and all we found out was some very vague shit about Canadian wolves!" Ruby's voice rose with each word and Rafe could feel the pack perk up around them.

He tugged her closer. "Keep your voice down," he warned.

Ruby blew out a frustrated breath, but whispered when she spoke. "I thought we came to help Lena. We need to figure out her visions."

Rafe glanced around them, but the camp was quiet. "You need to trust me." He waited, his gaze locked on Ruby's. She wanted to argue. He could see it in the grim set of her mouth and the furrow of her brows and the anger flashing in her dark eyes.

"Fine," she ground out. "I trust you. Let's go."

He took her hand and they strode back through camp, not bothering with goodbyes. His need to leave was stronger than his need to mend fences right now. Maybe someday he'd come back and try again, but five years hadn't been enough to close his old wounds. He still couldn't forgive what had happened here. Or his own role in it. Maybe he was a step closer than before, but today wasn't the day he rejoined the pack.

When they were finally far enough from the camp that Rafe felt safe again, he tried to explain. "I remembered something."

Ruby turned to look up at him. Her cheeks were pink with exertion. Rafe slowed the fast pace he'd set since they left.

"Oh?"

"The pack comes before everything else, Ruby."

"Okay. But what does that have to do with Lena? We still don't know what to do."

Rafe flinched at the accusation in her tone, but he went on. "If we told Knox what Lena was, the first thing he would do with that information was figure out how it could benefit the pack." He'd seen it in his brother's eyes, the calculations he'd made when Rafe told him about the wolf attack. He only agreed to increase patrols because it would keep his pack safe, not for Ruby. Not for Rafe.

What he would do with information about the first seer in over a century was anyone's guess, but Rafe didn't think it was worth the risk. A seer could be valuable to a leader, someone to guide the Alpha in his decision-making. Werewolves lived a precarious life. Whatever small assurance a seer could give would be welcomed. The more Rafe thought about it, the happier he was that he hadn't told Knox the whole truth.

"You think he would hurt her?"

"I don't know. But I do know his first thought would be for the pack. Not for helping Lena."

Ruby sighed, pushing the wispy hairs from her face. Curls stuck to the sweat on her brow. "Well, fuck."

Rafe grunted. "Yeah."

They walked on in silence, the afternoon hot and sultry around them, before Rafe spoke again. "I'm sorry I didn't think of all this before we left. I can be impulsive, I guess. Act before I think sometimes." More so when she was involved.

"You were trying to get away from me again." He hated the words, but Ruby's tone was light like she was trying to tease him.

"I'm sorry about that too." He said it even as Knox's warning rattled around in his head. Exhaustion settled heavily on his shoulders. He was so tired of fighting this thing between them. He wanted to sink into it, to give in and crawl into her lap like those damn puppies.

"Rafe, stop." Ruby tugged him to a standstill on the narrow trail.

"What is it?"

Her face was tipped up and he couldn't stop himself from brushing the damp tendrils from her brow.

"I know," she said, never taking her dark gaze from his face.

He swallowed hard, his blood suddenly speeding through his veins. "You know what?"

"I know what we are. To each other, I mean. At least I think I do." Her forehead scrunched in hesitation and Rafe pressed his lips to the creases, unable to stay away, to stay back, to resist.

"Say it," he whispered, needing to hear the word from her blood red lips.

"I think we're ... Mates."

His mouth crashed down on hers, all restraint breaking. *Mates.* And she felt it too, dear God, she felt it too.

She jumped into his arms, wrapping her thick thighs around his waist. "I thought I was going crazy," she said between kisses. "It was all so much, so fast." Her breath was coming in short gasps as he backed them up against a tree. He kissed down her neck, nipping and biting her soft flesh. She writhed against him and he pushed his hardening cock into her center, heat and need pulsing through him.

His Mate. His fucking Mate. Every instinct was clamoring at him to claim her, to make her his forever. But her words rang in his head, even as her body called to him. *So much, so fast.* This was all new to her, to both of them really. He pulled back, panting. Ruby stared at him with hungry eyes.

"Wait," he growled. "Slow down."

Ruby stilled in his arms.

He leaned his forehead against hers, their breath mingling between them. "Once we do this, that's it. There's no going back. Mates are forever."

"There's no going back for me regardless of whether or not you stick your dick in me, Rafe."

He huffed a laugh at her fearlessness. It was exactly how he felt too, that it was too late for them anyway, that nothing they did now would change what they were to each other.

"I'm serious." She wriggled from his grasp and put her feet back on the ground. "I want you. Mated or not." She wrapped her hands in the front of his shirt and tugged him close. "This thing between us is impossible to fight and I don't want to fight it. I want to be with you."

Rafe swallowed the emotions rising rapidly in his throat. It was everything he'd wanted to hear from her, but still his doubts lingered.

"I couldn't keep Scarlet safe."

"I don't want a bodyguard. I want a partner."

Rafe's heart pounded in his chest as though it were trying to leap directly into Ruby's hands. A partner. Such a human concept.

"After everything I've done—"

"It's your turn to trust me. Trust that I want you. That I know what I'm doing."

"I won't age like you," he said, the words burning his throat.

"I'll take as much time with you as I can get." She smiled weakly, tears brimming in her eyes. His brave girl.

He brushed away a tear with his thumb. He leaned down, kissing along the line of her cheeks. "Lena has magic in her blood," he whispered. "Maybe you do too." It was too much to hope for, that Ruby would have an extended lifespan, but it wasn't impossible.

"Fate doesn't make mistakes." He echoed the words he'd spoken to Knox earlier and they felt even more true with Ruby pressed against him.

"I feel it," she said, her breath skating across his neck. "I know you're mine."

His body trembled at her words. He would never be able to watch her age and die without him. It would be torture. "Seers, nymphs, werewolves. We all have extended lifespans. If you're one of us..." It had to be true. Of course she was one of them, she was his. "We'll figure it out."

She wrapped her arms around his neck. "We'll figure it out together. Please, Rafe. Don't run from me anymore." Her words were so sweet, so desperate. He'd made her feel that way: afraid that he would keep pushing her away. It was all he'd been doing since they'd met.

"I'm done running." He nuzzled her neck, breathing in her cinnamon-spiced scent. He'd known her for a week. He'd known her forever.

She sighed, dreamily, running her fingers through his hair.

"But Ruby..."

"Yeah?"

"I'm not fucking you for the first time up against a tree."

She pulled back, looking so indignant Rafe had to bite down on a laugh.

"What the hell kind of werewolf are you?"

"One that doesn't want to fuck his Mate so close to his shitty pack."

Ruby nearly growled and the sound shot straight to his cock. "Damn it. Fine. But maybe we could..." Ruby reached between them, gripping Rafe through his jeans.

"Shit, Ruby." He leaned his forehead against hers again, watching her ruby lips spread into a smile.

"Just to take the edge off. We'll be quiet. And quick." She rubbed up and down his length and he had no doubt he could be quick.

He captured her mouth again, pressing her against the trunk of the tree and her gasp tickled his lips. He slid his tongue against hers, lapping up her sweet moans. Her fingers fumbled with the fly of his pants and he reached down to help, freeing his aching cock. Ruby wrapped her fist around him and stroked.

Static filled Rafe's brain. Static and the overwhelming need to spin Ruby around and fuck her against this goddamn tree. But he was determined not to be a complete animal. Not their first time anyway.

Ruby picked up her speed and Rafe groaned.

"Stop." He wrapped his hand around hers and stilled the motion.

"Please, Rafe. I want to make you come."

Rafe struggled to control his breath, to control everything. Every muscle was rigid, every atom at attention. And then Ruby rubbed her palm over his tip, spreading the moisture that had gathered there and he let her. He let her slide her slick hand up and down a few more times. He let her bite and suck the skin at his throat while she did it.

"Shit, Ruby. Shit, shit, shit…" He growled as he came all over her hand like a goddamn adolescent. Pleasure shot through him and left him shuddering against her.

"Was it good?" Ruby peered up at him with dark eyes.

"Good?" Rafe leaned his forehead against hers, unable to right himself yet. "Jesus, Ruby. I just came faster than I have in the past two hundred years. Yeah, it was good."

Ruby's grin made up for his embarrassment. She stooped to

wipe her hand in the grass before standing to face him again.

"You deserve to feel good, Rafe." She ran her fingers through his hair and he sighed, his muscles relaxing.

"So do you," he murmured, sliding his hand down the front of Ruby's shorts. She was warm and so wet for him. He growled, scraping his teeth against her neck. He didn't waste time. Even through his lust fog, he had no intention of getting caught by his pack with his pants down.

He circled Ruby's clit and she arched into him. She had gotten this close to coming just by getting him off. That was so damn sexy. He worked faster, mimicking the things he'd seen her do to herself, remembering how her fingers had moved.

"That's it," she gasped. She tugged on his hair, her back arching away from the tree. She bit down on his shoulder to stifle her screams as she came, and the feel of her teeth on his flesh sent another bolt of lust to Rafe's cock.

"Holy shit," she said, pulling away. Her lipstick was smudged and her cheeks were flushed pink.

Rafe grinned. "Better?"

"Not really," Ruby huffed, fixing her shorts. "As soon as we get back, we're doing this mating thing."

Rafe's heart nearly burst. "Don't say shit like that, Ruby."

"Why not?"

He shook his head, but couldn't hide his smile. "I don't know," he admitted. "It just doesn't seem real."

"You're stuck with me," she said, taking his hand again. "Fated Mates or not, okay?"

He nodded, but words stuck in his throat. He wanted to believe her. He wanted to put his father and his pack behind him. He wanted to leave Scarlet to rest and forget the sins of his past. But the way Ruby looked at him still seemed too good to be true.

Chapter Thirty-Five

The trip back was tense and quiet and horny as hell. Hiking back to the truck had only taken a few hours, so they decided to forgo another campout and just drive home. But the whole day felt like it lasted at least a month.

Now that it was all out there, Ruby didn't want to waste any more time. Mates were forever. And that felt so right to her, so exactly right, she couldn't wait another minute for it to start. For Rafe to be hers. It was like every atom in her body called to every atom in his. And the best part was, she wasn't just a kinky weirdo who wanted to be stalked through the woods—although she definitely was—it was so much more than that. It was fate! It was love! It was magic.

Ruby hadn't stopped touching him the whole trip, even as he drove. She ran her fingers over his arm, through his hair, up and down his thigh until Rafe had grabbed her hand and warned her with a low growl that she needed to stop or they wouldn't make it home.

She'd voted for pulling over and fucking on the side of the road, but he said no. Not in the truck, not in the middle of the day on the side of the highway. He kissed the back of her hand while she pouted, and she soaked in every lopsided grin he sent her way. It was the longest drive ever.

But now they were home and Ruby dropped her bag in the living room, leaning her back against the front door. She closed her eyes and sucked in a deep breath. Her whole body was vibrating in anticipation. Rafe was her Mate. And they were about to seal the deal. She was ready to mate the hell out of her werewolf.

It was like some part of her had known all along, like the little girl who loved ghost stories and haunted houses, who liked to stay up late watching old werewolf movies had known exactly what was waiting for her. A small, smug part of her was vindicated by Rafe's existence. She was right. Things did go bump in the night and they were sexy as hell.

"Hey, you're back!" Theo's cheerful voice snapped her out of her thoughts.

Ruby opened her eyes to find him smiling at her as he came down the stairs. "Hey, Theo."

"Where's Rafe?"

"Unloading the truck."

Theo nodded. "How did everything go?"

"Uh … well, I met your mom." It was the first thing that came to mind that didn't involve entering into a mating bond with Rafe or bringing up their terrifying third brother.

The smile fell from Theo's face. He ran a hand over his curls. "Oh yeah? How is she?"

"I think she misses you."

It was the wrong thing to say. Theo's expression darkened and for the first time since she met him, Ruby could imagine him as an animal.

"Lena's a little shaken up," he said, gesturing up the stairs and bypassing Ruby's comment. "But I think she'll believe you now."

"What did you do?" Thoughts of mates left her mind as worry for her sister crowded back in. What if the stress worsened her condition?

Theo shrugged, his casual charm returning. He flashed Ruby a smile. "Seeing is believing. So I showed her a few things."

"You shifted in front of her?" Ruby strode through the living room, already heading for the stairs. "I wanted her to take me seriously. I didn't want to kill her!"

Theo laughed. "She's not dead. Just a little ... surprised."

"Surprised? Shit, Theo. You're the worst babysitter ever."

He laughed again before opening the front door. "She'll be fine. I gotta go. See you around, Ruby."

He was gone before she could tell him he was an asshole like his brothers. She took the stairs two at a time until she reached the top. Lena's door was closed, and Ruby hesitated, not really wanting to face her yet, but also needing to know if she was all right. Or as all right as she could be after witnessing a man turn into a wolf and back again.

She knocked and held her breath.

"I'm not letting you in." Her sister's voice was strong and angry from the other side. At least she wasn't cowering in fear or worse, slipping into another episode.

"It's me. I'm back."

Stomping footsteps approached, and then the door swung open. Lena's eyes blazed bright and her hair was a wild pale halo around her head.

"Jesus, Lena—"

"No." She held up a trembling hand in front of Ruby's face. "No, Ruby. I've had enough for one day. No more of this ... this ... whatever the hell this is."

"Okay, Lena, I'm sorry. I just—"

"Nope. No more. No more strange men staying here with us. I don't need a babysitter. I need everyone to leave me the fuck alone."

The door slammed in her face before Ruby could speak again. *Shit.* Ruby had never seen her sister that angry before, especially not lately, not with all her strength leached from her body. Maybe anger was better than submission to whatever this power was that was eating her from the inside.

Ruby knocked again. "Lena, I know it all seems crazy but—"

"Go away, Ruby."

She blew out an impatient sigh. "I tried to tell you."

"Ruby, I swear to God…"

"Okay, okay … you need a little time to process this."

Her sister scoffed and Ruby heard it loud and clear through the door. "I did warn you," Ruby muttered. "Just try and remember you liked Rafe before. And he's the same guy now. And you have to admit, Theo is pretty charming."

"Ruby…"

"Okay." Ruby held up her hands in surrender even though Lena couldn't see her. "I'm going. We can chat more about this … uh … later." She hesitated a minute longer outside Lena's door just in case she changed her mind. At least she was safe for the moment, Ruby told herself as she backed away from Lena's room. Safe and sound. And Ruby had unfinished business with Rafe.

Business she intended to finish very soon.

She hurried down the stairs and into the kitchen. Rafe was still out front with Theo. Ruby paced the small kitchen, her heart thundering in her chest. What the hell was he doing out there? Holding some kind of werewolf summit? Her foot knocked into the cat dish as she walked and it rattled across the floor.

"Shoot," she muttered. The dish was empty so she pulled out the catfood and gave it a shake, expecting Lucy to come running, but the little demon was nowhere to be seen. She poured it and still no cat. That was odd. The glutton always came when he heard the kibble hit the dish.

"Lucifer? Where are you, buddy? Did you return to the depths of hell?" She made the universal cat kissy-face noise, but still no cat. Ruby blew out a long sigh and opened the back door. It wouldn't be the first time he got out. Damn cat had a deep love for sparrows. Not to eat, just to stare at for hours on end. Sometimes he liked to get a closer look.

"Lucy? Lucy, where are you?"

How long had he been gone? she wondered as she stalked out into the yard. She hadn't even noticed with all the insanity of the past few days. A small stab of guilt hit her at not realizing sooner he was missing. She was a horrible cat mom.

"Lucifer, come on home. Who wants belly scratches?" she cooed.

She walked to the edge of the yard where she'd let the grass grow far too tall.

"Is that you, buddy?" She peered into the weeds and a set of golden eyes peered back. "Holy shit," she whispered. The eyes flashed and the beast's mouth tipped into a wolfy grin. That thing was not her pet. And she was so fucking screwed.

She turned to run, but the creature pounced faster than she could think. Her scream tore through the quiet evening as the werewolf knocked her to the ground.

Rafe froze.

Ruby.

Another scream.

And then, on the soft breeze of a summer's night came the scent of blood. His *Mate's* blood. Rafe was shifting faster than he could think, howling like his own heart had been ripped from his chest. He raced to the back of the house, a lone wolf once again. Theo was gone, already on the road back home. It was up to him to save Ruby. It was up to him to succeed where he had once failed.

He turned the corner of the house into the backyard and his world crashed down around him. Ruby was on her back in the grass. A huge brown and white wolf growled on top of her, his paws pinning her to the ground. Rafe nearly choked on the smell of her blood. It stained the grass around her and his reality flipped, circling back to the most horrific moment of his life. Scarlet dead in front of her home. Murdered by wolves. Except this was worse. So much worse. Because it was his Mate that lay in the grass. It was his own life that spilled out into the night.

"Rafe!"

Ruby's voice yanked him back to the present. She was alive! She fought from beneath the wolf, but he didn't budge. Just turned and snarled at Rafe, keeping Ruby pinned beneath his giant paws. He could have killed her by now but he hadn't. Why not? What the hell did he want?

"Rafe, get this bastard off of me!" Ruby tore at the wolf's fur, ripping out tufts of hair with her fists.

He leapt, a growl escaping his lips, and he knocked the other wolf off Ruby's body. She rolled away, panting and holding her arm. Blood, bright red and smelling like Ruby and life and eternity, seeped through her fingers.

He would kill him. He would kill this wolf and any others that dared to hurt her. He would fucking kill everyone.

His mind went blank of everything except the burning desire to destroy anyone that came near Ruby. He was only vaguely aware of her yelling at him. He only distantly heard her words pleading with him not to chase this bastard of a wolf into the woods. He only barely understood that she stood at the edge of the treeline, begging him to come back.

Rafe saw nothing but the wolf in front of him. He smelled nothing but the fear coming off the animal as he tore through the woods. He heard nothing except the wolves behind him panting as they closed in on him.

He knew their scent. It was the same one that had been around Ruby's house for days now. And one of the wolves on his tail was the wolf from the first attack. But he didn't recognize these wolves from anywhere else, not from his pack, not from any lone wolves within a fifty-mile radius.

Some distant human part of his brain realized that he shouldn't have run after them, that he needed these wolves alive to get answers about who they were and what they wanted. But he couldn't hear that part anymore because the rest of his brain was screaming for blood.

These bastards had attacked his Mate. Over and over again they'd come for her and they wouldn't stop until he made them.

He opened up his stride, gaining ground on the first wolf, dirt and pine needles flying beneath his paws. The coward should turn and fight him, not make Rafe chase him down like a fucking chipmunk, but he nearly had him now. He was nipping at the first wolf's heels when one behind him pounced, landing hard on Rafe's back. He rolled through the dirt and crashed into a tree. The impact slammed the air from his lungs and left him gasping for breath.

The lead wolf, the one with Ruby's blood still on his lips, stood over him now, the other two by his side. Rafe growled low in his throat. A warning.

The lead wolf growled in return and pounced but Rafe rolled and avoided his gnashing jaws. The two other wolves circled him as Rafe pushed to his feet, the trio surrounding him.

Again a distant part of his brain warned that it would be worse if he ended up dead, that it would hurt Ruby more if he never returned. But his wolf side howled for revenge.

These wolves threatened his Mate and neither side of him could let that go. He'd lost one woman in his life to the savagery of his kind, he sure as fuck wasn't going to lose another.

Rafe bared his teeth and pounced.

Chapter Thirty-Six

"Ruby! Ruby!" Lena's voice broke through the clouds of her despair. "Come on, we have to get you inside."

Ruby was kneeling in the dirt at the edge of the woods. Rafe was gone. She looked up at Lena, her tears blurring her sister's concerned face.

"Come on, Ruby-red. You're bleeding." Lena tugged on her hand, but Ruby couldn't find any strength to stand. Her Mate had just run off into the woods to chase a vicious werewolf with at least two more on his tail. Ruby saw them race after him. He was as good as dead. Her Mate was ripped from her, robbing her of a lifetime with him.

Another wail escaped her lips. Lena grabbed her under the arms and hoisted her up, shushing and whispering to her as they hobbled toward the house. Ruby was vaguely aware that she was bleeding and that her shoulder burned with every step. But the pain was nothing compared to the one tearing through her chest.

Lena dragged her back into the house, Ruby weeping and bleeding all over her. She helped her into a kitchen chair and gingerly cleaned her wound. Ruby winced at the sting of peroxide. The pain snapped her out of her spinning thoughts.

"He's my Mate, Lena. I know you don't believe it, but he's it. He's mine." Her voice was clogged with tears. She sounded pitiful.

Lena peered down into her face after wrapping her arm in a bandage. "I think you'll live," she reported.

"Not without him."

"Oh, Ruby."

"I don't know where he went or if he'll come back," she sniffed, wiping her nose on the back of her hand. "There was more than one, Lena. I saw them go after him when he ran. What if he gets killed?"

Lena passed Ruby the box of tissues, her pale eyes seeing everything. Ruby's blotchy face, her runny nose, her bloody shoulder. And maybe seeing more than that. Maybe she always had.

"I believe you. I mean after Theo's little trick, how could I not?" Lena gave her a rueful smile and Ruby couldn't help but return it. "This is all pretty nuts, you know."

"I know."

"Kinda like a dream come true for you though, huh?" Lena put the kettle on and grabbed two mugs from the cabinet.

"Besides the whole getting bitten thing, yeah, it's kinda perfect."

"Sorry I didn't believe you before. I couldn't. Or I didn't want to, I guess."

"I know. I don't really blame you." Honestly, Ruby was impressed her sister hadn't gone running from the house and never come back after Theo's little show. Most people would have, but then again the Bellerose sisters were not most people.

Maybe years of living with Ruby and Millie had desensitized Lena to the utterly bizarre and mildly creepy.

Ruby took a breath, "Lena, I have to tell you something. The day of the accident, I didn't want Mom and Dad to go. Remember?"

Her sister poured the tea and brought it to the table. She slid into the seat across from Ruby. They rarely spoke about that day. "I remember. You threw a fit about it."

"I think I knew."

Lena paused with her mug halfway to her lips. "What?"

Ruby took a breath and plowed forward, finally saying things she'd kept bottled up for years. "I think I knew what was going to happen. I tried to stop it."

Ruby's thoughts filled in the silence that hung heavy in the room. Everything Rafe had told her, everything she'd felt as a child. The way Aunt Millie seemed to have an uncanny knack for knowing where the girls were even when they tried to sneak out. The fact that they could never seem to pin down an exact age for their aunt. Maybe Rafe was right. Maybe they all had this ... this thing. Not that it had happened to her in years, but maybe it was still in there.

"So what are you saying? We're both... what did Rafe call it? Seers?"

Ruby shrugged. "I guess?"

"You saved me that day."

"I should have done more." She'd managed to convince her parents to let the girls stay home alone for the first time, but she couldn't convince them to cancel their plans.

"Ruby, you were eight."

She nodded, her hair swishing over her shoulders. She knew she shouldn't feel guilty about it. It wasn't her fault that the roads were slick, icy weather coming before anyone expected it, but that didn't stop her from waking up in a cold sweat sometimes, the fear and the panic so close to the surface she couldn't breathe.

"It didn't happen again after that. I thought it was a weird coincidence, a dream. And then after a while I let myself believe it had never happened at all."

Lena grabbed her hand. Her fingers were cold and frail, and Ruby squeezed them tighter.

"But now, it's happening to you."

"I don't know what it means, Ruby. The visions are slippery, like I can't grab on to them and when I try to, they just slide through my fingers."

"Maybe this was it? Maybe this attack is what you saw? But I'm fine." Ruby swallowed the word "fine," not wanting to think about what was happening to Rafe. Not wanting to wonder if he was fine too.

Lena shook her head. "They were looking for me."

Ruby's eyes went wide. "For you? How do you know?" She felt guilty for the barrage of questions but this was more than Lena had ever shared about any of this, more than she had ever admitted.

"I saw it. Or pieces of it anyway. When you left my room. They wanted me, those wolves that came. I could feel it." Her sister's eyes were haunted, fear shimmering in their pale depths. "I don't understand why they keep attacking you."

"They must think I can do it too."

"Shit."

Ruby shrugged. "Maybe all seers smell alike? Or maybe they don't realize there's two of us? I don't really know how any of this works."

Lena blew out a long breath. "Well, shit, Ruby. If you don't know after all those years of scary movies and books, then I don't know who would."

Ruby gave her a small smile. It was nice to feel like they were in this together. She leaned back in her chair and pain shot through her shoulder. She winced, a soft hiss escaping her lips.

"You're not going to turn into a werewolf, are you?"

"Uh ... probably not?" Ruby held her shoulder and squeezed her eyes shut, trying desperately not to think about the werewolf currently out fighting for her. He should have listened to her. He should have stayed. He should be the one tending to her injuries. She blew out a frustrated breath.

"He'll come back, Ruby."

Ruby nodded. She met her sister's gaze, feeling like there was more to say. About their parents, about Lena's visions, about being literally tracked and hunted by werewolves. But Ruby didn't know what to say or do about any of that.

Lena untangled her fingers from Ruby's and got up to pour more tea.

"What do we do now?" Ruby asked, her hands curling around her mug, her mind racing.

"We wait for your Mate to come home, I guess." Lena's lips tipped into a smile at the word "Mate." Dark circles hung below her eyes and she was far too pale today, but she was here. Safe.

"Okay, but I'm terrible at waiting."

Lena laughed and pulled out the deck of cards from the junk drawer. "I'll help you pass the time."

Ruby had managed to lose to Lena five times before the frantic knock on the door disrupted their game. She was out of her seat so fast, she jostled the table, spilling tea all over the cards, but still Rafe pounded on the door, the windows rattling in their panes.

She raced to open it, worried he would rip it from the hinges if she didn't get there quick enough. She yanked it open and found him standing on her back deck. Alive and covered in blood.

"Ruby." Her name was torn from the depths of him, rough and ragged. His gaze went immediately to her shoulder. He lifted a hand to touch her but then dropped it to his side. "You're hurt."

"Not really. It's nothing. What about you?" She couldn't stop the horror she was sure covered her face. Couldn't arrange her features into anything normal. Rafe looked like death himself standing among her wildflowers. Blood was splattered across his cheeks. His chest was covered in it. His arms. Jesus, how much of it was his? Was he about to bleed out on her doorstep? Should she call 911? Her head spun, her breath coming in short gasps.

"Ruby, look at me." Her gaze snapped to his. "They're gone. All of them. They can't hurt you anymore."

She swallowed hard. "But you—"

"I won't hurt you anymore either." He was backing away. Leaving.

Wait. Why the hell was he leaving?

"Rafe, stop."

He raised his hands, his fingers caked in dried blood. He looked bigger than usual, his teeth and fingernails longer, like he hadn't fully shifted back to his human form. Like he tried but couldn't find it. She was losing him.

"You're safe now."

"Rafe, please." She reached out toward him and he backed away, shaking his head.

"That's it, Ruby. It's over. We have to be over."

Ruby's throat closed up, squeezed by her overwhelming panic at the thought of Rafe leaving. Hot tears streamed down her face. She looked up at Rafe's tortured expression.

"You're scaring me," she whispered.

He flinched, and she immediately knew it was the wrong thing to say. She needed to explain. She needed to tell him that wasn't how she meant it. She reached for him again but he stayed out of her grasp. His gaze skittered from her face to her injured shoulder, fear and pain flashing in his silver eyes.

"It's better this way." He spit out the words like they were poison. They *were* poison. How could her Mate say anything so absurd? How could he believe it?

"Nothing is better this way." Her words came out strangled and garbled with tears and panic.

But it was too late. He wasn't listening anymore, his eyes scanning the yard one more time for danger before he turned and ran. Before she could say anything else, her Mate was gone.

Horror. Pure horror. It was etched on Ruby's face. Like she'd never seen something quite so disturbing. He'd seen the look before. He knew what it meant to have someone look at you like you were a monster. But he'd been foolish enough to hope he'd never see that look on Ruby's face.

He stumbled back through the trees, trapped somewhere between human and wolf. He didn't have the strength to shift completely. He'd killed all three of the wolves that had attacked Ruby, but they'd put up a good fight. He was exhausted and injured. And his heart literally ached.

Ruby's pale face and wide eyes flashed in his memory. The

way her chest rose and fell in rapid, terrified breaths. The way he must have looked to her, like a mutant covered in gore. How did he ever think he deserved to have her? How had he fallen into this same trap again?

He shook his head, causing a sharp pain to shoot up his neck. He'd been pinned at one point before he managed to flip the other wolf. His muscles ached from the effort. He'd let himself go soft. Maybe his father was right. Maybe for a moment he'd forgotten who he truly was. What he was built for. But once he was back in the fight, his body remembered what to do.

He could still taste the other wolf's blood, acrid on his tongue. He needed to get home and wash it away with a drink, or five. He needed to forget the last week of his life. Erase it. Erase her.

Ruby was safe. Lena saw wolves and blood and he'd taken care of it. Maybe he was wrong about the whole Mate thing. Maybe this was all he was meant to do for her.

His body rebelled at the thought, his muscles tensing as though they would run him back to Ruby against his will. But he couldn't go back. She'd never be safe around him. The last five years of his life had been a lie. He was still the monster his father raised. He had no trouble ripping those wolves apart. All his old instincts had come roaring back and it didn't matter how much time he'd spent working with his hands and sitting at the pub with the locals, pretending to be human. It didn't matter how hard he'd wanted to believe he could be what Ruby needed. In the end, he was still a killer.

All this time he'd been trying to convince her that he was scary and he'd finally done it. Now she'd seen it with her own eyes, how much of a monster he really was. He ran a hand through his tangled hair and his fingers got caught in the dried blood. He was a goddamn mess. No wonder she looked at him like he was a nightmare come to life.

She was better off without him.

The thought rioted against his ribs, his heart rampaging against it, fighting to the end to keep her.

Apparently, fate did make mistakes.

Chapter Thirty-Seven

Ruby staggered back into the house to find Lena wide-eyed at the table. "He left." She collapsed into the closest chair. "Again."

"Oh, Ruby."

She swallowed her tears, despair quickly turning to anger. "Is he fucking kidding?"

Lena drummed her fingers on the worn surface of the kitchen table, thinking. "You should go after him."

"Go after him? No way." Ruby crossed her arms over her chest, her shoulder aching in protest. "I'm done chasing him." Her throat burned with the words. She would never be done chasing him and exhaustion weighed down on her at the thought.

"And what about him being your Mate?" Lena raised a pale eyebrow.

"If this is what it means to have a Mate, then I don't want one." She tipped her head up and yelled at the ceiling. "Okay, universe? Fucking forget it!"

"Ruby, a few hours ago I had to drag you inside bawling

your eyes out. Crying about how you would never love again and that you'd lost the other half of yourself."

"So?" She was pouting but she couldn't seem to stop.

"So, now you're done? You're going to let your literal soulmate just walk out the door?"

Ruby thunked her head on the table and groaned. "It's too hard, Lena. It hurts too much."

Lena ran a hand over her hair, soothing her. It was a sensation Ruby knew well, her sister's comforting touch. Lena had always been there when the sadness about their parents would overwhelm her or when the kids at school got too cruel. Lena had always been her soft place to land and she'd missed it.

"I know. But maybe the hurt is worth it?"

Lucifer wound between Ruby's legs under the table, purring contentedly. Lena had found him after the attack, snoozing peacefully under her bed. Ruby glared at him. "I blame you for this." He stopped and blinked at her with golden eyes. "Okay, fine. It's not your fault." She turned back to her sister, the cat sitting contentedly on her feet.

"I feel like an idiot. I thought he understood me, but he's still convinced I'm better off without him. How many damn times can I tell this man that I want him?"

"Maybe one more? He did just save your life, after all."

Ruby growled. "Well, goddamn it. I never asked him to."

Lena huffed a laugh. "You've always been the brave one, Ruby-red. I just want you to be happy."

Ruby lifted her head. Lena studied her with worry in her clear blue eyes. If she had been the brave one, Lena was the sweet one, the kind and good one. Ruby hated that she couldn't help her.

"I can't leave you here by yourself."

"Ruby, enough with this. I'm fine. The threat is gone. Rafe took care of it. You are perfectly free to go."

"I'm so glad you came to terms with all of this in time to lecture me about what I should do next," Ruby said with a smirk. She never could have imagined having a conversation about her werewolf Mate with her unbeliever sister, but here they were.

"It's my job as the eldest." Lena grinned, her old self shining through again.

Ruby stuck out her tongue. "I liked you better when you were brooding in your room."

A shadow crossed Lena's face and Ruby immediately regretted her words. "Yeah, well…"

"I didn't mean it." Ruby grabbed Lena's hand across the table. "I'm really glad you're here. Even if it's to torment me." Ruby didn't want to be lonely anymore.

Lena smiled and gave her hand a squeeze. "Are you going?"

Ruby blew out a long sigh, delaying the inevitable. "Eventually."

"Eventually?"

It hurt her more than she could express that Rafe still didn't trust her, still didn't trust himself. That even after everything, he believed she didn't want both sides of him, the monster and the man. It was frustrating and infuriating, but breaking through hundreds of years of bullshit was going to take time. Ruby wasn't quitting on her Mate, but she sure as hell needed a minute to gather her strength.

"I think I'll let my wolf-man stew a bit first. Think about what he's done."

"And then?"

"And then I'll go get him." Because of course she would. Because just sitting here right now was taking all her strength.

Because her whole body felt like it was being pulled from her house by a giant Rafe magnet.

Because he was her Mate and she'd fucking fallen in love with him.

The knock on the door scared the shit out of him. He didn't get visitors. Had never wanted them. But now, the idea that Ruby could be on the other side of that door sent his heart racing. He yanked it open, ready to send her away, ready to list all the reasons they couldn't be together, ready to kiss her until she whimpered, but he didn't get to do any of those things. It wasn't Ruby at his door.

"Ma?"

"So this is where you've been hiding all this time?" she asked, her shrewd gaze scanning the outside of his cabin. She was bathed in the yellow glow of the porch light, looking eerily out of place on his doorstep.

"Not hiding," he huffed.

Nell hummed knowingly. Of course he was hiding. He'd been hiding for five years. He was hiding from Ruby right now.

"Can I come in?"

Rafe nodded, unable to turn her away, and let his mother glide past him into his cabin. It was the first time anyone from his pack had been in his space. Having her here sent a shiver of unease through his gut. This was his sanctuary and even though his stepmother had taken care of him in his childhood, she'd done nothing to stop his father's abuse as he got older. His feelings for the woman were nothing if not complicated and more complicated feelings were the last thing he needed.

All he wanted to do was curl up in the corner and lick his wounds. Alone.

Nell looked around, taking in the cramped space. She ran a hand over the stack of books on his end table, trailed her fingers over the blankets on the back of the couch, and let out a small sigh that Rafe found unreadable. Was she expecting more?

"What are you doing here?" Rafe sounded like an asshole even to himself but he didn't care. The woman who raised him hadn't come looking for him in five years, and he didn't need her here now.

Nell turned to face him, a crease in her brow. "You left without saying goodbye."

Rafe nearly laughed. Leaving without a goodbye was the least of his crimes. "Now's not a good time."

His mother's gaze landed on his chest, his various injuries still on display. "What happened?" Her pale green eyes were nearly translucent as she studied him. The concern on her face only tied the knot in his stomach tighter.

"A fight."

Nell blew out another long sigh, letting her gaze flick over him one more time. "I see you don't want me in your space. I—I only thought you might need someone to talk to. Family."

She moved back toward the door while that word "family" burrowed into Rafe's gut. Why would he need a family now? He'd survived this long without them.

He glanced down at his slashed torso, remembering the look on Ruby's face when he'd showed up on her doorstep. His stomach twisted again, the pain sharp and desperate.

"Wait."

Nell froze with her hand on the doorknob.

"Why now? Why'd you come? I know it's not about some bullshit goodbye."

She chuckled softly and turned to face him. "Let's make a cup of tea and talk about it." She was already moving toward the kitchen, settling herself down at his table, leaving him no chance to reject her.

He moved silently around the room, putting the kettle on and gathering mugs. He'd washed the blood from his hands, but he was still a mess. It was a small comfort that Nell didn't care. For years it was perfectly normal for Rafe and his brothers to return home bloodied and injured. Sometimes it was all in fun. Others it wasn't. Toward the, end it was life or death.

Rafe set a mug in front of his mother and wondered for the hundredth time how much she knew about his father's plans. Did she know before her sons entered that ring what the Alpha intended? It was clear to everyone that his father pitted his sons against each other, that their whole life was an endless stream of competitions. But did his stepmother know that their last fight was to the death?

He shook the thoughts free and sat across from Nell in the tiny kitchen.

She ran a hand over the top of the table, smoothing her palm along the dark wood. "I heard you were making things."

"How?"

She shrugged. "Nymphs talk. I always ask about you."

Rafe grunted.

"Where's the girl?" Nell cut to the chase, pinning him with her ethereal stare.

"Home."

"Oh, Rafe." Nell shook her head, her hair whispering across her back.

"What?" He couldn't seem to get more than one word past the hot ache in his throat. His mother was finally here and Ruby was gone. His poor brain couldn't seem to process it all.

She tipped her head, studying him. "The girl is your Mate. I was sure you knew."

Rafe's eyes widened, his heart tripping over itself just hearing his mother voice the truth. "It doesn't matter."

It was Nell's turn to look shocked. "Doesn't matter? Doesn't matter!" She slammed her hands on the table, rattling the tea cups. "How can you say that?"

"How can you care?" he fired back. "I thought we didn't believe in that bullshit in our pack? Remember? We mate for strength and humans are weak." He rose from the table and turned his back, unable to look at his mother's horrified face.

His breath heaved in and out of his lungs, burning with each inhale and exhale. His father had been right. Humans were weak, so easily injured, so quick to die.

Rafe's lungs squeezed tighter, his throat closing. Ruby's body in the grass, under that fucking wolf. Her blood. Scarlet's blood, her vacant eyes staring up at him. It was his fault. He'd done that to them. Ruby could have *died*. He should have never gotten near her. When will he stop being so goddamn selfish?

Nell's hand on his back startled him out of his spiraling thoughts.

"Just breathe," she whispered, the warmth of her fingers a small comfort. "We'll figure it out."

Rafe let out a bitter laugh. "There's nothing to figure out. I'm a fucking monster and now she knows it." His voice was raw, broken. "I can't let things end the same way this time."

"Nothing is the same."

He looked at her over his shoulder. "You don't know what you're talking about."

"She's your Mate, Rafe. That changes everything."

He let out a strangled groan, the word "Mate" like claws down his back.

"Tell me what happened. Why are you all torn up?"

Rafe sighed and turned, leaning against the counter. He took in the sight of his mother standing in his kitchen, her familiar scent filling his nose, and he was just so damn tired of being alone.

"The wolves following Ruby attacked again. I got there in time... She...she's okay." Even as he said it, he barely believed it. She was okay. "I chased the bastards down." He swallowed hard, the memory of the fight still fresh in his mind. "I took care of it."

Nell ran a hand down his arm, avoiding his injuries. "You always were the sensitive one."

A startled laugh escaped him. "The sensitive one?"

"These things always bothered you more than your brothers."

"These things? Killing? Seeing people I love get mauled?"

Nell flinched. "I should have done more. I know that, Rafe. But just know that as much as you were under your father's control, so was I. For decades that man controlled everything in my life." Shadows crossed Nell's face and a layer of guilt was added to Rafe's swirl of emotions.

"Well, the bastard is dead."

Nell huffed. "Yes, he is."

Silence stretched between them. Rafe didn't know what else to say. It didn't really matter if his mother could heal all the wounds of his childhood; he only brought danger into Ruby's life.

"How did you know she was my ... my Mate?"

"A mother knows." She gave him a rare smile. "That's why I came. I know what you grew up believing. I remember, of course. But I've seen it, Rafe."

He flinched. "Not you and my father?"

Nell shook her head violently. "Oh, God no. He wanted me for my speed."

Rafe swallowed the bile that rose in his throat at the mention of how his father chose his mates.

"But my sister, she left the pack before you were born. She found her true Mate, a lone wolf she met on a hunt."

Rafe's heart sped up just hearing that other Mated pairs existed, were even possible.

"Devon wanted to pair her with a member of the pack, but she couldn't bear it, knowing her true Mate was out there. So she left." Nell paused, her fingers squeezing his forearm. "She couldn't fight it and neither can you. It will kill you."

It already was killing him. He'd been apart from Ruby for only a few hours and already he could barely breathe, barely think. What would days of separation do? Years? Hot panic settled in his gut.

"And what about her? What if I led those bastards right to her?"

Nell shook her head. "It's bigger than just this girl. Something is going on. Knox is worried."

Rafe perked up at that piece of information. "Worried about what?"

She dropped her hand and went back to her tea, settling in at the table. "I don't know. He's been nervous, tense, like he knows something is coming but he hasn't told us yet."

Something's coming...

"Shit." Rafe scrubbed a hand down his face. "Ruby's sister keeps saying the same thing."

Nell went still. "What do you mean?"

His mother had beaten down his defenses and he no longer had the strength to keep secrets from her. "Ruby's sister Lena has visions. She has for a while, but she can't remember much.

She says, 'They're coming,' and she saw something about wolves. And blood."

Nell's eyes were wide. "A seer?"

"I guess."

She slammed her mug down. "That's what those wolves were after! You didn't lead them anywhere. They were obviously tracking down the sister."

A tiny trickle of relief coursed through his veins.

"Well, they're dead now. So it's over."

Nell raised her eyebrows. "Let's hope."

Fear quickly snuffed out his relief. "What do you mean?"

"There's too many questions left unanswered. Where were the wolves from? What did they want with her?"

"I don't know. Maybe they attacked Ruby to draw Lena out?" Rafe suggested. He'd been so hell bent on keeping Ruby safe he hadn't really given thought to the bigger picture. "They want to know what she knows?" Possibilities raced through Rafe's head. Maybe they wanted to get rid of Lena before she could decipher her visions and warn them about what was coming? Or maybe they wanted her for what she could do for them, for what she could see. Knowing what was coming next would make any pack stronger. But would they risk more wolves' lives to get her? Who were they?

Nell nodded. "Makes sense. What did Knox say about it all?"

"He blew me off. Said he'd send out more patrols." Rafe huffed in frustration.

"He really is trying. For the pack," she said, taking a long sip of tea.

"As long as he's taking care of you." Rafe blew out a long sigh, realizing as he said it that it was true. He wanted his pack to be taken care of, his people. If his brother was figuring out how to do that without terrorizing and manipulating everyone, then good for him.

"He is." Nell glanced at him, looking like she might say more, but she dropped the subject of his brother. "I should get back." She stood, her chair legs scraping along the floor boards. "Just think about what I said. Things are different this time, Rafe. This girl is the one for you. Don't let her get away because of some misplaced guilt. Don't be afraid." She squeezed his hand, her green eyes glinting with tears.

"I'll think about it." It was probably all he would think about for the rest of his life. He walked his mother to the front door. "If you can, I'd like to know if you hear anything that might affect Ruby or her sister. I still want to…" *Keep her safe, be with her forever, protect her at all costs, wrap myself around her and never let go.* "keep an eye on things."

Nell arched an eyebrow. "Of course. I'll see what I can find out." She opened the door into the muggy night, the sounds of crickets quickly filling the house. "And don't stay away so long next time, Rafe." She reached up on her toes and kissed his cheek.

He wanted to argue. To tell her he had nothing to return for, but maybe that wasn't true anymore. Maybe his family was worth returning for. "Yeah, we'll see."

"Goodnight, sweet boy."

A wash of tender memoires swept over him at the nickname she'd given him as a pup. The sensitive one. He nearly laughed again.

"Goodnight, Ma." He stepped out onto the porch to watch her go, nearly letting the next words dissolve in his throat, but he forced them out. "You could visit, too. I mean … you could come back again some time."

Nell's face lit up in the moonlight. "I would love that." She shifted into a sleek mahogany-colored wolf and raced off into the night.

Rafe lowered himself onto the old wooden steps and watched the fireflies flicker through the trees. The conversation with his mother ran through his mind on a loop.

She was probably right: he hadn't led the wolves to Ruby. They were on the trail of a seer. Thank God Ruby hadn't manifested any seer abilities. The one thing he'd prayed for when he thought they could be together was now the thing he was hoping never showed up.

He knew in his bones Ruby was his Mate. She hadn't run from him. She'd accepted what he truly was. Or she had until she'd seen it in action.

You're scaring me.

Her words echoed in his heart. He'd finally done it. He'd scared his fearless Ruby. It didn't matter if he let his guilt over Scarlet's death go, or forgave his mother, or returned to his pack. He'd never get over the look on Ruby's face, the terror in her eyes. He wouldn't do that to her again.

He had to stay away.

Right?

Chapter Thirty-Eight

R uby didn't know where Rafe lived but it didn't seem to matter. Her feet carried her down the overgrown path through the trees, never hesitating. It was late, dark except for the full moon and the occasional flash of heat lightning. It lit the path in front of her at random intervals, allowing her only glimpses at where she was going. The dark silhouettes of the trees reached up toward the sky.

But it didn't matter. The darkness, the hour, the impending storm—none of it mattered as long as she got to him. She was still hurt. Hurt that he'd left her, hurt that he still didn't trust her. But nothing compared to the fear and the ache she felt when thinking about living without him.

She had known from the beginning that she would fight to keep him. She knew it like she knew her parents still existed somewhere, like she knew the chill of fall would follow this record-breaking heat. Ruby knew Rafe before he appeared from the shadows, before he fought those other wolves, before he realized she was his Mate.

He belonged with her, *to* her. He always had.

She knew it wouldn't be easy to convince this man, who had been told his whole life he had to be violent and strong and stoic, that he could be soft and open and safe. But she was damn well going to keep trying.

The crickets buzzed around her, louder in the direction she needed to go. The path seemed to clear in front of her, fireflies lighting the way. Ruby's feet kept moving down the trail. She knew the way like she'd seen it before. She walked until her toes ached in her boots and her back was tight and sore.

When the little cabin appeared between the trees, the porch light glowing in welcome, she knew without a doubt it was his. It was time to be as brave as everyone seemed to think she was. It was time to lay her heart at the feet of her wolf.

One knock on the door was surprising, but the second in one night was unheard of. Rafe shuffled to the door. Everything hurt, but not from the fight. His body ached with the loss of Ruby. It had been less than twelve hours and he was about to say uncle, to show up at her house and throw himself at her feet. He was a weak son of a bitch and he was almost done caring. Nell was right. He couldn't fight it. Living an eternity without Ruby would slowly and painfully kill him.

He opened the door and found her standing on his porch. He blinked, thinking he'd hallucinated her, but there she stood, hands on her wide hips, the dark of the woods all around her. He gripped the door frame tight to keep from keeling over.

"You are an idiot." The first words out of her mouth startled a laugh out of him.

"I know."

She narrowed her dark eyes at him. "Are you hurt?" She

glanced over his body, cataloging his new wounds. He'd showered the blood off after his mother left, and his injuries were already healing, but he had a patchwork of scratches and scrapes along his arms and torso, and a pretty big gash in his side. His hair hung damp around his bare shoulders and he wished he was wearing more than just a pair of gym shorts.

"Not really." His gaze fell on her arm where someone, Lena he imagined, had bandaged it up for her. "Your arm, how is it?"

"It's fine." She crossed her arms over her chest and continued to glare at him. Crickets and cicadas buzzed around them, and the moths fought for the best spot in front of the porch light. The night was still and humid. Another storm, besides the one Ruby had brought to his doorstep, was in the air.

"You shouldn't have come here at night. How did you even find this house?"

Ruby huffed. "I could find you anywhere."

Rafe's heart flipped at her words. "Ruby—"

"Don't you dare." She cut him off, poking him in the chest with a single finger. "Don't you fucking dare say a word about me staying away from you or so help me God..."

"Why are you doing this?" His words were ragged, broken. Why was she making this harder? Why drag out his misery? "You've seen for yourself, I'm not hurt. Go back home now, Ruby."

"Fuck you, Rafe." He flinched at her words but she kept going, closing in on him until his back was against the door. "I didn't come to check on your boo-boos. I came to ask you why you left me. Again." Her voice broke on the last word and Rafe's world shattered.

He grabbed her face in his hands and she gasped. "I had to," he growled.

Ruby blinked, tears sliding down her cheeks. "Why would you think that?"

Rafe leaned his forehead against hers and breathed in her cinnamon-spiced scent, letting his fingers slip into her hair. "I killed them. I know how I looked when I showed up at your door. I saw your face, Ruby."

She was shaking her head, rolling her forehead against his.

"You were terrified," he insisted, remembering the look in her eyes and the monster he'd seen reflected in them.

You're scaring me.

"Terrified that you were hurt! Terrified that some of that blood was yours!" She put her hands on his chest and pushed away from him again. "Just like I had been terrified the whole time you were gone, out there fighting by your damn self. Damn it, Rafe." She turned and put her hands on the railing, looking out into the night. Her shoulders rose and fell with every breath. His whole body screamed at him to go to her, to wrap her up in his arms and never let her go, but his fear kept him rooted to the spot. Those old voices, the ones that said he was a monster, that he wasn't good enough, were hard to silence.

"I can't promise you'll be safe around me. As much as I try to escape it, my life is violent and dangerous. I killed without thinking tonight, Ruby. I can't promise I won't again."

She didn't answer, continuing to stare out into the trees. He would never forgive himself if anything ever happened to her. His heart would stop with hers.

"I'm not good for you, Ruby. I don't belong around humans. You saw it. You saw me."

She spun to face him, her eyes wide and cheeks flushed with anger. Her voice was raw when she spoke. "There are no guarantees, Rafe. I lost my parents when I was eight years old, not because of monsters but because of fucking icy road conditions." She took a long shuddering breath. "This is the only promise I can make you. I see you. And I'm still here. That's all I want from you in return."

He shook his head, trying to force the voices of the past to leave him, Ruby's words thundering through him. It was time to listen to the woman right in front of him. Not the voices of people long dead. But the voices were loud, persistent. He couldn't silence them, even for her.

"Ruby, I'm sorry. I can't." His voice cracked miserably, but he forced the words out.

Tears streamed down her face and he reached out to touch her, wanting to comfort her even as he hurt her, but she backed away. "Don't do this. Don't throw this away." Her voice was thick with pain.

"It's not natural!" he snapped, grasping for anything to make her go, to make this end before he lost the strength to push her away. "We don't make sense."

She flinched at his words, at the thunder of his voice.

"Tonight reminded me of that." He kept going, severing their bond for good. "I'm a killer, Ruby. I tore those wolves' throats out and I would do it again. You need to stay away from me before you end up like Scarlet."

She shook her head, looking like she would say more, like she would fight him. Fight *for* him. But he watched as resignation settled over her like a fog rolling in over the fields. She was done. His brave girl was done fighting.

He'd made sure of it.

Chapter Thirty-Nine

O n the second day of battling every instinct in his body to go throw himself at Ruby's feet, Rafe returned to his pack. There was no way this thing was settled just because he'd killed a couple of rogue wolves, and Rafe hadn't slept in days. He needed assurance that Ruby really was safe. He needed to know it was over and that he could walk away. Rafe needed every excuse to hover around Ruby gone.

He meant what he told her that night on his porch. The worst night of his miserable life. Taking down those wolves reminded him of exactly who and what he was. A killer and an animal. He had no place in a human's bed or heart.

But his body wouldn't rest. He couldn't eat. He couldn't sleep. He was haunted by thoughts of Ruby's life being in danger. If there was still a threat out there, he needed to know and he needed it gone. It was the only way to get Ruby Bellerose out of his life for good.

The thought made bile rise up in the back of his throat. Any thought of removing Ruby from his life caused a violent physical reaction. He'd thrown up everything he'd eaten ever

317

since the night she ran from his porch crying. But Rafe didn't have time for that now and he certainly didn't need his pack seeing him lose his lunch while he cried. Rafe pushed it all down and strode into the werewolf camp.

Not surprisingly, Knox was thrilled to see him.

"Fuck, Rafe. Again?" His brother rose from his spot by the fire and strode to where Rafe stood on the edge of his campsite. The smell of roasted rabbit wafted to Rafe's nose. His stomach turned.

"Twice in one week. What now?"

"Three more wolves, Knox. Another attack," Rafe growled, his blood heating just thinking about the fight. "What the hell is going on?"

Knox ran a hand through his hair and then gestured for Rafe to follow him away from the other men seated around Knox's site. Curious pack members watched them go, eyes sharp and assessing, but Rafe didn't have time for all that today. He just needed answers, needed to settle the anxiety simmering under his skin, needed to fucking rest.

"What happened?" Knox asked when they were at the edge of the camp.

"I killed them."

"Jesus Christ, Rafe. This isn't the dark ages. You can't just go around killing—"

"They attacked my— Ruby." The word Mate echoed through his skull but he couldn't bring himself to speak it. He didn't deserve to, not since he sent her away.

Knox's eyes widened a fraction of an inch. "Where is she anyway?"

"Home. Safe." He hoped. Being this far away from her even during the day made him feel like his skin was too tight, like his lungs didn't work.

"Does she know?" Knox cleared his throat. "That you think she's your ... Mate?" He said the word like it left a bad taste in his mouth.

Rafe knew if Ruby was there right now, she would warn him about his murder face. But she wasn't, so he let his face do what it wanted. He bared his teeth at his brother. "She knows. But it's not worth it."

"Oh?"

Rafe kicked a rock and watched it skitter through the trees. "Devon was right about humans. Too fragile."

Knox gave a stiff nod, his silver eyes so like their father, studying Rafe while they stood in the dappled sunlight of the afternoon.

"I didn't come here for that," Rafe continued. "I came to find out what you know about these attacks." Rafe lowered his voice and leaned in closer, fully aware of the perked ears all around them. "Nell mentioned you were worried about something. She said she felt like there was something on the horizon. Something bad."

His brother narrowed his eyes. "There's nothing to worry about."

"There is!" Rafe nearly exploded. "There clearly is, Knox! What are you going to do about it?"

Knox growled low in his throat. A warning. "I'm protecting my pack. My concerns don't extend beyond that."

Rafe opened and closed his fists at his side, for once wishing he could get back in the ring with his brother and kick the shit out of him. He nearly turned to storm off, but the image of Ruby lying bloody in the grass wouldn't leave him. If there was some way to help her while still keeping his distance he needed to do it.

"Lena is a seer. Ruby's sister. I think it's connected somehow."

Knox froze, surprise written across his face. He quickly schooled his features. "Can't be. There hasn't been a seer around here in decades."

Rafe pushed forward. "She has visions."

"And what does she see?" Knox crossed his arms, leaning back against the trunk of a tree. Calm, cool, completely in control again.

Rafe hesitated. How much should he tell his brother? "She can't understand them. She doesn't remember when she wakes up."

"Hm." Knox nodded. "What good is a seer if she can't remember her visions?" He smirked.

Rafe growled in frustration. "You don't think it's odd that these sisters are being attacked and one of them has visions?"

"Well, only one sister has been attacked. Technically."

"Lena never leaves the damn house! But Ruby—" Rafe swallowed hard, the breath leaving his lungs in a painful rush. Ruby was out there every damn night. An easy target. What the hell was he doing here arguing with his asshole brother?

"Never mind. Forget I said anything."

"I said I would send out more patrols, and I will."

Rafe huffed. "A hell of a lot of good that does me."

"You could come back."

Knox's words dropped between them like stones into a still pond. They stood and silently felt the ripples.

"Come back to the pack?"

"Yeah." Knox cleared his throat. "If you're tired of being alone."

"I don't think that's a good idea."

His brother pushed away from the tree, coming closer. "You

could bring those sisters. We'd protect them. We'd protect your Mate."

Unease settled in Rafe's gut. "You don't believe in Mates."

Knox shrugged. "Maybe you changed my mind." His smile was slow and calculated.

Rafe shouldn't have come back here. He was right when he told Ruby that Knox would only use Lena to help the pack. He didn't know what his brother was plotting but he knew he didn't give a shit about Ruby and her sister. Or him. He just wanted the power a seer would give him, the edge he would have against other packs and a future he couldn't control.

"Well, change it back. I didn't claim her as mine. And I'm not going to."

Knox shrugged again, casual even as he held Rafe's stare with his own. "The offer stands if you get tired of protecting her by yourself. You know how that turned out last time."

Rafe's body slammed into Knox's before he could stop himself, his hands fisted in his brother's shirt. He pressed Knox against the tree he had been so casually leaning against, scraping his back against the bark.

"Fuck. You."

Knox didn't bother to struggle in his grasp, not even giving Rafe the satisfaction of fighting back. "I'm just reminding you what's at stake here, little brother. You couldn't save that other pretty human from our own father. How are you going to save this one?"

Every word sunk into the marrow of Rafe's bones, his every fear laid out in front of him. He released Knox's shirt and stumbled backward.

"I'm not bringing her here." He was breathless like they'd fought physically and not with words.

Knox held his hands up in surrender. "I'm just trying to help you out. Two human women under my protection is the last thing I need. But if you don't want my help, stop showing up here." Knox's expression was tight, his stare hard. The coolness had left his demeanor, replaced with something else. Something like hurt and, simmering beneath it, worry.

His brother was a good liar, better than most wolves. But Rafe could see it now. The Alpha was scared.

"Consider this my last visit." Rafe stormed away from his brother, praying he hadn't just made things much, much worse.

Ruby managed to pull herself out of bed today. It had been three days, seven hours, and fifty-two minutes since Rafe stood on her porch covered in blood, and three days, three hours, and forty-one minutes since she stumbled away from his cabin a broken mess. Not that she was counting. Not thatevery minute was imprinted on her soul. Nope. Ruby was really fucking fine.

And werewolf drama aside, she had bills to pay. So she'd forced herself to get up, stuffed her feet into her boots and her tits into her bra and clocked in to her shift.

Any hope she'd had of forgetting about Rafe while she was at work quickly evaporated when she walked into the dining room. Rafe was imprinted all over this damn place. His favorite seat at the bar, his beautiful tables that Ruby couldn't seem to stop running her fingers over every time she went by, the spot where he almost killed a drunk frat boy for her. Being at work was like wading through one long "Ruby and Rafe's best moments" montage.

Getting out of bed was a grave error.

"Jesus, Ruby. You look like crap."

She rested her tray on the bar while Macy filled the drinks for her table. "Thanks, Mace. Sweet of you to say."

Her boss gave her a lopsided smile. "Sorry, but I mean really, you okay? What's going on? You never miss a shift."

What was going on? Well, she and her sister were being hunted by werewolves, her one true Mate had rejected her, and she was really tired of trying to convince him he was exactly what she wanted. But none of those things felt acceptable to say out loud.

"Rafe and I got in a fight." Got in a fight, broke up forever. One of those.

Macy's eyebrows rose. It was more than Ruby had ever shared with her; Ruby always opted to keep things professional. But at the moment, the confession seemed like such an understatement, Ruby let it spill out.

"I can't seem to convince him that we make sense together." Ruby bit her bottom lip. She would not add crying to this little girl-talk moment.

Macy studied her with sympathetic eyes. "Men, am I right?" she said after a beat, and Ruby burst out laughing at the comment from her spectacularly gay manager.

"You are definitely right."

"So what happened?"

Ruby shrugged, unable to put the full weight of the past few days into words. "I don't know. He seems convinced that he's doing me a favor by staying away. Like he's protecting me somehow when all he's doing is hurting me."

Macy nodded, considering. "So what are you going to do?"

Ruby balanced the tray on her hand and spoke the words over her shoulder. "I wish I knew."

Macy's concerned gaze followed her through the bar.

Ruby let the hum of the crowd and the monotony of the work wear away the tension of the day. Would she ever feel normal again? Would she ever feel like she wasn't missing a chunk of herself? She didn't know. Certainly not today. Today she felt like she was walking around without her heart, like the space behind her ribs was hollow. But that wasn't right either. She wasn't empty. She was aching, like a giant walking bruise.

It was different from when her parents died. Her parents' death had left her feeling alone and scared, like the world no longer made sense. But her aunt helped put the pieces back together. The loss of Rafe was like the world itself had gone dark. If only she could find him lurking in the shadows.

Part of her screamed to try again, to never stop fighting for what they had, for what they could have. But every time she thought of doing it, all she could see was his face set in that tormented grimace, the certainty that they shouldn't be together stamped across his features. How could she possibly fight that? How could she battle what was in his own heart?

"I forgot to tell you," Macy said as she went back to the bar for another round of beers. Ruby rested her tray on the bar, happy for the distraction from her swirling thoughts.

"Yeah?"

"Some guy came looking for you this afternoon."

Ruby's heart stopped and the tray wobbled in her hands. She steadied it on the sticky surface of the bar. "Who?"

"He didn't say."

It wasn't Rafe, of course it wasn't Rafe. If it had been him Macy would have just said so. *Calm down, stupid heart.*

"So what did he want?"

"He just asked if you were around. When I said no, he left. Didn't even bother ordering anything."

Ruby swallowed hard, her mouth suddenly bone dry. Werewolves weren't always wolves. Sometimes they were men. Could one of them have been sniffing around here? Were they back, more of them?

"What did he look like?" Ruby asked, trying to keep her voice calm.

"Tall. Like really tall. Dark hair with gray at the temples. A beard." Macy wiped the sweat from her brow with the back of her hand. The AC was on the fritz again. "Actually he kind of reminded me of Rafe."

Knox. The name rang through her like a warning bell. Knox, the Alpha of Rafe's pack, was here looking for her. What the hell was that all about? Maybe he thought of more to tell them after they left? Maybe he wanted to help?

As much as Ruby wanted to believe that, her strangled heartbeat said otherwise. There was no way in hell Knox being here was any sort of good omen.

"Hm. Strange." She scrunched up her face like she was trying to think of who this mysterious man could be. "Not sure. Maybe some long-lost cousin," she said with a forced laugh.

"Well, don't worry. I never give out my employees' information."

The tension in Ruby's body eased, even as she glanced over her shoulder at the door as if expecting Knox to saunter in at any moment.

"Thanks."

"If he wants to track you down, he can use the internet like the rest of us."

Macy meant it as a joke, but the idea of Knox trying to track her down sent shivers down Ruby's body. And not the good kind.

Macy's gaze flicked to where Ruby held the tray. She'd been avoiding her injured shoulder all night, but had forgotten in her muddled confusion about Knox. She hissed in pain and switched the tray to the other side. The damn bite was still sore.

The other woman's brow crinkled in concern. "If you ever need anything, just let me know. Okay, Ruby?" Macy's smile was kind and genuine, and Ruby allowed herself to smile back, nodding at Macy's offer, before returning to her customers. Maybe she'd had a friend here all along. Even with her broken heart maybe she had at least two people who would help her pick up the pieces.

Her shift was nearly over when she spotted Callie in the corner booth.

"Hey, we're closing up soon, but can I get you something?" Ruby asked, leaning against the edge of the table. She was surprised Callie was alone tonight. She rarely came in without Sawyer.

"Actually, I wanted to talk to you for a minute. If you can spare it."

Ruby glanced around the empty bar. "Yeah, I think I can spare it." She slid into the booth next to the little blonde witch, sighing in relief to be off her feet. "What's up?"

Callie studied her in the dim light of the bar and Ruby knew she was seeing exactly what Macy saw. She looked and felt like shit. Callie's eyebrows drew together in concern but she didn't comment on Ruby's less than stellar appearance.

"My grandmother sent me some books that I thought might help you with your … uh … situation." Callie pushed the stack of books toward Ruby and she ran a hand over the top. The covers were soft and worn, old and exactly how you would picture a book filled with ancient wisdom. If she wasn't exhausted and heartbroken, she would have been psyched to flip through them all night.

"Can you give me the Cliff's Notes? I don't think I'm up for studying right now."

"Sure, of course." Callie scooted closer, dropping her voice, not that there was anyone around to hear them. "From what I could find, clairvoyance seems to run in families."

Ruby groaned. "Yeah, that seems to be the case."

Callie blinked her blue eyes in surprise. "Have you started having visions too?"

Ruby shrugged. "Maybe? Maybe a prophetic dream or two. I'm not sure it matters anymore."

"What's going on?"

She couldn't bear to tell the story again. "It just doesn't matter. I appreciate this though. I really do, but the attackers are gone, and me and Lena just want to get back to normal."

"But they can be controlled. The visions. She just needs to learn how." Callie put her hand over Ruby's on the table. "I understand how overwhelming it all is, trust me. I tried to run away from my powers, but it didn't work. You can't outrun it."

"Are you like two hundred years old too?" Ruby asked, examining Callie for any signs that she might be older than the very young twenty-one that she claimed to be. She didn't want to talk about Lena's powers or her own, or the fact that she had no idea if her parents had them too, or why no one bothered to tell them about it. It was all too much.

"No. Witches are more human than most other … uh … others. We live a little longer than the average human, but that's mostly because we're just very health-conscious."

"Oh, right. Of course."

Callie smiled at her sympathetically. "I'll leave these with you. They might help."

"Thanks. Sorry, I'm kind of a mess right now."

"No need to apologize." Callie stood to leave but paused beside the table. "Witches don't have Mates, but I know what it's like to be apart from your person."

Ruby slumped down in the booth. "Were we that obvious?"

She remembered that day at Callie and Sawyer's apartment. At the time she had no idea what Rafe was to her, only that she wanted to jump his bones.

Callie shrugged. "Witch's intuition, I guess." She ran her hand over the top of the table Rafe had made. "I'm around if you need anything."

Ruby nodded and Callie gave her one last smile.

"It'll work out in the end, Ruby."

As her witchy-friend walked away Ruby really hoped that little comment was a witch's intuition too. She needed all the help she could get.

Chapter Forty

He was here. Every hair on her body stood at attention. Rafe was in the woods. She could feel him. Ruby sucked in a deep breath as though she could inhale him into her lungs and keep him locked inside her chest.

She'd thought she sensed him the night before but hadn't been sure. Now she was sure. He was there again. Their old game was back in play, but now with the familiar zing of excitement came the desperate longing for what she was missing.

She strode down the path, pretending to ignore the weight of his stare from the shadows, pretending to be immune to his presence when all she really wanted to do was drop down in the dirt at his feet and beg him to come back to her. But she didn't. She wouldn't.

Instead she let him walk beside her, his steady breathing and quiet footsteps comforting her aching heart. Neither of them spoke but Ruby knew he was getting closer, and could feel his warmth beside her. Perhaps if she turned and peered into the darkness she would catch a glimpse of her wolf. But she kept her eyes on the path ahead of her, using her phone to light only the dirt in front of her feet.

"I miss you," she whispered to the darkness.

No answer other than rustling leaves in the branches overhead.

"I miss watching movies with you. I know *Twilight* was secretly your favorite." She paused, hoping he wouldn't be able to resist arguing about his least favorite werewolf portrayal in a teen drama. "Team Jacob all the way, right?"

Nothing.

She kept walking and felt him keep stride beside her. "I definitely miss you making me breakfast. Lena tried yesterday and I had to pretend to like my toast burnt and my eggs runny."

Still nothing.

Ruby blew out a sigh and adjusted her bag on her shoulder. "This purse is awfully heavy. I sure wish a big strong man would come out and carry it for me," she said in her best damsel-in-distress voice, hand on her forehead for dramatic effect.

A wolfy huff cut through the sound of the crickets. Ruby bit down on a smile. "I miss that wolfy sound you always make."

He did it again, the low breathy noise teasing Ruby with its closeness.

"I'm glad you're still there. Even though I should be pissed at you. Even though I kind of am."

They were nearly at her house now and she dreaded the moment he would leave her again. "For a minute there, I really thought this would work. I thought we understood each other. I thought we were inevitable…"

She swallowed the tears that rose up in her throat. She considered telling him about Knox's little visit. It might draw him out; his instinct to protect her was clearly still intact. But she'd told him before, she didn't want a bodyguard. She just wanted him.

"If this is the only way I can have you, then I'll take it. Just knowing you're there, listening. I'll take it."

The light from her windows spilled into the yard, and she stopped at the edge, not wanting to leave him. She turned in time to see silver eyes watching her from the dark before she made her way slowly to the door.

The wood was covered in scratches, a permanent reminder of how this all started, of why Rafe was so terrified to be with her. How her sweet werewolf could ever think he was anything like the deranged wolves who attacked her was incomprehensible. As angry as she was with him for turning her away, Ruby knew Rafe was the one in more pain here.

She just hoped it didn't take too long for him to realize what she already knew. She would love him for the rest of her life. He'd been right all along. Fate didn't make mistakes.

Rafe waited for her every night for a week at the edge of the woods just like before. He walked her home just like before. He stuck to the shadows just like before. His life was running on a tortuous loop and it was his own damn fault.

Knox's words about keeping Ruby safe were like a toxin in his blood. Every time he thought he was close to purging them, they came back to the surface. But Knox had forgotten something. A truth Rafe kept reminding himself of, the fact like a balm to his wounds. Scarlet didn't want him, didn't accept him. But Ruby did.

She had all along. Even her terror had been for his safety, not about his misdeeds. And still he'd pushed her away. Still he balked at being with her, at having the one thing that would make him happy after living centuries with only half a soul.

He was an idiot.

And for some reason she was still talking to him, still holding on to this thing between them because it was too fucking precious to let it go. Still acting like he wasn't a monster at all. And slowly it was sinking in, slowly it was replacing things he'd thought about himself for years.

Ruby's steady belief in him, along with Nell's words, worked to chip away at the image he had of himself. He'd always been the sensitive one, she'd said. Had everyone seen him differently than he'd seen himself for years? Even Knox, underneath his posturing bullshit, seemed hurt that Rafe had left and never returned. The brother he was sure wanted him dead wanted him to come home.

With every day that passed, every night spent walking beside his Mate, Rafe's confidence in his decision to stay away from Ruby wavered. He'd acted out of decades-old fear and a lifetime of believing he wasn't worth loving.

But Nell loved him. His brothers … tolerated him. Maybe even wanted him around? Could Ruby love him too?

"Macy sent home chicken parm tonight." Ruby's chatter interrupted his thoughts and Rafe smiled. Chicken parm was her favorite.

"That should make me happy." Her voice was too far away so he slunk closer, stealthy even in his human form. "But food can only do so much, you know?"

He winced. He couldn't keep doing this. He was hurting her. His Mate was in pain because of him. It was worse than finding her bleeding in the grass. He could see that now. That wolf attack was not his damn fault, but this ... this sorrow in Ruby's voice, this was his fucking fault.

"It's hard being without you. Do you feel it too?"

God, yes, he felt it in every inch of his body. He ached with it.

She turned suddenly on the path and stared into the shadows. He could tell by the way she squinted that she couldn't actually see him yet, but she spoke into the darkness anyway.

"Why are you doing this, Rafe?" Her voice broke and so did Rafe's restraint. He stepped into the light and Ruby flinched, startled. But the smile that crossed her face at the sight of him set his heart racing. How could she still look at him like that? He didn't deserve that smile but God he wanted to earn it.

"I thought you wouldn't want me anymore after what I did." His voice was raspy from a week of speaking to no one but the ghosts in his head.

Ruby's eyes widened. "You thought I wouldn't want you after you saved my life? My sister's life?"

Rafe shook his head. "I don't know. I just ... I thought that wasn't me anymore. I thought I could be..." He growled in frustration, his thoughts scrambling in Ruby's presence. "I thought I could be more human for you."

"Oh." Ruby's response was small and quiet in the expanse of the woods.

"But I can't. That attack made it perfectly clear, Ruby. I'm still a beast."

"And what if I want the beast?"

Rafe huffed. "We have to stop playing this game."

"It isn't a game, and protecting people you care about isn't a sin!"

God, he wanted to believe her. His body called for hers; keeping his hands clenched at his sides was taking all his strength.

"You didn't leave," Ruby continued before he could piece together an explanation, before he could collect the reasons for his self-hatred.

"What?"

"You said it was over, that we were over, but you're still here." She put her hands on her hips, ready to fight, and hope surged in Rafe's chest.

"I can't stay away. You know that."

"Then why do you keep trying?" Ruby's voice rose. "I don't know how many more times I can tell you that I want you. Both sides of you. That I'm not scared of you. That I fucking love you!"

Her arms were across her chest, and she was scowling at him, and her words were sharp and angry, but all Rafe heard was that she loved him. Ruby, *his* Ruby, loved him. And everything else faded into the background. Every doubt. Every fear. He'd be insane to turn her away now.

"Tell me again," he demanded.

"What?" Ruby asked, brow furrowed, frown pulling down her red lips. She'd painted them to walk through the woods with him and he loved that. He loved her.

"Tell me again. And again. Please." He stepped closer until he could feel her warmth. "I'll try to hear you this time. I'll keep trying."

Her face crumpled and she leaned into his chest, her cheek pressed against his heart. "I love you, you big idiot. I love you and I want you and I need you."

She *needed* him. Ruby, who tried so hard not to need anyone, had just admitted to needing him. Couldn't he do the same? Couldn't he leave all his bullshit behind for her?

"Shit, Ruby." He wrapped his arms around her and pressed his lips to her hair. "I love you too. I'm sorry I'm so screwed up. I wanted to be something better for you." He breathed her in, crushing her to his body. How had he thought for a second he could live without this? Why had he even tried?

"We're all screwed up. And I don't want you to be different. I want you to be you." Her words were muffled as she spoke nuzzled against his chest. "Just stay with me."

Rafe grabbed her by the arms and pulled her away so she could see his face, so she could see how dead serious he was. He was going to do this. He could be the man she needed, the man she wanted. He could trust her like she trusted him.

"Always." Knowing Ruby loved him burned down all his doubts. Nell was right. Ruby was different. This time was different.

"Even if my face is doing something weird?"

He huffed a laugh. "Even if your face looks absolutely horrified. I won't leave. You're stuck with me."

She grinned through her tears and he pulled her close again. He held her like that for a long time, lingering on the overgrown forest path where he had first seen her. His fingers wove through her hair and down her back. He let them trail over the tempting curve of her ass and back again. Ruby sighed against him and he thought he could stay here forever, listening to the crickets and the distant thunder and the heartbeat of his beloved.

"Walk me home?" Ruby asked, eventually emerging from their mutual stupor.

"Of course." Rafe took her hand and led her through the dark woods back to the little house on the edge of the trees.

"Hey, Rafe?" she asked when they stood in her yard under the soft glow of the lights from Lena's window.

"Yeah?" He didn't know what was supposed to happen next and his heart clenched at the thought of letting her go inside alone. But as for the next logical step, he was at a complete loss.

"Want to make it official?" She raised her eyebrows suggestively and heat shot through Rafe's body.

"What did you have in mind?"

Ruby ran a hand down his chest, her fingers skating across his abs, skimming along the waistband of his pants. A low growl started in his throat. Ruby smiled wider.

"I thought instead of running away from me, we could switch it up. Maybe I could do the running…"

A dozen images crowded into his head, Ruby running, Ruby pinned down… He groaned.

"What are you asking for, Ruby?"

Pink crept up her cheeks and she bit down on her bottom lip. "I want you to chase me."

Fuck.

The chance to release all these human emotions and let his inner beast play was so damn tempting. He could show Ruby how much he wanted her so much better than he could ever tell her.

Rafe stepped closer and dipped his head. He whispered, "And what do you want me to do when I catch you?" He brushed his lips along the shell of Ruby's ear and she shivered.

"I want you to make me yours."

His teeth scraped the soft skin of her neck. "You're sure?"

"Yes." The word was nothing more than an exhale but it rang through his body and left him trembling. There was no coming back from this, but if she was in then so was he. Forever.

He held her closer, his lips pressed against her racing pulse, her fingers raking through his hair. He kissed her hard and fast and then let her go. She leaned back against a tree with a gasp.

He let his lips tip into a predatory grin as his gaze raked over her. "Well, brave girl, you better run."

Chapter Forty-One

Ruby tore through the woods, underbrush scraping at her legs as she ran. Somewhere in the distance, thunder rumbled. The sound echoed in her chest.

Rafe must have given her a head start because she didn't hear him behind her. It was dark. Almost impossible to see more than a few feet ahead. Ruby ran with her hands out in front of her, stumbling her way through the trees.

Her heart raced. Something like fear prickled along her spine. Even though it was Rafe following her, even though she wanted to be caught, it was like some primal part of her body didn't know that. She was nothing more than prey in these dark woods.

Her hand skimmed along a tree trunk, scraping the skin from her palm. She stopped running and pressed the hand against her chest to ease the sting.

Leaves rustled somewhere to her left. She peered into the darkness and saw nothing. She kept going, slower now, her breath shallow and unsteady. More rustling. Silver eyes watched her from the shadows. A familiar thrill crept up Ruby's spine. He was there.

She kept going, picking up her speed again, not wanting to end their little game yet. Her boots crunched over dry leaves and her skirt flapped against her legs. She'd skipped the underwear and her thighs were slippery as they rubbed against each other.

A low growl traveled across her skin. He was close. Her heart rammed against her ribs, waiting to get caught, running to stay away. It was the sexiest, most terrifying game of tag she'd ever played.

Another growl and this time Rafe's breath ghosted against her ear. She bit down on a scream as his strong arm banded around her waist and scooped her right off the ground. He held her tight, her back against his chest. She could feel the steady beat of his heart.

His teeth scraped against her neck, sharp against her skin. The teeth of an animal. "Caught you," he whispered.

Ruby whimpered.

He lowered her, letting her feet settle back on the earth, but his arm stayed tight around her waist. His other hand snaked around the front of her and lifted her skirt, exposing her to the summer night air. He growled when he found her naked under her skirt, his fingers skimming over her sensitive skin.

"Shit, Ruby. You're so wet for me."

The world was black around her, the only sensations Rafe's voice in her ear and his fingers stroking between her thighs. She moaned, tipping her head back to rest on his chest. He sucked the skin along her neck as he circled her clit. Her legs trembled but he held her up, pressing her against him, rubbing and kissing until she lost all sense, all thought. Until she let herself be caught.

The orgasm built higher and higher until she shook with it, pleasure and relief pouring through her. Her body quaked in Rafe's grasp, his breathing harsh and ragged on her neck, but she twisted from his arms. She wasn't ready to give in yet. She wanted more from him. More proof that he would follow her anywhere. More evidence that he wanted her as much as she wanted him.

So she ran again, her legs weak and shaking. She ran, and again Rafe must have given her a head start, letting her get away before he chased her. He was enjoying the game as much as she was.

Distant thunder, her pounding footsteps and her own ragged breaths were the only sounds as Ruby groped her way through the trees. She stumbled her way into a small clearing. She glanced back. Silver eyes flashed in the darkness.

Ruby stood rooted to the spot. Unable to look away as Rafe stalked out of the shadows. He was huge, his muscles tense, his chest rising and falling with each heaving breath. She turned to run again, but he lunged for her, grabbing her before she could move.

She shrieked and he paused.

"You okay, brave girl?" he whispered in her ear.

She wrapped her arms around his neck and tugged his hair until he looked at her. "Yes."

He didn't ask again. He found a much better use for his mouth. He slammed his lips down on hers and kissed her, hard and hungry. She kissed him back like she would devour him, like she was the beast and he was her meal.

His growl vibrated through her, sending little waves of pleasure through her body. Rafe's hands lifted the back of her skirt and squeezed the flesh of her ass. "Fuck, Ruby," he groaned, breaking their kiss.

"Yes, exactly."

He huffed a laugh, his breath skating across her face.

"You want me to fuck you?"

"God, yes."

Rafe swallowed hard. "You want to be my Mate?"

"Yes, forever."

He blew out a long breath. "But what about—"

"I'm on the pill."

He nodded, his hands still moving over her body, squeezing and grabbing, pushing clothes aside. He dipped his head to her neck again, and she could feel his pointed teeth on her skin. "And what about this, Ruby? You want me to mark you as mine?"

Heat pooled in Ruby's core at the word and shivers raced across her skin.

"Yes. I want all of it. I want everything."

Rafe groaned.

She wanted everything and he wanted to give it to her. He was done running away from her, from his life. He thought he didn't know how Mates worked or how to lock in the bond but chasing Ruby through the woods made everything abundantly clear. They were locked in whether he fought it or not. This woman was his whether he bit her or fucked her or asked her to marry him.

And he was so damn lucky she wanted him back, that she loved him and trusted him enough to play this game forever.

"Rafe, please." She writhed against him, her sweet little body stroking against his chest, his cock. He still had a hand full of her ass and he gave it a squeeze before moving his hands to the hem of her shirt and lifting it over her head.

It was dark, but even in human form he had better eyesight than most. He could see perfectly well the soft swell of Ruby's tits over the top of her bra. He could see her wide eyes and slightly parted lips. He could see the pulse racing in her neck.

Ruby held his gaze as she tugged the waistband of his shorts down and freed his cock. Her hand was soft and sure on his flesh as she stroked him. The growl that escaped him was involuntary but it made her lips tip into a smile. He pulled down the cup of her bra and let her tit spill over the top. He grazed it with his thumb and Ruby moaned.

Shit. He would not last long if they kept this up.

"In the dirt or up against the tree, brave girl?" he asked, rolling her nipple between his fingers. Her up and down motion on his dick slowed as she thought about it.

"Tree."

He tugged her other cup down and sucked her nipple into his mouth before answering, "Good choice." Any inclination he'd had to not fuck Ruby up against a tree like an animal had evaporated as soon as she asked to be chased. She wanted it like this and so did he.

He turned her around, maybe a little roughly, but his brave girl just whimpered with pleasure. "Put your hands on the tree and bend over."

She did as he asked and he brushed kisses along her shoulders. He avoided her injury, the sight of it causing anger and guilt to coil in his gut, but he breathed it out. Let it go. He could do this. For Ruby he would do anything.

He ran his hands over her back and lifted her skirt. She swayed toward him like she couldn't wait any longer. Shit. Neither could he.

He slid his cock along her slick entrance and they both groaned.

"Please, Rafe."

That word. That fucking word.

He slid into her, painfully slow, giving her time to adjust, to stop him, to come to her senses. But she just pushed back into him, until he was buried inside her. He held tight to her hip with one hand, his fingers digging into her flesh and reached around to grab her breast with his other. He held still for a moment longer, breathing her in. And then he started to move.

The sound that escaped from Ruby's lips could only be described as a growl and Rafe bit down on a smile even as he felt like his world was imploding, his entire life distilling down to this one moment. He pulled out and thrust in again. Ruby's fingernails scraped along the tree bark.

He was probably hurting her.

"You okay?" The words were barely human. He was barely human. And for the first time in a long time, it felt good.

"Yes. Fuck yes," she panted. "Keep going."

Who was he to argue? He was done doubting her. Ruby knew what she wanted. So he gave it to her.

Rafe fucked her hard against that tree, the sound of their bodies slamming together and their grunts and growls filling the small clearing. Not a single thought entered his brain. Nothing but the need to keep fucking Ruby until they both fell apart. Until the entire world fell apart.

He was practically lifting her off the ground now, the toes of her boots barely clinging to the earth. He moved a hand between her legs and stroked her clit as he moved inside her. And when he felt her clenching around him, when he felt his own world shattering, he did the only thing he could do. The only thing that made sense.

He leaned forward and sank his teeth into Ruby's neck.

She screamed his name, claiming him as much as he claimed her.

His Mate.

His Ruby.

Forever.

Chapter Forty-Two

R afe scooped her up in his arms, grabbed her shirt from a nearby branch, and started walking home. Ruby considered protesting. She was perfectly capable of walking. But of course Rafe knew that and he was carrying her anyway. It was kinda nice.

Ruby snuggled against his chest and breathed his piney scent. It was really nice, actually. Supremely nice to be carried for once. To have someone to lean on. For the first time in a long time, Ruby could rest. She could listen to her Mate's steady heartbeat and not worry about bills or her sister's episodes or her next shift at the bar. Not that those things wouldn't still be waiting for her in the morning, but now she'd have someone by her side when she woke up to face it all again.

And being back with Rafe made her feel pieced together again. Her heart seemed to beat in sync with his, her breath matching his inhales and exhales. Being held by Rafe lit her up inside, filling in all the dark spaces.

They made it to his cabin just as the first drops of rain began to fall. Lightning lit up the trees around them, thundering crackling in its wake.

"Guess you'll have to stay," Rafe said, setting her down on the porch. "Think Lena will be okay?"

"She basically kicked me out. She's done with babysitters."

Rafe huffed and pushed open the door. His home was small and cozy and far messier than Ruby would have expected, but Rafe didn't give her much time to explore.

"Let's get you cleaned up." He tugged her into the bathroom and ran the hot water in the shower.

Ruby bit her bottom lip, happiness bubbling up so fast and fierce she thought it might spill out. "Okay, fine, but later I'm snooping through all your stuff."

He gave her a shy smile. "Fine."

"And I want to see your workshop."

He removed her bra with a deft flick of his fingers and let it drop. Ruby shimmied out of her skirt. Rafe's hands skated over her hips and into the dip of her waist. Steam filled the small space.

"You can see everything."

"Hm, okay." She reached for his shorts but he grabbed her hands.

"Ruby," he warned.

"Yes?"

"I'm trying to take care of you."

She pulled her hands from his and slid his shorts over his hips. His cock was hard and heavy in her hand. *Werewolf genes. Goddamn.*

"I think this is a very good way to take care of me."

"Ruby, you're hurt." His fingers ran over her bandaged arm and for the first time in the past several hours, she felt the pain emanating from the wound. "You need to rest." He pressed a kiss to her forehead and ushered her into the shower.

"At least you can join me." She tugged him in with her, making it far too crowded in the tight space, but seeing Rafe wet and soapy would be totally worth it.

Apparently, he felt the same way about her because he wasted no time lathering her up. His big hands gently washed away the dirt and the sweat from their little romp.

He eyed her injury like he wanted to resurrect those wolves just so he could kill them again. She ran a hand across his chest. "It's okay. They're gone. I'm safe."

Rafe blew out a long sigh. It would take him a long time to believe she was safe, she knew that. After everything he'd lived through, she knew it would take more than a little fucking and biting for him to trust that she was really here and safe and his, but Ruby would tell him every damn day.

"And what if they're not?"

"Rafe—"

"No, really. This isn't me being … me." He shrugged and ran a hand through his hair, sending water droplets down his forearm. "What if they keep coming until they get what they want."

A shiver ran up Ruby's spine, remembering Knox's little visit to the bar. But bringing up Rafe's brother was the last thing she wanted to do right now. "Then we'll face it together."

He stared at her a moment longer before nodding. "Together." He ran his assessing gaze over her one more time. His eyes turned dark with hunger and Ruby bit down on a smile. His thoughts had turned to more pressing matters. He tore his gaze away to pour shampoo into his palm and Ruby groaned as he massaged it into her scalp.

"Turn," he commanded and she did.

He lathered her hair, his fingers digging into her scalp as the warm water ran over her breasts and stomach. She moaned and she felt his cock slide against her ass.

"Turn."

She giggled and did as she was told, letting him rinse the suds from her hair. Face to face now, his cock slipped against her soap-covered stomach.

"Rafe, please."

He groaned, pressing against her more urgently, water trickling down between them. She ran her fingers through his wet hair and licked the water dripping off his jaw.

"Not here. You're hurt enough for one day." He turned off the water and they stepped out of the shower into the steamy bathroom. Ruby was wrapped in a towel and hoisted onto the bathroom counter before she could protest, Rafe's mouth between her legs before she could breathe.

"Shit." She leaned her head back against the mirror as Rafe worked his tongue over her clit, sending pleasure skittering down her legs and curling her toes. He hummed against her, the vibration making her moan.

"I knew," he said, his head still between her legs. "I knew as soon as I tasted you that you were mine."

"Rafe." She groaned his name, all other language evaporating from her head. It didn't take long, her orgasm winding tighter and tighter until finally rolling through her like a wave. Rafe placed a kiss on her thigh as she ran her fingers through his hair. "Seriously, so good at that," she murmured.

Rafe huffed a laugh. He stood, his gaze landing on her hands. "I did that?" His eyes went dark as he studied the scrapes on her palms.

"Nope."

He narrowed his eyes at her.

"I crashed. It was dark. It's not a big deal."

"Not a big deal," he repeated in disgust as he lifted her off the counter and carried her to his bedroom. He deposited her on the bed.

"Are you going to carry me everywhere now?"

"Maybe."

He left the room and Ruby could hear him digging around in the medicine cabinet. The rain was pouring down outside, drumming loudly on the tin roof. Every few minutes a flash of lightning lit up the cozy room. Ruby grabbed one of Rafe's oversized T-shirts from a chair in the corner and pulled it over her head.

Rafe returned with a small white box in his hands and his shorts back on his beautiful body. "Gimme your hand." He sat on the edge of the bed, his brow furrowed in worry as she presented her scraped palm.

"It's fine."

"It's not fine. You're hurt." He wiped peroxide on the scrape and Ruby hissed. He glanced up at her, the furrow deepening.

"Just stings a little." She gave him a weak smile.

He huffed and gingerly unwrapped a Band-Aid and pressed it to her hand. "Next time we have sex in a bed. Like normal people."

Ruby scrunched up her nose. "But do we really want to be normal people? Sounds kinda boring."

Rafe bit down on a laugh. "I don't think we could pass for normal."

"Me neither." Ruby patted the spot beside her on the bed. "Come keep me warm."

Her werewolf moved his little first-aid kit aside and sprawled out next to her on the bed. Ruby rested her head on his chest, listening to the storm howl outside the window. Rafe stroked a hand through her hair and down her back. He traced circles on the skin of her arms, his fingers moving back up her body until they found the bite mark on her neck. Ruby closed her eyes, savoring the feeling. The feeling of his hands on her and the feeling of belonging to someone.

"I think you were right."

"Oh?" His voice was a rumble beneath her ear. "About what?"

"Maybe I am like Lena. A little bit anyway." She lifted her head, leaning on her elbow beside him.

"Why? Did something happen?" His expression turned immediately murderous like he could terrify any visions she might have right out of her body.

Ruby shook her head, her hair ghosting along Rafe's skin. "Just a memory about a dream I had a long time ago. I think maybe it was a vision. According to Callie's big, ancient books, clairvoyance runs in families, and the more I think about my aunt, the more I'm convinced she had that type of power, too."

Rafe tucked her hair behind her ear, studying her like he was waiting for her thoughts on the matter before formulating his own.

"And when I was coming to find you, it was like I was pulled here. My body knew where to go. I don't know." She shrugged. "Felt kinda magical."

"Sounds kinda magical." His lips tilted into a smile. "It's how I felt about you from the start."

She leaned down and pressed her lips to his chest, right above his beating heart. "Who knew werewolves were so romantic?"

He flashed her a rare grin and she lifted her face to his to kiss it. His lips were warm and soft against hers and as they kissed, the years and years ahead of them spooled out in front of her. A lifetime longer than she ever thought possible stretched out into the future. If she really was a seer like Lena and her aunt, she could live as long as Rafe. They would be together for all of it.

Rafe broke the kiss first. "You hungry?"

"I could eat."

Rafe slipped his arms under her body as though he was trying to lift her again. Ruby squirmed from his grasp. "I can walk!"

Rafe kissed a line down her neck, murmuring against her skin. "If you insist."

"I do. I do insist." She swung her legs out of bed and followed Rafe to the kitchen. She sat at the small table, running her fingers over the smooth wood.

"Did you make this?" she asked as he pulled bread, cheese and butter out of the refrigerator.

"Mmhmm."

"It's beautiful."

Ruby watched in delight as a slow blush crept over Rafe's cheeks.

"Thanks."

"You're beautiful," she said with a grin.

"Ruby..."

"Too far?"

"A bit," he said, the pleased smile returning to his lips. "Grilled cheese okay?"

"Grilled cheese is perfect. I like any food as long as someone else makes it."

Rafe huffed a laugh. "I'll keep that in mind."

"For all the days you're going to cook for me in the future?" she teased but Rafe held her gaze, his silver eyes flashing.

"Yes, exactly."

Pleasure rushed through Ruby's body. She could really get used to this. "Okay," she squeaked, her voice tight with the emotions of imagining decades of Rafe cooking her meals at three o'clock in the morning.

"I plan to make it up to you," he said, assembling the sandwiches and laying them in the hot pan. The smell of buttered bread filled the kitchen and Ruby's stomach grumbled.

"Make what up to me?"

He looked at her, eyebrow raised. "Ruby, we both know I have a lot to make up for. I put you through hell. I put both of us through hell."

Ruby opened her mouth to argue, but changed her mind. "Well, you're not wrong."

Rafe laughed, low like thunder. "I know."

He slid the sandwiches onto plates and sat next to her at the table.

"Ooo … diagonally cut. Nice start."

"Glad you like it," he said through big bites of his dinner. They ate in comfortable silence after that with Ruby studying the quaintness of his house and Rafe never taking his eyes off Ruby.

Her gaze returned to his to find him staring. "What is it? Do I look scared? Because I'm only appalled at how many throw blankets you have on that couch. Are you a little old lady in disguise?"

"I get cold!" he said in mock outrage and Ruby giggled as he beamed at her.

"I never said thank you," he added when she was done laughing.

"For what?"

"For not giving up on me. Even when I was being a stubborn asshole."

"You're welcome." She pushed the hair back from his face, reveling in the look of him. A sight she'd now get to see every day for the rest of her hopefully very long life. "Thanks for finally hearing me."

His lips tipped into a smile and he took her hand in his, laying a kiss on her palm. "Let's go to bed."

Rafe led her back to the bedroom and tucked her into bed. He flopped down beside her and Ruby giggled as the bed rocked with his weight. She burrowed into his side and he wrapped his arms around her, his fingers trailing up and down her body. They skated over his bite mark again. Her skin tingled when he ran his fingers over it like her body recognized his touch.

"Is it freaking you out?"

He blinked. "What? No."

"You keep touching it."

He shook his head. "I still can't believe it's real. That *this* is real."

Ruby ran her finger along his neck. "Maybe I should give you a matching one. You know, so other ladies don't get any ideas."

His eyes darkened at the thought and Ruby grinned. She leaned forward and sucked the sensitive skin of his neck, nipping and biting until he groaned. She pressed a kiss to his pulse and pulled away.

Rafe gazed at her, his pupils blown wide.

"Nah, your skin's too pretty to damage. I'll just get you a flashy piece of jewelry instead."

A surprised laugh escaped Rafe's lips. "Jewelry?" He flipped Ruby onto her back and she squealed as he licked her neck. She giggled as he nuzzled against her, kissing and biting her sensitive skin. "No jewelry. No mark necessary. Although you're free to bite me whenever you like." He held himself over her, his hair shadowing his face, but his silver eyes glowed from the darkness. "I'm yours, Ruby. Have been from the start."

She reached up and tangled her hands in his hair, sighing his name as he kissed her neck again. And again. She tugged his shorts down and he slid into her, forgetting her wounds, forgetting everything except their bodies coming together. He fucked her long and slow like they had forever. He fucked her until they both came apart and held her until they were pieced back together. Until they both fell asleep in a tangle of limbs and blankets, the rain dripping through the trees and the magic strumming through Ruby's veins.

It was close to dawn; weak gray light trickled in through the window. Rafe had been relegated to one quarter of the mattress, one of Ruby's arms draped over his chest and her leg tangled with his own. And it was perfect.

He ran a hand down his face, preparing to get up and make some coffee, wondering what they would do today. What would a normal day look like? Would they stay here? Go back to Ruby's? He knew she would sleep for a few more hours but he was too keyed up, too excited to start his new life to sleep anymore today.

Ruby probably had work tonight and he had commissions he'd put off for the past two weeks. It would be normal. Nice. Easy. And they would be together.

He could do that, right? He could do normal. For her, he could do anything. And they had so much time ahead of them to figure it out. The more he thought about Ruby and her family, about her being his Mate, about Lena's visions, the more he was convinced Ruby wasn't a normal human anyway. She was magic and she'd be his forever.

Ruby, *his* Ruby, didn't want normal. He bit down on a smile, watching her chest rise and fall, her dark hair spilling out across the pillow. For a minute he felt like he'd stolen her, ransacked a village, stalked her through the night to get her here. But he hadn't. She'd come because she wanted to, wanted him. And as for the stalking, she'd liked that part. Rafe's blood heated at the memory of last night and his heart raced at the promise of all the nights to come.

His Mate wanted both sides of him and he never in his hundreds of years had imagined that was possible. He didn't have to pretend to be human anymore or disown his people or become the killing beast his father wanted him to be. For the first time in centuries, he could be himself, and he would spend the rest of his incredibly long life showing Ruby just how much he appreciated it.

He should have listened to her sooner. He would probably let her hold that over his head for the next century or so. That and unlimited grilled cheeses and orgasms and he figured they'd be even.

He rolled to his side, dislodging Ruby's limbs from his, soaking in the sight of his Mate next to him. If his father had only known how powerful it felt to have found her, their pack would have been unstoppable. Rafe would tear the world down for her. She was the ultimate motivation to be a better man, a better wolf. Devon was wrong about so many things. His hatred could never have motivated Rafe like Ruby's love did. The old man had it all wrong.

Rafe breathed deep, letting Ruby's scent fill his soul. She was here with him and that was all that mattered now. Or he hoped it was all that mattered.

He tried to push aside the prickle of unease that had nothing to do with thoughts of his father. The wolves that attacked Ruby were dead, but Rafe couldn't help but feel like it wasn't over, like there were more pieces to the puzzle they hadn't figured out yet. Seers were valuable and he now knew two of them.

He should have left one of those wolves alive. They would have had to shift eventually and he could have questioned them, but at the time he'd wanted only one thing.

He didn't know what the odds were that those were the only wolves interested in Ruby and her sister but now that Knox knew about Lena there was no telling what the new Alpha would do.

Maybe they shouldn't have left her alone.

Ruby stirred next to him and he pulled her closer, breathing her in. All thoughts of Lena and Knox left his head as he drifted back to sleep.

Chapter Forty-Three

The wolf streaked past her, his gray fur glinting silver in the sunshine. Ruby smiled from her perch on Rafe's front steps, the old wood warm beneath her thighs. It was early. Early by Ruby's standards anyway. Well before noon. It might as well have been dawn. But the past few weeks she'd developed a habit of waking up in time to see Rafe running through the trees in his wolf form. It was worth it to see this side of him. It felt like a privilege.

She sat with her coffee mug balanced on her knees and sipped in the quiet morning as she waited for him to come back. It was peaceful out here beneath the towering pines. It felt like home.

A twinge of guilt settled in her gut at the thought of home. Lena insisted she was fine but Ruby didn't need superhuman powers to see right through her sister's lies. Despite the fact that all had been quiet since Rafe'd killed those wolves, Lena still looked like hell warmed over. Ruby hadn't witnessed any more of her episodes but she was sure Lena was still having them.

Only now Lena wouldn't tell her about them, wouldn't let Ruby in at all.

Her sister had been slowly pushing her out of her life for weeks now, happy to use Ruby's new Mate bond as the reason. Lena more than encouraged Ruby to spend most of her time at Rafe's. She'd practically kicked Ruby out on her ass.

But if Lena needed space, Ruby was willing to give it to her. Not that her sister had given her much say in the matter.

At least Lena was safe. Rafe's morning runs had started as a safety check, a way to assure himself that all was well, that no one was after her or her sister anymore.

But the past few days something had shifted in him. Ruby could feel it. She could feel the happiness radiating off him as he raced off, wild. Free. Her own heart soared as he raced away each morning.

So with her Mate happy and her sister needing space, Ruby had allowed herself her own space, her own time to relax. And these mornings with Rafe were perfect for soothing her weary soul and her perpetually aching feet. The fact that Rafe gave her a ride to work every day helped too.

She wiggled her bare toes on the bottom step. They were neon pink today, very pleasing in the morning sun. She took another sip of coffee and scanned the trees for her wolf-man. His steps were so quiet she usually didn't see him until he was close to the house. She'd made a game of it, of trying to spot him from further away. So far she was terrible at it.

She leaned back, letting her hair fall over shoulders, and the sun warmed her face. Birds chirped and chittered in the branches above her. It was going to be another hot day, but on the edges of the heat, Ruby could feel the chill of fall creeping in.

The idea of sitting on this porch, breathing in the scent of dry leaves and watching the trees change color around her brought another smile to her lips. It was like she had finally settled into her real life and everything else had been a dream. Like a really boring dream.

She was so wrapped up in her thoughts, her eyes still closed against the brightness of the day, she didn't hear Rafe until his wolfy breath was skating across her wrist.

She dug her fingers into the thick fur at his neck and savored his contented huff as he rested his head on her lap.

"Good morning."

Wolfy sigh.

"Did you have a good run?"

Wolfy nuzzle against her hand.

"Oh, good."

He closed his eyes as she stroked between his ears.

"I was thinking of making pancakes."

One highly skeptical wolfy eye opened.

"What? I'm not going to get better if I don't keep trying."

Wolfy huff.

Ruby laughed. "I really think I have it figured out now. I had the burner turned up way too high last time."

She tried to get up to begin her breakfast experiment, but the giant wolf in her lap wouldn't budge.

"Rafe." She shoved his big shoulder but he just snuggled against her. "Rafe, come on. They couldn't possibly be that bad."

Low wolfy growl.

She laughed again. "Okay, fine. You win." She settled back on her step, grabbing her mug from the top step and taking another sip. "You can cook again."

Relieved wolfy sigh.

Ruby's fingers sank into his fur, the weight of him reassuring against her. They sat like that until her coffee went cold and her butt went numb on the step and the body leaning against hers wasn't an animal anymore. Another little privilege, a sign of his trust, that he would shift in front of her.

She ran her fingers through Rafe's hair and he smiled up at her.

"You're going to get splinters in your ass."

He huffed a laugh. "Not worried." He sat up, his hands roving over her bare thighs.

"Aren't you going to get dressed?" she asked as his lips found the soft skin of her neck. His teeth scraped along her throat, sending heat directly to her core.

"Seems silly," he growled.

"To get dressed?" Her voice was breathy, giving away exactly how she felt about the futility of Rafe getting dressed.

"Why put clothes on to just take them off again?" She could feel his grin against her neck, his hands working their way up her skirt.

"What about breakfast?"

"Fuck breakfast."

The laugh escaping her lips quickly became a gasp as Rafe's fingers found where her underwear was already soaked.

"I don't know why you wear these."

She didn't either. Nine out of ten times her peaceful mornings ended exactly like this, with Rafe's hands up her skirt and his teeth and tongue on her neck and her senses flung far up into the trees. It was a really good thing Rafe didn't have any neighbors.

Especially since she hadn't gotten over her desire to be

chased, to be pinned down in the dirt by Rafe. If anything, her little kink had only grown.

She shoved him away and took off down the steps. But her Mate was fast, breathing down her neck before she'd made it far.

"You gonna make me work for it today, brave girl?" he asked, his growl curling up in her belly like a pet.

He caught her before she was even out of his small yard, pressing her back to his front, his arm banded across her waist. "Want you too bad to chase you today." He spun her, his hands rough, demanding.

His kiss was the same, urgent and hard against hers. She loved it, loved when he let go, when he stopped worrying about breaking her.

"Get on your knees for me," he rasped, his voice rough in her ear. "Please, Ruby." He kissed along her jawline, each nip of his teeth followed by the softness of his lips, his demand followed by a request.

Ruby dropped to her knees in front of him, her hands on his thick thighs. He towered over her, huge and solid, the sun streaking across his tanned skin. The muscles in his thighs twitched beneath her hands. She smiled up at him before she took him in her mouth.

A strangled groan escaped his lips. "Goddamn," he said, his hands tightening in her hair.

She took him deeper, letting the silky hardness of him slide past her lips until he hit the back of her throat. She pulled back and then swallowed him again.

Over and over she worked him from base to tip until his legs were trembling and her jaw was aching. Her lips tingled with the sensation of his skin coasting past them again and again.

Her awareness distilled to the cold dirt under her knees and the tugging of his hands in her hair. The world had gone quiet except for Rafe's words, skimming over her.

"So, so good. My brave girl, my sweet, sweet girl. Take all of me."

And she did. Over and over she took him into her body like she could consume him, like she couldn't remember doing anything but this. Rafe's cock between her lips and nothing else. Nothing else existed.

Until Rafe tugged her back by her hair, angling her dazed gaze up to his.

"My Mate," he growled and her swollen mouth tipped into a slow smile at his words. He dropped to his knees then, taking her mouth with his, his tongue replacing his cock. Ruby groaned and clutched at his bare shoulders, her nails digging into his flesh.

He tipped her back into the dirt and drove hard between her legs, giving her no chance to catch her breath.

"You are everything." His voice was ragged in her ear, his breath hot against her skin with every thrust. *Everything.* Yes. She wanted everything and he was it. Her everything.

The earth was cool and damp on her back, a stark contrast to the heat of Rafe's body on hers. Leaves tangled in her hair as Rafe stroked into her fast and hard. She wrapped her legs around him and rocked up, angling herself so every thrust built the pleasure higher and higher.

Rafe kept up his punishing pace, sweat slicking their bodies until Ruby squirmed beneath him. She was so close, but her orgasm was just out of reach.

She whimpered her frustration. Rafe nipped at her neck before shifting onto his knees, taking Ruby with him. His arms were under her thighs angling her up to him, his cock hitting a tender, aching spot inside of her. He found her clit with his thumb and rubbed. Hard. Fireworks flashed behind Ruby's eyelids.

She moaned his name to the treetops.

"Better?" he asked, the grin apparent in his voice even when she wasn't looking at him.

"Keep going," she panted.

He gripped her ass tight with one hand, supporting her weight and rubbed her clit with the other hand, thrusting into her with long, slow strokes.

"Come for me, brave girl."

His gruff words, his bruising grip on her body, the way he held her gaze as he gave her what she needed. It was too much. Ruby shattered. Tears streamed down her face as she let loose, spewing an unintelligible string of words and gasps and moans.

Rafe gave her no time to recover before her ass was back in the dirt and he was plowing into her, growling her name. It didn't take long. He had been close since she had him in her mouth, but he'd held back. But now, he came hard, shudders wracking his big body.

He half collapsed onto her and Ruby kept her legs wrapped around him, not ready for him to go yet. He pressed his forehead to hers, his silver eyes flashing.

"I love you," she said, her voice weak but sated. She planted a kiss on the tip of his nose.

A slow smile crossed his face like it still took him a minute to believe it was true. "I love you, too."

Ruby grinned, letting the words settle in her veins, the truth of them. The permanence. She ran her hands over his back, damp from sweat. She knew if they stayed like this long enough, Rafe would get hard again inside her. *Very tempting.*

But she had shit to do today.

And they had forever.

So she pushed Rafe off and he huffed as he landed in the dirt beside her. "Done with me already?" he asked, smiling up at her as she stood. She primly brushed the dirt off her skirt as though she didn't have leaves in her hair and that the whole back of her wasn't filthy.

"I have to shower before work."

"I should probably come with you. For safety," he said with a sly grin. He was quicker to smile these days, but Ruby's heart still raced at the sight of it. Her Rafe. *Happy.*

Except when she burnt the pancakes, then he was exasperated. Or when she left her dirty clothes strewn around his room, then he was annoyed. Or that one time when she borrowed his toothbrush, then he had been appalled and utterly grossed out even after she pointed out that her tongue had been in his mouth on numerous occasions.

And all those little moments just made this real, made being here with Rafe her real life and everything else that boring dream. She was finally where she was meant to be. And despite the minor spat here and there – she had no interest in Rafe bringing home his hunting trophies, for example – they were blissfully happy.

"I really don't think that's necessary," she said, fighting the laughter in her voice, but Rafe was already up and prowling toward her. "Rafe, I'm serious," she squeaked as he chased her into the house, her giggles filling the quiet forest.

Maybe everything she had to do could wait a little bit longer.

It had been one month since he'd claimed Ruby as his Mate and she'd claimed him every day since. One month of her telling him she loved him and him doing his damnedest to believe her. One month of late-night runs through the woods, of waking Ruby slowly with his tongue between her legs, of endless grilled cheese sandwiches, of rides to work over bumpy backroads. It had been one month of piecing his soul back together, of trying to see himself the way Ruby did.

And that seemed worth celebrating. Right? That was something humans did, celebrate relationship milestones? He was sure they did, but *he* never had and now this whole thing seemed ridiculous.

He glanced at where Ruby was still asleep in his bed and then to the wildflowers clutched in his fist.

Maybe this was stupid. It was only a month. The best month of his entire life, but still.

Ruby moved suddenly, startling Rafe from his thoughts. She sat up straight in the bed, flinging off the blankets as she moved. He was beside her just as quickly, the flowers tossed aside.

"What is it?"

Ruby stared at him wide-eyed, her hair a nest of black around her head.

"Ruby." He grabbed her arms and gave a little shake until she blinked, recognition returning to her face. "Ruby, what is it?"

She blinked again, her brow furrowed. "It's Lena." Her voice was raspy from sleep and her sister's name came out choked and scratchy.

"It's okay. We'll go check on her." Dread pooled in Rafe's gut like he knew what Ruby would say before she said it. He'd let his guard down. He'd let himself believe that everything was fine, that there would be no consequences for his actions.

Ruby shook her head, suddenly frantic, grasping at his shoulders. Her fingers dug into his flesh.

"No. We can't."

"We can. Ruby, she's fine—"

"She's not fine. She's gone."

Epilogue

Theo wasn't surprised to find Phoebe sipping tea in his kitchen when he woke up, but his heart fluttered anyway. His stupid heart was always doing shit like that around her.

"Morning, Fee." He padded out into the kitchen, running a hand across his bare chest. It had been a while since he'd seen her, but his best friend had a tendency to disappear sometimes.

"Hey. When did you get back?" Phoebe asked, peering at him over her mug. He paused to look at her before tearing his gaze away. He never really could get over how distractingly beautiful she was. Even now, as he made his coffee in his own kitchen, he had a hard time concentrating, knowing that she was watching him with those big brown eyes.

"A while ago."

"So how's the seer?" she asked, digging for details. She couldn't help it. The nymph in her could never get enough gossip.

"Fine. Well … mostly fine." Theo couldn't stop the grin on his face when he thought about the look on Lena's face when he shifted in front of her. A werewolf had to find fun where he could these days.

"What did you do?" Phoebe raised a copper brow, tension coiling her muscles. Jealous. She was jealous of what he might have done with the seer. And Theo was just enough of an asshole to run with it.

"Nothing." Theo shrugged, pulling down his mug from the cabinet. "Just had a little fun."

"God, Theo." Fee thunked her mug down in disgust. "Is there no one you won't fuck?"

He turned to her, leaning his back against the counter, a slow grin crossing his face. "Just you, I guess. But only because you won't let me."

Pink bloomed across Phoebe's cheeks. "You know why it's not a good idea."

"Remind me."

She huffed out a sigh. "We're friends, Theo. If we sleep together, it will just get weird." She held his stare until he had to look away, knowing he revealed too much when he looked at her. "I can't have you falling in love with me," she said, gently. "Nymphs aren't built for that."

He held up his hands. "Hey, neither am I. I'm offering a fun night, Fee. That's it."

She smirked like she could see his lie from a mile away, like she knew he wanted to keep her. Like she knew that he hadn't actually slept with anyone else in months and currently had the worst case of blue balls just from looking at her in her oversized sweatshirt and leggings.

But he'd blown his shot with Phoebe years ago.

"There was another attack, though."

"Really?"

"Yeah. Rafe took out three wolves on his own, apparently."

Phoebe's eyes widened, impressed. "Maybe he should have been the Alpha after all."

Theo shrugged. He didn't feel like rehashing the events that led to Knox becoming Alpha and him and Rafe becoming exiles. "That's what happens when someone attacks your Mate, I guess."

Phoebe rolled her eyes. "Mates."

"Yes, I've heard your thoughts on the matter many times."

"It makes you wolves all crazy." Phoebe sipped her tea. "It's the only thing I've ever agreed with your father about."

Theo groaned. "It's way too early in the morning to talk about Devon." Especially with Phoebe. He shouldn't even have said the word Mate in front of her. It made him feel all squirrelly like his insides were trying to crawl out. Maybe he should lay off the caffeine.

He turned to pour himself some cereal and avoid Phoebe's gaze. There was a time he thought maybe Fee could be his—

"So what do you think these attacks are about?"

Theo shook his head like he could scatter his thoughts like water from his fur. "Uh ... don't know." He spoke between bites of cereal. "I figure they either want the seer dead or want to use her for her visions. Right?"

"Could be."

"You mean you haven't heard anything through the extensive nymph grape-vine?"

The little dryad blinked innocently. "Nothing too out of the ordinary. Canadian pack is on the move again."

"Hm." Theo had zero interest in the inner workings of werewolf pack politics. It was one of the many reasons he'd never wanted to be the Alpha. Not that anyone believed he would be. People didn't tend to expect much from Devon's youngest son.

"All I know is Rafe is real fucking keyed up about the whole thing," he said with a mouth full of Fruit Loops. Phoebe wrinkled her nose in mock disgust and he grinned through his sugary cereal. He swallowed before adding, "You know how he gets."

"Well, he always was the sensitive one."

Theo huffed. "And what am I?"

Fee smirked. "The pretty one."

He set down his bowl and stalked closer to where she sat at the counter. "That's all I am to you? A pretty face."

She giggled and he had the fleeting and ridiculous thought that he could listen to that sound forever.

"Everyone knows Knox is the brains."

"Ouch, Fee. You wound me." He rested his hands on the counter, leaning forward until he could smell the steam from her herbal tea rising between them.

"Poor pretty baby," she teased, but the color had risen in her cheeks again, her gaze flicking down to his bare chest. "Must be so hard to have women throwing themselves at you."

"That has nothing to do with my pretty face," he purred. "I do have some skills."

Phoebe's lips parted like she might say something or like she might lean forward and do the one thing Theo had been wanting her to do for the past decade...

His phone buzzed aggressively on the counter. Fee straightened on her stool.

"Jesus," he muttered. Theo glanced at his phone to see Rafe's name on the screen. "What the hell does he want now?"

"Might be important."

Theo rolled his eyes. "I'm sure Rafe thinks it is, but I'm done being his errand boy."

"Well, he did save your—"

"Don't finish that sentence. I'm perfectly aware of what I owe my brother," he grumbled as he unlocked his phone.

Lena's gone. Need your help.

He glanced up at Phoebe. The delicious blush was gone from her cheeks; her eyes looked at him with concern and not possible lust. Fucking Rafe and his drama cockblocked him again.

"I gotta go. Rafe lost the damn seer."

"Maybe I should come." Phoebe hopped down from the stool and Theo let his gaze rake up and down all five feet two inches of her. How was it possible that after seeing her nearly every day for the past ten years, his blood still heated at the sight of her? Pathetic was what it was.

"Nah. I should go alone. No need to complicate things."

"Right."

No need to complicate things, because things with his best friend were complicated enough.

Acknowledgments

The road to publishing a book is never an easy one (at least as far as I know!). This book was accepted for publication on the heels of a rejection. So first, thank you to the team at One More Chapter, especially Charlotte Ledger, for seeing something in my writing and encouraging me to resubmit. A big thank you to my editor Ajebowale Roberts for all her help making this book into the best version of itself.

Before this book ever made it into the hands of publishers, it was read by my critique partners. Ginny, Christine, and Love read this book when it was unedited, unpolished, unfinished, and their thoughts and notes (and love for Rafe) contributed so much to the final product. So thanks, ladies for making the writing of this book a less solitary endeavor. And thanks to everyone who expressed their enthusiasm and excitement for this series online and in person.

My mom has been looking forward to this book ever since I mentioned werewolves, so I hope this book lived up to your expectations, Mom, and thanks for being excited about the weird stuff I write. Thanks as always to my Dad for knowing I was writing romance before I did. I guess I have to keep thanking you for that forever.

And lastly, thanks to all the people that live in my house. The pets, the kids, the husband. Thanks for letting me hide and write sometimes. Thanks for getting excited about publishing contracts and cover reveals. Thanks for thinking I can do this. I love you guys.

ONE MORE CHAPTER

The author and One More Chapter would like to thank everyone who contributed to the publication of this story...

Analytics
James Brackin
Abigail Fryer
Maria Osa

Audio
Fionnuala Barrett
Ciara Briggs

Contracts
Sasha Duszynska
Lewis

Design
Lucy Bennett
Fiona Greenway
Liane Payne
Dean Russell

Digital Sales
Lydia Grainge
Hannah Lismore
Emily Scorer

Editorial
Arsalan Isa
Charlotte Ledger
Federica Leonardis
Bonnie Macleod
Ajebowale Roberts
Jennie Rothwell
Tony Russell

Harper360
Emily Gerbner
Jean Marie Kelly
emma sullivan
Sophia Wilhelm

International Sales
Peter Borcsok
Bethan Moore

Marketing & Publicity
Chloe Cummings
Emma Petfield

Operations
Melissa Okusanya
Hannah Stamp

Production
Denis Manson
Simon Moore
Francesca Tuzzeo

Rights
Vasiliki Machaira
Rachel McCarron
Hany Sheikh
Mohamed
Zoe Shine

The HarperCollins Distribution Team

The HarperCollins Finance & Royalties Team

The HarperCollins Legal Team

The HarperCollins Technology Team

Trade Marketing
Ben Hurd

UK Sales
Laura Carpenter
Isabel Coburn
Jay Cochrane
Sabina Lewis
Holly Martin
Erin White
Harriet Williams
Leah Woods

And every other essential link in the chain from delivery drivers to booksellers to librarians and beyond!

YOUR NUMBER ONE STOP

ONE MORE CHAPTER

FOR PAGETURNING BOOKS

One More Chapter is an
award-winning global
division of HarperCollins.

Sign up to our newsletter to get our
latest eBook deals and stay up to date
with our weekly Book Club!
<u>Subscribe here.</u>

Meet the team at
<u>www.onemorechapter.com</u>

Follow us!
🐦 <u>@OneMoreChapter_</u>
f <u>@OneMoreChapter</u>
📷 <u>@onemorechapterhc</u>

Do you write unputdownable fiction?
We love to hear from new voices.
Find out how to submit your novel at
<u>www.onemorechapter.com/submissions</u>